INK, Inc.

Dawn M. Lewis

Dedication

This book is a work of fiction! Most of my stories come from watching people in public places and this book came from conversations with virtual strangers. I meet people and I love to find out what makes them tick, so I listen and ask questions. Sometimes, a story presents itself and this book is the culmination of listening and asking questions. A spark appears and then it has to be written! I hope you enjoy this story.

Other Books I've written:

Christmas Magic

Accidentally Yours

Always Yours

Forever Yours

Secrets of Oak Mountain

Not That Different

Brave ~ Courageous ~ In Love

A Family for Christmas

Christmas for Heroes

Secrets of Simon Island

Chapter One

"That's a wrap everyone. Thank you." Erin called to her crew. "Great job team." She turned to Cassi. "Ms. Reynolds, you and your kids did an excellent job, and this garden is fabulous. Thanks for letting us showcase your project. I got some great footage, great interview clips, and it will make a terrific production for the Hometown Heroes segment." Erin smiled at her friend and teacher.

"Ms. Bradford thanks for making this a reality. The kids have worked so hard on their project and it will make a huge difference in this community. The garden is going to be very helpful for so many, including our students and their families."

"I agree. My angle on this story is to tell how the children and their teacher were able to find a way to serve this community in a way that is sustainable, while teaching the kids about plants, how they grow and how to use them, how to give back. It's a great story and one that needs to be shared with this community. We didn't show any of the kids' faces, but rather hands and over their shoulders as they worked to plant the garden." Erin handed off the microphone she had unclipped from Cassi, and a couple of cables to the production assistant and she started wrapping up her camera gear. "Ms. Reynolds, can I ask you a question?" Cassi turned back to her friend after seeing all the kids off to their parents. The classroom was empty of students.

"Sure. What's on your mind Ms. Bradford, now Erin because the kids are gone?"

"Well, I saw your hunky man the other day when he came to pick you up and I noticed the beautiful artwork on his arms. Do you know where a girl could get amazing art like that?"

"Erin, are you thinking of getting a tattoo?" Cassi was really excited.

"Yes." She said blushing. "But I don't know how to pick a tattoo place and I want to make sure they are reputable and trustworthy, and aren't scared off because this my first time. I don't know how to do this."

"Erin, my man does that for a living! He and his brothers run a shop called Ink, Inc. and they do art and piercings. I know he would love to do this for you."

"Do you think they, or your Alex, would do an ink for me? I've never done anything like this before but I've been creating what I really want and I'm so ready for it! This has been a dream of mine for so long now and it would help me to keep my mom close to my heart too." Erin was so hopeful.

"Erin, let me call Alex and see if he is willing. Do you have your drawing with you?" Erin nodded and handed her notebook to Cassi, opening it to the right page. Cassi stepped to her office which was behind her classroom, and called Alex taking the notebook with her. She took a picture to text to him.

Erin turned back to her equipment and finished stowing everything away. Erin sent her production assistant to the car with the first round of equipment and she swept the area to make sure she had everything. She straightened up the row of desks they had moved, and she looked over her notes. She put the SD card in her pocket and picked up her phone and her clipboard.

"Ok Erin, you have an appointment with Alex on Saturday morning at 9. He loves your design and is excited to do this for you." Erin stopped, shocked.

"Really?!" She was excited and nervous at the same time. Cassi handed her the notebook back and Alex's card so she had the address.

"He's looking forward to meeting you in person. I've talked about you over the last few weeks and he's really excited to meet you. He wanted to know if you wanted colors on your ink."

"Yes Cassi! I was thinking to start the ribbon with black and move to teal and then to purple as it trails away with shadowing. I'd also like the rose to be red for my mom."

"Oooh that will be awesome. Let me make a quick copy of this and I'll share the colors with Alex tonight. He can be prepared when you get there." Cassi and Erin walked to the office so that Cassi could make a photocopy. They talked about getting together next weekend and having a girl's night; Cassi said she would get ahold of Mariah too, and Erin told her she would call Kiera. Cassi made notes on the colors for the tattoo, explained to Erin to wear her black corset so her bra wouldn't get in the way and finally they parted ways.

"Thanks Cassi. Great job with your students! The piece should air this weekend, but I'll let you know for sure. Talk to you soon." Erin hugged her, turned, waved and headed to the car with her crew.

*****

Saturday morning Erin made her way to Ink, Inc. and parked. She had her gear in the trunk because she was doing a shoot in the afternoon. Deep breathing, she exited her car and headed inside. A very handsome man sat behind the desk as she entered. He was the spitting image of Cassi's Alex, just a bit younger. She wondered if they were brothers.

"Morning!" He greeted with a huge smile.

"Good morning. I'm Erin and I have an appointment with Alex." She smiled at him.

"Good to meet you Erin. I'm Michael, Alex's brother." He could sense her nerves as she waited at the counter. "This is your first time huh?" He asked her, smiling.

"Yes. Is it that obvious?" She laughed nervously, but kept her composure.

"You'll be just fine darlin'. My brother is very good at what he does." She nodded. "How did you hear about us?"

"Cassi, Alex's girl, is my best friend. I saw Alex and all his artwork and realized I wanted to do this, and now I see your beautiful artwork too, which makes me want this even more. Cassi helped me get connected with your shop." She smiled at him and he realized that she radiated sunshine. "Do you do ink also Michael?"

"Nope. I'm the piercer in the family! My brothers Alex, Anthony and Kade do the inking and I do any piercings that need to be done." He gave her a killer smile. "Do you want something pierced while you're here?"

"Umm, I already have my ears pierced twice, I think that's enough." She blushed, swallowed hard, and he loved that he could make her off-balance. "I can't imagine needing anything else pierced or what I would have pierced for that matter." She was really red and that made Michael laugh out loud. She realized what she just said and she was mortified. He had an amazing laugh and she was totally embarrassed by her comment.

"You should see your face darlin'." His laughter continued a moment. "I pierce a lot of different body parts, but if you ever decide to give it a try I'll be happy to help you out." Her blush just deepened. The door opened and another gorgeous, hunky man walked in. This had to be Alex; he looked familiar, but Erin was reeling from her encounter with Michael and she couldn't think straight. She was so inexperienced with men! She was totally out of her comfort zone.

"Hey Alex. Your first appointment is here! This is Erin." Alex could see the blush and figured something happened before he got here. He'd have to ask Michael about it later.

"Morning Erin. It's nice to officially meet you. My brother treating you ok?" She nodded and shook his offered hand. "Come with me and we'll get started." He turned toward his work area after sharing a look with his brother over Erin's head, and headed to his bench. Erin followed. She kept deep breathing and mouthing her mantra that this was all ok. Alex and Michael watched her, fascinated. She was nervous and trying to appear stoic, in control.

"Ok Erin, Cassi told me she explained the process to you and that this is your first time." Erin nodded. "You can put your things down here and you need to take your shirt off so I can work on your shoulder." She moved to the table and put her cell phone and bag down, then she took her shirt off. She had worn a strapless corset underneath. It was beautiful on her; black lace against her creamy skin. She had a beautiful figure, tiny waist and small frame, creamy, ivory skin that was flawless. The shirt she wore over the corset didn't do her figure justice. She was tiny and exquisite. It was like she was trying to hide her true beauty. She was deep breathing and trying calm herself.

"Erin, I promise to be gentle. Please don't be scared darlin'."

"Sorry Alex. I was actually admiring your artwork. Your arms are beautiful. Michael has impressive art too. Thank you for agreeing to do my first, maybe only, artwork." She smiled at him. She was nervously fiddling with her fingers.

"Breathe Erin. Come here honey and sit at my work chair. You need to straddle the bench and lean forward here. I'll place your arm in the right position and we'll take this nice and easy. Please trust me." He held his hand out to her and she took it. She took a deep breath, nodded, and lowered herself to the workspace, leaning into the soft leather of his work chair, grateful for the coolness against her overheated skin. Alex got out his tools and the drawing she had given to Cassi. Erin glanced over and saw that he had re-drawn it, adding in the colors, shadowing, and enhancing her work, to make it look amazing. He came to her left side and positioned her body, trying to help her relax her muscles, moving her arm and hand to the handle on the back side of where she was sitting. "You'll be more comfortable if you hold on here." She smiled at him. She kept trying to relax her body, but she was very tense.

"Ok Erin, breathe for me darlin' and just relax. I'm going to clean your shoulder with alcohol, and then I'll show you how I enhanced your drawing. It's going to look amazing!" She rested her chin on the leather edge and Alex moved her hair out of the way tucking in into the space between her neck and her right shoulder, cleaning the left shoulder area. Her hair was silky and beautiful, just like she was. The alcohol was cool and turned cold as he finished. She shivered just a bit. While it was drying he pulled the piece of paper and showed her what he planned to do on her shoulder.

"That looks amazing Alex. I'm so excited. I have wanted to do this for a really long time, but didn't know how to go about doing it. Cassi was happy to recommend you. Thank you for making my dream come to life." She smiled at him. Her excitement just radiated off her and made Alex smile.

"Did you draw this design Erin?" She nodded. "You have an eye for design. What do you do?"

"I'm a television producer. I met Cassi doing a project for the news station about the school where she works and yesterday I finished shooting a production about her class and the community garden they started. We hit it off and have been best friends ever since. I have to edit Cassi's project and then it will be part of the local series on hometown heroes that plays on the weekends."

"You do those programs?!" Alex was impressed. She nodded again. He turned back to the drawing and showed her how he enhanced her design to make it dance off the page with shadowing and told her he would do the same with the shadowing on her shoulder. She smiled at him and managed to catch her lower lip in her teeth. She captured his attention. Alex wanted to know more about her; perhaps Kade or Anthony could be her match. Alex was always trying to help his brothers find the woman of their dreams. He knew she was inexperienced with men, so they would have to take things slow if Kade or Anthony was interested in her. Cassi had cautioned him about her inexperience and innocence.

For the next hour Alex worked on her shoulder, telling her every step of the way what he was about to do. She talked to him, asked and answered questions, and didn't flinch as he worked the outline of the design across her flesh. He had the design marked on her skin with the black color, adding the shadowing, and rubbed some salve into her skin when he finished the initial design. His fingers were warm, like a caress, on her skin. He asked if she was doing ok. She told him she was great. He told her they would take a short break and she could move her arm, stretch a bit. She was grateful for the pause. Alex got up and cleaned out his tools from the black color. Erin sat up and stretched, reaching her hands above her head. She was very limber and in good shape. They heard the front door open and she heard voices, both decidedly masculine. One was Michael, whom she already met, and the second turned out to be their brother Anthony. She heard Michael telling Anthony that Alex was working on a client.

"Hi bro!" Anthony said as he made his way into Alex's work space and stopping short as he took in the sight of Erin. She just captured his attention. He was drawn to her immediately. Alex tried to hide his smile.

"Anthony. Do you have a client today?" He shook his head.

"I just came to see what you were up to." Anthony could not draw his eyes away from the beauty sitting at Alex's work area. "Bro, are you going to introduce me?"

"Erin, this is my brother Anthony. Anthony, this is Cassi's friend Erin." Erin looked up at Anthony and caught her lower lip again in her teeth. She smiled shyly at him.

"Erin, it's a pleasure." He walked toward her and held his hand out.

"Nice to meet you Anthony. So all three of you own this place?" Erin asked surprised as she shook his hand.

"Yep. There are four of us! Alex, Kade and I do the ink and Michael pierces things."

"Yeah, he already asked if I wanted anything pierced." She blushed. That made both of them bust out laughing. She smiled at them. Alex understood now why she was blushing when he first arrived. She was very innocent and didn't understand much about their rough and tumble world, their lifestyle. She was naïve in the nuance between men and women too. Innocent and very special. She oozed sunshine; she brightened up the place. She would be good for Anthony.

"Is this your first tattoo?" Anthony asked. She nodded. He moved her hair to see what Alex had already done and his fingers brushed her neck. "Such a beautiful canvas." She shivered slightly under his touch, but she was definitely attracted to Anthony. The blush creeped up from her neck to her cheeks, and her breathing hitched as Anthony's hands brushed over her shoulder.

"Ok Anthony, I need to get back to work on this beautiful lady and her design. You can pull up a chair and talk while I work." Alex motioned to him to move. Alex repositioned Erin's arm and helped her find the handle on his chair; he moved her hair again so he had room to work. Her auburn hair was long and silky, and it felt good on his fingers. It hung almost all the way to the middle of her back. She was a very beautiful woman; Alex was surprised she was still single. Everyone had a story and he wondered what Erin's story was.

Anthony moved a chair from the side of the room and straddled it close to Erin's right side. He exuded strength, masculinity and charm. He was sexy as hell. Erin was off her mark with Anthony. She really didn't know how to navigate things, but she was attracted to him. Alex was telling her that he was starting on the teal color, and prepared her for a bit more pain than the black color. The two brothers talked to each other and Alex told Anthony that the design he was doing was something Erin had drawn up herself to help her remember her mom. Anthony was impressed by that comment.

"Erin, how do you know Cassi?" Anthony asked.

"Your brother and I were just talking about this. I am a television producer and I string for the local news stations, as well as working for TK Productions. That means that I get sent out on news stories to bring footage back and edit the stories for the evening news. I met Cassi when I did a story about the school she works at and I just finished up a piece on Cassi and her class with their community garden project. That piece will air on Sunday night as part of the hometown heroes segment, providing I get the editing finished. Cassi and I hit it off right away and we've spent a lot of girls' nights together over the last year with another lady named Mariah, and two other friends Laurel and Kiera. Cassi has talked about Alex a bit." She shared with them both the different kinds of programs she liked to create and that she wrote, shot, edited and post-produced most of her pieces, as well as creating graphics. She liked to tell stories through her video production. He asked about her mom and she told him that she had lost her mom a couple years ago, wanted this ink to memorialize her. She didn't elaborate much.

While Alex worked Anthony asked more about Erin's work and she told him she was heading to another shoot after she finished with Alex. She asked if he wanted to tag along and see what she was working on. She really hoped he would say yes! She let him know she was taping a story at the beach, a piece dealing the ecosystem and a rare species the scientists had found. The scientists wanted to showcase the species and help beach goers understand the importance of treating the beach with respect. She told him the beach was one of her favorite places. Anthony told her he would love to go with. That thrilled Erin to no end.

With Anthony keeping Erin occupied Alex was able to finish the design on her shoulder and she didn't flinch or move. He was pretty impressed that she sat through all of the work he did. Even some of the big guys Alex worked on couldn't sit as still as Erin was sitting. He wondered if she had a way to rise above the pain, and if she found something else to concentrate on. She was engrossed in her conversation with Anthony and never moved as Alex made the design come to life with all the colors. Her shoulder was pretty red when he finished, but the design was amazing.   He cleaned her shoulder and rubbed more salve into it to try and relieve the pain. She just let him work. It was beautiful. Alex got up to clean up the tools. Alex loved to create with color, shading and blending them. He liked that Erin wanted her piece to pop with color and shadow.

"Are you all done Alex?" Erin asked, a hint of awe in her voice.

"Yep. It looks amazing." She seemed surprised.

"Can you take a picture of it for me? My phone is on the table by my shirt. I'd love to see it." She didn't move. Anthony reached over and grabbed her phone. She unlocked the screen and pulled up the camera app handing it to Alex. He snapped a few pictures and handed her back the phone.

"So do you boys have website, a social media presence, for your shop?" She looked from her phone to the two men. Alex noticed she had a text message, but it seemed to be from an unknown number. Anthony wondered about the message too and the look on Erin's face. A moment of panic, frustration, and then back to professional. She tried to ignore the message and hoped Alex hadn't read the words.

"No. Mostly we get clients through word of mouth." Alex stated.

"Do you want more clients, a bigger following? The reason I'm asking is that I could do a series of videos showing you completing an ink artwork or a piercing and I can help drive more business to your shop. We can do a slideshow of the different artwork you've done over time set to music too for each of you, or even the different kinds of piercings that Michael does. It would showcase each of your talents, if that's something you want. I love to create with video, tell stories with images, music and narration; what you do is so amazing, it would lend itself so great to the video medium – I mean I'm overwhelmed looking at you both and your artwork, and what you've created here, bringing my design to life." They both looked at her and then at each other.

"Erin, do you do videos for social media and websites?" Anthony asked.

"I do. I create websites too. I work for the news station and a small production house, but I also freelance, so I get to do the kinds of productions I want to do." She smiled at him. "I would love to help showcase your talents. You do incredible work. But, I don't want to overwhelm you with clients, if that's not something you want, and I don't want to exploit your talents either." She took a breath. "I could also just do a production for you instead that you could play here in the shop. It could be something on a loop and it could run on a screen as your clients wait for their appointment. If it's something you want to do, here's my card and contact info, although you can find me through Cassi too." She finally took a breath. She got carried away because she could see the potential. She realized she may have overstepped. "I'm not trying to tell you that you need to do this; I'm just offering. Sorry, I sort of got carried away." Both of them smiled at her. She was so genuine and she had a unique passion for her work. They were both trying to process all that Erin had just shared with them and she was chastising herself for getting carried away again. They could see her berating herself. She knew she overwhelmed them with this information and she felt bad for that. Anthony watched her with a smile on his face. She was so cute, and he was attracted to her.

Alex gave her instructions on how to care for her ink and what to do in the next two weeks while it was healing. He added more salve and massaged the area for a few minutes. Then he added a clear sticky bandage to her shoulder, completely covering the design. He told her to leave it on through the next seven days. She could shower and just pat it dry, but no beach swimming or laying in the sand. She agreed.

"Thank you Alex. It's so beautiful. You made me so happy. I've wanted to do this for so long and now I've memorialized my mom on my shoulder. Thank you so much." She smiled at him. She got up with Alex's help and put her t-shirt back on. Anthony was sorry to see her cover up her beautiful body. He really needed to get himself under control. Alex realized that Anthony was drawn to Erin. That made him incredibly happy. She was a beautiful lady and she would be a great match for Anthony. Anthony's eyes were a dead giveaway to his feelings. He was definitely attracted to her and Erin was enamored with and drawn to Anthony. Alex could see the way her breathing hitched when Anthony got close to her. This would help get Anthony settled down a bit more, and he had no doubt that Erin needed someone like Anthony in her life. He still wondered about the message on her phone. She didn't seem excited to read it and looked rather upset and panicky. He needed to caution Anthony.

Erin headed out to settle her bill with Michael after gathering her belongings. Alex and Anthony stayed behind and talked a bit. Alex asked if Anthony was really going to accompany her to her video shoot and Anthony said yes. He told his brother that he was curious about her work and there was something about Erin that drew Anthony to him. Erin was talking with Michael and she showed him the picture that Alex had taken of her artwork. They were deep in conversation and he told her that he kept the books and made sure the business was moving forward, did all the scheduling too. She let him know that she could do videos for them if that's something they wanted and that she had already talk to Alex and Anthony. They could just call if they wanted to explore that. She saw the text message again on her phone, but she didn't want to read it.

"Erin, are you sure it's okay for me to tag along today?" Anthony asked.

"Absolutely. I would really love to show you what I do. It's pretty low-key today and I can show you what I do. I am just getting shots of the area, and the rare species. I call this my cover footage trip, my establishing shots, for the project to help show what the subject matter expert is talking about, where they found the species and how it integrates into the ecosystem. Plus I would love the company. I can show you how I put together a production. It's been great to talk with all of you and get to know you, so I'd love to continue our conversation, if you want to do that. The scientists will be there to show me what they want for footage, but we aren't doing any interviews or other audio, so it's a great time for you to come along. I'd really love to show you what I do." She smiled at him. "My car's out front. Do you want to ride with me or follow me?" Alex liked her spunk and she was confident in her work. That made him smile. No wonder she was a friend of Cassi's.

Anthony decided to ride with Erin. Erin thanked Alex again and bid them all good-bye. Anthony followed her out and they climbed into her car. She drove them to the beach location, a place that Anthony loved to be. They chatted the entire drive and Anthony found himself even more drawn to her. She parked the car, and Anthony watched in amazement as she gathered her gear. He asked to help her carry it, and she finally relented. She told him she was used to being independent, but he insisted.

Anthony watched her in wonder; she set up her gear, talked with the experts and then as she captured all the footage needed and conversed easily with the scientist who wanted to demonstrate the habitat; she talked to Anthony too and kept him engaged in her process. Erin was the consummate professional. She and the scientist showed him what they were looking at and Erin showed him some of the shots she was able to obtain. She spent about two hours gathering all the footage and shooting from different angles. Because of Erin's personality none of this felt like work to Anthony and the time flew by. He really enjoyed getting to be part of her world. He could get lost in Erin and the work she did. She was special and just drew him in.

Erin thanked the scientist and he headed back to his other work. Erin turned and started to pack up her gear while conversing with Anthony. She brushed the sand out of the gear and packed it away carefully. Anthony stood by watching and completely captivated by Erin. She kept him engaged in conversation with her. Her phone buzzed again with another message and this time she looked at it. Her body language indicated she wasn't happy, but she regained her professional, carefree status and tried to bring herself back into the moment. Anthony wondered what made her stiffen, but she returned almost immediately to their jovial conversation and packed up her gear. Besides her gorgeous body, she exuded confidence and sunshine and she treated everyone with dignity and respect. She finished packing the gear up and straightened up just as a guy came running up toward them. She didn't seemed at all pleased. Her fear and anger radiated off her.

"Erin," he called out. Anthony watched Erin's face change dramatically; she was cringing, with an almost angry demeanor. "Hey Erin, babe, it's good to see you again."

"What do you want Devin?" It was an exasperated question and she didn't seem at all pleased to see him. Her body language was stiff and unyielding, no longer fun and playful. Anthony felt a vibe from Erin about the guy, and the guy struck him as sleazy. He started getting close and Anthony watched, fascinated as Erin backed up away from him, keeping distance between them. She was actually repelled by him.

"I wanted to see you baby. Didn't you get my messages? I think we need to give us another chance. It's been much too long." He kept coming toward her and she put her hand out on his chest pushing him back. It was a football stiff arm move.

"Devin, for the last time there is no us, there never was us, we are not together or connected in any way, shape or form. Get that through your head. Leave. Me. Alone. I have a restraining order on file against you and you need to back up now. I will call the cops." Her voice was raised and she was trying to make her point, but she was radiating fear of this guy. Anthony was ready to intervene. "You are not welcome here Devin. We are not a thing. We never were. And we never will be. Go away Devin."

"C'mon baby. We can work this out."

"I'm **not** your baby. I'm nothing to you. There's nothing to work out. Quit this now Devin. We are nothing, **not now, not ever**, we never were, and never will be. Go away!" Her voice kept rising and she was emphasizing each word clearly. She bent down keeping her eyes on Devin, picked up her gear, grabbed Anthony and headed off to her car.

"You can't get rid of me Erin. I just bought the house across the street from you. I moved in today and so we're neighbors now. I'll see you every day." Erin went rigid at that statement. She kept walking and her anger was now radiating off her.

"Erin, darlin', who is that guy?" Anthony finally found his voice when they were away from Devin.

"Anthony, let's stow the gear in the car and I'll tell you over dinner, my treat. My favorite taco place is just over there. It's been a really long day and I need a minute to decipher all of this, and figure out how to tell you all about him, and we need sustenance." She was taking really deep breaths of air and trying to regain some control. Devin stalked off the other direction and headed toward a group of people on the beach. Anthony watched him as the other group moved away from Devin.

"Ok. I'm here for you darlin'. That guy looks like trouble. You're Cassi's friend and so a part of this family. I can help if you will let me. I don't want you hurt." She smiled at him but he could feel her anger at Devin and see the fear, anger in her eyes. She had beautiful hazel green eyes and they darkened with the fear and anger, making the gold in them stand out; they glittered with her anger and fear. Anthony knew she was in over her head with that Devin guy. They walked over to the taco place, the owner called her by name and she ordered two specials for them with drinks. She introduced Anthony to Ari. Ari told her he would bring their meal out shortly.

Erin led Anthony to a table that was farther away from the crowd so they could talk. She made sure she was sitting where she could keep an eye on where Devin was and if he was approaching. Anthony was impressed with Erin. She didn't let her anger for Devin show when she interacted with Ari. She was trying to keep it from him too, but he needed to know. So, he pressed her a bit. He knew this guy was trouble with a capital T.

Over dinner Erin told Anthony about Devin and the events that transpired to date; answering questions that Anthony asked. She let him know that no one else knew about this except the police for the restraining order. She told him that after a couple of months at the production house Devin had asked her out and she declined. Devin pushed and pushed, kept at her and asking her out, and she repeatedly told him that she would not go out with him ever. Devin figured it was because they were co-workers and it was against the company policy, so he found another job elsewhere and tried again. He kept turning up everywhere and inserted himself in her life, but she still wouldn't go out with him. He did that for months and finally stopped, for which she was grateful. Today she received two text messages from him, after months of no contact, and it totally rocked her world.

"I heard you tell him that you had a restraining order. Is that for Devin to keep so many feet away?"

"Yes. He's not supposed to come within 100 feet of me." She pulled the document out of her bag and handed that to Anthony. She was still shaky.

"And now he's moved in across the street which totally freaks me out and makes me want to move, except that I love my house and it's all mine, free and clear. I worked hard to pay off all my bills, my mom's medical bills, final expenses, my house, my car. I don't know what he's capable of. He scares the hell out of me. He won't back down and won't take the hint that I want nothing to do with him. I'm sorry for my language." She buried her face in her hands. Anthony could see that she was freaked out and very rattled. This situation was over her head and she had no way to protect herself against Devin. The restraining order wouldn't do anything either, not the way it was written.

"Erin, darlin', look at me." Erin finally looked up at Anthony. He could see the hurt, the pain and the fear. She finally let down and let Anthony in.

"I want to help you. This is a bad situation, and it's getting deeper for you. I know you don't have anyone else to turn to. Do you have security cameras around your property?" She shook her head no. "I have a cousin, Stefano, in the security business. I'll have him install cameras and motion lights, sensors around your place tomorrow. In the meantime, do you want company tonight? I can sleep on the couch."

"Anthony, thank you for that. I really like you and have enjoyed our day today, but I don't want to get you mixed up in this and I don't want you or your family to get hurt because of me. I find myself drawn to you. Thanks for wanting to protect me, I'm so grateful you were here with me today and all your help. I'm just totally freaked out right now and don't know what to do. There isn't anyone else I can turn to. I don't have any family; I've tried so hard not to burden anyone with my problems, but I don't know what to do anymore. I'm totally at a loss and I really don't know where else to turn."

Anthony and Erin talked about her life. She explained that growing up it was just her and her mom, and she lost her mom a couple years ago after a long illness. He offered again to stay with her and tomorrow they would get security cameras to help protect her. Finally, she agreed that she would like to have him stay with her tonight, he would bring her some sense of peace, plus she was attracted to him. He could see the visible relief in her body language when he pushed enough for her to say yes. He knew she was independent from all her experience and taking care of her mom, and wouldn't readily accept help, except this situation was out of her control. She didn't know how to let people in. She needed him and she knew that.

"You don't have to sleep on the couch though. I have a spare bed for you. Anthony, seriously, thank you for your help. I thought Devin had learned his lesson but now I don't know what to do, the restraining order doesn't seem to deter him. He's relentless. Thanks for helping me have some peace tonight." Anthony got up and came around sitting down by Erin and wrapped his arm around her, pulling her close.

He told her he would be there for her and she could count on him. She leaned into his embrace and he realized how nicely she fit in his arms. He could feel her shivers and he pulled her closer to protect her and help her warm up a bit. This Devin could become a huge problem. He needed to dig into Devin's past and see what they were up against. Anthony wanted to protect Erin. Anthony and his family had enough reach they could help her with this situation. Erin snuggled up into his embrace and just wanted to stay there. It was so nice to have someone to help and look out for her. Plus he was hunky! It had been so long since she had had some sort of support. He took a picture of her restraining order and then handed it back to her. Erin shared the text messages with him too. Anthony was worried about this Devin character. The text messages were suggestive and very menacing. There was nuanced meaning and Anthony realized Erin didn't fully comprehend how much of a threat Devin actually was. She was innocent and way over her head with Devin.

*****

Devin arrived back at his new house and started to unload his pickup. He was going to keep a careful eye on Erin and he would find a way to take her. She belonged to him and only him. Somehow he needed her to see that and he would do anything to make her his. She couldn't just tell him no; he had invested too much time into winning her over and she would be his. She belonged to him. He didn't know who the guy was she was with at the beach, but he would take care of him and then find a way to get Erin to trust him. She was the one person who could elude him time after time and he aimed to make her his. She belonged to him. She was the only girl who had ever said no to him and he couldn't abide that, so his mission now was clear. He had to have her, even if that meant kidnapping her and holding her hostage. She would be his. He started to gel a plan in his mind. He knew her work schedule and he knew her movements around the city. He just needed to figure out when and where to strike. Devin set his plan in motion in his mind.

Devin unloaded four boxes and hefted them inside. He went back for his clothes and a couple of smaller boxes. He needed to check with Richard to see how far he could push the restraining order. Erin was determined to keep Devin out of her life, and he needed to know how much leeway he had. He had spent too many nights in jail because of the restraining order and he didn't know how many more chances he had. He sent another menacing text to Erin reminding her that she belonged to him and only him, and then he called Richard. Erin ignored the text but Anthony asked her to forward it to him. She did that and Anthony's mind started to put his own plan in place. He needed to help her and protect her. This guy was a definite threat. Erin didn't have enough experience but Anthony did from his time in the SEALs and he was going to protect her. Anthony knew that Devin was capable of destroying Erin; he had dealt with Devin's type before. Anthony may even need to call in his friend Jake for help. He was going to protect Erin.

As Devin wandered his new house, he picked out the first bedroom on the west side of the house to be the perfect location to tie up and keep Erin confined. It faced an empty quad, so no one would be the wiser when he had her captive in his house. No one would question why there were bars on the windows. His goal was to kidnap Erin, tie her up in the room that had no escape because of the bars he would install on the windows, and the special locks on the doors, and he would have her at his beck and call no matter when he wanted her to satisfy his needs, his cravings. She would beg him to satisfy her too and she in turn would slake his lust for her. She had told him no too many times and this time she wasn't getting away. She would pay dearly for telling him no. He laughed to himself. This was almost too easy.

*****

Erin and Anthony headed to the production company office to drop off the gear and then headed to Erin's house. She asked if Anthony wanted to go to his house first and then to Erin's but he declined.   She got him situated in her spare room, brought him towels, a toothbrush, toothpaste and a brand new razor with shaving cream. He got settled and then headed into the kitchen. Erin was standing, staring out the front windows looking at the house that said 'sold' on it across the street. She was keeping away from sight, but she just watched. Anthony could feel her anxiety and fear across the room.

"Erin, darlin', don't think about him. I'm here and you're safe with me. Ok?" He walked over and put his hands on her shoulders. He could feel her trembling. He gently turned her to face him and wrapped her in his arms. She clung to him and tried to compose herself. She didn't like to show weakness and this brought out her fear in spades. Devin could see Anthony wrapping Erin in his arms through his binoculars and he seethed under the surface. It should be him comforting her, not this tattooed guy. What was Erin thinking? She was his and only his. This other guy was trouble.

"Thank you Anthony." She took a deep breath and wrapped her arms around his waist and laid her head on his sculptured chest. "I'm sure you didn't expect this today did you?" She took a couple more deep breaths. "I'm sorry to involve you in this. I don't know what Devin is capable of, but he's relentless. He scares the hell out of me. Sorry for my language." Anthony liked to be needed and Erin was amazing. She fit his body so well and she had the most unique scent of flowers. She had definitely captured his attention and he would do anything for her. He didn't want her hurt. This guy Devin was a menace; Anthony was aware of what Devin was capable of. He'd seen it a thousand times in his Navy service. Erin was lost in Anthony; the feel of his arms around her made her feel safe and cared for. She could feel his well-defined muscled torso and his strong arms, his heartbeat. He also heightened her senses with his cologne. It was like a spicy suede and she could easily fall under its spell, just like she was under the spell of the man who wore it. He exuded confidence and she was aware of his magnificent body under her hands. She wanted him with her entire being. She had never experienced this kind of want before and it scared her.

Anthony walked her away from the window, shutting the blinds, effectively shutting Devin out. He sat her at the counter and found her kettle. She directed him to the tea bags and the cups. They sat and talked for another hour or so. Anthony asked a lot of questions and she helped him to understand that Devin needed more than a restraining order, but the police and sheriff told Erin that their hands were tied and they couldn't do anything until Devin actually made a move against her physically. She said that she felt the police were just placating her with the restraining order. Anthony knew the restraining order was no match for Devin and his antics. He didn't want Erin hurt. Erin shared that her fear is that Devin would strike and she would be dead before the police did anything.

Anthony had already called his cousin and the security system would be installed tomorrow morning. He got as much information about Devin as he could from Erin and he called his other cousin, Thomas, and had Thomas run a background check of Devin Traeger. He sent the texts too. Thomas told him he would see what he could do to help, and Anthony sent him the restraining order. Thomas told him that the way the order was written nothing would stop or deter Devin, and Thomas confided that the system didn't do much to protect women like Erin. Thomas thanked Anthony for staying with Erin, suggesting that perhaps he needed to move in with her permanently to keep her safe, seeing as how Anthony didn't have a house of his own; he also ordered extra patrols in Erin's neighborhood. No one deserved this kind of treatment, or to be made to feel threatened.

Erin checked all the doors more than once, and made sure the blinds were shut. They headed to their rooms and Erin crawled into bed after changing into a simple oversized t-shirt to sleep.   She trusted Anthony so wasn't worried that she was just in a thin cotton t-shirt. He was so amazing and the fact that he wanted to help protect her was in itself a way for her to put her trust in him, plus he was soon to be Cassi's brother-in-law. She hadn't had that in a long time, and she was grateful for his help and protection. She had dealt with Devin on her own for so long, and it was nice tonight to have a bit of protection. She really was out of her league here, but Anthony was able to allay her fears at least for tonight and help her.

Shortly after midnight Anthony heard Erin and she seemed to be in the throes of a nightmare. He quickly headed to her room, which was right next door to his; she was thrashing about and Anthony gathered her in his arms and held her against him while trying to wake her. She fought him for a bit, and he realized she was really strong, but she finally opened her eyes and realized he was only trying to help. She had tears streaming down her cheeks and she was very tense. She kept saying no over and over again. He rubbed circles on her back, held her against his very solid frame and whispered to her that she was ok. Erin, though freaked out with her nightmare, was very aware of Anthony's body molded to hers. She absorbed his warmth, strength and the peace he brought to her. He was comforting and sexy as hell. She wanted to get lost in Anthony; she had been alone for far too long. She wanted to be loved, protected, and held; she wanted Anthony to tell her it was all going to be ok. It was times like this she wished she had more experience with men and she would know how to handle all the feelings running through her body.

"Shhhh Erin, its ok honey. It's Anthony and I'm right here. I've got you and you're in my arms darlin'. You're ok honey; you're safe." She clung to him, sobs wracking her body. "It will all be ok darlin'. " She finally unclenched her fists, relaxed a little, and her arms wrapped around Anthony in a big hug. "You're safe darlin'. I'm here with you. I'm not going to let anything happen to you honey." He enjoyed her soft curves pressing against him through her thin t-shirt, but he really needed to change his line of thinking. She needed him to keep her safe and he needed to help her relax. Her breathing came back to normal and she clung to him, wrapping him more fully in her arms.

"Thank you Anthony. I didn't mean to wake you. I'm so glad you're here though. That dream was too real." She said all of this through the hiccupping sobs. She curled into Anthony and laid her head on his shoulder absorbing strength from him. "Thank you for keeping me safe. I'm totally freaked out right now after the text messages, Devin moving in across the street, and just everything." Anthony laid down in her bed with her nestled in his arms. He pulled the covers over both of them and tried to help her relax. She felt so good against him, soft and small, perfect, and he wanted to protect her. He needed her to rest and she needed to feel safe. Thomas was right, he needed to be here permanently for her. He needed to move in with her. He caressed her back with his free hand and held her tightly with his other arm. She melted into him, her head on his shoulder, and finally relaxed enough to go back to sleep. Anthony murmured to her that she was safe and he kissed her forehead. Finally, Anthony drifted to sleep with Erin snug in his arms. He could get use to this.

*****

Sunday morning, with sunlight streaming in the upper windows, Erin stirred and felt Anthony's body under her hands and his arm wrapped around her. Her hands moved over his upper body, reveling in the feel of his muscles, and she panicked momentarily, then remembered he helped her last night as she was dreaming her nightmare. She opened her eyes and dared to look up into Anthony's beautiful, handsome face. He was watching her with a smile on his face and she blushed.

"Mornin' darlin'." Anthony drawled with a smile on his lips. He had watched her for the last few minutes.

"Morning Anthony. Thank you for your help last night my sweet hero. I truly hope I didn't hurt you when I was thrashing about." She tried to smile at him.

"No you didn't hurt me, but I was surprised at how strong you are. You can take care of yourself." He smiled at her.

"Probably comes from lugging all my gear around and my self-defense training. I like to work out and lift weights." She smiled back. "Did you sleep or did I keep you up?"

"I slept. It was nice holding you in my arms." She blushed a beautiful shade of red. "Sorry, I had to get that in beautiful!" Her blush deepened and she started to extract herself from his arms. "Where are you going?"

"I should get up and give you some space." She didn't know how to navigate this. He realized she didn't understand what was happening between them.

"It's early darlin'. Just stay here a bit and let me hold you, relax honey, you're safe in my arms, I promise. We're going to talk about today." She looked up at him quizzically, apprehensively. She swallowed hard and grabbed a breath of air. She tried to re-center herself. She was so out of her league here. She had no idea how to navigate this situation, but she found herself very attracted to Anthony.

"Before you say what you need to tell me, can I please first just say thank you for being here for me last night and with me at my shoot, protecting me, keeping me safe. I do so appreciate you. I don't know how to navigate this, whatever this is between us, but thank you. I'm just very inexperienced, but I'm really attracted to you." She raised up, sliding up his body and making Anthony totally aware of her soft curves, and kissed his cheek. He tightened his hold on her, cupped the back her head with his hand, turned his head and captured her lips with his own and turned her innocent kiss into a full-blown kiss experience. She gasped momentarily, relaxed with the sensations she was feeling, and then instinct kicked in and she moaned into his mouth as he thoroughly ravaged her mouth with his own. She kissed him back with fervor, her hands sliding up into his hair and around his neck, instinct kicking in. She ended up laying on Anthony's chest and feeling his warmth. Her eyes were closed, savoring the moment, and she was enjoying the sensations of his lips on hers. She almost whimpered when he pulled away, breaking the kiss.

"Wow that was amazing!" She whispered when she came back to earth and her eyes finally flickered open. Anthony looked at her and realized that she had never been kissed like that before. He tried to wrap his head around that fact and just how innocent she was. He didn't want to corrupt her, ruin her, but he was attached to her, attracted to her, and he wanted so much more of her. He wanted to make her his. He just needed to take it slow and help her to learn. Alex was right about that.

"Sorry Erin darlin'. I just had to taste your lips." She blushed fiercely. He chuckled at her reaction. She slid off his chest and laid back on the side of him with his arms still around her. "Ok, so what I was about to say, before I got distracted with you in my arms, is that my cousin Stefano will be here at 10 this morning to install security cameras, motion lights and security devices on your windows and doors. He'll make sure that you can see your house at all times through your phone and he'll give me access too so I can help keep you safe. Then, we are heading my folks' house for family lunch." She started to protest but he put his fingers on her lips to still her.   His arm around her waist tightened its hold on her and she relaxed a bit more against him.

"This afternoon we are going to my gym and we're going to see what you have for self-defense strategies, and we're going to work on some things to help in case Devin shows up again unannounced. I want you safe honey, and my brothers, my family, and I, are going to make sure Devin doesn't hurt you. The police and sheriff have their hands tied in what they can do, and your restraining order is no threat to Devin, but you have family now to watch over and protect. You have me." He paused and watched her for a moment. "Erin, darlin', I want to move in here with you to keep you safe." She panicked and tried to process everything.

"Anthony, you have done so much for me already.   I don't want to intrude on your family lunch and I don't want you or your family hurt because of me." Her eyes were full of fear. "I like you a lot Anthony, and your brothers that I met too. And I could definitely get used to your kisses too. I love being in your arms, feeling protected and safe, but I don't want any of you hurt or having a target on you because of me. I am so sorry I got you involved in my mess." She was desperately trying to get away. She really cared about his family and his well-being. Anthony was not about to let her run. He held her tightly to him. He reached up and cupped her cheek.

"Erin, darlin', I'm involved now and I'm glad to be able to help. I like you too, very much and I want to help protect you. No one should have to go through this without help, and you are on your own; I want to change that. I want to be here to help you through this. I want to see where this thing between us goes. My cousin Thomas works on the police force and he has checked into Devin's background, and the restraining order. Devin has a rap sheet a mile long, but none of the charges have stuck; he's hurt a lot of women, and I'm going to ensure you are safe beautiful lady. I am here to keep you as safe as I possibly can; you are amazing and I want you to have some peace of mind. Besides, I really like you; I'm very attracted to you. You have a family now to back you up. I know you're used to being independent, but I'm here now and I'm ready to help. You can't fight this on your own darlin' and I'm here to help. I know Devin's type, he thinks he invincible and that nothing can stop him, he doesn't take no for an answer; I've dealt with people like him before in my military career. We can protect you and ourselves too. You aren't going to get rid of me sugar; I'm here to stay and help keep you safe." He was trying to be gentle with her. He just needed her to understand that this situation was way over her head and she needed him.

Erin sat up abruptly, pulling away from Anthony, and covered her face with her hands. She was reeling from all Anthony just told her and she was trying to figure out how to protect Anthony and his family from all of this. Anthony sat up and wrapped her in his arms. He could feel her trembling and knew she was truly scared of everything that was happening. She turned toward him on her knees, looked up into his beautiful electric blue eyes and lost herself. She put her hand on his jaw and caressed him as she talked.

"Anthony, sweetie, I can't risk you or your family being hurt. Devin is not ever going to stop his pursuit of me; he scares the hell out of me because I know he's capable of destroying me and the police/sheriff won't do anything until Devin makes a move to hurt me. By the time he makes his move it could be too late for them to help. I don't want you hurt. You are too important to me to see you hurt. I'm so very sorry I dragged you into my problems. I can deal with whatever he does to me, but I can't risk you and your family, my friends Cassi, Mariah, Laurel and Kiera. Devin is obsessed with me and I know he's after my virtue, my body, but I can't risk you getting hurt; you mean too much to me to have you hurt." Tears, unbidden, slid down her cheeks. Anthony picked her up and sat her on his lap, wrapping his arms around her.

"Erin, beautiful, you didn't drag me into anything, I came willingly, and my family is going to protect you. You are one of us now, you're mine. You're Cassi's friend and I hope my friend too, maybe more than friends; I want to explore this chemistry between us. I am very attracted to you and don't want you hurt. You have people in your corner now that will help to make sure you are safe. We have a large extended family with lots of resources to help. I know you are used to taking care of yourself, fighting the world all on your own, but I want to help. It's ok to ask for help honey. This is more than you can handle on your own; Devin is a monster and he is driven to get you alone. You're right, he can destroy you and I'm not going to let that happen. I really like you and I want to help keep you safe honey. Ok?" He brushed the tears off her cheeks. She wrapped her arms around him, buried her face in his shoulder, and held on. She tried to pull herself back together and reveled in the feel of Anthony's arms around her. She was very aware of his magnificent body that was molded to her own. She was also very aware of her own body and its reaction to Anthony, and she wanted more than anything to run her hands over him. She had no idea where that thought came from, but he could kiss too and she could let herself get lost in all of what made up Anthony. She leaned in and tentatively pressed her lips to his, which helped Anthony to pull her even closer and kiss her senseless.

Chapter Two

Stefano and two members of his team arrived at 10, and Anthony helped them get started. He introduced Stefano to Erin and Stefano set his crew to work. His two helpers put up cameras in front, along the sides and back outside covering her entire yard and house, and motion lights all around her property. Stefano came in the house, working with Anthony, and put sensors on all the windows, all the doors, and in the garage, as well as cameras in strategic places inside. They wired everything into her internet connection and provided her with a secure internet connection so that outsiders couldn't break in and tamper with it. Erin was impressed with the work they did. Everything they did blended in with her décor and didn't stand out like a sore thumb.

While Anthony and his cousin were working Erin edited in the room just off the kitchen and finished the piece about Cassi and her students, and their community garden. Anthony checked on her a couple of times; she showed him the piece when she finished it. Anthony was very impressed with the segment she put together. It didn't take her long and by the time she was done with the editing, Stefano and his team were done with their installation. Erin uploaded the finished project to the drive and emailed it to the station for airing later tonight. Erin tried to settle up with Stefano for the equipment and service, but Stefano told her he just wanted her safe and taken care of. He asked for her phone to install the app, and by 11:30 everything was done. Erin pulled a tin of homemade cookies together for Stefano and his team as a small token of her appreciation. Stefano and Anthony hugged and Stefano and his team departed.

"Ok Erin, darlin', are you ready to head to my folks' place for lunch? Cassi will be there too, as well as Michael's girl." Erin nodded and tried to quell her nervousness. "Don't be nervous darlin'. My folks, my family is going to welcome you with open arms; they know you're coming with me, and they are ready to help. None of us want you hurt honey."

"Am I dressed ok? Do I need to change?" She was fidgety.

"No sugar, you look beautiful. Just relax and be yourself." Anthony came over to her and wrapped her in his arms. She looked up at him with huge, green, gorgeous eyes, and he leaned down, capturing her lips with his own. The electricity arced between them. Her knees went weak and she leaned into him for strength standing on her tiptoes to deepen the kiss. Anthony held her and kissed her thoroughly. Her arms wrapped around his shoulders and she held on because her knees were threatening to buckle.

"Let's go darlin'." Her eyes finally flickered back open and she regained her feet. Together they locked up her house and headed to her car. Devin was watching from his front window across the street. Anthony saw him, knew he was there, but Devin decided to bide his time, not come busting out the door and tackling Anthony. He would figure out how to make Erin his and how to get rid of this new wrinkle named Anthony.

Devin snarled at the thought of someone else being with his Erin. She belonged to him and he meant to make her his. He compared every woman he'd ever been with to Erin. She couldn't escape him. He knew she would be sweet and his mouth watered just thinking about her delicious flavor. He would find a way to get her in his house and keep her there forever. She would be his. To say the least Devin was obsessed with Erin and he would do anything to make her his. He just needed to carefully plan and make sure her room in his house was ready and inescapable. He had work to do. The cage still needed to be built and the bars needed installing on the windows. He needed to get to work and make sure everything was set. She would be his, only his, and she would never escape; no one but him would ever touch her.

*****

Anthony directed Erin to his parent's home and she parked out front. Another deep breath, she exited the car placing her hand in Anthony's. Together they walked to the front door and they met Anthony's brother, Alex coming out of the living room. Cassi and Alex were already there and shortly Mariah and Michael joined them. Erin hugged Cassi, greeted Alex and then turned to see Michael and Mariah.

"Erin you remember Michael and this is…."

"Dr. White?!" Erin exclaimed and gathered her in a hug.

"Erin, call me Mariah like you do when we're out at our girls' nights." They hugged again and both Anthony and Michael stood there speechless that they knew each other.

"How do you two know each other?" Michael asked.

"Dr. White, sorry Mariah, is, was, my doctor until she moved to the free clinic permanently."

"Erin, Cassi and I have girls' night out once a month with a couple others. Erin how do you know Michael and Anthony?"

"Alex did my tattoo yesterday and I met these wonderful gentlemen at Ink, Inc." Michael and Anthony exchanged a look and Michael mouthed "wonderful gentlemen' to Anthony. Both of them smiled. She had them pegged all wrong. Erin was one of those people who saw the good in everyone until they disappointed her or made her see them differently.

They came further into the house and Anthony introduced Erin to his mom and dad. They both welcomed her and told her they were glad she was here today. They kept moving and eventually stopped outside in the backyard. Cassi, Alex, Michael and Mariah were standing facing the house discussing something and Anthony and Erin came to join them but had their backs to the house.   They were all in conversation, with Erin doing more listening and tuning into her surroundings.

Erin was trying to relax but her muscles were tense, her eyes darting all around, and she was keyed in on the goings on around her, on edge. She was afraid Devin would jump out from behind a bush or the fence or something. She was in a new place and keeping herself ready at all times was just her norm. Her demons chased her no matter where she went. All of them were talking, conversing easily, when all of a sudden Erin felt a presence behind her and changed her stance subtly. She braced herself for the worst possible scenario when Kade put his hands on her shoulders. Erin's training kicked into high gear and she reached up, grabbed his wrist, brought her elbow into his ribs and kneeled down and threw Kade over her shoulder to the ground. Everyone stood there stunned. As Kade was heading over her back Erin realized this was not Devin so she helped to break his fall so he wouldn't get hurt. She knew how to help alleviate pain as he fell. Kade sort of floated to the ground with Erin's help, and landed gently on his back. She could see the surprise in his eyes; she was mortified.

"Hey Kade," Anthony said when he recovered and tried to keep the smile off his face. "This is Erin. Erin, this is my brother Kade." Erin's eyes grew large, she let go of Kade who was safely on the ground now, mumbled an apology, abruptly stood, turned and ran out of the backyard through the gate.

"What in the hell was that?" Kade said, still stunned that he was laying on the ground. He was not prepared for a woman of her stature to throw him to the ground. Kade was 6'4" and about 230 pounds. He had at least a foot on her and 100 pounds or more. He had electric blue eyes with dark, wavy hair, just like Anthony.

"Sorry man. Erin has self-defense training and she's on edge right now. There's a lot going on in her life right now.   I'll explain in a bit, but right now I need to find Erin before she bolts." Alex and Michael helped Kade off the ground and Anthony took off the way Erin ran.

"Kade are you ok?" Mariah asked as she ran her hand over his ribs.

"Yeah doc. Stunned, but not hurt. She surprised me with the hit to my ribs and then flying through the air. She seemed to realize I wasn't a threat and she helped me to fall without getting hurt." Michael said it was like Kade floated to the ground. All of them rallied around Kade. "Who is Erin?"

"She's Cassi and Mariah's girlfriend. She came in yesterday and I put a tattoo on her shoulder. Anthony was taken with her and he accompanied her to one of her video shoots, but still not sure why she's here. Anthony told mom and dad that he needed all of our help. I guess we need to wait and see. Just so you all know Anthony is very interested in Erin. She captured his attention. Hopefully Anthony was able to catch up to her."

"Should I go help and let her know I'm ok?" Kade asked.

"Might not be a bad idea."

Anthony caught up to Erin. She was sitting on the front porch steps with her head in hands down to her knees, buried away from everyone and everything. Anthony perched next to her and pulled her to him. "Hey darlin', you ok?"

"I'm so sorry Anthony. I'm on edge with Devin and I just reacted. I didn't mean to hurt your brother. I'm so very sorry." She still hadn't looked up yet; Anthony could hear the distress in her voice. Kade came into view and Anthony motioned him over.

"Erin, honey, look at me please." He waited and she finally raised her head from her hands and risked a glance. "Erin this my brother Kade. Kade, this is Erin."

"That was some greeting Erin. Nice to meet you." Kade said smiling.

"Kade I am so sorry.   Did I hurt you?" She was definitely reeling.

"No, just surprised the hell out of me. Is everything ok?" Kade was looking between the two of them. He could feel the electricity arcing between them. He was genuinely concerned about Erin. She seemed on edge and worried.

"Kade, Erin is dealing with a huge problem and I'm helping her. She is like family, and I am finding myself wanting to be with her, attracted to her. Anyway, I need all of my family to help and see what we can do to keep this little lady safe."

"I'm intrigued Anthony." Kade sat down on Erin's other side and she felt small nestled between them and completely overwhelmed. Tears of frustration and fear slid out of the corners of her eyes. Anthony put his arm around her.

"Erin, honey, please don't cry. We're going to figure this out and I'll keep you safe; my family will help." She held herself rigid. She was afraid to relax. "Kade, we'll tell everyone at lunch, but I went with Erin to one of her video shoots yesterday and this guy named Devin ran up to her as we were finishing up. Erin here has a restraining order against him, but the police and the sheriff won't do anything about that until Devin makes a move physically. Devin has sent her some menacing text messages too. Anyway, Devin wanted to get a rise out of Erin here; it turns out he bought the house across the street from her and just moved in. He's trying to intimidate her. So she's a little bit on edge."

"Whoa!" Kade looked at Anthony. "Erin," Kade reached down and turned her face gently so she would look at him. "I'm ok, not hurt at all. My brother and my family and I are going to do what we can to protect you. This Devin guy sounds like a real peach, but we will help you, protect you and keep you safe. I know that restraining orders don't have any real protection for those they are designed to protect." Tears still managed to trail their way down her cheeks. "Don't cry sugar. We're here for you. You have a very large family now that will work together and help keep you safe." He pulled her into a bear hug. Anthony hugged her from the other side. Kade could feel her trembling. She was so tiny and he was very concerned for her well-being. He would help Anthony and they would protect her.

"Kade I am so sorry, I never meant to throw you to the ground. Thank you both. I've never had anyone to look out for me before and I really don't know how to deal with this situation. I have been dealing with Devin on my own for so long. I appreciate you both. Thank you." She looked up at him and he was lost in her beautiful eyes. Erin worked to pull herself back together and brush the tears off her face. She took some deep breaths and tried to smile at both of them.

"Damn girl, you can take care of yourself! You're one tough cookie." Kade gave her a killer smile. She smiled back at him while tears slowly slid down her cheeks. The three of them got up and headed back to the backyard. Cassi and Mariah came over and intercepted Erin. They could see the tears on her cheeks and her eyes swimming. She was their friend and they wanted to help. Erin didn't want them hurt. The boys headed to talk to their brothers. Cassi and Mariah were worried about Erin, but she told them they would understand soon. She only wanted to explain things once. Erin worked hard to pull herself back together, and make herself smile again, brushing the tears off her cheeks.

"Kids, come eat!" Mom said as she peeked out into the backyard. All of them headed towards the door and Erin waited for Anthony. He wrapped his arm around her as they walked inside. Anthony kept reassuring her that all was ok and she was safe with him and his family. Erin was still deep breathing and trying to get herself back to center. Once everyone was seated and served, after grace was said, Anthony started to tell them about Erin's predicament. He explained what happened yesterday at the beach. He also regaled them with the fact that Erin drop-kicked Kade to the ground in the backyard. Erin turned several shades of red, but Anthony told them he wanted to figure out how best to help protect Erin.

"I had cousin Stefano install cameras, motion lights and sensors in Erin's house this morning, and Cousin Thomas ran a search on Devin. Devin has a rap sheet a mile long but the police and sheriff can't do anything until he tries something physically against Erin. None of the previous charges have stuck; he has a lawyer that gets him off on loopholes every time. I don't want Erin hurt. Her restraining order is no match for Devin."

"Anthony, my boy," Dad said. "We need to protect this young lady. She's family now. Let me make a few calls and see what I can figure out to help. In the meantime, Erin, girl, tell me about your work weeks. Are they normal hours or erratic?"

"Mr. Romano I don't work regular hours. I'm a news stringer so I can be sent out on the weekends, evenings too during the times I'm on call. I usually work mornings at TK Productions, but then I work odd hours for the station gathering news footage or editing pieces. In fact this evening, Cassi's kids and her community garden project will be featured on the 'Hometown Heroes' segment." Cassi smiled and inside was secretly thrilled that the project was going to get recognition.

"So your hours could present opportunity for this Devin character. Erin, child, please call me Roberto." He smiled at her. Erin relaxed just a little bit more. "Boys, after lunch come with me and we'll figure out how to protect this little lady. Anthony I want you to move into her house with her and be there to protect her." Anthony nodded. Erin started to protest, but Kade and Anthony wrapped their arms around her to reassure her. Everyone returned to their food and the conversation turned to Angelina asking her boys about their weeks. Erin had never had a large family gathering like this so she just absorbed the love and the laughter around the table, and she enjoyed the bantering. Kade was sitting on her left and he occasionally engaged her in conversation and she again apologized to him. Kade assured her he was ok.

She watched this family. All four boys and their dad were big, strong, muscled and tattooed. She admired all of their artwork including the dragon with their last name wrapped into the design. She asked Kade about his artwork, telling him how much she liked what his ink looked like, and they talked through lunch. Erin tried to make herself present in the moment. She tried to participate in the conversation and let things go.

The boys headed with their father to his study after the meal while Erin, Cassi and Mariah helped Angelina with the dishes and cleaning up.

"Erin, did Devin hurt you?" Mariah asked very concerned about her friend.

"No Mariah. He's trying to intimidate me, but he hasn't made a move yet physically, but he can really make me panic. He's good at playing mind games. He is keeping me on my toes. I know he's after my virtue. For some reason he's obsessed with me."

"Is this why you asked me about birth control?" She nodded. "I'm glad we got you protected that way, but now we need to keep you safe. How come you didn't tell us about your situation with Devin?"

"How did you meet him and how did this all start?" Cassi demanded.

Erin looked at them and sighed. These were her girls and they intended to help protect her. She felt loved.

"Mariah I didn't want you to be hurt by Devin. I thought I could protect you both by not telling you and not letting Devin know about you. He's hurt a lot of women. He's not a nice person and I didn't want you to be burdened with him knowing who you both are. Cassi, I started working at TK Productions four years ago and about a month after I started they hired Devin. He asked me out and I told him no. He kept asking and my answer was always the same. Devin strikes me as smarmy, only after one encounter, and his nearness was a turnoff. I just get a bad sensation up and down my spine when he's near. He just won't accept that I want nothing to do with him. I'm really inexperienced as you both know with dealing with men and innuendo. I don't think he's used to being told no. He's obsessed with me for some reason. He told Terry, my boss, that he was resigning because of company policy of dating a co-worker, and he took a job at another production company. I thought, naively, that was the end of it. But then he started showing up at every shoot I had for TK Productions and the news stations, and inserted himself into the productions I did off-site and tried to pursue me harder. He would call my office phone and leave suggestive messages, sometimes I had flowers or other gifts delivered via courier, and he had my company cell number where he would leave text messages and voice mails. I kept telling him no, I told him I wasn't interested, told him to leave me alone, and finally asked the police what I could do; I got a restraining order, and finally after about six months and two nights in jail he stopped, disappeared. I hadn't heard from him in almost two years, until yesterday. I'm also equally distressed about the fact that he knows where I live so he could buy the house across the street." She took a deep breath and a drink of water. All of them watched her carefully. She was reeling from all this, and Mariah was worried because it had gone on for such a long time. She looked up at them all and started again.

"Saturday, I took Anthony with me to my beach shoot after Alex finished my ink, and once I finished my shoot and was packing up the gear while talking with

Anthony, Devin comes running up to me and you heard the rest. I was so glad to have Anthony was with me. I'm not sure what Devin's capable of but he doesn't take no for an answer. He scares the hell out of me. It's unsettling. He's started sending text messages again too. They are very suggestive and very scary." Angelina came over and wrapped her in a hug.

"Erin, my Anthony will take care of you. Let us help keep you safe. We need you! You bring sunshine and just light up this family, and you have captured my Anthony's heart, which is a good thing. There is electricity between you. That's a good thing too!" She held Erin in her arms pulling Erin's head to her shoulder and holding it there. "Erin dear, do you have family?" Angelina was a little taller than Erin, and she was warm and wonderful. Erin missed having a mom and Angelina fit the bill!

"No Angelina. Growing up it was just my mom and I and I lost my mom a couple years ago, so now it's just me."

"Well you have family now. We're all here for you and my Anthony is going to help protect you." Mariah and Cassi nodded and it became a group hug. Erin felt safe in their arms and protected with these women. This was her group of sisters. She loved them all.

****

Kade and Anthony took Erin to the gym, a gym that their cousin Marco owned. Marco gave them access to the boxing ring and the weights, punching bags. Erin headed into the locker room and changed into her workout gear. Kade and Anthony changed too. She changed quickly and headed to the mats to stretch. Anthony came back out and stopped short watching Erin. She was limber, muscled and he was just taken with her. Kade came out, appreciating the view as well, and clapped his brother on the back.

"You ok bro?" Anthony nodded. Kade laughed. "You have it bad bro. She's beautiful and you should make her yours." Kade clapped him on the back again and headed over to where Erin was stretching.

"Ok Miss Erin, let's see what else you have!" Erin looked up at Kade and finished stretching. She stood up and walked with Kade into the boxing ring. "Tell me about your self-defense training."

"Well, I'm a black belt in judo." She said that simply and without hesitation. He looked at her surprised.

"Damn girl! No wonder you had that throw down to perfection. It's ingrained in you." She nodded. "Ok, I don't know judo, so let's work on a few scenarios and we'll see if we can teach you some new moves to add to your arsenal." He looked up to see if Anthony was joining them. "Yo, Anthony, get your ass in gear and get up here and join us. We haven't got all day." Kade's voice cut through Anthony's daydream and he moved his feet toward the ring.

"Kade," Erin asked smiling, "are you the oldest?"

"How did you know?" He smiled at her.

"Just the way you talk to Anthony. You just seem like the oldest." She smiled back at him and Kade could see what drew Anthony to Erin. She was pure sunshine and she radiated good vibes. Erin didn't realize how many shades of electric blue there were. Kade had really bright electric blue eyes and Anthony's were a shade deeper, but just as electric. A family of very good looking men!

Anthony joined them and for the next two hours they did different scenarios and coached Erin in other ways to help her with Devin. Erin told them about her SING method and she demonstrated using Kade as her assailant. She also showed both of them the other scenarios she knew how to deflect. She had Anthony come at her with a 2x4 and she disarmed him leaving no doubt in either of their minds that Erin could protect herself, but they also knew that Devin wouldn't be easily deterred. Devin was determined and so they all needed to be on their toes.

They worked the punching bag and watched her form, correcting things here and there, and they worked on weights to tone her muscles even more. Kade showed her ways to add more to her punch without expending more energy, and she tried many times, finally got the hang of it and really nailed the punching bag. He told her that his training would help her with stamina and power. As they finished their workout Kade could see part of her ink and he asked if he could look at the whole tattoo. Anthony helped move her hair and the strap of her tank top. Kade told her it was a stunning piece. Anthony told him that Erin created it, a way to memorialize her mom, and Alex executed it. It was still covered with the clear sheet Alex had put on it yesterday.

"Erin, can you work out with us every morning this coming week. We can do early, say six and then you have time to shower, and change for work." Kade asked.

"That would be awesome, yes. Thank you both for the pointers, the help and for the protection." Erin answered. "I don't know how to be part of a big family, but I sure appreciate you both." She hugged both of them and headed to locker room to change. Erin dropped Anthony off to get his bike from Ink, Inc. and she headed home. The brothers had put Anthony's bike into the shed to keep it safe while he was with Erin yesterday at the shoot.

Erin's phone rang just as she arrived home. Anthony told her, as they were leaving the gym, he would be back this evening and to keep vigilant until he returned. She promised that she would be watchful and be careful. She locked all the doors and retreated to her office area, away from the windows. She made sure her car was in the garage too. She cleared space to put Anthony's motorcycle into the garage when he came. She didn't want Devin to have opportunity to hurt Anthony.

"This is Erin." She listened. "Hi Brad." She listened more. "I'm glad you liked the project. Is it airing tonight?" She talked further with him and he told her he had two more segments for next week that he needed her to work on. She noted all the details and finished her call with him. She started to put things into her calendar program. She had a busy week coming up, but she thrived on work; work was pretty much all Erin knew. She didn't date, she just had girls' nights out occasionally, but mostly she edited, worked on client projects and she took care of her gardens of roses. She texted Cassi to let her know the piece was definitely airing this evening.

Her phone buzzed as she hung up and it turned out that her security system was letting her know there was activity at her front door. She quietly headed to the door and made sure it was locked and the deadbolt engaged. She checked every door in her house. She stayed out of range of the windows and watched her screen as Devin wandered her front porch searching for her and perhaps a way in. Anthony's phone was alerted too. He immediately recorded the images and sent it on to Thomas. Anthony was in route to Erin's, so he stepped up his pace a bit. He didn't want her alone for too long. Erin pulled out a spare key to give to Anthony so he could have access to her house, and she put it on a spare key ring. She also made sure Anthony could park his bike in the garage, double checking the space available. She stacked up a few more plastic bins full of her baking pans and tools. Anthony could easily fit his bike into the garage now and maybe keep it safe from anything Devin could do to it. She had a second garage door opener, so she would give that to Anthony.

Erin wasn't breathing normally, but she was prepared to fight if necessary. Her house was locked up and she knew she was safe if she stayed inside. She took all her notes and computer and set up at the kitchen counter so she could be away from the windows. She worked on her projects, added things into her calendar, and watched Devin as he wandered her front porch and tried the front door. He knocked a couple of times, but she wasn't about to answer the door; that would just be inviting trouble. Anthony crested the hill on his Harley and Devin heard him coming. Devin turned and hightailed it away from her front door. Anthony watched him go and watched as he headed back home. Anthony parked in the driveway, locked up his bike, grabbed his bag and headed to the front door.

"Erin, darlin', its Anthony." She opened the door and let him in. He closed the door, locked it and Erin threw herself into his arms. She was trembling but trying to keep it together. "It's ok beautiful. I'm here now." Anthony dropped his bag and gathered her into his embrace.

"Thank you Anthony. I'm guessing Devin heard you coming. I am so glad you're here with me." She took his hand and led him into the house further. Anthony settled into the spare bedroom in her house while Erin started dinner. He unpacked some clothes into the dresser Erin made sure was ready for him and his toiletries in the adjoining bathroom. Anthony came back and perched at the counter. She told him he could move his bike into the garage, which Anthony did and returned to the kitchen counter.

"Anthony, sweetie, I want to give you access to my calendar so you will know what I'm working on and where I'm at every day. I keep it as detailed as possible with addresses and contact names of the places I need to be. The news team called me about an hour ago and I have two new projects to work on this week, which will take me out of the office and on site."

"Darlin, I'm sticking to you like glue this week. My schedule is such that I have inking to do in the mornings while you are at TK Productions editing, and then I'm with you in the afternoons and evenings." Anthony laid that out there. Erin ran around the counter and grabbed him in a big hug. He pulled her up into his lap.

"Thank you Anthony." She kissed his cheek and he held her, pulling her mouth to him and devouring her mouth. She moaned and deepened the kiss. This was pure heaven. Feelings that Erin had never experienced before were running through her and she wanted to just lose herself in Anthony. Erin gave Anthony a key to the house, trying to break the spell. She really wished she had more experience with the feelings that were developing between herself and Anthony. Maybe she needed to talk to Cassi and Mariah. Maybe they could help her navigate this.

*****

Anthony and Erin settled into a routine where they headed to the gym at 6 every morning and worked out with Kade. Erin was getting stronger, leaner and more in tune with how to throw a punch, and be more effective with her judo. They worked on stamina and pushed Erin to her breaking point. Kade and Anthony were impressed with her skills and her ability to learn from their teaching. She didn't back down from the challenges, she didn't complain, and she didn't let them rattle her. She pushed hard every morning. Then, Anthony would drive her to TK Productions where she would edit on the three projects she had all the footage for. They were learning all about each other and learning to live in the same house.

Erin was learning to be on the back of Anthony's motorcycle. She was enjoying the feel of him and he loved having her arms, her body, wrapped around him.   Erin met Anthony at noon, they headed home and did lunch; Anthony accompanied her to all the video shoots in the afternoons taking Erin's car. He was like her production assistant and got really good at helping her with the gear, setting the shots and putting things away. Erin saw Devin several times, and Anthony knew he was there too. Devin didn't make any moves; he was just watching and waiting for an opportune moment.   Devin was trying to see any weaknesses that Anthony might have. He kept his distance but he wanted Erin rattled and off-guard. He accomplished that easily, except Erin didn't let it show to her clients; Anthony was the only one who knew.

This same scenario played out for the next few weeks. Anthony was settling into the spare bedroom at Erin's house and they grew closer every day. Erin enjoyed Anthony's company and his kisses. Devin left Erin alone for the time being, mostly because he was figuring out how to get rid of Anthony. Anthony and Kade, and the rest of the Romano clan kept vigil to help protect Erin. Anthony had family all over the city and they were all aware of the events. Everyone was trying to help. They kept checking into Devin's background, but had no way to get the restraining order or other charges to stick. Most of the women he had hurt didn't remember who he was or were too scared to come forward and press charges. Devin knew how to intimidate and how to cover his tracks or have his lawyer find loopholes in the charges.

Devin had a plan in mind and he just needed a few minutes without Anthony around to execute it. He had designed on paper a special room he would build in his house; his goal was to get Erin alone, lock her away and she would be his to use for his pleasure whenever he wanted. He had gathered enough information about Erin, where she went during the daytimes, and the stations she worked for, as well as her car make and model. Devin had amassed a lot of intel about Erin. He had the parts ordered for the special room in his house and would construct and install once it all arrived. She would belong to him. He would be patient, bide his time, and then Erin would be his. He would kidnap her and lock her away in his house and use her body to satisfy his needs. He knew his plan was brilliant. Erin, the one person who could elude him, would soon be his and only his.

*****

Saturday morning came with bright sunshine. They were into their fifth week together. Erin made breakfast and shortly after they finished eating, Anthony's phone rang. He needed to go into work and complete another ink for a buddy. The guy really wanted Anthony to do his artwork.

"Erin, darlin', I need to go to Ink, Inc. and work on a tattoo for a buddy of mine. Do you want to come with or will you ok here alone?"

"I really need to do some yard work Anthony. It's my first Saturday with no productions. If it's ok with you I'll work on my roses and my flowers, get the dead parts out, prune and maybe mow the lawn. I'll be vigilant. I'll be ok." She kissed him.

"Ok. Do you want me to have one my brothers come by and spend the morning? I should only be gone for a couple of hours."

'I should be ok. I will just trim my roses and my flowers and wait to mow the lawn until you are back. You'll be able to see the yard with the cameras. I'll keep my eyes open and my ears perked up. The motion detectors will help me keep vigilant. Thanks handsome for worrying about me." He wrapped her in his arms.

"I'm sorry I have to go do this." He held her to him and kissed her forehead.

"I'm a big girl and I'm tough! You and Kade have taught me well. I will be ok and you have a job to do! Will I see you around lunchtime?" He nodded. He kissed her soundly and prepared to head to work.

Anthony went to his room and grabbed all the things he needed while Erin found her gardening gloves, and grabbed her pruning shears. She found her yard bags and prepared for her morning of taking care of her gardens. Erin walked Anthony to his bike and kissed him goodbye. Anthony knew Devin was watching out his window and he prayed that Erin would be safe. She headed back to the house, locked the front door and headed out the back to work on her flowers. This was the first time, in as long as she could remember, that she didn't put her headphones in and get lost in her country music. She needed to be totally aware of her surroundings in case Devin got any ideas. She needed to hear any movement from the front of the house. Her phone was in her pocket and would vibrate if Devin made a move.

Anthony arrived at the shop and texted Thomas to see if he could take some extra laps by their house letting him know Erin was alone with Devin across the street. Anthony was considering Erin's house his! He was just taken with her. He also let Kade know he was at the shop and the Erin was alone. Kade said he would wander over to her place in about thirty minutes. Anthony breathed just a little easier. His family was amazing. They protected and watched over Erin and made sure she had knowledge of how to protect herself, and building her muscles and stamina. Anthony loved his family and they were all loving having Erin in their midst. Erin was relaxing into the family element too. This was all good. He was falling head over heels in love with Erin.

Erin made her way across the back of the house clipping the dead flowers and vines off the roses, shaping the bushes, making sure the new buds could grow, and she trimmed the other perennials in her yard. She checked her water lines too. She filled her first bag, tied it up and set it aside, then grabbed for the second bag. She kept her eyes open, her ears tuned into every noise and nuance of the breeze. She could smell her roses and was thrilled they were thriving. She was on high alert, rigid and ready to strike if she needed to. She seemed to always be in defensive stance these days.

Forty minutes into her work Kade stopped by and came around the back to find her. Her phone indicated movement at the front of her house. She about jumped out of her skin, and was ready to tackle him, but he was prepared for her to throw him to the ground again. She was in her defensive stance and prepared. She had her hands up and ready to take him on. They laughed about that and he stayed with her as she finished the back yard. He helped her take the two bags to the trash on the west side and she started on a third bag as she came to the east side of the house.

"Kade, thank you for helping me and keeping me company. Did I take you away from something important today?"

"Nope. I just wanted to talk with you and get to know you a bit more. Is that ok?"

"It's awesome. Thanks for letting me get to know you a bit more too! Do you want some lemonade, maybe some cookies?" He nodded eagerly and she put her gardening gloves and pruning shears on the rail of the front porch and they headed inside through the back door. She poured them both lemonade, brought out some cookies, and they chatted. He asked her about Devin's house and she sat him where he could see the house. They talked about her program for Cassi's students and he told her how much he enjoyed it. He told her he was impressed with how she told the story. They kept their conversation light and steered away from Devin. Kade asked her a lot of questions about her work.

Devin was biding his time. He didn't know the man that was with Erin right now and he hoped that the man would leave soon so he could put his plan into action. He texted Erin a picture of the room, but a close-up that wouldn't reveal much, because he didn't have it fully set up yet. Erin ignored the text because she knew it was from Devin. Kade asked about it, she told him it was Devin trying to make her afraid. He asked her to forward it to him, which she did. Kade watched Erin closely. She was on edge, but she seemed to be taking everything one moment at a time. She wasn't panicking, yet. Kade knew the demons were just under the surface though, waiting to strike. He was trying to keep her off the ledge. The picture Devin sent made her edgy.

Erin and Kade headed back outside and Erin picked up her tools and gloves to start on the east side of the house. Kade grabbed the bag and held it as she trimmed her flowers and rose bushes. Kade told her she had a beautiful garden. She told Kade that she loved her flowers, spent a lot of time finding the right tea roses to plant, and she liked to keep them growing and prospering. It was like everything was normal, only Erin was churning under the surface trying to keep her face passive. Kade knew that she was on alert and on edge, but he tried to keep things normal too. His goal was to make his presence known to Devin. They finished the trimming, threw the bag away and Kade was getting ready to leave her. She asked if he wanted some roses to take home and he agreed. She found a plastic vase in the garage, added water and sugar to it, then cut several long stems of roses for Kade, trimming the leaves off and making a very pretty bouquet. He especially loved the dual colored roses with the bright, vibrant magenta and tipped with yellow. Erin told him those were her favorites too.

Kade was the only brother of the four who drove a pickup and not a motorcycle most of the time, so he could put the vase of flowers in his cup holder as he drove home. She instructed him to change the water out daily and add a little bit of sugar to keep them fresh for a long time. He thanked her and told her they would look so pretty on his table.

While she was cutting the flowers Kade texted Anthony that he was preparing to leave Erin since she was done with her flowers. Anthony said he was wrapping up at the office and would be heading toward Erin's in about five minutes. Kade felt like she would be ok. He took the flowers, gave Erin a hug and climbed into his pickup. She stood at his window and talked to him for a few more minutes and soon he was backing out of her drive. They were laughing at something and that made Devin crazy. Devin was watching and waiting for his moment to pounce. Kade could see Devin at the window. He hoped and prayed that Erin was ok and would remain safe after he left. As Kade drove off, Thomas, his partner, and another police cruiser drove by in opposite directions. Thomas stopped and talked to Erin for a few minutes. Devin was getting antsy. Erin could see him and she knew that he was prepared to act.

"Detective Thomas, good to see you." He smiled at her. "Just so you know I see Devin watching out his window. Can you not go too far away, but still be close enough in case he makes a move? Anthony isn't back yet and I still have a few flowers to work on in my front yard."

"Erin, I've been watching him for a bit now. I know he's up to something. I'll go back to my position. Please be careful, stay vigilant. I've got you covered. Remember that Devin has to make a move before we can take action." She nodded.

"I'm going to work on my flowers near the front of the house. I'm on guard. Thank you for being close." She kept her smile on her face. She didn't want to give anything away.

She waved goodbye and turned back to her house and flowers. Thomas pulled away while still watching Devin's house. Erin decided that in order to pull Devin out she needed to turn her back to him and work on her flower pots. She started pruning her carnations and the two small rose bushes up near her kitchen window. She checked the water lines too. Devin watched as the police cruisers disappeared in opposite directions. It was time to make his move; she had no one around to help her. Erin heard his door open and close; she knew he was coming for her. It was quiet in the neighborhood today and her ears were tuned into where the sound was coming from. One of her neighbors was watching too, and captured video on their phone of Devin walking toward Erin. She stood, keeping her back to him, but she could see him in the reflection of her silver trim on her door. She was prepared. He was heading her way. She shifted her stance. Breathe, she kept reminding herself. Her heartrate quickened and she ran her scenarios through her head. She was as prepared as she could be and she knew Devin was going to grab her from behind. She watched the reflections and Devin just walked over like he owned the place.

Devin quickly made his way across the street and to her front yard, walking through the gate. She could hear his footfalls and she made herself calm as she could. She knew she needed to wait for him to touch her and she would jump into gear. She kept her breathing normal and as even as possible, but every fiber of her being was poised to jump into action. Devin crept up behind her, as quietly as possible, and reached out to grab her around her shoulders, dragging her back against him. The neighbor zoomed their video in capturing every moment. They needed to help her.

"Finally, I have you to myself," he hissed. "You're mine Erin and always will be. I just had to bide my time, but you're mine. I am going to enjoy you; enjoy watching you squirm and moan." His words and his voice creeped her out. Devin's meaning was crystal clear. He meant every word. He was definitely obsessed.

Erin didn't flinch, didn't respond verbally, tried hard not to give away what she was planning, but she was disgusted at his implications; she kicked her training into high gear. She glanced up and saw her neighbor videotaping. She held his arm with her non-dominant hand, brought her elbow back hard into his rib cage with gusto and heard him grunt and his ribcage cracked; at the same time she stepped as hard as she could on his instep and felt his grip loosen. She quickly slipped out of his grasp, turned to face him, brought her hand up to break his nose thrusting upward hard, and her knee up to kick him in the balls. He fell to the ground in pain and she stepped quickly back out of his reach. He recovered though, got up and grabbed for her again and this time she reached, grabbed his upper arm, kneeled down and threw him to the ground using his momentum against him. He flew from his feet over her back and to the front of her. She heard his breath whoosh out of his body as he hit the driveway on his back, and his head hit with a sickening sound moments later. She grabbed a really deep breath of air. She kept her distance, still in defensive stance, but he needed to hear her.

"You just never learn do you Devin. **Stay. Out. Of. My. Life**! I want nothing to do with you. I've told you no a thousand times. Leave. Me. Alone!" She was winded but ready to do more damage if necessary to put him out of commission. Her stance was defensive; she was ready to strike.

Anthony was headed into the driveway as she threw Devin and Thomas' patrol car pulled up at the same time from the other way. Anthony stopped on the street and waited for Thomas and his partner to handcuff Devin, read him his rights and escort him away to the car.   Anthony jumped off his bike and grabbed Erin in a bear hug taking her off the ground. She wrapped her arms around him. She was so glad he was back home with her. She was trembling.

"Erin, sugar, are you ok?"

"I'm good Anthony, my handsome hero. I'm shaky but I'm not hurt; I'm just angry and full of adrenaline. He never learns. Oh, my neighbor across the street was videoing the event. Maybe we need to get their footage." Anthony put her back on the ground but kept his arm around her.

"Erin," Thomas said, "can I see your restraining order?" She pulled it out of her back pocket and Thomas took a picture of it with his phone.

"Detective Thomas, thank you for your help and driving patrols by here. Be careful with Devin and watch your back. He's unpredictable. Also, my neighbor across the way was videoing the entire thing. We should have that video."

"He's restrained now Ms. Erin, and will soon be behind bars. I'll get your neighbor to give us their footage. We have all the footage we need of him trying to kidnap you from your security cameras that Anthony just sent us so I can guarantee with this restraining order his lawyer will not get him off or out of jail too soon." Thomas and Anthony shook hands and Thomas headed back to the patrol car to head to the station with Devin. Devin was shooting daggers at Erin and Anthony from his seat in the back of the patrol car. Anthony was impressed. Erin had it together and she was keeping vigilant. He was so proud of her.

"Hi handsome." Erin said as she pulled Anthony into another hug. He could still feel her shaking but she was holding it together.

"Hi beautiful. I'm so proud of you." She melted into his arms. Together they turned and headed into the house after Anthony moved his bike into the garage. "You're one tough cookie darlin'." She smiled at him.

"Thank you and Kade for helping me with my strength, stamina and power. I can guarantee you Devin will feel all the hits he took today from me." She giggled a little at that. Anthony was so proud of her. She washed her hands and made them lunch. They talked over lunch and he regaled her with stories of the buddy he did the artwork on earlier. Together they mowed the lawn in the afternoon and spent the evening enjoying a movie together.

"Anthony, sweetie," Erin turned toward him, "I don't know how to say this or how to do this, but I wanted you to know that I am becoming attached to you and I hope we can continue to explore what this is between us. I'm having a hard time keeping my hands off your gorgeous body, but I am also not sure what I'm doing."

"Sugar, come over here and sit with me." He pulled her to him. "I am becoming completely attached to you too. I know that you are inexperienced and probably scared of your feelings for me, but I want nothing more than to make you mine." He leaned into her and kissed her. Her arms wrapped around him and she found herself in his lap. The movie forgotten, both of them got lost in the sensations of lips, hands and arms. They were breathing heavily when they finally broke apart.

"I just want to keep doing that Anthony, my sweet, sweet Anthony. You know how to make me forget about what happened earlier today." Anthony leaned his forehead against hers.

"Darlin' you are amazing and I want to just be here to protect you, love you and hold you." He leaned in to kiss her again.

"Anthony, my hero, will you hold me tonight in my bed. I don't want to have another nightmare after what happened today and I don't want to be alone."

"Darlin' it would be my pleasure." She smiled at him and he was lost. They shut down the house and headed to the bedroom. Anthony crawled in beside her when they were both ready for bed and she asked him about his ink. He told her that his family crest was the dragon she saw on his right side and she traced it with her fingers. He loved the feel of her fingers on his skin. She told him how amazing it looked. She asked about the crossed swords on his upper left arm and for the next forty minutes or so they talked about his ink on his upper body with her tracing each one of them with her fingers. He explained that most of the ink on his body was from his time with the military, specifically the SEALs. She loved listening to him talk about his artwork, and his service to the country.

Erin finally got brave enough to ask Anthony about the piercings. He had both nipples pierced and a barbell of sorts running through each one.

"Anthony, handsome, did this hurt to have done?" She was completely overwhelmed that anyone could sit through having that pierced.

"No, not at all. Michael does great work and makes it painless." He smiled at her.

"Do you have other piercings too?" He nodded. She blushed. "I don't think I'm ready to know more." That made Anthony laugh. She loved the sound of his laughter. It was deep, harmonious and sexy as hell. He watched her face for a few minutes. He was totally lost in her beautiful face, and she was definitely his weakness.

"Darlin' you should see the blush on your face. Let's leave our conversation about piercing for now. Just know that if you want your nipples pierced Michael would be happy to help you out. It really gives an amazing sensation with the piercings and I know they would look beautiful on you. Michael could do the ones with the delicate chains and it would be so pretty, very sexy. I would love to see them pierced." She turned another few shades of red. Anthony gathered her into his arms and tucked her into his side. He could feel the heat on her cheeks as she lay in his arms. He kissed her forehead and wrapped her more fully in his arms. Her fingers splayed across his chest and she toyed lightly with the piercings; that made Anthony smile.

Chapter Three

Devin was processed and given jail clothes to change into; a jail guard accompanying him to change. The infirmary had taken care of his injuries. He was led to a holding cell and he finally had the chance to call and talk to his lawyer Richard. Richard told him he needed to sit tight for tonight and he would see him in the morning. He was gathering all the details now and would find a way to get him out. Devin thanked him and told him more of what he was planning for Erin. He told Richard that Erin deserved everything he was about to unleash on her. Richard told him to stand down and be patient. Devin didn't care who heard him at this point. Erin had hurt him deeply, both physically and emotionally and she had to pay. There were one or two people in the adjoining cells listening intently to Devin's conversation.

Devin relaxed into his bunk and started planning his next moves with Erin. She hurt him deeply with the broken rib, the broken nose and her knee to his groin. She actually threw him across the grass to the driveway. She was going to pay for hurting him and for telling him no. No one said no to him. She had no right to express that opinion because she never gave him a chance. He was going to make her pay dearly. Satisfied with the direction he was headed, Devin allowed his body to slip into sleep. The infirmary had set his broken nose and taped it, and put tape on his ribs too. He had bruises that needed to heal now. That made him even angrier with Erin.

His cellmate was watching with interest and took notes of everything Devin said. He would pursue questioning Devin tomorrow to find out exactly what he had planned for this girl he was miffed at. Quatro was a snitch for the police and he wanted to see what this guy was up to. He had listened to Devin talking about this girl who bested him. Quatro didn't take kindly to guys wanting to hurt girls and he had ways of finding out information to help the police. Quatro's goal was to protect even though he was in jail. He also knew how to make new inmates his friend.

Quatro's own sister had been stalked by a guy just like Devin and that guy eventually ended up killing her because the police couldn't protect her, and Quatro killed him. That's why he was in prison now. He turned his experience into helping the police by finding out details of those who were arrested because of a restraining order violation. Quatro was doing his service hours and trying to protect other women, because he couldn't protect his sister. Devin did not know how to treat a lady and that made Quatro very upset. Too many men like Devin had gotten away with injuring and killing women who said no to them. He was determined to make sure Devin paid. He didn't know how, but somehow Quatro would help the police and perhaps if Erin had a special someone, he could help him too. He hoped that this work he was doing would help him to get out prison sooner, and maybe he could find a niche in helping others with the restraining orders. There had to be a way to strengthen that so called protection. He would see if he could find a way to work on that.

*****

Erin and Anthony fell into a companionable routine over the next several days, and Anthony moved more things into Erin's house. She told him repeatedly to think of the house as his too. Anthony loved being part of Erin's world and he loved holding her in the nights keeping her safe and helping her navigate her nightmares. She was getting stronger all the time with the work he and Kade did with her at the gym. He was so proud of her because she didn't shy away from hard work and she diligently tried without complaint all they threw at her. She mastered much of it too.

"Erin, darlin', we're going to family dinner at my folks' place tonight." Anthony said when he called her at work. It was Friday and almost two weeks to the day from the last events with Devin. Erin was still vigilant. They hadn't seen anything from Devin's house since that Saturday. It was quiet and Erin was content with the quiet.

"Can I bring anything?"

"Nope. Mom has it all prepared. She just wants to have her family all together tonight. Ok?"

"I'm looking forward to it. Anthony, thank you. I love being part of your family."

They talked a few more minutes and Anthony told her he would see her at the house later. Both of them were breathing a bit easier with Devin out of the picture for now. It was an uneasy breath because they had no idea when Devin would be released. He was still in jail, having been denied bail by the judge, with his lawyer working on finding a way to lessen the charges against him. He had been locked up for almost two weeks now. Quatro made friends with Devin and gathered quite of bit of evidence as to what he was planning. Devin was hard up for friends and he was so willing to share his plan with Quatro. Quatro was disgusted by Devin's plan. He needed to be taught a lesson. When Quatro had his meeting with Detective Thomas he would share what he knew of Devin's plan. He would make sure that the detective had enough for his files. Perhaps he could help keep Devin off the streets for good.

Erin hadn't heard anything but she knew soon the trial would come up and she would have to testify. They signed off and Erin headed to the news station to edit the last piece they needed for the evening news. She did a fluff piece on the downtown business association's newest project. She interviewed the head of the business association and she even got an interview with the mayor. All she needed to do now was edit the package and get it to the director for the evening news. She was really happy with the piece and made sure it was what the director wanted. Todd told her it was exactly what he was expecting. She thanked him and headed home. She wanted to shower quickly and change clothes before dinner.

Meanwhile, Devin's lawyer, his very corrupt lawyer, was able to get Devin off on a technicality with the way the restraining order was worded. He was working right now to make sure Devin would be a free man by dinnertime. Devin could find a new way to get to Erin, and Richard would help him figure out how to do that.

Devin was putting a new plan in place because in his mind if he couldn't have Erin then no one was going to have her, even if he had to kill her to make that a reality. Devin had shared that tidbit with Quatro who shared it with Detective Thomas. He meant to make her pay for breaking his ribs and his nose; she would have a slow, torturous life with him, while he satisfied his own sadistic needs. She was going to pay for her sins and for rejecting him, of that he was sure. She had made a fool out of him and he wasn't about to let her live her life on her own terms. She would be his prisoner or she would be dead. The choice would be hers. Quatro did his best to control his anger and not punch Devin out. Quatro would be up for parole in the next year, so he didn't want to jeopardize anything.

*****

The family gathered and had dinner together. Conversation and food flowed freely, coupled with love and hugs, exuded from the house. Erin was thrilled to be part of such an amazing family environment; something she hadn't experienced before. After they finished dinner and the boys moved to the living room, Erin and the girls helped Angelina in the kitchen. All of them asked about Devin and Erin said as far as she knew he was still in jail awaiting the next step. All of them realized that Erin didn't want to think about Devin so they changed the subject.

The girls talked about Cassi's class and how the garden was coming along and Mariah shared with them the good news that their clinic had received another grant to provide even more care to the homeless population in the city. Cassi said the kids had harvested the first part of the garden and had planted new items. The kids were giving their excess produce to the food bank so those who really needed help could get some fresh food. Mariah talked about how the clinic was expanding and now doing women's health and working to keep the homeless healthy. Erin said they needed to do a follow up video project on both of their causes and get the word out. Perhaps they could set up a 'GoFundMe' page for both of them with video vignettes to help get more donors and keep the good work flowing. Cassia and Mariah were thrilled as they listened to Erin detailing what she could do for them. They made plans for the video segments in the next week, and Erin would set up their pages. She said that perhaps even some large companies would see what these two ladies were doing to make a difference and could possibly provide funding and support. Both Mariah and Cassie loved the idea.

While the boys were talking and watching the game, Anthony's phone rang. It turned out to be Thomas who let him know that Devin was out of jail on a technicality that his corrupt lawyer Richard found. It was a loophole in Erin's restraining order and he was now a threat to Erin again. Richard found a way to exploit the system and Thomas warned that Devin was now out for blood where Erin was concerned. Their snitch in the jailhouse had given the police good information on the despicable things Devin bragged he was going to do the Erin. Thomas eventually wanted Anthony and his snitch Quatro to meet. He wanted Anthony to be on his toes. He also told him that he had patrols increasing again in Erin's neighborhood. Anthony's brothers and dad watched his face as he talked. They knew something big was going on.

"Anthony, son, what's going on?" Roberto asked as Anthony hung up.

"Well, Devin's corrupt lawyer got Devin off on the charges from the restraining order with a technicality and Devin is now out of jail and once again a threat. Her restraining order has absolutely no teeth. The jailhouse snitch gave the detectives information on Devin's plan for Erin and its bad." Anthony scrubbed his hands over his face. "I need to tell Erin some of this. We have to be vigilant and I'm guessing Devin is even more of a threat now that Erin got the best of him the last time he tried to kidnap her. If I know the way that man thinks, he's going to want to make her pay for the broken bones and bruises, and for embarrassing him by besting him, and for telling him no repeatedly."

"Anthony, we may need to think about having you and Erin move into mom and dad's house, or you can move in with me since I have a better and more secure area; an area where she can have some freedom but be safe. I have plenty of room. We need to get Erin out of her neighborhood until we can find a way to permanently remove Devin." Kade said.

"I hate to uproot her but I think you're right. We need to tell her. This is going to stir up her nightmares again. I don't want her hurt." Anthony was in love with Erin. All of the brothers and dad could see it.

"Anthony, my boy, let's have you and Erin move in with Kade, and you two can keep her safe. I will work with Uncle Mory and we will see what we can find out about Devin's lawyer, and figure out how to change her restraining order so that Devin can't keep getting off on a technicality." As Roberto was finishing this statement, Erin walked into the living room, and overheard the last statement. She dropped the glass she was carrying, luckily it was empty and plastic, and sucked in a deep breath.

"Devin's out of jail?!" Her eyes were wide and she was on the verge of panicking. "When did this happen?" Instantly, Anthony and Kade were by her side.

"Darlin' look at me." Anthony turned her and tipped her face to look at him and Kade held onto her from behind her; he could feel her trembling. She looked like she could crumble right there. "I just got off the phone with Thomas. Devin's corrupt lawyer got him off on a technicality and he's home as of twenty minutes ago." She almost collapsed right there, her knees turning to jelly, but Kade scooped her up and they moved to the dining room. Kade sat her in Anthony's lap and sat down beside them both. She was tense and almost over the edge with the news she overheard. She was not only afraid for herself but for Anthony's family too.

"Erin, honey, we're going to protect you. We have a plan to help you be safe." She watched them both with fear laden eyes. "You and Anthony are going to move into my house with me. I have plenty of room." She started to protest. "Erin, we need you away from the situation and out of Devin's reach. He's angry that you got the best of him and he couldn't take you two weeks ago. I'm sure his rage has increased tenfold what with being in jail and awaiting trial, the damage you did to his body when he tried to grab you, and we need to get you out of the line of fire. He has a corrupt lawyer who is helping him, so we need to make sure you are far away and out of his reach."

"Darlin' it's also time to talk with your boss at TK Productions and the news stations. They need to be made aware of the situation and why we need you to work from a distance. We need to have you work from a secure location and not be visible or anywhere that Devin can find you. You have to be off the map for a now and we need to get you a new cell phone with a number that Devin doesn't know." Her eyes drifted up to catch Anthony's gaze and finally she nodded in agreement. "I know you're scared darlin' but we are going to protect you. Ok?" She nodded and buried her face in Anthony's neck and held on. Kade rubbed her back to let her know they were going to protect her.

"This nightmare is never going to end, is it?" They both could hear the fear in her voice. "He knows you are all trying to protect me and I don't want any of you hurt. You all mean too much to me to see you hurt. He could easily figure out who you are and he could try to hurt this family, my family. I can't abide that. I don't want any of you to suffer because of me. Perhaps I just need to face him and figure out how to end this once and for all, one way or another. Maybe if he takes me, does his worst to me, the rest of you will be safe and I can rest easier. This is my cross to bear. I didn't mean for you all to be involved this deeply in my life. I love you all, you are my family, and I can't have you hurt."

"Darlin' that's not happening. You are my life Erin. This family here is your family and we protect our own. We will find a legal and permanent solution, but Kade and I need some time and we need you removed from the situation. Don't give up sugar; don't let Devin win. Please trust us. We have eyes and ears all over this community and we can and will protect you and ourselves. We can handle this honey." Kade and Anthony did their best to reassure her that she was going to be safe. Anthony just hoped they could convince her they were going to protect her. Anthony and Kade made plans to help get her packed up tonight and close down her house. They would have Thomas and his partner make their presence known, and once she was away from the house, the police would continue their patrols, but everyone would be able to breathe a bit easier with Erin sequestered someplace safe. She would not be alone; one of the brothers would be with her twenty-four/seven.

The rest of the family joined them for dessert around the table while Kade and Anthony briefed the family on the events of the last half hour. All of them tried to reassure Erin and Erin did her best to keep the demons away and be present in the conversation, but her mind was churning up all kinds of scenarios, none of them good. She told them all they needed to be vigilant too because Devin could hurt them. She wanted to protect them, but didn't know how to do that. She told them all she loved them and didn't want them hurt. She made sure they knew what Devin looked like. Anthony had Thomas look at ways to patrol the free clinic, the school where Cassi worked and their parents' house. Thomas and his chief were able to help and told them they would do their best. Anthony asked Thomas how they could strengthen Erin's restraining order and he told Anthony he would look into it. Thomas told him that restraining orders were crap and they did not protect those that needed it most like Erin. He also told Anthony that the way Erin's was worded was just to placate her when she brought the situation to the police's attention.

*****

Devin started to work on another plan where Erin was concerned. She was tough but she couldn't best him. He needed to find a way to get her alone and make sure she paid dearly for the pain and suffering she caused him. He talked with Richard and asked how best to proceed; Richard told him that the restraining order would kick in if he came within one hundred feet of her and the police were stepping up patrols because of the number of times it had been acted on, but it said nothing about sending her emails, texts or leaving voice messages. Devin smiled his most sardonic smile. He could make her life a living hell and that's exactly what he intended to do. He needed to figure out how much of his hand to play, but if he showed her snippets of her life with him, and the torture he had planned, he could drive her slowly insane. That thought thrilled him to no end.

Devin laid out his plan and had Richard help him. He took pictures of the room he started to set up to hold and contain Erin, and he took pictures of all the toys he had amassed that he planned to use on her too. Once he had all his pictures, he started to form his messages to her. He found lines from movie thrillers that would help slowly drive her to madness and laid out his plan for her life. She hadn't returned home yet, but he set up his cameras to watch her house and figure out when she was home, without that Anthony guy. He needed her to be alone when he executed his plan. Richard warned him to be careful of Anthony and Devin said he needed to find out who this Anthony was.

Devin got his hands on a picture of Anthony and started searching to figure out who he was. Anthony did not have a social media presence and so Devin spent his next few days trying to figure out who this guy was and if there was a way to exploit him too. Erin had not returned home in several days and he wondered where she was living. With her disappearing, he was at a loss as to how to put his plan to kidnap her into gear. It crossed his mind that perhaps he could lure her out by sending the first message. She would react to what he sent, which was a picture of the bars on the windows and a description of her life with him. Devin started his plan in motion. He also asked Richard if there was a way to charge Erin with assault for the broken bones. Richard told him he would look into it.

*****

Mory worked with Roberto and they contacted the judge for the case of Erin and Devin. The judge confided to them both that she was disgusted by the sloppy work on Erin's restraining order and she was working on drafting legislation now to see if she could help people like Erin. Mory told her he would help, but in the meantime they needed to figure out their next steps. They needed to protect Erin now; the legislation she was proposing wouldn't help Erin in this instance. He told the judge he would be in touch soon.

Mory went back to his office and dug into Richard's background. With the help of his partners they found several black marks on Richard's dossier and it was time to make trouble for Richard. They needed to keep Richard on his toes so he couldn't as easily get Devin off the charges. Mory was now on the board of the bar association and his committee was responsible for taking care of corruption where the lawyers and attorneys were concerned. He took his job very seriously and he wanted to help Roberto and the family protect Erin. They had a zero tolerance for lawyers who used and abused the system, and they were looking into several attorneys who had bucked the system and put bad people back on the streets with technicalities. Mory and his colleagues were going to clean up the riff raff lawyers in the city and region; the corruption had to stop. Richard was their first target.

These lawyers, like Richard, took bucket loads of money from clients to work the system to their benefit, no matter the cost to the victims.   They also were working to figure out how to better protect women like Erin from the haphazard way restraining orders were written and conducted. Restraining orders left too much ambiguity and left women totally unprotected, vulnerable. It was like the police couldn't be bothered to actually write something that would protect a woman from harassment and from hurt, sometimes even death.

Quatro met with Detective Thomas and the police chief. He detailed to them Devin's plan for Erin. They both asked lots of questions and Quatro gave them explicit details that Devin had shared with him.   He told them that Devin's goal was to kidnap and hold Erin hostage in his house. Devin was sick and twisted and he was a definite threat to Erin, but without a means they couldn't get him off the street. Detective Thomas and the police chief commended Quatro, sent him back to his cell and tried to figure out how to help Erin and get Devin off the streets. Thomas wanted Quatro to help with the legislation that Mory had told him about. They were working to get Quatro released on parole too.

****

Erin and Anthony got settled in at Kade's house and Erin realized Kade had a very secure location, one that would help keep her and them all safe. Kade set up a space for her in his office to do her editing and work; he had a second desk with a window view of the beach that wasn't being used so he gave her that. She had secure internet access and Terry, her boss from TK Productions was very understanding. He assigned two production assistants to capture whatever footage she needed, set up videoconference meetings for her to meet with her clients, and they would upload footage, finished projects to the secure drive for Erin to access. She could just send them what she needed and they would get all the footage, upload it and she could edit and complete the productions, then meet with her clients via the videoconference connection. Terry made sure her phone number was changed on the phone she had so they could reduce Devin's access. That happened by the end of the day. Erin could breathe just a bit.

The news station wasn't as understanding. They were not happy losing one of their best stringers, but Kade talked with the managers of the station and finally got them to give Erin a leave of absence so she could still do the fluff pieces they needed from afar. Kade also asked him to make sure the staff did not tell Devin where she was working and what she was working on. They needed to help protect her. Todd and Brad agreed and said they would tell the staff too. If she needed footage someone would be with her as she did her shoots. Erin was going to be protected up close and from afar. She would not be alone, and they would all do their best to make sure that Erin was safe.

Erin felt like she had put her new family in so much danger and she was finding it difficult to relax. She was on edge and she didn't sleep much. The demons were greater at night. She paced the floor in the house most days and never stayed in one place very long. She wandered from room to room. Her fear was that if she slept Devin would find a way to hurt her family and so she needed to stay awake to protect them. If she concentrated on her projects she would sit for a time and work, but soon she was up and pacing the floors again. Her life was turned upside down, and she was worried about her girls and the Romano family. Kade and Anthony were worried about Erin. She was fidgety and on edge. She workout harder every day and just tried to keep the demons away.

Stefano contacted his associates and they provided a plainclothes security person for each member of the family. Cassi had a protector at the school who was there every day and made sure she was safe to and from the school and Alex guarded her at night while they slept; Mariah had one at the clinic and there were two stationed at Ink Inc. Stefano also made sure that Angelina and Roberto had protection. Anthony called his friend and SEAL brother, Jake, and asked him to help with Erin. He quickly explained the situation and Jake was more than willing to come and help. He told Anthony that he would be there in the morning. Anthony breathed a bit easier knowing that Jake was coming to assist. Jake was his brother from his SEAL days, and he was an incredible protector. He could also help Erin with her nightmares and with her uneasiness too. Jake knew how to keep the demons at bay and change Erin's focus.

Erin got acclimated with Kade's house. He had a four bedroom house with an attached gym/workout area, huge kitchen and large living space. Kade told her she could make herself at home and the three of them would workout daily trying to help Erin be stronger and more prepared for anything that might happen. She asked if she could cook their meals, do laundry, and Kade readily agreed. Erin busied herself in the kitchen so she wouldn't think so much about what was happening. She helped Kade clean and prepare the cottage for Anthony's friend Jake. It gave her work to do and kept her busy. She had to direct her energy elsewhere because she wasn't able to relax or settle down. Kade and Anthony tried to change her focus, but Erin couldn't seem to let down or relax. She worked on her projects, she cleaned and cooked, she did laundry. She kept very busy, but rarely sat down or stopped for any length of time.

The three of them settled into an easy routine, but the nights were the worst for Erin. She had nightmares almost every night and it took Anthony a lot to get her to resettle back down. Some nights Kade could hear her whimpering and Anthony trying to comfort her. He wished he had the words to help comfort her, but he didn't know what to do. The demons chased Erin hard and she couldn't get away from the images that had begun arriving in her email. Each one more menacing than the last with words that could haunt even the strongest, bravest person. Devin knew how to play mind games and both Kade and Anthony worried that this would all be too much for Erin. She was already fragile and these images and words were threatening to push her over the edge.

Kade took all the emails and put them into a folder for Thomas. He then called his friend to see how to forward just the one sender so that Erin wouldn't keep getting the messages. Jack was able to access Erin's email and route Devin's email to a ghost account for Kade. She was strong, but her strength only went so far. The demons drove her to push herself in the gym and Kade knew Devin's face was on the punching bag every night. She put everything she had into the bag, and the weights, trying to chase the demons away, and tire herself out to sleep. Kade was worried she might break something as hard as she hit the bag. She was a mad woman as she punched the bag and lifted weights. She wore herself out. She pushed herself beyond the breaking point. She couldn't let down and she was beating herself up. The lack of sleep and the lack of food was making Erin fragile and vulnerable.

Jake arrived the next day and Kade settled him into the guest house. Jake asked a lot of questions and Kade did his best to provide answers. He had copies of the emails, letting Jake know he had a friend of his redirect these emails to a separate account so Erin wouldn't continue to see them, and the pictures of the first courier package contents, which Jake was disgusted in seeing. This guy Devin was one sick puppy and the sooner they could take care of him the better. Jake, unfortunately, had dealt with Devin's type on numerous occasions. He wanted to find time to talk with Quatro at the jail in reference to Devin. Kade told him that he would get Thomas to arrange that.

"Jake, tonight over dinner, the four of us will talk and you can ask Erin all the questions you need to, to find out what else you need to know, get to know her a bit, see where her head is at. She's fragile and almost over the edge. The demons are chasing her hard. Thanks for coming and helping us out."

"My pleasure. I would do anything for Anthony and his family." Kade smiled. "Kade, is Anthony in love with Erin?"

"Yeah, I think so. The family can see the love between them but I don't know if Anthony is willing to admit it just yet. Erin is very inexperienced when it comes to men and so I think he doesn't want to scare her off. She's already fragile with this situation, but she's strong too in spirit and she's protective. She's a black belt in judo and she was able to take care of herself with Devin three weeks ago when he tried to kidnap her. She put him out of commission. More details for you." Kade smiled at him.

"I'm intrigued Kade. I can't wait to meet this lady who's captured Anthony's heart. You seem pretty taken with her yourself." Kade realized that not much got by Jake. He told Jake of his first meeting with Erin and the fact that she laid him out on the grass in his parents' backyard. Jake laughed at that one. "How big is she?"

"She's a tiny thing. She's maybe 5'4" and small in frame, maybe 100 pounds. She's beautiful, sweet, caring, and I don't want to see her hurt. She's one that would give anyone in need the shirt off her back. This Devin guy is a monster." Jake agreed. "I'll leave you to get settled. Come up to the main house and we'll have dinner together. Erin's cooking. She's a good cook." Kade shook his hand and left him to get settled. Jake thought about the information Kade had shared with him. His first thoughts went to the fact that Erin was probably having nightmares and trying to protect everyone around her. If he knew how her mind worked, she probably had the demons chasing her, and she didn't know how to let down and let go. He also suspected that she wasn't eating either. She might know how to cook but his guess is that she didn't eat much of what she put on the table for the boys. He needed to get her to trust him.

A couple hours later Erin put dinner on the table with homemade French bread, fettucine with Alfredo sauce, grilled chicken and fresh veggies and a green salad. She bustled around the kitchen, not yet ready to light and face Jake, scared because another person was in danger because of her, but finally sat down between Anthony and Kade. She tried to be present in the moment but she was clearly rattled. Jake was here to help protect her and she put someone new in danger now. It was almost too much. He could see the exhaustion in her face. He knew she wasn't sleeping and she was worrying about everyone and everything, and all of this was out of her control.

"Erin, honey, this is my buddy Jake. He's a former Navy SEAL, my brother from my time in the SEALs, and he's here to help us protect you. He's in security and so his role is to stick with you when you have to leave the house for any reason. He knows television production techniques so can help you with any shoots you need to do as well. We're all here for you and with you in this." Erin smiled at him, but the smile didn't reach her eyes. She was clearly on the edge of disaster here.

"Erin," Jake started, "can I ask you some questions about Devin?" He watched her facial expressions. Jake was really good at reading body language and Erin was screaming her fear to him. He knew she was completely off her game and overwhelmed.

"Umm, yeah I guess. I'll do my best to answer." Erin said guardedly.

"Tell me about how you two met and how you know each other." Jake invited.

"I was hired at TK Productions a little more than four years ago. I had been there for about a month and had helped to bring more business into the production house. Terry, my boss, needed to bring on another producer/director and Devin was his candidate of choice. Devin has a way about him and he can seem like the perfect fit, but then turn in an instant if something doesn't go his way."

She took in a very deep breath, as quietly as she could but Jake knew this was difficult for her. "Anyway, Terry told the staff, now that it was growing fast, that he didn't tolerate personal relationships between staff – no dating, no anything. We even had to sign off on the company policies stating that we agreed to them – because it was detrimental to moral and the workplace, especially if it didn't work out. It was just fine with me because I wasn't interested in dating anyone, I was still taking care of my mother who was very ill. I was her advocate, her caregiver, and did my best to make sure she was ok. I worked hard to make sure my mom had nothing to worry about and then after I lost her I kept working extra hours and more jobs to pay off the medical bills, all the expenses." She toyed with the food on her plate, but hadn't taken any bites of food. The men watched her and ate their dinner, but Jake realize Erin was reeling from all of this and it was taking its toll on her.

"Devin asked me out a week later, after that meeting with Terry. I told him emphatically no but he kept asking every day being very pushy. I told him I would not, under any circumstances, go out on a date or anything else with him. There was something about Devin, he made my skin crawl, and he made me very uncomfortable. I'm not very experienced with relationships or men, but I knew what I didn't want and I don't think Devin was used to being turned down. He kept asking and I kept telling him no. He was very insistent, but I'm pretty independent and stubborn. I know my own mind and that didn't set well with Devin. He was pretty frustrated that I wouldn't give in to him." She took another shaky breath.

"When did you know he was a threat Erin?" Jake asked her gently.

"Devin pursued me very hard for almost six months and he was not someone who took no for an answer. He quit TK Productions, realizing that the company policies would prevent anything from happening, and got hired on somewhere else. I thought that it was over and I hoped he was moving on. My mom was taking a turn for the worse and I brought in hospice to help, my mind was distracted taking care of her, making her comfortable. Anyway, I'm getting off track here. Devin started turning up at all of my productions that were off-site and not at the production house, and somehow he learned about my schedule with the news station too. I think he had someone at the news station who would tell him where I was at with my productions.

He would show up, insert himself into my production work, trying to coerce me out to dinner or something else, and I kept asking him to leave me alone, telling him no, trying to be professional, but firm. He would always cause a scene in front of my clients and talent leaving me to apologize to them for the intrusion. Finally, it got to the point that I needed to find a way to stop him from being there altogether, and I sought out help from the police who suggested a restraining order. I explained to the police and sheriff and they wrote up a restraining order which I needed to carry with me at all times, and if I needed to call for help, they would take a copy of the order and take care of Devin. Finally, after several months of this and Devin being hauled away because of the restraining order four times, he quit coming around. I guess I thought, stupidly, he had learned his lesson and would now leave me alone. I was just naïve and living in a rose-colored world.” She looked down at her plate, put her fork down, and tried to re-center herself. She was really on the edge.

“Erin,” Jake said, and waited for her to look up. “You are not living in a rose-colored world. Devin is a sick bastard, sorry for my language, but he’s not going to be deterred, restraining order or not. People like Devin don’t care about anyone except getting what they want at any cost. They don’t like being told no and you’ve repeatedly told him that. I’ve dealt with many like him before.” She held his gaze, her eyes full of fear, tears. “You did all the right things and the system once again has failed you. Restraining orders aren’t designed to protect anyone or anything, I’m sorry to say.” Anthony knew she was on the verge of tears. He tried to convey his support to her.

“Erin, darlin’ help me understand what happened when Devin was put in jail this last time.” Anthony reached over and massaged her shoulder. He needed to give her some of his strength.

Erin drew in a shaky breath as a couple of tears slid down her cheek, and told Jake about the latest episode. She quickly brushed the tears away. Jake took notes in his tablet and asked questions trying to determine all the aspects of what happened. Anthony let him know about the first day he met Erin and went with her to the beach video shoot, Devin had shown up and caused her a bit of unease. By the time dinner was finished Jake had a pretty good idea of who Devin was and how much he had already hurt Erin. Devin was a master at mind games, manipulation, and he knew how to push her buttons. Somehow he needed to help her navigate this and be strong through this process.

“Erin, are you having nightmares?” Jake asked.

“Almost every night. My biggest fear is that I’m going to hurt Anthony when he tries to comfort me and wake me up out of the dream. I’m sure I’m keeping Kade awake too.”

"Jake, she's strong and she has self-defense training, so she worries that she is going to hurt one of us."

"Understandable, but Erin darlin' these two boys here are pretty much able to take care of themselves. Anthony is a former SEAL so has training in how to protect himself and you too." He smiled at her. She was on the verge of collapse. "Erin, can I do some hypnosis therapy with you and see if we can't change the images in your head so that you can sleep at night? You really need to relax and sleep, recharge your batteries. It will help with perspective too on this situation."

"That's a good idea Jake." Kade said. "We workout with her in the evenings before bedtime to see if we can't tire out her mind and body so she will sleep."

"That's good too, but perhaps we can change the images and help ease her out of the nightmares." He looked back at Erin who had a fearful look on her face, and her eyes were swimming with unshed tears. "Erin, can I try to help please?" He held her gaze. He was so gentle and caring. Finally, she relented and nodded her head. Erin's plate was still filled with food. She had barely touched anything, which Jake noted too, and as she looked back down nothing looked appealing. Erin got up and started to clear the table while the men talked. She took all the plates off the table, brought them coffee and took the dishes of leftover food, and kept herself busy in the kitchen. She brought them cookies for dessert while she cleaned up. She put the food away, washed and dried the dishes instead of using the dishwasher, cleaned the cooking pots, and cleaned up the counters, as well as the floor. She was doing everything to keep busy and not the let the demons in, but they were chasing her just the same. Jake finished up with Kade and Anthony and told them he would spend some one-on-one time with Erin and then they could all workout in the gym.

Jake watched Erin as he talked with the boys. She was on edge and beside herself because she couldn't protect everyone. Her life was spiraling out of her control and she was off-kilter. Her independence was gone and her life was in someone else's control. She didn't eat much and she wasn't resting; her mind wouldn't shut off so she could relax. He told Kade and Anthony to go relax while he talked with Erin in the kitchen. He needed to get her to trust him. They agreed and headed to catch the game.

"Erin, darlin', can I join you?" Jake asked gently as he came into the kitchen. Erin realized that Jake was huge and all muscles, tattoos, just like her Anthony. He filled up the kitchen area and that caught her off-guard. She tried to bring herself to center but Jake could see she was overwhelmed.

"Of course. Can I get you anything?" She asked trying to keep it light and conversational, but her body language gave away to Jake that she was edgy and scared of him, of Devin, of everything. He smiled at her.

"Come sit with me for a bit. I won't bite I promise! I want to talk with you and get to know you more, and help you to know me too." He smiled at her trying to reassure her that everything was going to be ok. She paused for a moment, put down the dishtowel and walked around the counter. He held the stool for her and sat down with her. They spent the next forty minutes talking where Jake asked her lots of questions and worked to find out more about her. He held onto her hands so she couldn't leave, run away from him, and he gave her time to ask questions of him. She had lots of tears and he could tell she was fragile in her emotions where Devin was concerned, plus she was still grieving over the loss of her mother. She held it together pretty well, but if he pushed in the right direction she would completely fall apart. He could see the lack of sleep, restfulness too, and she barely ate. The dark circles under her eyes made it clear that she was existing, but just barely. Jake was very concerned about her. She wanted to take care of everyone, protect everyone, but didn't have the ability to do that. He asked more about her mom and realized how hard she worked to make ends meet, care for her mom and take care of herself. She was amazing. She tried so hard not to burden anyone and she never had a support system in place until now. She didn't know how to navigate it, but she was definitely in love with Anthony.

He told her how he wanted to work with her the following day and he had some exercises for her mind that might help. She held his gaze but he saw the fear in her eyes. She was hanging on by a thread. He could see the vulnerability and he knew Anthony made the right choice to call him in. He could and would help. This was right up his alley so to speak, and he would protect them all. She was strong but all of this was taking its toll on her. She was a special lady and she was fighting for her very existence right now and she wanted her family to be safe too. He was doing his best to reassure her, and doing his best not to gather her into his arms and protect her. She didn't know him well enough yet. He just wanted to hold her and keep her safe. He needed to change his line of thinking.

Kade was right that she drew people in and made them want to hold her in their arms, protect her, keep her safe. She didn't have much of a support system until she met Anthony and his family. It was fortuitous that Anthony agreed to go on the shoot with her that first Saturday. She took care of her mom and her girlfriends; she tried to take care of the world. Jake realized how special she was to everyone who knew and loved her. She trusted and held that trust until it was broken. She would fight to the death to protect. He vowed to make sure she was safe, and that she would stay safe. He realized he would put himself in harm's way if he could protect her and save her from any more pain. She was that special. Jake was especially glad that Anthony was enamored enough with Erin to help keep her safe.

****

Devin made four more messages and courier packages to send to Erin. He was upset that she hadn't been back to her house and he didn't know where she was. He tried to call her number and it was disconnected; he was even more frustrated when he learned from the news station that Erin had taken a permanent leave of absence from her job. She was really making him angry because he couldn't find her, couldn't contact her and he was beside himself that she was gone. He called TK Productions too, but Terry and his staff wouldn't tell him anything. Terry had instructed all of his staff to not talk to Devin, period. Where could she have gone? Her house wasn't for sale, so she was planning to come back, but how was he going to flush her out so he could grab her if he couldn't find her? She had no productions on the schedule that he could find out about, and Terry wouldn't tell him anything. He knew her car, but he hadn't seen that either. She hadn't driven her normal routes, not gone shopping for groceries, and Devin was beside himself because he couldn't find her.

He called his courier service and had them deliver a package to Erin at the production house. He hoped that Terry would get it to her, wherever she was. He didn't put a return address or any notation that it came from him. This package, the first of four, would give her an idea of the plan he had for her when he finally got her in his house. He had created a replica of the room he was planning to use to hold her and it would show her in great detail what his plans for her were. That would be the start to her demise. Most of his packages to finish building the room would arrive this week. Once he had the room assembled and ready he would find a way to grab Erin and keep her locked up forever. She would be at his beck and call whenever he needed to satisfy his urges.

*****

Over the next week the three men and Erin got into a routine. Jake and Erin worked on hypnosis therapies in the morning after breakfast while Kade and Anthony headed to Ink Inc. to do their work. She was starting to trust him a little more every day and he worked hard to help her feel safe and secure when she was with him. Jake used different therapies where he told her how strong she was and how capable she was while she was under the hypnosis and he tried to change the picture of Devin in her mind. Anthony told him how much she loved the beach, so he coaxed her out to the beach to sit with him. He did a lot of therapies there with the sound of the water and shore birds, the feel of the sand. He also asked questions and learned more about her life under hypnosis. He planted code words in her head that he could use to trigger the strength thoughts, and used the Katy Perry song *"Firework"* to help her believe in herself, as well as the song *"The Climb"* by Miley Cyrus. She told him much while she was under hypnosis and helped Jake to find ways to change the images in her head. She was a fighter and he could see that in her. She was a protector too.

All four of them always had lunch together and Jake headed to Erin's house in the afternoon with Kade to see what was up with Devin, and so Jake could learn more about him. They watered the plants, checked the doors and windows, and made sure Devin hadn't touched her house. They also picked up her mail and checked the cameras' recording to see if Devin had touched anything or came near the property. Kade cut some of her roses and made bouquets to bring to Erin and help her feel like everything was normal. He had watched her when she cut roses for him, so he did his best to replicate what she did. Erin edited, had client meetings virtually, and spent time in Anthony's arms, or they walked the secluded beach area of Kade's yard. Erin would pick up shells and the white or black round stones on the beach. She used those to decorate around the house. Anthony just loved having time to spend with her, and she relaxed some when she was with him, shutting the world out.

Jake watched Kade's house in the nights as he was putting more plans together realizing that Erin edited in the office when the others were sleeping, late in the night, or rather early in the morning. He knew she was afraid to sleep for fear that she would hurt Anthony or scare Kade with her night terrors. Jake wished he had the words to help her, but until Devin was out of her life permanently she couldn't let down. He could see the exhaustion in her eyes, and she looked like she was losing weight, she didn't have much more to lose. He knew she wasn't eating. All of this was taking a terrible toll on her own health. He needed to try the music he planted during hypnosis; something had to work, there had to be a way to break through the walls.

"Hey Kade, did you know that Erin is up late in the night, editing I'm sure, to keep her mind occupied so she doesn't have nightmares?"

"I suspected as much. She looks so exhausted and when I ask her about it she brushes me off telling me she's ok. I know she's trying to protect all of us, but I'm really worried about her. She's going to collapse and we won't be able to bring her back, or she's going to end up in the hospital. That's my fear right now."

"Me too. She works out with us like the demons are chasing her and she tries so hard to be brave. I think Devin's face is on the punching bag for as hard as she hits it. I just can't break through her barriers. Even the therapeutic massage doesn't work. She has a wall up so high, but I'm afraid she's going to crash and burn someday soon. I know she's dealt with a lot in her life to this point and doesn't know how to let people in. She's hanging on by a thread."

"Maybe I can get Mariah, my soon to be sister-in-law and Erin's former provider, to come and talk to her. Perhaps Mariah can give us something to help Erin sleep and relax. She needs rest."

"That's a great idea. Maybe Mariah can give me some additional insight that I can use with Erin during our hypnosis sessions." Kade nodded and stepped to the kitchen to call Mariah. Jake wandered to the front window and discovered what he'd been waiting for – he saw Devin in his house, and he got his first glimpse of the man that was toying with and upsetting the balance in Erin's life. Jake watched him as he unloaded stuff from his front porch and put things together in the living room. Jake took his binoculars out and watched, fascinated, as Devin put together a cage of sorts that had chains and handcuffs attached. The cage was big enough when Devin had it all assembled to house a person. Jake suspected that was his plan – to kidnap and tie up Erin in that cage. The man was beyond sick. He was inhuman.

Devin put a mattress and frame in it and strapped that to the floor of the cage, and strung the handcuffs and chains out on it. Kade came back in with the roses he cut for Erin, and Jake told him what he saw. Kade took the binoculars from Jake and saw the same thing. Both of them were livid.

"Mariah is going to come with Michael for dinner on the weekend, but she has time right now to meet with us at her clinic. Shall we go?" Jake nodded. They closed up Erin's house, grabbed the two things Erin asked for from her kitchen and headed to the free clinic to talk with Mariah. As they left and secured the house, Terry came by and dropped off a package that had been delivered to the production house. Kade took it and asked if he knew who it came from, but Terry did not know. Nothing indicated who sent it. They thanked Terry, put the package in the car and headed to the clinic. Kade tried to handle the package by the string only so as not to mess up any fingerprints. They headed to see Mariah.

*****

Mory and the judge were conferring in the judge's chamber. Mory brought to her all the documents on Richard and together they came up with a plan to make Richard's life a living hell. The judge found three areas where Richard would have to explain his actions before a review board, and Mory had the case built up with the bar committee on ethics against Richard. They decided to start their impact on Richard with the bar sending Richard the complaints lodged against him as well as the manner in which he needed to respond. This first step would take him away from Devin and make him focus on his own career, if he was going to keep his license to practice. Richard would be tied up for a time answering to all the charges and black marks on his record.

The judge decided that this needed to be delivered by a court courier today with signature of receipt to ensure that Richard couldn't ignore the summons. That had to happen today before the close of business. They wanted a trail of evidence to help in their quest. Mory agreed. For the next hour they worked together to lay out the plan and organize the documents that Richard would need to address and provide documentation. Judge Kafner set up the courier and told Mory what she wanted to see in the file for Richard's case with the charges being pressed against him. The judge was trying to help keep Richard very busy so as to deter him from his mission with Devin. Mory told the judge he had it under control and would work with the committee to ensure that all the required steps were taken and documented. Richard would need to meet several times with the ethics committee to sort all of this out or risk losing his license to practice.

Mory called and talked with Roberto as he was heading back to his office. Roberto was glad to hear that the State Bar Association was tying up Richard's efforts and making him inaccessible to Devin. Roberto told Mory that he had some additional ideas and perhaps Mory needed to look into any other lawyers that Richard would use to help out Devin. Mory agreed.

*****

Jake and Kade made it to the clinic and spent half an hour with Mariah. Kade introduced them and Jake told her what he needed. Mariah provided a bit of background on Erin without revealing anything that could be a HIPPA violation, and told both of them that she too was very worried about Erin. She prescribed for Erin a relaxant/sleep combination med that she couldn't get addicted to, and told both of them precisely how to use it with Erin. She cautioned them that Erin would fight them over using it, but they could tell her it was safe, tell her that Mariah wanted to help her get some rest; Erin would rest, relax, and be able to see things with fresh eyes and maybe a fresh perspective. This med would help her body relax and in essence help her forget for a bit about Devin. She told Jake that perhaps the pill and some therapeutic massage would relax her enough to make her sleep. She also told them that if this didn't work she would come by and give her a shot, but she might need help holding her down. That made Jake chuckle. Mariah was a riot and it was no wonder that Michael had latched onto her. Jake and Kade took the pills and headed back home. A comfortable silence settled in the car.

"Kade, what do we want to do about the package Terry brought for Erin. It could be something that will set up more demons and push her further over the edge." Jake asked.

"I've been thinking about that package. I think we need to work with Anthony and open it ourselves. If it's from Devin, I don't want to push Erin any farther over the edge with it. That bastard is sick and twisted, and he has a deep hold on Erin's emotions and psyche right now. I need to protect her."

"Agreed. I'll take the package to my cottage and when you or Anthony have time, we'll open it together.   We need to use gloves. If it's not from Devin, we can figure out how to give it to Erin." They agreed and headed into the driveway. Jake held the package by the string like Kade had done and headed to the cottage. Kade turned and headed into the main house.

*****

Devin was smiling. His package had been delivered and now these two guys would make sure that Erin would get it. This would be the start of driving her over the edge. He just couldn't send her text messages anymore because she disconnected her phone. He could though, still send her email messages. He needed to get to work on those new messages. They would be suggestive and would hopefully make her crazy. She would learn what it meant to cross him and make him look like a fool. Her email was still connected so she was still doing productions. He would use that vehicle to push her to brink of crazy. His plan was genius.

Chapter Four

Kade came into the house and looked up to see Anthony motioning him to be quiet. He indicated that he had just gotten Erin to sleep in his arms and he wanted her to stay that way if possible. Her sleep was restless, but she was almost relaxed in Anthony's arms. Anthony shifted so Erin was laying on his chest. Kade helped by putting a blanket over them both. Anthony rubbed her back in soothing circles and kept her wrapped in his arms as she sank deeper into sleep. There was music playing on the sound system and it seemed to be lulling Erin into resting. They both knew how much Erin liked country music, especially the love songs of the 90's. Kade headed to his office, found his box of gloves and headed out the back door to Jake's cottage.

"Hey Kade." Jake greeted.

"Anthony was able to get Erin to sleep in his arms for a bit so I thought while she was out you and I could open up that package." Jake welcomed him inside and the led the way to the kitchen where the package sat on the table. Kade handed him gloves and together they carefully opened the package. What they saw inside made them both sick. "This really is one sick bastard! I'm glad we intercepted this package and we're the ones opening it. He is twisted and he's definitely obsessed with Erin. This is cruel."

"It looks like he created a replica of what we saw him building in his house. He's seriously out of touch with reality. How in the hell has been freed from jail? He deserves to be locked up and the key thrown away. People like him don't change. He must have one slick lawyer who keeps getting him released. He is twisted."

"We need to get this to Thomas." Jake took pictures and Kade called Thomas to tell him what they had. Jake was creating a profile and file on Devin. Thomas told them he would be by to pick up the box soon. Kade told him to come to the cottage in the back because Erin was not aware of the package. Thomas agreed.

*****

Devin set up two email messages to send one tomorrow morning and the second one tomorrow night. He would keep her off guard and do his best to drive her insane. She would more likely accept his advances if he could make her crazy. Once she was over the edge he could promise the torture would stop if she let him protect her. However, Devin did not know that Erin would never see those messages. Kade and the others had a way to re-direct Devin's emails so that they went to a ghost inbox. Devin called Richard to see what was up and to get his help with his plan. He really needed Richard's expertise.

"Hey Richard, its Devin. Do you have time to talk?"

"No actually I don't Devin." He sounded strange on the phone, distracted and frustrated. "I am dealing with my own set of problems man. The state bar association is after me for my extra-curricular activities and the work I've done to get you off on these charges. The ethics committee is breathing down my neck, so you're on your own buddy. I have to get my act together because I have to face the ethics committee tomorrow morning with documentation of all my legal work. They need all the evidence that I haven't been doing the wrong things here."

"Bullshit Richard! I need your help! That stuff can wait. To hell with the ethics committee. I'm paying you a shit load of money to help me with this project. I'm so close and I need you tonight. You can't say no to me."

"Sorry Devin. You have to figure this one out on your own for a little while. I have to save my job and protect my license. Otherwise everything I've done for you over the last four years will implode and you will go down with me in flames. We will be cellmates in the state lockup for a long time to come if I can't get them to back off."

"You can't do this to me Richard. I'm paying you good money. I'm so close to getting what I want and I need your help. You're my lawyer for God's sake. Please don't abandon me when I am so close to the promise-land."

"Goodnight Devin. I have my own problems to worry about. Stay out of jail until I can get this all straightened out. You can deal with Erin on your own for now." He hung up the phone and Devin seethed. Richard couldn't do this to him. No one treated Devin like that and got away with it. This was the second person to tell him no in his lifetime and he didn't like it. He would make Richard pay too. He had money to burn so he could afford to do all the stuff he had been doing. Maybe Richard needed more money to continue to help; Devin needed to look into a larger retainer.

*****

Erin woke up in Anthony's arms. She scooted up and kissed him as his arms tightened around her. She realized they were out on the sofa, but she was comfortable.

"Hi sugar. Did you rest?" She nodded and continued planting feather light kisses along his jaw. "Careful sugar." Anthony cautioned. She was starting a fire and he needed to keep a clear head. Erin was so fragile right now. He didn't want to take advantage of her. He heard Alex's warning.

"Anthony, my sweet handsome Anthony, this is so wonderful being in your arms." He smiled at her and she kept kissing along his jaw and her hands roamed over his torso and shoulders. "Thank you for letting me sleep in your arms and shut the world out for a bit. I feel secure in your arms." Her hands threaded through his hair and she roamed her hands over his torso, appreciating the feel under her palms and fingers.

Anthony sat up, cradling her and sitting her in his lap. He needed to break the spell so this wouldn't go too far. She was so on edge and he didn't want to hurt her. Alex's words kept repeating themselves in his head to take things slow. "I'm so glad you slept darlin'. You haven't slept in the last several nights and you're exhausted." She wrapped her arms around him and straddled his legs while hugging him to her.

"Anthony, my hero, can I tell you something?" He nodded and watched her face carefully while holding her at arms-length. "I was thinking this morning and I decided that I needed to tell you what I was thinking and feeling." She took a deep breath and tried to center herself. "You are everything to me Anthony, handsome. I love you so much." There she had said it and it was out there.

"Sugar, I love you too. I have loved you for a long time, but I didn't want to scare you away. You are the air I breathe darlin' and I want to love you, keep you safe, hold you, and just be with you. You had me from that first moment I saw you sitting at Alex's workspace. You were so brave and you didn't flinch with the work Alex did on your shoulder. Your smile just drew me in and I want nothing more than to love you, hold you and be with you."

"I want that too. You are my life Anthony and I love you with every fiber of my being. I never thought I could find love and I found you. You are everything to me. Thank you for loving me too." She leaned in and kissed him passionately. Anthony's body was responding to her and needed to keep his head. "Now, I need to go get dinner on the table. Jake and Kade should be home soon." She kissed him again and got up, heading to the kitchen. She was oblivious to the effect she had on him. Anthony worked to shut down his reaction. Anthony texted Kade to see if he could join them at Jake's. Kade told him to come over, they had something to share with him.

"Erin, darlin', I need to go to Jake's cottage. We'll all be back in an hour for dinner." He came over, wrapped her in his embrace and kissed her again. She told him to be good as he headed out the back door. Erin checked all the other doors and made sure they were locked, then she returned to her kitchen to finish her dinner. She turned on the radio to her country station and got to work. She had made chili earlier which was in the crockpot simmering and now needed to make the cornbread, and pull the rest of the meal together. She gave the chili a stir, and headed to the refrigerator to pull some other things out. She lost herself in her music, singing along when she knew the words. Music soothed her. It was her sanctuary, her release. She also headed to the laundry room and dropped in a load of towels.

Jake welcomed him in and together they told Anthony about the package that Terry had given them. Anthony was outraged that Devin was planning to lock up Erin and abuse her. All of them needed to deal with their anger because Erin didn't need to know about the package. Jake explained that they had re-routed her emails from Devin and they were filing them, sharing them with Thomas for Devin's file. They hoped they could stop any more packages and either intercept them or get them re-routed before Erin saw them. Kade said he would call and talk with Terry. Maybe Terry could hold them and let Kade know when he could pick them up. Thomas came and picked up the package the men had bagged up and took it into evidence. All three of them were glad they had been able to change her phone number, but they needed to be on guard with her email now; they hoped Devin didn't have more than one email account, but they would stay apprised. Devin was relentless. They each needed to keep vigilant with her email on her computer. At least Erin was ok with leaving her computer out on the counter and when a message came in it pinged. Maybe they could convince her to let them check it first. Kade needed to look into that with Erin.

*****

Mory called Roberto to let him know what else he was able to accomplish with Richard. He told him that the Ethics committee would be tying up Richard's time for the next several weeks.   Richard would need to prove that he was worthy of keeping his license to practice, and if the evidence presented itself, maybe they could take Richard and Devin down together.   Roberto asked several questions which Mory was able to answer with ease and gave him a couple other ideas to keep Richard occupied. Roberto said he suspected that Devin wasn't too pleased at having his lawyer unavailable. They laughed about that. Both of them agreed to keep in touch and to keep working on ways to frustrate Richard and Devin both. Roberto was glad to keep his hands in the work he used to do. If he could help clean up the smarmy lawyers he would do his best to help.

*****

Devin was furious about Richard. He needed his lawyer at his side so that he could pull off the work he wanted to do. He was obsessed with Erin. He also wondered why he hadn't heard back from Erin with the emails he sent. Maybe she had him blocked and maybe he needed to try with a new email address. Surely the several he had sent would have an effect. He checked his email again, but still no word from Erin. He didn't know how much more she could take with the stuff he sent, but perhaps he needed to step up his game and send the same messages from several different email addresses. Something had to shake her loose and let him know where she was hiding.

He sat down at his computer, found all his past emails to Erin, and flooded her inbox from different email accounts. That should get a rise out of her, he thought. He really needed to figure out where she was hiding herself. Richard hadn't found anything out about Anthony, so Devin still didn't know how to make Anthony's life hell too. He kept searching, trying to figure out who Anthony was and how to get to him. Devin was frustrated that Anthony didn't have a social media presence so he couldn't search for him and what he did or where he lived. He also called the news station to find out about Erin and asked his old buddy Justin. Justin told him that Erin was no longer stringing for them and he had no idea where she was or how to get ahold of her. Devin pushed, but Justin cut him off. He told him that Erin was not working as a stringer anymore and if Devin needed more info he could call the station manager. Justin hung up the phone and went back to work. Devin was furious. Why was everyone telling him no? And now Devin was desperate. He had to find some way to get to Erin and he really needed to know where she was. Desperation drove Devin to do stupid things; things he didn't really think through. He was seeing red and everyone was putting roadblocks in his way. He would show them; he would have the last laugh. Erin would be his.

*****

While Thomas was there picking up the box, Jake asked Thomas if he could spend some time with Quatro and learn more about Devin's plan. Thomas told him he would arrange it and get back with Jake. Jake needed to see what he could do to get to Devin, and get him locked up for good. Thomas made a call and set up an appointment for Jake to meet Quatro. Devin wouldn't accept help; that much he knew because nothing deterred him, not even spending nights in jail. Jake was going to talk with Quatro tomorrow morning. Jake needed to put some questions in order and see what Quatro could share with him and help him with.

Erin put the cornbread in the oven, set the timer, and started to set the table. She put salads together and dished up corn chips, diced onions, cheese and sour cream too for them to garnish their chili. Her kitchen was her sanctuary. She also cut up jalapenos and found salsa in the refrigerator, in case her chili wasn't hot enough for them. She even whipped up brownies to go with ice cream for dessert. She checked the washer, put the towels in the dryer and headed back to the kitchen. Her computer was open on the counter and she heard it ping with the new messages being received. She finished putting everything on the table, took her cornbread out of the oven, and turned to see what the emails were about. She didn't think she had anything on her schedule, but perhaps Terry found another production she needed to do. Kade came in the backdoor and intercepted her; he knew she was heading for her computer.

"Hey Erin. Whatcha doin' darlin'?"

"I'm finishing making dinner Kade and my inbox on my computer is going nuts. I was just going to check the emails." That statement put Kade's hackles up and his suspicious nature overcame him. He tried to keep his face passive.

"Erin, honey, can I look at the emails before you do? It's just me being protective." He was holding onto her shoulders and trying to stop her from her computer. She smiled up at him.

"Sure Kade, if that makes you feel better. I don't have anything to hide. It should be business emails and nothing more. Thanks Kade for your protection." She hugged him and stepped back into the kitchen to get drinks on the table. She figured they might enjoy beer with their chili. She also thought about crackers, so she put those out too.

Kade wandered over to her computer and opened the mailbox. He knew his gut was right. Devin had sent her more disgusting emails from three more accounts. Kade forwarded them to the ghost inbox making sure the ghost account had them, deleted them out of her inbox and sent mailbox, and texted Jack to re-route those addresses too. Jack sent back a text that he was on it. Kade checked all her new messages and left only the two that pertained to her work. He made sure those showed 'unread' so that she could deal with her business email. He loved that Erin cleaned out her inbox and filed everything. This made everything so much easier; he didn't have to sift to find all the unread messages. Kade loved a woman who was thorough and kept her inbox tidy. She was organized and he really liked that about her. He removed all traces of these emails from her view.

Erin came back out of the kitchen and put the pot of chili on the table, and she put the butter and cornbread out too. Jake and Anthony came in. Kade joined them and they took their places at the table.

"Erin, darlin', this looks delicious. You gave us so many choices for our chili." Jake said and beamed at her.

"I'm going to suggest that you taste it first and if it's not hot enough then you can add the hot stuff. I tend to make a spicy chili using a chile called tepini; it's how I was taught to make it." She smiled at them and they were hopeful she was settling down a bit.

"Erin, Jake and I brought what you wanted from the house, and we brought some of your roses too. Everything is good there, secure, and we put your mail on the counter."

"Thanks Kade. Thanks for cutting some of my roses. They are still going strong. They make me feel like home. Thanks very much."

"We also went to see Mariah today." Erin looked up at Jake and then to Kade. "Mariah wants to help you Erin, she's worried about you honey, and we all want you to rest without the demons. I know you edit late at night because you are afraid to sleep." Her face registered her surprise at his statement. She didn't think they knew. "Mariah gave us a non-addicting sleep relaxer for you; she wants you to sleep, and get some rest. We're all very worried about you honey. We just want you to rest. So we are asking you please to try this tonight so we can help you relax and rest. You need your strength darlin'. We don't want you to end up in the hospital." They all watched her process this.

"Am I really that far over the edge? I don't mean to be like this, but I'm afraid to let down. If I let down and Devin gets to me then I can't save myself or all of you. I'm really sorry for causing you to worry about me." The tears were balanced on her eyelashes and her eyes were swimming.

"Sugar, look at me." Anthony said gently. He tipped her chin up and held her gaze. "You are completely exhausted love and you are frightened. We understand that, but you also need to rest and keep your strength up. We want you to rest so that you can see things with a fresh perspective and maybe regain some strength. You barely eat, you don't sleep, and you pace constantly; I know you are losing more weight and you can't afford to lose any more darlin'. Devin doesn't know where you are and we won't let him get to you. The whole family is concerned about you. We just want to keep you safe and keep you with us. We don't want you to end up in the hospital." A couple of tears slipped down her cheeks. Anthony brushed them away and cupped her cheek. "Darlin' we are so very worried about you. Mariah said that you can try this and see if you can sleep, and if not she'll come give you a shot of something stronger. We just don't want you sick and ending up in the hospital."

"Ok." She acquiesced, the tears started to fall in earnest, and she fell into Anthony's arms. He held her, pulled her into his lap, and caressed her back until the sobs quieted down. She knew they were right, but she didn't like not being in control. Anthony motioned to Jake and Kade to eat while he comforted Erin. Finally, Erin pulled herself back together and moved back to her chair after kissing Anthony's cheek. She started to eat her chili and they changed the conversation to fun stuff. Kade told her he liked the new additions to his bookcases and end tables. Erin had put the shells and stones she gathered on the beach into different places in the living room. She smiled at him and all of them enjoyed their dinner. She tried desperately to pull herself back together. She didn't want to make them worry any more about her than they already did, and she really didn't want to end up in the hospital. They'd probably put her in a rubber room or at the very least in restraints!

Kade told them all that Michael and Mariah would join them for dinner on Saturday night. He suggested that they grill steaks and Erin said she would make potato packets, green beans and a green salad, and she would figure out something to make for dessert. All of them gave her ideas of what they liked. She was starting to come back to them, and starting to understand their worry over her demeanor. Maybe tonight would be a restful night for her. She forced herself to eat about a 1/3 of a bowl of chili and a small piece of cornbread. It was progress.

After dinner Erin cleaned up and the boys found a movie on TV. Erin checked her email and read through the two messages for the productions discovering that she needed to shoot an interview at the beach on Friday morning, and two interviews and cover footage at the pier in the afternoon. Terry tried to schedule it all for just one day. She added everything for these two productions to her calendar and Anthony got a notice of the change on the calendar, and filed her messages. He didn't mention anything to the boys yet. He wanted to talk with Erin first. Erin finished the dishes, cleaning the kitchen, and headed upstairs to the bedroom. She cleaned up a little, brushed her hair, changed into her oversize t-shirt, put on her robe and footies, brushed her teeth and came back downstairs. She climbed on the sofa next to Anthony, curling her legs under her, and he draped his arm around her bringing her close to his side. Kade brought her the pill from Mariah with a glass of water. She took it and they all watched as she swallowed it. Anthony tucked her further into his side and they watched the movie.

"Thanks for the movie guys and for being patient with me. I'm sorry I'm causing you all to worry so much. That wasn't my intention. Thank you all for keeping me safe." Erin said.

"We thought we could stand a rom-com tonight. Is this movie ok?" Jake asked grinning. She nodded. He got a small smile out of her. They talked during the commercials and she seemed to be in the moment. Anthony regaled them with stories about the two people he did ink for earlier in the day and Kade said he had one appointment for tomorrow. He told Erin that they wanted to explore the video idea and building a website for the shop. Erin smiled at him and said they could talk about that maybe at the next family dinner. Kade agreed and Erin snuggled more deeply into Anthony's embrace. Her limbs were feeling really heavy; she was fighting the effects of the medicine. Jake watched her eyes as they slowly drifted closed. She kept trying to fight it but the meds were doing their thing. The pill must be kicking in.

All of them turned their attention to the TV and the movie, waiting for Erin to fall into a really deep sleep. Anthony didn't want to move her until they were sure she was fully out. He was enjoying having her in his arms and resting against him. He knew she was finally completely at rest. It was close to ten and the movie was almost over. Kade offered to carry Erin upstairs so Anthony could get settled to hold her. Jake gave him the music to play low in the disk player in their room and bid them goodnight; he headed to the cottage locking the doors behind him. Anthony climbed the stairs with Kade and Erin close behind. He got ready for bed, sleeping in just his boxers. Kade helped him get Erin's robe and footies off and Kade laid her in bed next to Anthony. She was like a ragdoll, and she was so tiny. Erin snuggled into Anthony's side with her head on his shoulder. They tried to make her comfortable. He wrapped his arm around her waist, putting her head on his shoulder, and Kade covered them up. Kade leaned in and kissed her forehead. He started the two pieces of music playing on low and put them into a loop.

"Goodnight bro. I think she's going to sleep well tonight."

"Thanks Kade. Appreciate you both taking the initiative to talk to Mariah. Erin really needs the rest. Goodnight Kade."

*****

Devin watched his computer waiting for a response from Erin. He had sent her more than a dozen messages and still nothing. She couldn't be that immune to the things he told her that he wanted to do to her. Maybe she had cracked and was now in a psych ward.   Perhaps he needed to step up his game. Thinking about her luscious body made him want. He needed release so he decided to head to the neighborhood bar down the street. There he could find a willing woman to relieve his tension and frustration. Maybe he should shoot video of what he did to her and send that along to Erin. She was so innocent, pure, that perhaps that video would make her respond to him. He could then find out where she was stashing herself. He smiled again to himself. This was the best plan yet in Devin's mind.

Devin headed to Brews Bros and found a willing partner for the night. He had set up a hidden camera in his room and he lured her back to his house. Devin basically created a porn movie with all the acts he did with this woman. She was pretty well wasted when he brought her home; Devin made sure she had a few more drinks with him at the bar and she was really out of it, she allowed him to abuse her body with all the sex toys he had. He made sure the camera showed everything in great detail he was doing to her. After he had his fill, all the video he needed, and relieved his sexual tension, he put the girl into a cab and sent her on her way. She wouldn't remember anything when she came out of her alcohol-induced stupor and she wouldn't be able to identify him either. This was a great plan in Devin's mind. She was over the edge with all the alcohol in her system and he was sure she wouldn't remember what happened to her. He just needed her for release and for his movie for Erin.

He grabbed the SD card from his camera, edited the video, added in commentary about what he planned to do to Erin when he had her in his grasp, and once he was satisfied, he sent the video to her email from three different email accounts. He wanted to make sure she knew what he wanted from her in living color. Satisfied with himself, he headed to bed and immediately fell asleep. He was spent from all the work of trying to coax Erin into his house.

*****

Kade was working in the office, finishing up some documents for Michael and for the winery when the ghost account that Jack had re-routed Devin's emails to beeped with new messages. Kade opened the account and was sick with the video he saw. Devin had used and abused an obviously intoxicated girl. Kade texted Jake who came over immediately. Together they decided to contact the police chief to see if they could get additional charges filed against Devin, and to see if they could identify the young woman. She needed protection too. This guy needed to be taken off the streets and locked away where he couldn't hurt anyone ever again.   He was beyond help. They both wondered how many women he had used and abused already.

"Jake, I don't know how the police can be so blind to what this guy is up to. There's no telling how many women he's hurt and now this video. It's disgusting. She's obviously intoxicated and totally unaware of what Devin is doing to her, but that's no excuse for his sadistic behavior."

"Kade, we can't do anything tonight, but we will deal with this tomorrow morning. Devin needs to pay for his crimes against women. He's sick, twisted and the very description of the devil. We also need to find this girl and see if we can't convince her to join the charges against Devin." Jake grabbed a still of the girl's face and took that with him to run on his computer for a facial recognition match.

The two men talked for another hour about how to deal with this situation. Kade said he saw Erin's email earlier and she had two productions to go shoot on Friday. Kade told Jake that Anthony had appointments in the morning, so he would work with Jake to accompany Erin to the locations. They would protect her in the event that Devin showed up. Kade said he wanted to know if the police informant Quatro could give any more information on what he and Devin talked about. Jake said he needed to contact his SEAL brothers and get some additional support for them. These guys would be good background help and Erin wouldn't need to know about them. They called it a night and both headed to bed. At least they had a plan. Jake was going to try and find out who the girl was in the video and they would help her press charges too. Before he headed to bed he started his computer running facial recognition software from three different databases on the picture of the girl. They needed to get some answers.

Jake headed back to the cottage and Kade peeked in on Anthony and Erin. Erin was curled into Anthony's side with her hand on his chest, her head on his shoulder, and both were sleeping deeply. Her face was relaxed and she looked to be peaceful for the first time in a really long time. It was good to see her sleeping fitfully. She looked like an angel who had no cares in the world. Kade smiled, closed their door quietly and slipped into his own bed. They all needed sleep. She slept restfully for the next few nights because of the med that Mariah prescribed. It was good to see her rested and eating meals again. She looked so much better and much more in control. She didn't look nearly as fragile and she had settled down a lot.

****

Friday morning Erin was up early. She got breakfast made and worked on the two scripts for the shoots that day. She developed her interview questions for each one and planned out exactly what footage she needed to shoot at both locations. She emailed her two production assistants and asked them to meet her with the gear and six SD cards. She printed out the questions and information for both Kade and Jake to help her, as well as her list of shots to check off. Erin and Anthony had talked about the day and Anthony told her that Kade and Jake were going with her. Unfortunately Anthony had to work. She told him that she would be fine. She had slept well the last three nights and she would be ok. She told him she was feeling stronger and was now fresher having rested. He hugged her to him, and she enjoyed being in his arms.

Jake knocked on the back door and Erin headed to let him in.

"Good morning Jake. Just in time. The coffee just finished brewing and the breakfast casserole is ready to come out of the oven." She hugged him briefly.

"Morning Miss Erin. Did you sleep well?" She nodded and headed back to the kitchen. She took plates out of the cabinet and set the counter for all of them to eat breakfast. Soon everyone was sitting and eating. Erin chose to stand in the kitchen facing the boys, but at least she was eating. They finished breakfast, cleared the dishes, and Anthony prepared to head to Ink Inc. Erin gathered her notes, her clipboard, her computer and her still camera bag.

"Erin, honey, do you have everything?" Kade asked.

"I do Kade. It's all packed up in my two bags over there." She walked over to Anthony, kissed him good-bye and wrapped him in her arms. "I love you handsome." She whispered to him. He held her a moment and then headed out to go to work. Erin turned back to Kade and Jake.

"Ok guys, are you ready to go with me? My production assistants are going to meet us at the first location. They have the camera, tripod and SD cards."

"Erin, honey, please walk us through exactly what we are doing at the first location. We'll talk about the second one while we eat lunch."

Erin gave them each a rundown of the morning shoot. She explained that they would first do an interview with the SME and he would talk about his research, the new species he discovered, and where he found it. Next they would walk a short distance and he would narrate as he showed the habitat, explained the excitement behind this new species, and how the ecosystem needed to be maintained. Erin wanted to shoot more cover footage too. Kade and Jake asked questions about their role, and they worked through all the details. Finally, they were ready to head to the beach.

*****

Once on location Erin introduced Jake and Kade to her production assistants. Carl and Derek brought the gear and worked to get everything set up.   Both of them wanted to please Erin, and she tried to make them feel important, comfortable and helped them see what she needed. Erin praised her team and Jake realized the assistants would do anything for her.   She taught them things and helped them to see how they could work together. Carl held the reflector for light once Erin placed it correctly, and Derek monitored the audio as they videotaped; Jake ran the camera. Erin asked questions and the SME was very happy to answer her questions. When they finished the interview portion he told Erin he was thrilled with her choice of questions and told her she made it easy for him. Kade was impressed. Erin stood toe-to-toe with a scientist who was clearly very educated, and Erin didn't bat an eye. She asked the questions she had on the clipboard, and Kade checked them off, but she also asked clarification questions that he wrote down too. It was an amazing interview and Erin worked to make it understandable for the general public.

Jake and the production assistants moved the gear to the habitat area and Erin followed with the SME and Kade. Kade and Jake were keeping their eyes peeled for any sign of Devin, and they knew Erin was on her guard too. She worked well with her talent and with the team; she didn't let anything with her personal life show. By 11:30 they had all the footage for this first project and Erin headed them to the food trucks for lunch. Carl and Derek stowed the gear in their vehicle, while Erin took Jake and Kade to her favorite Mac Attack food truck. Over lunch of different kinds of mac n' cheese Erin filled them in on the afternoon production.   They had two interviews and more footage to do at the pier location. Carl came and told her they were heading to set up at the second location. Erin told him they would be there soon. Erin and her men finished their lunch, got into the car and headed to the pier. Devin spotted her car in the parking lot and decided to follow to see where she was going. He was fuming because she wasn't alone. She had two biker type men with her and her production crew. It would be harder to get to her, but Devin was undeterred. He would find a way.

Erin pulled into the parking lot at the pier. She saw Devin's pickup pull in shortly after. She didn't know if Jake or Kade knew he was there, but as they were taking all the gear out she quietly told them that Devin was on site. Jake told her he had seen him while they were eating lunch and suspected that he followed them. She smiled at him, handed him the clipboard and her tablet; she gave Kade the list of questions again and the SD cards. Jake told her they were on high alert and he would make sure the beach police were apprised too. Together they made their way to the location and met Carl and Derek. Erin was trying to breathe normally, but at least she was more in control today having rested the last few nights.

Erin greeted her talent and they walked through the production. She did the two interviews, adding in additional questions when she heard their answers. This time Derek held the reflector for her and Carl monitored the audio. She had Dr. Jordan read the two prepared statements for the narration pieces to the camera; Dr. Jacobson followed suit with his pieces, and then she told both talent that she was going to shoot the cover footage necessary to make the project complete.

"Erin, when do you anticipate having the production wrapped up?" Dr. Jacobson asked.

"Dr. Jacobson, I plan to take all the footage from today, and the footage from the last two shoots we already did and start editing on Monday. I should have a fine cut for you both to view on Friday next week; do you have time to meet with me via videoconference at 1?" They nodded and added that to their calendar. "Once we are in agreement on the piece I can finalize it, add in the credits, and my hope is to be done before your deadline!" He thanked her and they both headed back to their offices. Erin changed out the SD cards, walked to her three different locations and got all her footage. This production location took them about two and half hours to complete all that was needed. Jake and Kade saw Devin in the distance, he seemed to be waiting for something; Jake's SEAL buddies were made aware of his presence too; Jake also alerted the beach police and had one standing nearby.

"Carl and Derek, thank you both for your help today. Great work!" Erin said to them and they both beamed at her.

"What do you need us to do now Erin?" Carl asked.

"Let's clean the sand out of the gear and put the gear away, then you both can head back to TK Productions. I'll take the SD cards so I can upload them and start editing. Carl why don't you take the audio bag and the reflector back to the car once you finish packing it up, and I'll send Derek with the camera and tripod shortly." Carl nodded and started to gather his gear with the help of Kade. Her team would soon be safely away from here. Erin quickly put everything else in order, slipped the SD cards into her camera bag, put her notes and clipboards into her briefcase, which she handed to Jake, and sent Derek on his way with the camera gear. She glanced up and Jake was talking with a beach police officer a ways away from her and Kade. Kade was across from her with his back to Devin. Devin saw his opening. Erin stood up and saw Devin running toward her and Kade with a big piece of driftwood in his hands ready to take Kade out.

"Kade, when I tell you to duck do it fast." Erin instructed. She moved into a defensive stance. "Duck now!" Kade did that Erin put her arm up to connect with Devin's arm protecting Kade. She hit him on the nerve of his arm and he dropped the driftwood which hit Erin when it fell, but that didn't deter her. She really didn't feel the driftwood hitting her leg. She could see the fury in his eyes. Devin was out to take her away. Quickly she turned her hand and body in a fluid motion, grabbed his wrist and flipped him off his feet onto the sand. Jake and the officer watched all of this unfold with shock, as did Jake's SEAL buddies, and the three different groups of people who had heard the commotion. Jake realized the weights and workout had given Erin more power behind her judo. All of them headed to help. Devin was looking at the sky in just a heartbeat. Jake reacted with the beach police officer and headed towards them quickly. Kade got to his feet and wrapped himself around Erin from behind her. She backed up into Kade and pushed him backward, keeping her defensive stance ready to strike again if necessary, putting distance between her and Devin. She didn't let down.

"Devin get away from me and my crew. You just never learn. You don't belong here or anywhere near me." Devin jumped up after he got his air back and prepared to grab for Erin again, but she was too quick for him. She backed up even farther with Kade, protecting him, and Devin kept approaching. Jake and the police officer reached them. Erin kept her eyes on Devin but could see the police officer and Jake out of her peripheral vision; her hands and arms were up in a defensive stance. "Officer please take this man into custody. I have a restraining order against him and he's violating it again." Her eyes never left Devin and where he was at; she continued to back Kade up with her. Kade's arm was around her waist. The crowd had gathered around them.

The officer forced Devin to his knees and cuffed him. Jake was ready to lend a hand if needed. He radioed for back up and Devin was hauled to his feet and taken into custody. Erin gave her statement to the police officer and he took a picture of her restraining order.   He took Kade and Jake's statements too. Erin was still in defense mode and she hadn't let down yet.   They had caused quite a commotion and were surrounded by beach on-lookers. A couple of people offered to help if they needed it but Erin just thanked them, smiled and turned back to her gear. She was reeling from her encounter with Devin, but she tried to maintain her professionalism.

Jake tried to disperse the crowd and he talked to his four SEAL buddies in the process; these buddies were in the crowd and prepared to help, but Erin didn't know they were there. Kade was close to Erin; she was still edgy and in defense mode. Her eyes were darting all around her and she wasn't relaxed at all. He could feel the tension radiating off her. He guessed it would take a while to come of the high of fighting with Devin again.

"Kade, sweetie, are you ok?" Erin asked when she finally came off her adrenaline rush some. She realized she hadn't asked him how he was doing and if he was ok. She was still breathing hard.

"I'm good Erin. I didn't think when I turned my back to Devin. Thank you for saving me from some serious pain. Are you ok darlin'?" She was rubbing her arm where she connected with Devin's arm. He took the camera bag and the computer from her. He could see some pain in her eyes. She was trying to remain professional and brave.

"Yeah. I'm sore, my arm really hurts and my leg stings where the driftwood hit me; I'm going to have a bruise on my arm but we're all in one piece, Devin didn't get me and didn't hurt you, so that's all that matters. And, Devin is going to be locked up again." She smiled at him, but he could see the pain in her eyes.   She was trying to be so brave. "Let's get Jake and call this day done. I'm exhausted and we need food." Kade wrapped his arm around her and took all the rest of her bags to carry for her. She stopped short. He couldn't make her budge.

"Erin, honey what's wrong?" Kade asked very concerned.

"Kade, I didn't plan very well today. I didn't make anything for dinner and didn't even think about it. We're also out of leftovers. What are we going to do?"

"No worries Erin. We can just order something in. Please don't let it get to you, don't worry. You needed to work on these two productions; that had to be your first priority. It's really ok. Besides, you need a night off from cooking!" Kade tried very hard to reassure her. She nodded finally and started walking with him again. Jake caught up to them and they headed to the car. By the time they reached the car Erin was shaking from the adrenaline letdown, so Jake took her keys to drive them home.

As they loaded stuff into the car one of the beach police ran up and offered an ice pack which they gratefully accepted.

"You should probably get someone to look at your leg too young lady. Driftwood has lots of splinters and sand. It could be embedded in your leg. You might also want to get that arm x-rayed to make sure it's not broken. It sounded like you hit pretty hard."

"Thanks officer and thanks for the help today." He tipped his hat to her and shook Jake's hand.

"Kade, can you call Mariah and see if she can fit Erin in for an x-ray and her leg?" Kade nodded and Erin protested. "Erin, darlin' your arm may be broken so let's just rule out everything ok. It will make me feel better." He smiled at her and she relented and hugged him.   He texted and got an immediate response.

"Mariah will be waiting for us." They started to get into the car and Erin started shaking uncontrollably. The adrenaline rush overwhelming her and she was shivering too. "Erin, honey, you're going to sit here with me in my arms while Jake drives." He scooped her into his arms and held on. Jake helped them into the car, Kade placed the ice pack on her arm, guiding it up to hold onto his shoulder, and wrapped her against his chest. Her shaking was making her teeth chatter too. "Hold on honey." Jake drove them to the clinic.

"Hey doc!" Jake greeted as they came in. "Erin is coming down off the adrenaline of fighting with Devin. We need to get her arm x-rayed and we need to get her leg cleaned up too."

"Hi Erin. Let's go to room one Kade." Kade carried Erin to room one and kept her wrapped in his arms. She was still shivering and shaking. Jake stayed in the waiting room and called Anthony to prepare him for what happened.

"Erin," Dr. White started, "can you tell me what happened today?"

"Dr. White, Devin came after me again but was intent on taking out Kade first. I intervened and used my arm to stop him from hitting Kade with a big piece of driftwood. Jake said he heard my arm connect with Devin's, but I was so focused on saving all of us that I just turned my wrist and body, grabbed Devin's arm and threw him to the ground. The driftwood hit the back of my leg as Devin dropped it." She was still shaking but settling down some. Erin had on yoga pants, but they were short and revealed her lower legs.

"Mariah, one of the officers gave us an ice pack, but her arm is already bruising. She said her leg was stinging too." Kade offered.

"Ok, I'm going to have the x-ray tech come and x-ray your arm, and I'll go get some stuff to get any slivers out of your leg and we'll bandage that too. Kade, just keep her wrapped in your arms for now ok? Erin I'm going to give you a shot of pain meds that will help with shaking." Kade nodded and held Erin closer to his chest. Mariah grabbed her medicine and syringe and gave Erin a shot right away. She was in shock and was trying hard to be brave.

"Hey Anthony, its Jake."

"Jake, are you guys done with the shoot. Are you heading home?"

"Well, yes and no. We finished the shoot and Devin showed up at the pier location. Don't panic bro." Jake heard Anthony swearing on the other end. "Devin came after Kade with a piece of driftwood and Erin intervened. Kade is fine but we think Erin broke her arm protecting Kade and she has a cut on her leg from where the driftwood hit her. Devin's on his way to jail and we are here with Mariah. Don't worry bro. We'll be home soon."

"Thanks Jake. That guy is making me want to hit him hard."

"I know bro. Erin is ok – just shaking from the adrenaline rush, but we'll get her fixed up and we'll be home. We need to think about dinner because she's going to need to rest."

"I'll take care of dinner. I'll order Chinese."

"Sounds good. We'll call when we are on the way home. It's all good. She's strong Anthony and Mariah's taking care of her. Keep your head bro."

"I will Jake. Thanks bro." They signed off and Jake paced the small waiting room. He was livid with Devin. While he had time he checked his search using his facial recognition software to figure out who the woman in the video was. He got a hit while they were at the beach and did some research on her. They needed to approach her and figure out if she remembered what happened with the video and Devin. He hoped she would be open to pressing charges and helping them get Devin off the streets. He also hoped she had gotten a rape kit done.

Mariah got the x-ray and discovered that Erin had a hairline fracture in the outside bone of the forearm. She debated and then decided to put a cast on her for the first three weeks and then move to a splint. Erin was very active and so a cast to start with might help with healing properly. Erin picked purple as her color of choice and Mariah got out all the parts to put the cast on her. The cast was a fiberglass one and Erin watched as Mariah expertly put the stocking on her arm, rolled on cotton batting and then wet the cast material and smoothed that over her arm too. As she finished forming the cast it started to get warm. Mariah told her that was normal because it was setting, it wouldn't burn her.   The cast set up hard in just a few minutes. Mariah had Erin move her fingers and thumb, and then she put an ice pack on it and taped it in place.

"Ok Erin, we need to get those splinters and sand out of your leg."

"No!" Erin was adamant and trying to scramble away from Kade. Kade held her tightly to him and tried to soothe her.

"Erin, it will get infected if we don't take care of it now. I can numb it or you can just stay in Kade's arms and I'll be quick. We need to keep you healthy my girl." Erin finally relented and buried her face in Kade's shoulder. Kade readjusted her so Mariah could work on her leg. She cleaned it first with a soapy substance and a soft brush, and then used her tweezers to remove four long slivers of driftwood and several pieces of sand. Erin sucked in air frantically and clung to Kade. He kept murmuring to her and telling her she was ok, brave and strong. After about twenty minutes Mariah finished and cleaned the leg again with another soapy treatment and soft brush. Her leg was very red and a little bit swollen. Mariah put antibiotic ointment on it that had some numbing qualities to it, and covered it with a bandage. She taped all the way around it with paper tape so that it wouldn't pull or hurt when she took it off in the morning.

"Ok Erin, all done sweetie. You did great." Mariah said. Erin's face was still buried in Kade's shoulder. Mariah put her hand on Erin's head and tried to reassure her. "Kade, here is more ointment and bandages for her to use over the next couple of days. Erin, you can take it off to shower, but please put more ointment and the bandage back on during the day. Ok?" She nodded but she still was buried into Kade's neck and shoulder. Kade could feel her tears running inside his shirt. Mariah smiled at Kade and led them back to the waiting room where Jake was.

Kade and Jake thanked Mariah and told them they would see her and Michael tomorrow for dinner. Erin mumbled her thanks too, but still hadn't looked at them. Kade carried her out to the car followed by Jake. They headed home. Kade tried to coax Erin to look at him, but she was overwhelmed with the pain her leg and her arm. She was embarrassed by her lack of strength when Mariah was cleaning out her leg, but Kade kept telling her it was ok and she was brave, strong and doing great.

*****

Devin was once again processed at the jailhouse and placed in a cell. Quatro was in the adjoining cell awaiting his parole hearing in the morning; his hearing had been moved up because he was recommended for good behavior. Devin struck up a conversation with him and Quatro asked what he did this time to get back in jail. Devin told him that Erin had hurt him again when he tried to take out one of her production crew. Quatro asked a lot of questions and Devin was eager to share with him; he was very eager to blame all of this on Erin. Devin helped Quatro with a lot of information to provide to Detective Thomas. Devin felt that he and Quatro were kindred spirits so he found himself willing to share all the gory details and the information on what he was going to do to Erin.

Quatro kept his cool and kept his face passive as he asked questions that the chief and Detective really wanted to know. He asked about the cage Devin said he built at his house and Devin was all too eager to tell him all about it. He told Quatro he wished he had his phone so he could show him the movie he made to send to Erin. Quatro listened carefully. He asked Devin to describe the movie he emailed to Erin. Quatro was livid and trying hard to remain passive. He was grateful when Devin left to call his lawyer. Quatro asked to see Detective Thomas.

Devin finally got a chance to talk with his lawyer and Richard told him he would send someone to help him tomorrow. Richard asked why Devin was back in jail and Devin told him. Richard was still dealing with the ethics committee and his hands were tied right now. He told Devin that until he was cleared with the Ethics committee he couldn't see or help clients, which included Devin. Devin wasn't happy but acquiesced to having a different person that Richard hand-selected and would send to him.   Devin was returned to his cell and he engaged in further conversation with Quatro. Quatro asked lots more questions and added to his evidence to give to Detective Thomas.

Quatro got an audience with the chief and Detective Thomas and gave them a lot of details about Devin's revelations. Quatro told them that Devin had sent a porn movie to Erin that he made with another woman and Detective Thomas said he had the video. He also told Quatro and the chief Jake had found out the woman's identity and they were going to help her press charges too. Quatro said that perhaps they needed a warrant to search Devin's house because Devin said if he was able to get Erin he was going to lock her up and tie her up in his house. Detective Thomas said he was working on that right now.

*****

Kade had alerted Anthony that they were on their way home. He also told him through text that Erin was reeling from the process with Mariah cleaning her leg out. He just wanted him to be prepared. Jake pulled the car into the driveway and pulled up to the garage. Anthony saw them drive up and headed out to help. He saw Erin curled up in Kade's arms. His brother took such good care of her. He helped by opening the door and Kade handed Erin to Anthony. She had tears in her eyes but went willingly into Anthony's arms. Anthony tried to be gentle with her.

"Hey sugar. You did a good thing today. Thanks for protecting Kade and Jake honey. I'm sorry you got hurt beautiful. You are so brave." He kissed her and kept her wrapped in his arms.

"I'm sorry I wasn't very brave with Mariah." She whispered, tears still running down her cheeks.

"Is that why you have tears honey?" She nodded. "It's ok. None of us think any less of you for shying away from Mariah cleaning your hurt leg. It's ok sugar." She smiled up at him and kissed him again. He carried her into the house while Jake and Kade got her things out of the car, locked everything up and headed inside. Anthony took her upstairs to their room and helped her to change from her work clothes into baggy sweats and a t-shirt. He marveled at how beautiful she was and his body responded to her beauty. She was everything to him and he wanted to love her completely. Shortly after Erin changed clothes into something looser the food arrived and they sat down to eat. Erin hobbled around and set the table for them, found drinks and they all came to the table.

"Kade, Jake and Anthony, thank you all for your help today. I'm sorry how things ended and I'm sorry for my reaction with Mariah." She took another breath. "I don't handle medical pain well. Thanks for taking care of me." She looked up at them all.

"Erin, it doesn't make you any less in our eyes because you reeled from what Mariah was trying to do. We just want you to stay healthy and to do that we had to get that leg fixed and cleaned out. It's ok." Jake said and smiled at her.

"It's just me being silly. I don't like to show weakness and dealing with that stuff is a definite weakness for me." She glanced back up at them. "Thanks for putting up with me."

They changed topics while enjoying dinner and Anthony talked about the shop and what they had planned for tomorrow. Anthony asked about the productions and Erin came to life talking about all they did today. Jake and Kade filled in some of it too. She told Anthony that her plan for next week was to edit both projects, but concentrate on the pier one to get it done for the client.

Chapter Five

Devin was arraigned on Monday and preliminary hearing was scheduled for evidence identification in two weeks. Devin was remanded into custody in the regional prison with no bail because of the multiple times he had been arrested for the same thing, and for the new charges pressed against him from the young lady he abused while she was drunk. Jake had found her and Kade, Jake and Anthony convinced her to press charges. She told them she didn't know how it happened but she had the rape exam the next morning. Jake had also had an audience with Quatro and he now had a great deal more information to go on. They helped with the evidence. Now, the three of them needed to talk to Erin. She was better rested and healing, but she needed to know about this other young lady and all the evidence before she ended up in court.

"Erin, are you in a break from your editing honey?" Anthony asked on Friday afternoon.

"Actually, I finished the production, it was approved by the client just twenty minutes ago, and so I'm rendering it and then will send it to Terry for duplication and completion of the project. I have some time now."

"Come sit and talk with us." Erin watched the three of them and wondered what this was about now.

"Erin," Jake started, "we all have to be in court next week to present evidence in Devin's case. Our goal is to get him put away so he can't hurt anyone ever again."

"Has he hurt someone else?" Her eyes were large and she was preparing herself for their answer.

"Yes honey." Kade said and her eyes moved to him. "Do you remember several days ago when I intercepted you and checked your email?" She nodded warily. "Well, Devin has been sending suggestive and explicit emails to your account which we forwarded to a ghost inbox, he's playing mind games, but we intercepted them before you saw them." She sucked in huge breaths to keep herself centered. "We didn't want you to be affected by these emails because you were already on the edge, but we have to tell you before we end up in the courtroom because a lot of it will be brought out in detail."

"Did he hurt someone else with these emails?"

"Kind of." Jake said. Her eyes, hurt and reeling, shifted to Jake. Anthony moved closer to Erin and wrapped his arm around her. "Erin, honey, Devin abused a girl who was very much intoxicated and he videotaped what he did to her. He made basically a sexually explicit porn movie and emailed that to you to tell you what he was going to do to you once he had his hands on you." Her mouth fell open and her eyes got wider, larger. Fear was evident.

"We will not let that happen Erin, but you need to be aware that we found the young lady, she has pressed charges with our help, and so all of those charges along with yours will be presented in court. She had the wherewithal to get a rape kit done the next morning and the evidence is all on Devin. The video will be submitted as evidence, but will not be shown; it's just disgusting and too graphic. We just need you to be prepared so you won't react to it. We didn't want you to be blindsided."

Erin sat in Anthony's embrace, dumbfounded that someone as cruel as Devin could hurt so many people and not pay for his crimes. All three of them watched her and wondered what was going through her mind. They tried to give her some time to process the information. All of them wanted to be there for her to give her as much support as possible. Finally, she gathered her courage and formulated her questions. She didn't know what to ask or how to deal with all of this new information.

"I don't know what I am doing or saying here. Not sure even what to ask you, so will start with this. What will be expected of me in court next week?"

"Erin, darlin', the judge is the only one besides the attorneys and those of us who are testifying who will be in the courtroom. This is not a jury trial, but rather a preliminary hearing to see if there is enough evidence to remand Devin into custody for a trial, and to lay out all the charges against Devin. Devin has already been arraigned."

"Ok, I understand that. Will Devin be in the courtroom? Will I have to face him?"

"No Erin he won't. He's being held in the regional prison and we've asked that he be brought in via video conference. You will see him on video monitor and he will see the entire courtroom. The judge, Judge Kafner, has agreed to that so that you and Erica can be protected." Anthony wrapped his arm tighter around her and Erin relaxed into his embrace. She was reeling from all this information. Jake went on with his information. "Erica was very drunk at the bar Devin picked her up from; we've been able to identify her using facial recognition, and the bar owner of Brews Bros. Erica is a regular there so the bar owner knew her. He cooperated and gave his surveillance footage to the police. Anyway, Devin took her back to his house and well basically abused her sexually. He put her in a taxi and sent her home when he was done with her; she had the wherewithal the next morning to go to her provider and a rape kit was done in the office. All of the DNA they found on her, and the fibers, bruises, fingerprints, etc. all belong to Devin. There is a plethora of evidence to hold him over for trial, it just needs to be presented in court to the judge. We don't anticipate him being eligible for bail after all the evidence is presented. The judge we have is tough on these kinds of crimes and she will make sure he spends his days in the regional prison until trial."

"Well that's the first positive thing to happen in this situation. I'm sorry for Erica having to go through all of this. Hopefully she has a support system in place. Thank you all for finding her and helping her add her charges to this case. Maybe we can both get some benefit from Devin being locked up." Erin thought for a moment. "What will I have to do?"

"Erin, honey, the judge and the DA will ask you questions as to what happened with the restraining order, how you know Devin, all the details leading up to this last arrest, and she will ask you about all the past times that Devin has been taken away for the restraining order violations. She may even ask about your self-defense training and how you protected yourself, and the rest of us."

"So basically you're telling me to really listen to what the judge is asking me and provide her the best answer possible."

"Yes Erin. We call it active listening." Jake said. "My best advice to you is to listen, really focus on what the judge is asking, and only answer what she is asking you, be specific, succinct. Ignore Devin and the monitor he will be on. Don't embellish, don't add anything, just tell her the answer to what she asked. It's a just the facts ma'am kind of thing." He stopped a moment. "Truthful answers!" Erin smiled at him.

"I try to always be truthful Jake. I don't think I should lie to the judge!" That made them all smile; she was trying to tease him a little. She needed to lighten the mood a bit. This was all overwhelming and had her completely off her game.

"The judge is a great lady, she is tough, and she's working on new legislation to try and strengthen the restraining order process. Plus she's working with our Uncle Mory to clean up the bad lawyers, judges and their ethics or lack thereof." Kade said. "I talked to dad and what else we know is that Richard, Devin's lawyer, is tied up with the ethics committee and Uncle Mory. That means that Devin will have a different lawyer representing him. Not sure that that matters, but Richard can't get him off this time and with all the new charges Devin is in for the fight of his life, especially with Judge Kafner presiding. She will take him to task on the people he has hurt and the despicable things he has done."

"Can we find out who the attorney of record is before we get there?" Anthony asked.

"Uncle Mory is working on that for us as we speak. We hope to know before Monday morning." Kade turned to Erin. "Erin, honey, how are you doing with all of this?"

"I'm scared out of my mind if the truth be known and reeling a bit about Erica and what she went through, but I'm tough and I know I can do this. I'm also thankful that you are all protecting me and that it wasn't me in Erica's position. I know that sounds bad of me to say. I am strong and because of all of you and Mariah's magic medicine, I have more of my wits about me. I'm sorry I fought you all so hard when you were only trying to help. I've just never had support before and I was so worried about all of you putting your lives on the line for me because I didn't think I was worth it. I didn't mean to sound like I had given up; I just didn't want any of you hurt. I have spent the last five years taking care of my mom, advocating for her, being alone in that task, fighting the system, and trying to take care of myself. I didn't know how to accept your help." She looked at all three of them and tried to hold the tears back. "Thank you all for not giving up on me and for helping me stay alive, and out of Devin's grasp." She hugged Anthony and kissed him. She held onto him for a moment longer trying to compose herself. She then got up and hugged Kade, kissed his cheek, and hugged Jake too with a kiss on his cheek. They all could see the tears she was holding back.

*****

They tried to do fun things over the weekend to keep their minds off the upcoming hearing. Erin asked Anthony if they could take a motorcycle ride. She missed the time she had to spend with him alone, but also wanted to do something fun with all of them, and she really like the freedom of feeling the wind in her hair and the open air. All four of them got on the bikes, Erin riding behind Anthony, and they headed for a nice ride to clear their heads, and to have some semblance of normal.

She had packed them a picnic lunch and Anthony directed them to one of his favorite places. Erin reveled in the feel of Anthony's body as she nestled against him and wrapped her arms around him. Anthony was very aware of Erin pressed against him, but he wanted to make sure she had a little bit of normal activity in her life. He had to breathe and not let himself show what she did to him. Her nearness to him made his body react. He was still in shock that she loved him. He kept pinching himself to make sure he wasn't dreaming. He kept promising himself that he would take things slow with Erin, but her nearness was almost making that impossible.

They headed down the open road and rode for about an hour. Anthony led them to the secluded and private beach he loved to spend time at. They parked and walked down to the beach. Jake had brought a volleyball with him and Kade had the picnic lunch in his saddlebags. They spread a couple of blankets on the sand and spent the next couple of hours relaxing. Erin's leg was almost fully healed, just a small scar remained. She still had a cast on her arm, which would come off late next week when she started PT, but she was using it like it didn't have a cast on it at all. Erin walked with Anthony barefoot in the sand next to the water. She picked up several shells and some different colored rocks to add to her, well Kade's, collection. All three men were happy that she was able to relax a bit. Kade had brought plastic bags for her to put the shells and rocks into. They added that to Anthony's saddle bags.

They played volleyball, had their picnic, played in the surf and just had an amazing time. Finally, they climbed back on bikes and headed for home. Anthony led them a different way home this time giving them more scenery to look at. It was a leisurely trip back to Kade's house using the backroads instead of the main road. Anthony wanted to feel Erin pressed against him, so he took a longer trip back to the house. While they rode Erin started to think about her house and about her life. She needed to talk to Anthony. If they were able to get Devin put away, she didn't know any more if she wanted to go back to her house. The house was hers, but perhaps it was time to find a new place to live, make some new memories that were good. She was thinking of Kade's house as home and it had good memories for her.

Erin wasn't the only one thinking about the future. Jake wasn't sure he wanted to leave either. He enjoyed being here, he had found family too, and wondered if there was a way to relocate and stay here permanently. Jake realized that he could virtually work from anywhere, after all it was his own business and he wanted to be around Erin, Anthony and Kade. He had talked to his SEAL buddies who came to help at the beach and they liked the area too. Perhaps it was time to relocate and move his business here. He needed to explore this and figure out how to do this. Jake realized he liked being part of this family they had formed. Erin had definitely captured him like she had done with the Romano family. Sometimes relaxing and doing something different helped to clear the mind and focus the path a bit more. Jake was ready to find a woman, settle down and put down some roots. Perhaps he could find someone as wonderful as Erin and find his own happily ever after.

Sunday found the group assembled at Anthony's parents' house for dinner. They all talked about the upcoming hearing and everyone asked questions, gave advice and enjoyed the evening together. Erin was doing her best to stay calm and to focus on the positives of the day. She had a family and she was over-the-moon happy with her life. She was so in love with Anthony and wanted to make their situation permanent. She decided that she needed to talk with Anthony about the future and what it held.

"Can I say something?" Erin asked when a lull appeared in the conversation. Everyone looked to and waited for her. She grabbed Anthony's hand under the table. "I first just want to say thank you to you all for rallying around me and accepting me into your family, even though I threw Kade to the ground before I knew who he was." She smiled up at Kade who grabbed her hand and kissed it. "Thank you for protecting me and your patience with me as I navigated this situation. Thank you for rallying around me and Mariah for helping Jake and Kade find some way for me to sleep at night without the demons." She stopped and took a breath. She looked up all of them. She took another deep breath.

"I have also been thinking. I know I made a big deal about my house, but after living at Kade's house and feeling more comfortable there, than I have in a long time or anywhere else I've lived, I'm thinking I don't want to ever go back to my house. Too many bad memories of Devin living across the street, and too much bad stuff there. I don't want to keep reliving it all. I can start my roses and flowers somewhere new. I can just get clippings and restart all my roses or just find new ones." She stopped again and looked at Anthony.

"Darlin' I agree with you. There's no reason to keep the memories of the bad stuff mixed with the good." She smiled at him wistfully. "Did your mom live with you in that house?" She nodded. "We will take all her memories with us too, ok?" She nodded again.

"I agree Erin." Mariah said. "You can take the good memories with you, and your roses too, and start fresh when this is all over." Everyone thought that was a good idea. They resumed their dinner and had a great evening.

*****

Tuesday morning found all of them up early, dressed in professional clothes and prepared to head to the hearing. Erin was deep breathing and using her self-defense training to center herself. Jake and Kade came into the living room and Anthony was coming down the stairs. All of them stopped and watched Erin. She had her eyes closed and was practicing breathing in through her nose and out through her mouth while moving her arms in and out, up and down. They had no idea how long she had been doing that, but they watched for about another five minutes before she finally opened her eyes. Anthony finished his descent of the stairs.

"Erin, honey, are you ok?" Kade asked walking over to her. He wrapped her in a hug. She held onto him and looked up at him. Kade was lost in her beautiful, expressive eyes. He really needed to find a girl of his own.

"I'm good. I needed to center myself and make myself relax. This is a technique of my judo training and I needed it to center, get myself back on an even keel. I know I can do this today, but it's the thought of seeing Devin that I needed to relieve the stress of. Does that make sense?"

"It does honey. We, all of us, are going to be there with you. Just look for one or all of us to re-center ok." She nodded. They walked to the kitchen and had breakfast.

*****

"Good morning. All rise for the honorable Judge Kafner." Everyone stood up and waited for the judge to tell them to sit.

"Our case this morning is a preliminary hearing for charges levied against Devin Traeger. Is the defendant present?"

"Yes your honor. We are present via videoconference from the regional prison." Mr. Connor said. Anthony could feel Erin stiffen next to him and he tried to reassure her with his hand on her arm.

"Mr. Connor, your client Devin Traeger is charged with several things. The first is violating for the sixth time a restraining order held by Miss Erin Bradford. Mr. Traeger is also charged with statutory rape, attempted kidnapping with intent to harm, assault with a weapon, and creating and possessing pornography. How does your client plead?"

"Judge Kafner, my client pleads not guilty."

"Very well. Please enter a not guilty plea into the record." The judge made some notes and then addressed the court. "The goal of today's proceedings is to have the prosecution present their initial evidence in this case and then I will render a decision as to whether there is enough evidence to remand Mr. Traeger over for trial. Once the evidence is presented, a decision made, I will also make a determination on bail or denial of bail, if there is enough evidence." She paused again. Finally she looked up at the District Attorney and invited him to present his evidence. "Mr. Donaldson, you may begin your presentation of evidence."

For the next hour, Mr. Donaldson presented the chain of evidence starting with the first time Devin was jailed for the restraining order violation. He moved into the graphic emails, the video from Erin's security system, the restraining order itself, the porn video Devin had made and emailed with a caution to the court if they felt the need to view it, the packages Devin couriered to Erin's workplace, and the police records of the arrests of Devin. He basically created a timeline and established a pattern of behavior for Devin's charges and how he hurt Erin and Erica. After he had entered all the evidence into the court files, he was ready to call his first witness.

"Your honor, I would first like to call to the stand Ms. Erin Bradford." Erin stood with the help of Kade and Anthony and the bailiff escorted her to the stand. She was deep breathing as she walked with the bailiff. She was sworn in and she climbed into the witness box, took another deep breath, centered herself and looked to Mr. Donaldson. "Ms. Bradford can you please tell the court how you know Mr. Traeger?" Erin could see the video feed from where she sat and Devin was smiling his most evil smile. She glanced at Anthony who gave her the ability to do this, took a deep breath and answered the attorney. Her voice was strong, sure and she kept the emotions at bay. Anthony kept his eyes glued to her so she had a place to re-center herself.

Erin told them how she met Devin at TK Productions and his repeated attempts to ask her out. For the next forty-five minutes Erin answered questions succinctly and without emotion about the times Devin broke the restraining order, his latest episode at the beach when he tried to hurt Kade, and her self-defense training. The judge asked about the cast on her arm and Erin told the court that it occurred when she was protecting her production assistants from Devin's attacks with the driftwood. The judge asked then about her self-defense training, how she used it and learned it, and Erin told the court that she was a black belt in judo.   She confirmed that she had taken, and continues to take judo training classes. She could see Devin's surprise when she let the court know that little tidbit. Finally, Erin was excused and Mr. Donaldson called each of Erin's guardians forward. Anthony, Jake, and Kade all presented their information which gave Devin their last names and a way to find out more about their family. Unfortunately that couldn't be helped.

"If it pleases the court I would like to round out the testimony piece and call Miss Erica Stanton to the stand." Erin watched Devin as Erica came forward to testify. His eyes were huge and he was literally shaken at the sight of Erica taking the stand. This was something he did not expect. He realized it explained the additional charges against him.

Mr. Donaldson questioned Erica for the next 30 minutes and she told them she was drinking the night Devin came into the bar. She remembered him asking her to dance; he told her he wanted to get to know her, and they drank more. She didn't remember much after that, but when she woke up the next morning, still dressed in the same clothes, with bruises and pain, and realized she had been sexually assaulted she went to her provider and had the rape kit done. It confirmed she indeed had been raped and assaulted. Her provider gave her the morning after pill to ensure that she wouldn't have a baby. Erica had a few tears. Mr. Donaldson provided the report from the rape kit identifying Devin Traeger through DNA as the perpetrator, and he provided the footage from the bar's cameras too that showed Devin taking advantage of Erica, walking out with her. Just before lunchtime the prosecution laid out their entire case against Devin Traeger.

"We will take a recess for lunch. Ninety minutes. When we return this afternoon I will render my decision and will decide on bail. Court is in recess." The bailiff had all stand and as soon as the judge left the room the videoconference was disconnected. Erin was breathing again.

"You did it sugar. I am so proud of you." Anthony scooped her into his arms and held her. She wrapped her arms around him savoring his closeness. She buried her face into his neck and held onto her love.

"Anthony, can I talk to Erica?" Kade heard her question. They both nodded and took her over to talk with Erica.

"Erica, I'm Erin. I just wanted to say how sorry I am that you are going through this and what you've already been through."

"Erin, we need to make sure Devin is put away for a very long time. He's a horrible person. Thank you for helping to charge him too."

"I agree. The restraining orders I had didn't do anything to stop him and I'm sorry you had to get hurt physically to make this all come to light."

"Erin we are both in this together. You have an incredible set of men watching your back. I'm glad they found me and were able to help me with this. It's nice to have their support." They talked for a bit longer and Erin assured her that all of them had her back and would help her through this. Erin asked if she had someone to support her and Erica told her she had a special guy who was helping her through all of this. She told Erin that Drake was amazing and he was always here for her.

They finished their conversation and Erin hugged Erica. She turned to her men and they headed to grab some lunch. When they returned and court was resumed, the judge asked one more time if Devin wanted to keep the plea of 'not guilty.' His lawyer confirmed he was staying the course.

"In this matter of these charges levied against Devin Traeger this court finds there is more than sufficient evidence to remand the defendant over for trial. Mr. Traeger is denied bail at this time due to the heinous nature of the charges, and will spend his time at the regional correction center. He is to surrender his passport. He can work with his lawyer from there. Trial will be scheduled for September 1st to provide sufficient time for both sides to pull their witnesses and evidence together. Court is adjourned." The bailiff had everyone rise and once the judge was gone they could breathe again. Mr. Donaldson immediately asked the judge for a warrant to search Devin's house. Judge Kafner signed off on the warrant which Mr. Donaldson would give to the chief of police.

"We did it you guys. Let's go home." Erin said and hugged Anthony. Kade and Jake hugged them both. Erin was finally breathing and the weight on her shoulders was lifted a bit. They turned and headed home. Erin was thinking of Kade's home as her home too. She was content to spend her nights in Anthony's arms and her life at Kade's for now. They needed to celebrate this first victory.

*****

Life got back to almost normal for the next few weeks. Erin was able to finish her projects and resume working for the news station because Devin was locked up, as well as making appearances at TK Productions. She was busy and her work was always in demand. Jake, Kade and Anthony relaxed their watch a bit knowing that Devin was in prison for now and they kept their ears to any information that would put Erin back into seclusion. Anthony found the perfect ring for Erin with his brothers' help and he planned dinner at Kade's house for his entire family. He wanted to move their relationship to the next step.

Erin started working with Ink Inc. to create their videos and she worked in the evenings with Kade and Anthony on the basic design of their website. She asked all four brothers to give her ideas for their stories and she took their information and wrote the narrative for each one. In order to get at their story she asked them questions about how they got into the art world, what inspired each of them, and how they learned their craft. It took a bit to get at their stories, but Erin was pleased when she finally had them written and ready for the boys to look over. Erin was good at digging for information and asked the right questions to get to the heart of their stories. They made her work hard for the information, but Erin had a way to ask questions and make it sound conversational. All of them eventually gave her what she needed and she was able to come up with the perfect story for the website pages.   She had a unique way to tell each of their stories.

She gave them what she had written from their answers, and asked them to read through it when they had time, and she made changes until all of them were happy with the wording. They went through a few iterations, but the brothers liked the way Erin told their stories. She made them sound amazing and heroic for the work they did. She took their pictures in their workplaces, and a few candid photos while they were at their family home. The next thing she did was take the images for each brother's artwork that they wanted to share, and created a slide show for their individual pages set to music. Alex had Erin's ink featured prominently in his pictures. That thrilled her to no end. She also asked for additional images for the splash page too. She even asked if they wanted space for clients to write reviews, which they readily agreed to, and she created a way for future clients to request scheduling appointments. She asked Michael for any letters to start the reviews on the website. Michael also gave her their rate card for piercing, tattoos and special requests.

"Erin, honey, this is amazing!" Anthony said. "I love how you showcased my artwork and the tattoos I've done. You set it to my favorite style of music and made them move in the frame. You really brought it to life. It's wonderful." She smiled at him and he captured her lips in a kiss that rocked her world. He held her in his arms and she caressed his shoulders, loving the feel of his muscles and his body wrapped next to hers.

"Anthony, my handsome sweetheart, your artwork was easy for me to showcase, but I don't know if I'm ready to handle the piercing side of things. I know that Michael has lots of pictures which he has given me, but I'm blushing just thinking about what I might see when I edit the pictures." Anthony smiled and chuckled.

"Darlin' I know you are inexperienced, innocent but you know that people love to show off their bodies, especially if they are pierced or have artwork, and I can guarantee that Michael will be very disappointed if he doesn't have a slideshow like the rest of us. It's his art, his life's work."

"I know handsome. I don't want to disappoint him and I promise I won't; I will showcase his work well. I'll make it work, because I am a professional, but I just had to share that with you my initial thoughts." She took a deep breath trying to clear the blush on her cheeks. "I was also thinking that perhaps we needed to explain what each type of piercing is. Michael was throwing out names of the piercings he does, it made my head spin with all the names, and I thought that perhaps we needed to explain that on the website too. It would be kind of like a dictionary of piercings. That way the clients could ask for exactly what they wanted."

"I think that's a good idea." He walked over to the bookcase and grabbed a book. "Here's a book that might help give ideas of what the different piercings are. This is a dictionary of sorts that we used when we all were first getting started." He came back over and sat with her on the sofa. He turned to the page showing her the barbell piercings he had. She took the book and looked at it for a bit, and turned the page to see the really pretty ones with the delicate chains on them for women. Anthony watched her and just smiled. She blushed a little as she looked through the book, but she was completely captivated by the images and descriptions.

Anthony left her perusing the book and headed to the kitchen counter to work on his surprise. He talked with Kade and for now they were going to live with him. Kade was loving having all of them there. His house finally felt like a home. But, Anthony had a plot of land just to the west of Kade's property and he wanted to build a house for them there. Their two properties were adjoining and they would share the secluded beach. He just needed to ask her to marry him, and then they could pick the number of rooms, the style of house and the colors too. He was ready to put down some roots and he couldn't wait to marry Erin. This was the first time, in a really long time, that Anthony felt settled with his life. He just wanted Erin to be safe too. He hoped this would be the end of things with Devin, but he was also realistic that it might not be over this easily.

Erin took the images that Kade had given her and started to work on his slide show. She wanted to make all three of the artwork slideshows different. With Anthony's show she made the images flip from one to the next like turning pages of a book, and added movement into them by zooming in on them or pulling away; with Kade's and the style of work he did, she opted to do dissolves and allow more fluidity. She also picked music for Kade's that was more fluid and less edgy. Kade liked country music like she did, so she found country music in her audio library and used that to set off his images. After two hours of working on the slideshow Erin needed to stretch. She got up and wandered into the kitchen, moving her arms and trying to stretch her muscles.

"Hi Erin." Jake said. "Where have you been hiding?"

"I've been working on the website for Ink, Inc. I didn't think I was hiding!" She said smiling. That got a chuckle out of Jake.

"Can I see what you are working on?" She nodded, grabbed a bottle of water out of the fridge, and took him to her edit space.

"Here is Anthony's artwork slideshow. I just finished this one. You need to put the headphones on and push this button right here to start." She handed him the headphones and indicated the start button. She stepped back and let him watch. She watched his face as he watched the piece. He got a huge smile on his face, and his eyes revealed his enjoyment as the music and the images meshed and changed. This is the part she loved, watching others watch the work she created.

"Wow Erin, that's amazing!" Jake exclaimed. "You are really talented girl." He hugged her and pulled her close to where he was sitting. She wrapped her arm around his shoulders.

"All three of the tattoo pieces will be different. For instance you see Anthony's and the music is edgy because his style is edgy. Kade's, which is rendering in the background right now, is more fluid and I used dissolves rather than the page flips to transition, and set it to his favorite country music. His style is more laid back, so the music reflects that too. Alex is a combination of the two and he uses lots of color, so I thought I would use more color by putting the images over a color changing background, and have the slides move more across the screen with shadowing and light to music that is laced with steel drums."

"I like how you think Erin. You look at the artwork and you look at the style of the artist and you create from that. It's amazing to me how you see the big picture and then can form a final product from that. What are you planning for Michael's side of things?"

"Thanks Jake. I'm still working on Michael's piece with the piercing. I know people get lots of different body parts pierced and it's hard after everything that Devin has put me through to not see it as wrong showing body parts on the website. Well that, and my own inexperience."

"I understand that Erin, but what Michael does is art. It's beautiful art. Look at it from the art side and don't think about Devin, or your inexperience. Piercings can be really beautiful if taken in the right context. They can enhance a person's beauty, sexuality and they can be exquisite."

"Easier said than done, but you make a really good point. It is artistic and can be really beautiful. At least the pictures that Michael has taken show it as art, and the pictures I saw in the book of piercings show it as artistic. Thanks Jake." Jake left her in the office and headed outside to talk with Kade.

*****

Detective Thomas, his partner Dirk and two additional detectives searched Devin's house and took pictures of the rooms of the house, all the elements that were visible in the video the court had, and they cordoned off Devin's house with police tape. Detective Thomas was just sick with what he saw in Devin's house. Many parts were removed and taken into evidence for the trial. Devin had pictures on the wall of the den with Erin at various productions, and the plans spelled out for when he was able to get her in his house.

"Detective Thomas," Dirk said, "I think you need to see what else we found." Thomas took the rest of the pictures and walked with Dirk to the master bedroom. There Dirk showed him all the materials Devin had accumulated about Erin's mom, her illness, all her moves, her paths, from the house to work and to the productions she did. Devin had a complete dossier on Erin's activities and photos to match. He was using that to create a way to kidnap her when she was alone. He knew what kind of car she drove, the routes she drove, and his plans for Erin were very detailed. Devin even knew when she met with her girlfriends. All of that evidence was taken to the station.

Thomas moved through the cabinets in the master bedroom and discovered several more ladies that had been abused by Devin over the last few years. Devin needed serious help. He photographed everything he did to those women and used that to plan what he was going to do to Erin. All of the materials they uncovered made all the detectives just sick. They took pictures, then packed everything up and carted it to the station to enter as evidence. Somehow they needed to ensure that Devin never left the prison walls. There had to be a way to ensure that Devin's lawyer couldn't get him off on a technicality. They would work with the police chief to find a way to keep Devin contained.

*****

The Romano family gathered at Kade's house for dinner on Saturday night! Erin's arm was free of the cast and she had done a couple rounds of PT. The boys helped Erin make fettucine Alfredo with grilled, parmesan crusted chicken breast on top and lots of fresh veggies too. They made pasta from scratch; Erin had the attachments for her mixer to cut the fettucine and the sheets for the ravioli. She also made chicken and cilantro ravioli with a garlic white wine sauce. To round out the dinner she made homemade French bread and a green garden salad. Jake proved to be very helpful in the kitchen with the pasta machine.   She and Jake worked side-by-side running the pasta through the machine and laying it into the ravioli molds.

"Erin, honey, mom called and she insisted on bringing dessert tonight. I hope that's ok." Anthony said when he came in the kitchen.

"That's awesome. I didn't think about dessert. I was too focused on making dinner!" She said, smiling at him and leaning in for a kiss.

"What can I help with?" Anthony asked.

"You can help me finish these raviolis while Erin finishes the Alfredo sauce." Anthony washed his hands and headed over to where Jake was laying the pasta sheet into the ravioli mold. Anthony could sense Jake's frustration trying to do this on his own. The two of them worked together and they finished all the ravioli, putting them on a cookie sheet lined with parchment and semolina so they wouldn't stick. Erin was impressed that Angelina had taught her boys to cook. Kade came in and put the bottles of wine in the wine fridge, and then took the spoon from Erin to stir the sauce. A couple of times while they were working Erin had to duck under an elbow here or a hand there. She had good reflexes. She was short and always managed to be underfoot. Her guys were 6' 2" and 6'4", and she was almost a foot shorter than they were. No one knew where she would turn up because she moved so fast. She only ended up on the floor once and Kade picked her back up with a smile. The boys put the ravioli into the freezer as Erin requested and all of them turned to setting the table.

The family arrived while Erin was finishing up the French bread loaves. She was slicing them and arranging them in a bread basket. Cassi and Mariah, with Angelina, headed to the kitchen while the men stayed in the living room. Angelina wrapped Erin in a hug and put the dessert on the counter.

"Something smells good Ms. Erin." Mariah said.

"Thanks Mariah." She gave Cassi and Mariah hugs too. "I made French bread today, and I have the water boiling to finish my pasta."

"What can I do to help dear?" Angelina asked.

Erin put the ladies to work taking the salad, the dressings and stuff to the table. Angelina wanted to help cook the pasta, so Erin left her to cook the ravioli while she started on her sauce for it. In just a short amount of time the ladies put the steaming bowls of pasta and sauces on the table with the veggies and chicken. Erin had Anthony get everyone seated and pour the wine. They all sat down to the feast that Erin had created with lots of help.

"Erin, my dear girl, this is very good. You are an amazing chef!" Roberto said beaming.

"Thanks Roberto. I had lots of help." Erin smiled back at him.

The family all enjoyed their dinner and conversation revolved around Michael and Alex and their upcoming marriages to Cassi and Mariah. Cassi and Mariah shared more details about their weddings. It was exciting. They talked about everything revolving around the family, projects, the business, and kept the conversation away from Devin and the trial. Cassi said that her 'GoFundMe' page had netted them more money from corporations for the garden, they had expanded it and planted more plants, and Mariah chimed in that hers was providing for a new piece of equipment and supplies for the clinic. Erin just smiled bigger.

Roberto asked Kade what was up with the vineyard, and they commented on the great vintage of the wine they were enjoying with dinner. Erin was puzzled at those questions, but she didn't say anything. She had wondered about the wine in Kade's wine fridge, but she hadn't asked anything yet. She talked about the website for the boys' business and told them that she had finished Alex, Anthony and Kade's pieces, and she was currently working on Michael's video. That elicited smiles from all the brothers. She also told them about the projects she was working on. After dinner the boys headed to the living room and put the game on, and the ladies helped Erin clear and do the dishes. Mariah checked Erin's arm, now that the cast was off and she had done a couple of weeks of PT. Mariah seemed pleased with the movement and range of motion that Erin had regained.

"Mariah, thanks for all you did to take care of me that day. I'm sorry about my reaction to the work you needed to do on my leg. But I'm all better now thanks to you and to the boys with the workout we do every night!" Mariah hugged her and then Erin turned to Angelina.

"Angelina, what did you bring for dessert?" Erin asked.

"I made cannoli." She smiled at Erin.

"I guess I should get some coffee made and we can do dessert with the boys." Erin turned and plugged in the coffee maker. Mariah and Cassi got the dessert dishes down and took them to the dining room while Angelina arranged her dessert on a platter that Erin handed her. Erin got coffee cups, cream, sugar and spoons out which Mariah took the table. Cassi headed to the living room to get the men to the table for dessert. She overheard Kade and Alex giving Anthony advice on how to propose to Erin. She squealed.

"Cassi, sugar, you need to keep this to yourself. Let Anthony do this in his way and when he's ready." Alex said to his bride-to-be.

"I'm so excited! But I will tone it down." Anthony thanked her as she launched herself into Alex's arms. "Kade, when are you going to find someone special?"

"I guess I need to do that soon. Now that all of my brothers are set, I guess it's my turn." He smiled at her and led the way back to the dining room. Angelina was serving the cannoli onto plates and Erin breezed in with the coffee pot. She poured cups of coffee for everyone and headed back to the kitchen. When she returned, everyone was seated except for Anthony. He was standing apart from the table and was seeming to be practicing something. He looked nervous.

"Anthony, sweetie, are you going to join the family? Is everything ok? Are you ok?" Erin asked gently as she walked over to him and laid her hand on his arm.

"Erin, my love, I have to ask you a question first." She nodded and waited for him. He took her hands in his and took a deep breath. "Erin, my sweet beautiful Erin, you captured my attention while Alex was working on your ink that day in the shop. You captured my heart when you protected yourself against Devin that very first time at the beach, and when you protected all of us in one way or another over the last few months. You are strong, you are brave and you have such sunshine in your smile; you light up my life with that smile. You hold my heart in your hands beautiful girl, you are gentle, loving and amazing; I love you so very much." He paused and kneeled down while pulling something out of his pocket. "Erin, darlin' will you make me the happiest man in the world by marring me?"

Erin sucked in a huge breath of air. "Oh Anthony, my handsome hero, yes I will marry you. I love you more than anything and can't imagine a day without you. Yes!" She leaned down to kiss him as he put the ring on her finger. Erin was oblivious to the family watching. Anthony wrapped his arms around her and took her off the ground in his arms while he stood. The family clapped and cheered as Anthony kissed her deeply. She held onto her man, the man of her dreams.

"My boys, three of them, are getting married! Soon I will have lots of grandchildren! This is so exciting." Angelina exclaimed. Erin was blushing when she and Anthony came up for air. Everyone rallied around them and congratulated them both. After a few minutes everyone finally sat back down and had dessert. Erin was so happy and for tonight, life was good.

The family headed home, the house quieted down and Jake and Kade headed over to the cottage to play cards. They needed a break and some well-deserved downtime. Anthony and Erin sat on the couch. She was loving having a few minutes with her handsome Anthony. They needed some quiet time together.

"Anthony, handsome, thank you for making me the happiest person on the earth. You are truly my sweet hero and I love you so much; I can't wait to marry you." She leaned in and kissed him and somehow wound up in his lap.

"Wow, sugar that was some kiss. It's getting hard to keep my hands off you honey." She leaned in for more kisses and then whispered in Anthony's ear.

"Anthony, my handsome fiancé, will you make love to me tonight. I know I'm inexperienced, but I love you so much and I can't keep my hands off you either. I need you and I need to feel you."

"Erin, sweet Erin, it would be my pleasure. We'll take it slow ok?" He scooped her up in his arms and carried her upstairs while kissing her. They spent the night making each other incredibly happy and Erin learned about the rest of Anthony's piercings. They relished each other, relieving the stress and learning how to be with one another. The night was so perfect and she was so much in love with her handsome man. She never knew that love could be like this, or that someone would ever want to marry her, be with her. She learned so much, felt so much and was so much in love with her handsome Anthony.

*****

The next week brought more PT for Erin's arm and a glow about Erin that was very hard to hide. She was moving pretty well, and Mariah scheduled her for two PT appointments with Dak. The PT tech worked with her and helped her to move her arm, trying to get range of motion extended. Dak gave her exercises to do at home and she promised him she would do them. Mariah set her up to come in at 8 on Tuesday and Thursday mornings before she headed to TK Productions. Erin added everything to her calendar and headed to work. Anthony, Kade and Jake had her calendar and saw when she added something new. They were being vigilant.

"Morning Terry." Erin greeted as she came in the door of the production house.

"Morning Erin. When you get settled, can you come see me? I have a new production for you." She nodded and headed to her office to drop her things. She checked in with Kade, Jake and Anthony letting them know she was at the office and set up her computer. She grabbed her notebook and headed to Terry's office.

"Erin, thanks for coming in. I have a new production that requested your expertise." Erin was shocked at that. "Don't be so shocked. You do great work and it's getting noticed both by my clients and by the news stations." She smiled a little.

For the next half hour Terry told her about the production. A new player was added to the roster of the hockey team called the Raptors and their publicity folks wanted a video introduction of him for the news stations, as well as snippets of him working out and skating for the website, as well as featuring his clinics he did for the kids. Erin would be meeting Kyle Hunt at his home on the beach; she would interview him, shoot footage of his ice time practice in his personal rink, and do a video story of who Kyle Hunt truly was. Erin asked lots of questions and finally had all the information she needed, including the dates for the shoots. The team wanted her to come to their practices as well, to add to Kyle's introduction to the community, and the social media splash of the Raptors team. These videos would help garner interest in the hockey team. That would be scheduled at a later date, and Terry would get her passes to be at a couple of the games to shoot footage there too. Erin put all of the dates she knew about in her calendar so her boys would know her schedule.

Erin headed back to her office and did some research on the hockey player and on the game itself. She wasn't familiar with the sport and was confused as to why she was requested, but she worked to find out all she could about the team, the sport and this new player. That consumed her morning. It was time to head home and have lunch with her fiancé and her soon to be brother-in-law and friend. Terry was ok with Erin continuing to work from home. She was getting so much done and he had no problems with her work. Terry was also working on a way to make Erin's appointment with his company full-time with benefits. She was doing amazing work and he needed to keep her busy so that she was available for all the productions that were now requesting her services. Erin learned a lot about the hockey team and she needed to ask her boys if they knew about hockey. Maybe they could give her some ideas to help with this project. She did a lot of research on the internet trying to find out about hockey and how the game was played, but maybe one of her men could help her with additional details. She would just have to ask. She thought about all the questions she would ask them when she got home.

*****

Devin and his lawyer huddled daily at the regional prison and Devin asked Mr. Connor if he could see about getting Devin released on bail. Devin needed to get back home and put all the other evidence away before the police found it. Mr. Connor did everything in his power to get another hearing and a way to get Devin out of confinement, but so far had been denied at all requests. He told Devin he had one last card to play and would see if he could make it happen. Devin headed back to his cell and Mr. Connor made another push to have Judge Kafner's ruling overturned.

Chapter Six

The rest of the week flew by and by Friday Erin was ready to head to her appointment with Kyle Hunt. She was looking forward to meeting him in person. Erin had worked from home and finished up another project for Terry. Terry was very pleased with Erin's diligence and hard work. She made the clients happy and she always finished her projects early or on time. She had a unique style and the clients loved her work. She was getting his production company noticed in the best possible way because of how she treated every client with respect and did their productions brilliantly. Terry was kicking himself for having hired Devin and bringing him in Erin's life. He was trying to protect her, and he would do everything in his power to keep her safe.

"Anthony, Kade, Jake, I have my video shoot with Kyle Hunt today. Do any of you want to come with?" Erin said as she breezed out of the office with her bags which she set by the front door.

"Erin, my love, I have two tattoos to do today, so I have to be at the office." Anthony said as he wrapped her in his arms. "I'll miss being with you but you can tell me all about it tonight when you get home." Erin leaned in and kissed Anthony, holding him in her arms. She let him go and headed to the kitchen counter. Anthony headed to gather his tools.

"Jake and I will be standing by if you need us today Erin. We have a couple of things to work on from here if that's ok." Kade said.   "Unless you want one of us to go, we certainly can."

"I will be fine on my own. I just thought I'd ask." Erin smiled at them all while she was going through her checklist. She was relaxing a bit more, but none of them had let down their guard entirely. The system had failed Erin one too many times for them to totally relax. Erin texted her production assistants and gave them the address to meet her with the gear. They confirmed they would be there. "Have a good afternoon guys. I'll see you later this evening."

"Erin, please text us when you arrive at Kyle's and let us know when you are leaving, ok?" Kade asked. "Just to be sure all is ok."

"I will. Thanks for always being here for me." She walked over and wrapped Anthony in a big hug before he left for the day. "I love you handsome. Have a good day." He held her to him. "I can't wait to be in your arms tonight." Blushing, she let him go and he headed out the door. Erin headed to her office and gathered all her notes, her tablet, tripod, and her still camera. She made sure she had enough SD cards too. Kade walked her out to her car and watched, fascinated, as Erin buckled her gear into the passenger seat.

"Erin, honey, why is your gear buckled in?" He was smiling at her and there was a hint of laughter in his voice.

"Kade, if I have an accident, or something happens, if I have to stop suddenly, I can ensure my gear is safe if it's buckled in. I don't want it to wander all over the car and get broken. I've always done that. It's just a habit."

"It's a good practice; I've just never known anyone who actually does that. Cool." He gave her a hug and she climbed in. Kade waved until she was out of sight.

Carl and Derek met her with the gear and they set up on Kyle's back deck for the interview portion with the backdrop of the ocean, secluded beach and the horizon in the distance. Erin set up the shot with Kyle and attached the microphone to his lapel, making sure she hid the cable. She next made sure Carl was set with the headphones and had good audio. Derek was right next to her with a clipboard of the questions while running the camera. She asked Derek to zoom in occasionally and tighten the shot, then back out, doing the moving while she was asking questions. He agreed. She planned to ask a variety of questions so he was ready to check off what she asked, and poised to write additional questions as she talked with Kyle.

"Ok Kyle, we are just going to have a conversation, you and I. We're friends, just two friends having a good conversation, and I just want to get to know you better. Try to forget the camera is there and you can just talk to me, focus on me." She smiled at him and he smiled back at her. "Please take a moment after I ask a question to rephrase the question in your answer. My voice won't be part of this interview, rather your public will meet you and get to know you through your own words! So as best you can, use the question as part of your answer. When you pause it will give me edit space too."

"I think I can handle that Erin. Thanks for making this easy for me." She nodded and smiled at him.

"Ok Derek, let's roll in record."

"Recording Erin." She took a deep breath and started her line of questions.

For the next forty minutes Erin and Kyle conversed about Kyle's background, how he got interested in hockey, and his new team the Raptors. She asked him about the position he played, what made him stand out and his storied career from NCAA sports through the minor leagues all the way up to the majors. She asked about his family and life outside of hockey. Kyle was eager to share and told her he was former

Navy, didn't have much for family anymore, and he did work with the youth of the community to sort of give back. She asked about his military service and he told her where he had been stationed and the work he did. They wrapped up with his expectations of his new team, his life here in this new city, and Kyle's thoughts on their upcoming season. She asked if there was anything else he wanted to add, so he talked a bit about hockey in general and his passion with the game.

"Cut! That was a great interview Kyle, thank you!" Erin said.

"My pleasure Erin. You have a good handle on what the PR folks want. Thanks for making it so easy."

They struck the gear; Erin grabbed the SD cards and she sent Carl and Derek back to TK Productions, letting them go for the weekend. She wanted some stills of Kyle on the ice and she could also shoot video with her tablet; she didn't need her crew for that. She helped Derek and Carl take the gear out to their car, thanked them and sent them on their way. She wished them a great weekend and told them she had more productions next week, so she would get that to them.

"Erin, shall we get some of those stills?" Kyle asked when she returned. She nodded, grabbed her still camera, tablet, tripod and SD cards, and they headed to his ice rink. Erin was impressed with his set up. Kyle skated and warmed up a bit while Erin set up her gear; he showed her drills which she videotaped and took stills of, then he coaxed her onto the ice with him. He had skates for her and helped her get comfortable. She asked if he ever thought about teaching and he told her he ran a clinic for kids in grade school through high school in the off-season. She asked what he did in his clinics and he set up cones, pucks and handed her a hockey stick. She looked at him with wide eyes. For the next thirty minutes he taught her all about hockey and helped her get comfortable holding the stick, hitting the puck and scoring. She had a blast, and her camera captured it all.

"Kyle, thank you so much. This was so amazing to see into your world and the world of hockey. I learned a lot today! I can't wait to come to the practices and then the games to shoot more footage!"

"It was my pleasure Erin. You made this process very easy and I appreciate all you asked about and wanted to know about me. Most reporters, especially after the games, are looking for dirt and not the truth. They tend to twist words and make everything out to be scandalous. They can exploit the most innocent of comments. You really listened to me and made me feel like you really wanted to know about the real me. So thank you for that."

"Kyle, I really do want to know the real you, that's my secret weapon! I want to know all about the work you do, the kids you teach and how you got here to the Raptors, how the past shaped who you are today. My goal is to tell your story using your words. Perhaps we can help you with the kids' clinics to get sponsors or donations too with the footage. Maybe I can help you create a webpage or social media presence that can help solicit donations to the program." She smiled at him while she put her camera, tablet, and computer away. "I would love to show you the finished piece before I give it to my boss and your PR person." Kyle gave her his email and put his phone number into her phone, taking her phone number in return. She got all of her footage, packed her gear, thanked Kyle for access to his world and Kyle walked her to the front door. Before she left Kyle gave her a Raptors jersey, hat and pennant; they talked for a bit longer. She asked him to sign the hat and pennant, which he was glad to do. He walked her out and made sure she was in her car safely. He was a real gentleman. She thanked him again told him she would be in touch.

*****

While Erin was doing her shoot, Devin's new lawyer, Mr. Connor, was able to play his final card and finally got Devin out on bail. He found a judge that was willing, with the right pressure, to overrule Judge Kafner's denial of bail. Devin was able to walk out of the regional prison and he made it to his house by 2:30. He had an informant that told him where Erin was and what she was doing. He also said that she didn't have anyone with her today. At least he had one friend left that he could count on. However, when Devin arrived at his house and saw the police tape he was livid. His focus changed immediately. He frantically went through all his rooms and found out they had gone through everything in his house, and they had taken every file, every picture, and all his notes too. They had all the evidence they needed to put him away for a long time. He had only a short time to make Erin pay and she would pay dearly. This was going to end today.

His focus changed from taking her and holding her hostage, to taking her out completely. She was not going to survive this afternoon if he played his cards right. He quickly disassembled his ankle bracelet, rendering it useless, and grabbed his keys. He jumped into his pickup and headed towards the beach. His plan was clear; Erin had to pay for all the pain and agony Devin had endured these last few weeks in prison. If his life was going to be spent in prison for all of this, then her life would end today. Mr. Connor hadn't yet been able to charge her with assault, and Richard was tied up, so he needed to take matters once again into his own hands. He couldn't take her and lock her up in his house because the police would find him easily, so his next best plan was to take her out. If he couldn't have her for himself, then no one could, including that Anthony guy. Erin would die today.

Mark Connor, in the meantime, worked with Richard and they found a way to charge Erin with assault and battery. She would be served the papers on Monday and they got a court date for Wednesday to see if the charges would hold up. Richard told Mark that this was a long-shot but if Devin really wanted to pursue it, then he would help the best he could. Mark asked him about the Ethics committee. Richard told him that he had appeared three times already and given all the documents he legally could to them. He was just waiting on a decision, but he couldn't help Devin. The ethics committee was working to charge Mark next. Mark would be served with papers and an order to appear next week.

*****

Erin called Anthony as soon as she was ready to head home. She dialed and he answered after the first ring. "Hi handsome." Anthony could hear her excitement.

"Hi Erin. Did your interview go well?"

"It did. I'm in my car now and getting ready to head home."

"Drive safely sugar. I'm finishing my last customer's ink now, maybe another thirty minutes or so, and should be home soon."

"I love you so much Anthony. I'll see you soon handsome."

"I love you too honey." They hung up and Anthony headed back to his workspace. He needed to add two more things to the art he was doing, clean up, wash all his equipment, and make sure his client had all the instructions. Once he finished his paperwork then he could head home and spend the night in the arms of his Erin. She was incredible and made him feel loved, special and like the only man in the world.

Erin checked her two bags, as well as her camera gear, in the passenger seat and made sure they were strapped in and secure. She then called Kade using the car as her phone. She told Kade she was finished and heading home, just leaving now. He told her to be safe and signed off with her. Meanwhile, Jake was outside on the porch enjoying the afternoon sunshine. He and Kade had finished their work and were relaxing waiting to hear from Erin. His phone buzzed and it was Detective Thomas. He told Jake that Devin had been released from prison and wanted to know where Erin was and if he was with her. Jake told him that she was on a shoot and by herself. He quickly headed inside after signing off with Thomas.

"Kade," Jake said as he burst through the backdoor. "Devin was released earlier this afternoon and the prison lost the signal on his ankle bracelet already. I'm heading to where Erin is. I should have gone with her today."

"She just called and is on her way home. There was no way we could have known this Jake. Don't beat yourself up bro. She's strong. She'll be ok." Kade responded, angry that Devin had been released. They stood a moment and looked at each other. Both of them were processing the information they just learned about. This was crazy. The system just let him out of prison again!

"Ok. I'm heading toward her and will escort her home. You stay here in case she comes home a different way and I'll keep you posted." Jake ran out the front, jumped on his motorcycle and headed down Pier Street toward Erin. He called her from his motorcycle.

"Hi Jake." Erin said and she was happy. He could hear the smile in her voice. The shoot must have gone well. He hated to bring her this news. Life was just getting back to normal and she was happy with her life.

"Erin, honey, where are you right now?" Erin heard the panic and fear in his voice.

"I'm on Pier Street heading towards home. I just left my client. Why? You're scaring me Jake. Did something happen?"

"Erin, don't panic honey, but somehow Devin got out of prison and they've lost track of him from his ankle bracelet. We don't know where he's at. Where exactly are you?"

"OMG! Wow. Um, I'm about a half mile from the fourth street interchange. It looks like the light is red, nope it's green my way, but I think it will be red by the time I get there."

"Ok honey I'm headed your way. I'll call you right back. Don't panic." They hung up and Jake called Thomas to get him and others rolling. They needed to be prepared for anything and they knew that Devin would be out for Erin, especially since the police had already searched Devin's house. They could only hope that Devin had no idea where Erin was.

Jake was second-guessing himself for not going with her today. He was beating himself up for thinking all was ok and letting his guard down for the afternoon. He needed to protect her, it was his job to protect her and now this; he had failed at his job. He hoped and prayed things were ok and that Erin would be all right.

Erin's phone rang again as she came to a stop at the red light at the 4th street interchange. "Hi Jake."

"Erin, are you at 4th Street yet?"

"Yep. I just stopped at the red light."

"Ok honey, I'm headed toward you, I'm probably a mile away. Keep your eyes open Erin. You know Devin's truck. We don't have a clue where he's at or if he knows that you had a shoot today. Is there a lot of traffic?"

"No, it's pretty light for a Friday afternoon. I'm the first in line, and actually no one else is around me and there isn't anyone across from me either. This is odd for a Friday afternoon, but I'm grateful for the lack of traffic. Jake, its ok sweetie. We'll get through this and deal with Devin, whatever happens. You are my hero like my Anthony. It's all ok. Please don't worry and don't beat yourself up about not going with me today. We just need to be alert now. This is not your doing and no one is at fault here Jake. Whatever happens we will deal with it." Jake shook his head. Here she was calming him down and she was the one in danger.

They continued talking and Jake told her he was staying on the phone with her. She told him that the light just turned yellow on 4th Street and she would soon have a green light. She also told him she hadn't see Devin's truck yet. The light turned green and she started to cross the huge intersection once she was sure there was no traffic running the red light the other way. Fourth Street was an interchange with four lanes in either direction, two turn lanes and on ramps to each side, so she had a lot of intersection to traverse. She kept looking in her rearview mirror, to her right and to her left too, watching for any sign of Devin's truck as she picked up speed. She was on edge and trying to keep the panic out of her driving. She kept talking with Jake letting him know she hadn't seen Devin yet. Her eyes darted to the rearview mirror, out the side windows and up the hill.

Devin saw Erin's car start forward as he crested the hill and sped up quickly. He had the two inside lanes clear of traffic and now was his chance, his only chance to take her out. No one was coming from the other way and her car was alone in the intersection. She was going to pay dearly for all of this pain and suffering she caused him.   He gunned the pickup, surged forward, ran the red light and he headed into the intersection. Erin's car and his would collide in just moments. Erin looked to her left again, and saw Devin's truck hurtling toward her, only a few feet from her.

"Jake, Devin is going to ram my car! Tell Anthony that I love him. I can't avoid this collision. Thank you Jake for all you've done for me." He could hear her breathing, panicking, and he knew she was prepared to die in this crash.

"Erin, you can and will survive this. Move towards the center of your car, remember your self-defense training. I see Devin's truck too. I'm almost there honey."

The phone went dead as Devin's pickup crashed into Erin's car, head on into the driver's side door. Erin's airbags, side-curtain and front, all deployed helping to cushion the accident. Her car was pushed into the farthest lane before it stopped, skidding sideways. She also had her pillow tucked down on her left side. Devin wasn't so lucky. His truck's airbags did not deploy and he slammed into his steering wheel with his chest. Erin saw Devin's eyes in the moment before impact and his angry, evil smile as his pickup plowed into her driver's side door. She realized he was trying to kill her and that threw her for a loop. Erin had adjusted and moved toward the center like Jake told her, she tucked her chin to her chest and waited, tried not to stiffen when the impact hit; her left leg and foot was pressed against the drivers' side door to keep her in the middle of the car. She held the steering wheel steady so she didn't waiver, but Devin's momentum pushed them sideways across the lanes. Erin could hear the sickening sound of her car sliding sideways against the tires. Jake alerted Thomas and the cavalry was in route. Jake got to the vehicles just as Thomas pulled up. Devin was trying to get out of his pickup, and Thomas, along with his partner, was there to take him into custody. Devin was disoriented and unsteady on his feet from the impact, but determined to get to Erin, except he was stuck in his seatbelt and couldn't get away from the truck. Jake headed to the passenger side of Erin's car. He hoped she was ok. Prayers were in abundance for her safety.

"Erin, honey, it's Jake. I'm here."

"Jake." Erin's voice, shaky and in pain, was music to his ears. She was alive! Thank God she was alive. He got the passenger door open and he could hear sirens barreling their way to the scene. She opened her eyes and looked at Jake. "Jake, thank you for being here with me. Can you take my computer bag, camera bag and stuff to your bike? I'm sure my car is totaled and I need the footage I shot today." Jake smiled. This was Erin through and through. She was worried about her productions and not about herself.

"Erin, honey, yes I'll put your bags in my saddlebags, and I'll be right back. Hang on honey. Stay with me. Don't try to move." Jake unbuckled her gear and put the computer bag and her camera bag into his bike saddlebags, added the locks and hurried back to Erin. He called Kade and let him know what was going on as he gently climbed into the passenger side of the car.

"Kade, its Jake. Devin hit Erin's car, plowed into her at the 4th Street interchange. She's alive. I'm with her now and we're getting her help. Can you go get Anthony and meet us at the trauma hospital? Maybe call Mariah and see if she can help."

"Kade tell Anthony I love him." Kade could hear the pain in her voice. Kade cringed on the inside. His prayers too became more fervent. She had already been through so much and now this.

"Jake, take care of her." Kade was beating himself up for not going with her today. He should have protected her.

"I will bro. Just bring Anthony to the trauma center. We'll meet you there. She's strong, a survivor, and she'll be ok."

Jake crawled further in beside Erin and wrapped her in his arms. "How are you doing honey?"

"My left side really hurts Jake, especially my ankle. It feels really funny." She laid her head on his shoulder when she felt him get close enough. "My head hurts too. I don't want to hold it up on my own anymore. Thanks for your shoulder." Jake tried to comfort her. "Jake, thank you for staying on the phone with me, keeping me calm, and rallying the troops. I moved to the center like you told me to and remembered my training." Her voice was getting a little weaker. He watched her for a moment; she was thinking about something.

"Jake can you take off my engagement ring and move it to my right hand. I need to keep Anthony close by, but my hand is already swelling. I don't want them to cut off my ring." Jake gently took her left hand in his and worked to slide her ring off. He put her finger in his mouth to moisten it and make the ring slide easier, then he moved the ring to her right hand and closed her fingers over it to keep it in place and let her feel it. He looked back at her face and she seemed to be withdrawing from him. She was slowly slipping into another world, leaving this world filled with pain; she was seeking release from the pain. He didn't want her to give up the fight. There was a bruise forming on her left cheek and forehead too. Jake was trying to figure out what she hit and how those bruises got there. He raised his other hand and stroked her cheek being mindful of the bruise.

"Erin honey, stay with me. Talk to me honey." Jake said and tried to keep her talking. She opened her eyes and looked up at him. He was lost in her gaze. She had really beautiful eyes, even with the haze of the pain. He realized why Anthony was so drawn to her. Jake's goal was to keep Erin focused on him so she wouldn't slip away. He kissed her temple and talked to her in soothing tones. While he was talking to Erin the paramedic came up to the scene and tried to figure out how to get to Erin and how to help. Devin's truck was sealed against the driver's side door and front quarter panel. He saw Jake holding her.

"Hi sir, I'm Drake. I'm the paramedic and we're trying to figure out how to get her out of the car." Jake nodded. Erin stirred in his arms. "I need to put a cervical collar on her in case of neck injuries." He reached in through the driver's side window, doing contortions around Devin's pickup, and Jake helped him get the collar on Erin. Jake then directed her head back to his shoulder. He told Drake her name was Erin.

"Drake, I'm Jake. I think I can move her into my arms and take her out through the passenger side." Jake felt along Erin's left side while keeping her wrapped in his embrace, her head on his shoulder, and she didn't seem to be trapped in the car. He felt down along her ankle and leg, which made Erin moan in pain. Her ankle was pressed against the left side of car which explained why it hurt and felt funny. It took the brunt of the crash. He realized she braced herself using her foot/ankle to keep herself in the center of the car. "I think she's free. If we can raise the steering wheel up and slide her seat back, I can maneuver her gently and get her out. I just need to unhook her seatbelt. I think her leg, especially her ankle, is messed up." Drake nodded to Jake.

"Erin," a voice near her left side said, which she assumed was Drake. "Can you tell me where it hurts?"

"Um, my left arm hurts, my head really hurts, and my left leg, especially my ankle. Like Jake just said it's my ankle that's the worst. I think my pillow on the left side helped a bit." Jake smiled. This was definitely Erin through and through. He helped Jake to raise the steering wheel to the upmost position by crawling through the window laying on the hood of Devin's truck, unhooked her seatbelt, unthreading it from her left arm, and slid the seat back as far back as it would go. Jake was grateful that Erin was so small. He could hold her with one hand and help Drake with the other. Jake slid his seat back too. Her steering wheel was bent on the right side and Jake assumed Erin did that when the crash happened. She was probably holding herself to the center and bent the steering wheel.

"Ok Jake. I'll bring the stretcher around to the passenger side and we'll get her out." Jake nodded.

Jake continued to talk in soothing tones to Erin as he maneuvered his hands more fully around her back and under her legs, keeping her head against his shoulder and molding her to his body. He made sure he had a good hold on her. He told her to take a deep breath and hold it. He tightened his hold, moved his own body and lifted Erin from the driver's seat into his lap. Her head remained on his shoulder and she passed out from the pain from the movement, but she was breathing on her own. Drake reached in to help Jake up and out of the car, guiding Erin's legs and body, making sure Jake didn't hit his head on the frame. Jake laid her on the stretcher gently and helped Drake to put air splints on her arm and leg. Erin was so tiny and she looked so fragile laying on the stretcher.

They got her strapped onto the stretcher with blankets to keep her warm, and Drake got an ice pack for her head. Once she was secure Jake helped Drake and his partner to load her into the ambulance and told him he would be right behind on his bike. He leaned in and kissed Erin's forehead. Drake assured him he would take good care of her. Drake's partner headed to the driver's side and soon they were ready to roll. Jake checked in with Thomas and headed to the trauma center following the ambulance. She was alive, she was strong, and she would heal. He prayed to God to help her and keep her safe. Somehow they needed to make sure Devin paid dearly for this. At least she survived the crash.

*****

Kade called Anthony and filled him in on what happened. Anthony was swearing and pacing as he was listening to Kade's recount of the last forty minutes. Michael and Alex rallied to his side; they wanted to be there to help if they could. The look on Anthony's face told them this was bad. All of their customers were gone, so it was just the three brothers. Kade told him he was on the way to pick him up and they would head to the trauma hospital together. Anthony hung up the phone and filled his brothers in.

"Alex, Michael, apparently Devin got out of prison this afternoon and he just slammed his pickup into Erin's car on the driver's side. She's on the way to the trauma center. She's alive, but I don't know how badly she's hurt. She told Kade and Jake to tell me she loves me. I just need her to be ok." Anthony sat down and held his head in his hands. He was praying too for his Erin.

"Anthony, brother, she's strong. She will survive this. Do you want us to drive you to the hospital?" Michael asked.

"Kade's on his way here. He and I will head there now. Jake's with Erin. Can you please go and tell our parents and let Cassi know? Kade has called Mariah already." They nodded.

"Alex, can you call Terry at TK Productions and let him know too? She's going to need to heal from all of this and won't be doing a lot of productions right now. Well, at least I don't think she will, but if I know Erin, she will want to finish what she's started." He smiled at that thought. He prayed for her as he talked to his brothers.

"We'll take care of it bro. Don't do anything crazy Anthony." Alex cautioned. "Erin needs you to be strong, so don't give into the hate of Devin. Just be there for Erin. She's going to need all of us to rally around her now. She has a long road of recovery ahead." Anthony agreed and told them all he wanted to do was hold her in his arms. They could relate. He told them he would be careful and would just be there for Erin, not giving in to the need to punch Devin out. Alex and Michael both hugged Anthony and told them to give Erin their best wishes.

Kade pulled up and Anthony headed out to the truck. Alex told him they would put his bike into the shed and lock it up. Kade and Anthony headed to the trauma center.

*****

Erin awoke as the ambulance was making its way through the crowd of cars and emergency vehicles. She tried to glance around but the movement made her head hurt, so she instead tried to keep it steady, trying to relax into the pillow under her head. A second ambulance had been called for Devin and was trying to get into the scene. Drake looked down at her after finishing his notation, and she smiled at him. Erin was generally a very happy person and she didn't often frown. Her smile could light up the darkest of souls.

"Erin, I'm Drake." She nodded. "Can I ask you some questions?" Again she nodded. He grabbed his clipboard and pen. For the next few minutes he got all her information and let her know that he had started an IV to give her fluids and she was immobilized on her left side and her leg and arm were elevated. He told her he couldn't give her any pain meds until the doctor checked her out. She smiled at him. Drake loved her smile and that fact that she was responding to him. He knew she would be ok. She reminded Drake of his Erica. Once Drake finished asking her questions he checked her IV again, noted her vitals.

Erin asked him about how he became a paramedic and they got to talking. Drake told her he just moved to the city and was now actively looking for a house to purchase so he could settle down. He told her he had a girl, so he needed to get settled. That made her smile. He told her he was former military, an Army medic and she shared that Jake and her Anthony were both Navy SEALs. She also told Drake her house would soon be for sale and if he wanted to look at it, he could let her know. Drake was impressed by Erin. She was conversational, bright and her smile lit up the back of the ambulance. She had such beautiful eyes and so expressive; he was drawn to her. He did his best to reassure her she was ok, and soon they arrived at the trauma center. They talked about lots of things and Drake realized she was trying to keep the pain at bay by changing her focus to things other than her pain. That impressed him.

As they unloaded Erin's stretcher she saw Jake pull up on his motorcycle. He quickly locked it up and headed to the back of the ambulance. She tried to sit up but Drake encouraged her to lay still. She called to Jake instead, but her voice was weak.

She smiled at him and he got to her side as they wheeled her through the emergency room doors. He was reassuring her that everything was going to be ok. She was just holding Jake's gaze needing to reassure herself that this was real and that she was still alive. She couldn't move very well, but she needed Jake to help her stay calm. He tried to reassure her with his eyes, and his touch on her hair. Two nurses and an orderly met them at the door.

"Sir, please come with me. I'll get you to the waiting room. The doctor needs to assess her injuries and once he's finished you can come back in to see her." The nurse was guiding Jake away while Erin was reaching out to him. Drake held her right arm back to the stretcher. Jake smiled at her, told her to behave, and let the nurse lead him away. Erin was wheeled into a private cubicle and Drake, his partner and the hospital staff prepared to move her to the hospital bed. She didn't weigh much but they were worried about her injuries so they tried to be gentle.

"Drake, thank you for your help today and taking care of me." Erin said as they had her situated on the hospital bed. She gave him another smile.

"My pleasure Erin. Take care of yourself. I'll check back in a couple days and maybe I can look at your house after you are out of the hospital." He smiled at her and they left Erin with the nurse.

"Ok Ms. Erin, I'm Henry your nurse for today and we need to get you ready to see the doctor. You had quite the adventure this afternoon." Henry grabbed the hospital gown and a couple of plastic bags for her clothes.

"I know you have to cut my clothes off, but perhaps we can do it a different way?" Henry smiled at her. She told him she could get out of the right side of her clothes if he could help her, and together they managed to get her shirt off, then her bra and finally pants. She was small enough and Henry realized she could just shimmy out of the right side. Henry commented on her ink on her shoulder and she smiled at him. Henry took off her shoe and sock on the right side, and told her to lay still while he removed the splint on her leg, then her arm. Finally, she was completely undressed and in the hospital gown, which thankfully had snaps. Henry folded up her clothes and put them into the bag, and her shoes into the separate bag. He put the air splints back on, and then elevated both her arm and leg on pillows. He took her vitals and checked the IV. He made her promise she wouldn't tell the doctor that he took the splints off. Erin assured him it was their secret! Henry was good at his job and took good care of Erin. He was so gentle with her. She was adamant that she wanted to save her clothes, so he helped her and they were able to make sure he didn't have to cut them off her. He told her he would take her cell phone to Jake in the waiting room. Henry loved her smile.

She radiated sunshine. Usually his patients were grumpy and in pain, but Erin seemed to float above the pain realm. She oozed happiness and made Henry smile too.

"Erin, I'm going to connect you to the monitors and then I'll go get the doctor and take your phone to Jake. Can you tell me your name and date of birth?" She told him and he put the pulse oximeter on her finger, the blood pressure cuff on her right arm, and the leads for the EKG on her chest and side. He was getting ready to head out and find the doctor.

"Henry, before you go, can I sit up a little bit? I feel really nauseated. I think I want to throw up." Henry raised the head of the bed and then grabbed an alcohol pad, which he opened and placed over her nose. He also put a blue bag next to her in case she actually needed to throw up.

"This will help. Breathe through your nose Erin." Henry put his hand on her right arm. She did that and realized that the smell of the alcohol helped to ease her queasiness. "Better?" She nodded. He smiled at her.

Henry left the room and Erin tried to keep her nerves at bay. The pain was overwhelming but at least she wasn't going to throw up now. She closed her eyes and tried to rest a bit. She tried to practice her breathing and re-center herself above the pain in her body. She found her happy place, her beach and tried to relax into that picture in her mind. She was glad she had her self-defense training to help her relieve the pain. The beach and her laying in the sand was what kept her off the ledge.

*****

Kade and Anthony made it to the hospital and texted Jake to find out where to go. Jake texted back and told them where he was. Some of the hospital staff directed them to the waiting room. Soon all three were sitting in the small waiting room.

"I'm so sorry Anthony. I should have been with her today. I didn't mean to fail you both." Jake was really distraught over not being with Erin today. His head was in his hands. He felt so very bad for not going with her. He couldn't see that being there at the end was better than actually being the car with her.

"You didn't fail us Jake. You've taken really good care of Erin and the rest of us. The system failed Erin. That bastard Devin found a way to get what he wanted, with a lawyer who found a way to buck the system, but Erin is alive. She's strong, a survivor, and we're all going to be ok. Right now all that matters is that she's getting good care. No one failed at anything. The system failed her." Anthony hugged Jake. Mariah came in at that moment.

"How is she?" Mariah asked.

"She's in one of the trauma rooms. We haven't heard anything. Do you still have privileges here Mariah?"

"I have privileges. Let me see what I can find out." She left them and headed to the trauma bay. Henry directed her to Erin's room and told her Dr. Parker was already in with her. Mariah headed to the trauma room and knocked on the door. Dr. Parker beckoned her in.

"Hi Dr. Parker. Hi Erin." Mariah smiled at them both.

"Dr. White. What brings you in today?"

"Well this lovely lady you are fixing up is my soon to be sister-in-law and I wanted to see how she was doing."

"From my initial assessment she will need to go to surgery. We have to rebuild her ankle, it took the brunt of the trauma, and I think we will need to remove her spleen. I'm still waiting on x-ray. Dr. White do you want to scrub in and assist? I could use your expertise."

"Thank you Dr. Parker. I would like to assist." She laid her hand on Erin's right arm trying to reassure her. "Erin, Dr. Parker is the best orthopedic surgeon this trauma center has. He will make your ankle like new." Erin was trying to be brave.

Another knock on the door and x-ray was here. "Erin, we'll be back shortly. These folks need to take pictures of you. Ok?" Erin nodded. Dr. Parker and Mariah stepped out of the room.   While they were out of the room Mariah filled in Dr. Parker on the events leading up to today's accident. Dr. Parker, like the family, was livid that the system kept giving Devin opportunities to hurt her. Dr. Parker asked a few more questions to try and piece together all the events leading up to today. He told Mariah that he couldn't quite believe the system would leave someone so vulnerable. He wanted to throttle the system, but like the rest of them, had no real authority to make any difference. Mariah told Dr. Parker she would go and talk with Erin's fiancé and she would be back to scrub in.

Mariah headed to the waiting room to let the brothers and Jake know about Erin. She told them that she was going to scrub in and assist. Anthony asked if he could see her before she went into surgery and Mariah told him she would see what she could do. Mariah headed back to the trauma room. The x-ray techs had finished their work and she and Dr. Parker were about to head in.

"Dr. Parker, is it possible for Erin's fiancé to briefly come back and see Erin before we take her to surgery?"

"Absolutely. I'm sure this has been a nightmare for him. Perhaps he can get her to give him her ring. She wouldn't let me take it off her finger." Mariah agreed and headed to the waiting room to get Anthony. Anthony promised he would behave himself and he agreed to get Erin to give him her ring, so Mariah took him with her to the trauma bay.

They entered Erin's cubicle; her eyes were closed and she was breathing slowly. She looked so tiny laying there in the big hospital bed. Anthony could see the bruises on the side of her face. He forced himself to unclench his fists. He really wanted a moment alone with Devin, but he promised his brothers he would behave himself. He made himself be perky, took some really deep breaths, and put a smile on his face for Erin.

As he approached the side of her bed, he quietly whispered to her. "Erin, honey, it's Anthony." Her eyes flew open and she smiled at him. "Hi sugar." He leaned over and kissed her, stroking her head with his hand, being careful around the bruises.

"Hi handsome." She had tears in her eyes. "I'm so happy to see you. I'm so sorry for all of this, causing you more worry, pulling you away from your clients."

"Baby girl, there's nothing to be sorry about. I'm sorry that you have to go through more pain. But you have an excellent team of doctors here and I'll be waiting for you when you wake up. Ok?" She nodded and smiled at him. He brushed the tears off her cheeks being mindful of her bruises. "Sugar, can I take your ring and hold it for you? I don't want you to lose it." She nodded.

"I had Jake move it to my right hand because of the swelling. I didn't want them to cut it off and I wanted you with me, to feel you with me. The ring helped me stay calm and try to focus on you instead of the pain."

"I know darlin' but I'm right here now and I'll be waiting for you. Dr. Parker is going to help you with the pain and to sleep for a bit. I just want you well. I will keep it safe and then when you're better we'll put it back on your finger. Ok?" She nodded. He leaned in and kissed her again. She held her right hand up to him and he slipped the ring off her finger putting it into his pocket. He gave her one last kiss, told her to be good, he loved her, and he would see her soon. She relaxed back into the pillow and her eyes slid closed. Mariah led him out into the hallway just as Devin was brought in to the ER. She felt him tense beside her and she hoped she could convince him to return to the waiting room and not cause chaos.

"Anthony, go back to the waiting room now. Please don't cause a scene. Devin is in custody, but the state is also required to provide care. He will stand trial and we will get a conviction. Just don't make this harder. Please don't go after him. We don't want you to end up in jail." She headed Anthony to the waiting room and had Henry help her. They needed to diffuse the situation before it escalated out of control. Devin saw Anthony and knew Erin was here. Damn, he didn't kill her. He failed again. The paramedics wheeled him into a trauma room, the police officers following. Devin was handcuffed to the gurney, and he was struggling to get free. The police were trying to help the medical personnel keep Devin contained. He fought the doctors and the medical personnel, until they gave him something to make him sleep. Devin had a collapsed lung and contusions from the steering wheel impact; they also didn't know if he had internal injuries too. He really needed help, not just physically but mentally as well. The police officers and doctors all realized how much Devin needed psychiatric help, but all of them knew that the system probably wouldn't get him the help he needed or that Devin would be open to it.

*****

Mariah and Dr. Parker scrubbed in and prepared for Erin in the surgery suite. They spent two hours getting her fixed up. Dr. Parker started by working on her ankle, cleaning it up and locating all the pieces to put it back together, pinning them in place, adding screws and pins, while Mariah took out Erin's spleen using small incisions, laparoscope technology, and the small cameras. She would have minimal scarring and would heal faster. Mariah checked all other organs with the cameras, but nothing else seemed to have been affected. Erin was in good shape so this would be easy for her to come back from. Mariah then shifted and helped with the rest of the ankle restoration. They used a series of screws, glue, and pins to keep the small fragments together and both doctors were pleased at the outcome.

Dr. Parker reattached the tendon in the right place, and secured it with dissolvable stitches. They looked over the new x-rays after they got everything repaired, and put her into casts to keep her leg still, leaving space for swelling, and her lower arm in line. She had a full-leg cast to handle the fractured femur, and the ankle; she also reinjured her left arm which required another cast, and she had two dislocated joints – her left hip and shoulder. Her injuries could have been so much worse had Jake not told her to move to the center of the car. The pillow on her left also gave additional padding and saved her from more broken bones. She had lots of bruises, but those would heal. At least she had no head injuries or spinal problems. Once they were satisfied with the repairs, they wrapped up the surgery and started to bring Erin out of anesthesia. Fleetingly, Mariah had thought about giving her a cocktail for the nausea, but she forgot in the work they were doing to repair her body.

Erin was moved into recovery and Mariah stayed with her. Dr. Parker was needed for another trauma that came into the ER. Mariah monitored her vitals, which were strong, and charted from the surgery, what they did and the number of screws and pins in her ankle. Slowly Erin's eyes flickered open and closed a few times, and she was trying very hard to make sense of where she was. Finally, she spotted Mariah.

"Hey there pretty lady." Mariah said. She brushed the hair back out of Erin's eyes. "How are you feeling?"

"Hi Mariah. I think I'm ok. Is it over?" Her voice was rough from the tube they used during surgery to help keep her airway open.

"Yes. You did so great Erin. You're in recovery right now." She spooned some ice chips into her mouth. "Don't try to talk sweetie. Just rest Erin." She smiled at her. "We repaired your ankle, took your spleen out, and fixed everything else. You even have two purple casts now."

"Mariah, will I be able to still have a family once Anthony and I are married?" Erin seemed really concerned.

"Absolutely! By moving to the center of the car you prevented a lot more injuries to your body. The only internal damage was your spleen." Mariah smiled at her. "Now that you are on the road to recovery I'm going to see about getting you settled in a room. That way Anthony can come and be with you."

"Mariah, thank you for taking such good care of me, again." Erin smiled at her. Mariah gave her more ice chips. Erin's right hand came up to pull at her face. Mariah moved her arm back to her side.

"Erin, honey, you have oxygen on, so please don't pull it out. I know it feels strange, but please don't play with it." Mariah was holding her hand down on the bed.

"Ok. My face just felt funny, like there is a heavy weight on it. Sorry." She smiled at Mariah. Mariah adjusted the ice packs on her leg and arm, and the one on her face.

"Erin, do you remember if you hit the side of the car or if something hit you during the accident. I'm trying to figure out the bruises on your face." Erin shook her head.

"I remembered my training and tucked my head to my chest to help with any injuries to my back and my neck, but I don't remember getting hit in the head. I just know my head hurts. I remember the air bags inflated and those brushed me on the side of my face, and something brushed by my head, but no idea what that was. Mariah, I also feel like I want to throw up. I'm really queasy." Mariah set the head of the bed up a bit and put another alcohol pad on her nose. She asked the nurse to get her a nausea cocktail, and Mariah injected that into Erin's IV. "Thank you." Mariah gave her some more ice chips, charted the anti-nausea meds and took another set of vitals. She watched Erin for a few minutes making sure she was ok.

*****

Erin was moved to a private room on the surgical floor. The movement of the stretcher and the lights in the ceiling made Erin nauseated, but she did her best to breathe slowly through her nose. Erin remembered that she saw Devin at the trauma center when she was wheeled into surgery. She needed to ask Anthony about that. While the orderlies were getting Erin situated in a more comfortable bed, Mariah headed to the waiting room and brought the brothers and Jake upstairs. Erin's new bed was an air mattress and the air chambers ebbed and flowed with air as she lay on it. She looked so tiny in the large bed surrounded by lots of pillows. The medical team commented on that and Erin just smiled at them. As they were riding the elevator Mariah told them what they did for Erin and that she needed anti-nausea meds from the anesthesia. Mariah reminded them to be gentle with her. All three of them took deep breaths before they went in and tried to be happy, perky to keep Erin's spirits up. At least she wasn't on too many machines to keep her alive. She was so lucky with the injuries and the fact that she moved to the center of the car. That was thanks to Jake.

They came into her room, which was very bright. Erin had a private corner room with windows. She had a great view of the ocean from the vantage point of the fifteenth floor. Erin's eyes were closed and she was breathing slowly and peacefully. She still had the oxygen on just in case, but she seemed to be resting. They all smiled at seeing her, so little in the big bed. Anthony pulled up a chair by her right side and held her hand in his, stroking it. Erin opened her eyes and looked around the room seeing Jake, Kade and her eyes landing finally on her Anthony.

"Hi beautiful." Anthony said. Erin smiled at him and squeezed his hand.

"Hi my handsome Anthony. I made it through surgery."

"Yes you did. You are so brave." She smiled at him and he motioned the other two over. The both pulled up chairs and sat where Erin could see them.

"Thank you all. Jake, thanks for coming to me today and for keeping me on the phone, talking to me, giving me strength to survive. Thanks for keeping me off the edge with all the pain."

"My pleasure Miss Erin." He smiled at her.

"Erin, honey, how did things go with the hockey player?" Kade asked, changing the subject a bit. She came to life at that question.

"It was an amazing interview. He walked me through what he does and he even got me out on the ice with him to skate. He showed me how to hold the stick and how to hit the puck into the net." Just then they heard a phone ring. "That's my phone. Jake do you have my phone?" Jake pulled the phone out of his pocket. He told her it was Kyle Hunt. Erin reached for it.

"Hi Kyle." She said into the phone. Kyle told her he heard about an accident on Pier Street, and that the car in the news story looked a lot like hers, and wondered if she was ok. "Kyle, the accident you heard or saw was my car getting hit." She listened again and Kyle was asking all kinds of questions trying to understand. She seemed confused and trying to make sense of everything; the boys were watching her face. She needed to slow his questions down and have him talk to Anthony.

"Hang on Kyle. I just came out of surgery and I can't focus all that well because of the pain meds. I'm going to have you talk to my Anthony, my fiancé. He can fill you in." She handed the phone to Anthony who got up and walked to the windows while he introduced himself to Kyle and told him the whole sordid story through the questions Kyle asked. Kyle was furious and told him to take good care of Erin. He told Anthony that he thoroughly enjoyed getting to know Erin and looked forward to working with her in the future. He told him a bit about the interview too. He also asked what room she was in because he wanted to send some flowers. Anthony gave him the information. He thanked Kyle for calling and for the interview today. They signed off and Anthony headed back to his chair.

"So Kyle had you out on the ice skating with him?" Anthony asked.

"Yep. I had asked him about his give back program to the community and he told me he taught kids to play hockey, so you know me, I asked about that because I thought it was great PR, and the next thing I knew I was on skates, learning to play hockey!" She smiled at them all. "He told me he's former military, Navy." She could see the surprise in their eyes.   "I told him all about my wonderful men and their military service too! Oh yeah, Drake, the paramedic is former military too. He was an Army medic and he's looking to buy a house so I told him about mine." Anthony just smiled at her. She was incredible. She was just in an accident and she was trying to sell her house and keeping everyone else happy. That was extraordinary.

They talked for a few more minutes asking questions about Drake and Kyle, and Erin remembered about Devin again. Anthony watched her and saw the change come over her features.

"Erin, honey, is everything ok?"

"Um, no not really. I remember that as I was heading to surgery that I saw Devin in the trauma bay. He was surrounded by the police, but he was there just the same. That means he's here in this hospital somewhere. That totally freaks me out." All of them tried to reassure her.

"Darlin' you're safe. If Devin is here he's in custody, and you said yourself that the police were with him, so he can't get to you." Kade said. Jake and Anthony agreed.

"Will you all stay here tonight? I can guarantee you that I won't sleep unless I know you're all here with me."

Dr. Parker came in at that moment. "Erin, you have to rest. All the work I just did on your ankle, your body needs rest and you need to get your strength back."

"Hi Dr. Parker. I'm Anthony, Erin's intended. She's reeling because she saw Devin as she was being wheeled to surgery. Is he staying in the hospital?"

"Yes. He's on the floor below. He is handcuffed to his bed and he has four police officers – two in the room with him and two outside guarding him. I have also arranged for guards outside Erin's door too. You are safe Erin. We won't let him anywhere near you."

"I still want my Anthony, Kade and Jake to stay here too."

"I think we can accommodate that." Dr. Parker smiled at her. "There is a pull-out bed in that couch over there for one of you, this chair here reclines and can make a very comfortable bed too. I'll send in a rollaway for one of you."

"Anthony can share my bed, there's plenty of room and he can hold me." Erin said definitively. Anthony smiled, trying to hide his laughter. Dr. Parker started to protest, but then thought better of it.

"Ok, then it looks like you are all set. I'll send up dinner trays for you three. Is the salisbury steak plate ok for you all?" They nodded. "Miss Erin, is there something special you would like to eat?"

"What really sounds good is a grilled cheese sandwich on sourdough bread with a bowl of tomato soup."

"I can make that happen. With ice cream for dessert!" She smiled at him. "What would you like to drink?"

"Diet Pepsi." She was so definite. That got a laugh. He headed out the door and Erin tried to relax a little bit. "Thank you all for staying with me."

"We wouldn't be anywhere else darlin'." Kade said and smiled at her. They loved how she had the doctor wrapped around her finger already. This was their Erin. They enjoyed the time with her and tried to keep the conversation light, happy and away from Devin and the trauma.

*****

Devin woke up in an unfamiliar room and everything on his body hurt. He tried to move his arms and realized he was shackled to the bed. He was trying to remember what happened in the last few hours. He hadn't yet opened his eyes and he was trying to process the last few hours. He remembered getting out of the prison cell and heading home. He recalled that the police had already searched his house and then he remembered hitting Erin's car with his pickup. He smiled an ugly, evil smile thinking about the fact that he hit her driver's side door with his pickup truck. He remembered speeding up to hit her hard. He hoped he accomplished what he set out to do. Since he was moving the doctor figured he was awake.

"Welcome back to reality Mr. Traeger." A male voice said.

"Where am I?" Devin asked groggily, his eyes still closed.

"You're in the trauma hospital. You slammed your vehicle into someone else's this afternoon and your airbags did not deploy." Devin smiled bigger, a purely evil smile.

"I remember now. Did I kill Erin?" He was too eager in that question.

"Is that what you intended to do?" The voice seemed shocked at his question.

"Yes. She deserved to die."

"Why do you say that?"

"She had the audacity to tell me no every time I tried to get close to her. She hurt me with her self-defense tactics when I tried to take her to be mine and she was with some other guy named Anthony. If I can't have her, then no one will have her. Please tell me I killed her." He looked up at the doctor and locked eyes with him. Dr. Mendenhall saw all the anger and the hatred for Erin in his eyes.

Dr. Mendenhall was furious with the words coming out of Devin's mouth. The two policemen in the room were taking notes. Devin was basically convicting himself. "Mr. Traeger, why do you feel that she told you no?"

"Because she's a cold bitch. She's heartless. She had no right to tell me no. I was good to her and she never gave me a chance." Devin finally opened his eyes wider, glancing beyond the doctor, and saw the police officers.

"Mr. Traeger, you are in the hospital, shackled here to the bed, in the custody of the police for your antics today. Tomorrow morning you will be moved to the regional correctional facility and there you will stay until trial. Along with the other charges, you now face attempted vehicular manslaughter, attempted murder, and intent to kill with a vehicle."

Devin started pulling at the shackles on his wrists. "Let me go. I need to find Erin and finish her off. If I'm in the hospital that means she's close by too. Let me go so I can finish the job I started." Devin was creating a scene trying to get loose; he was pulling on the shackles on his wrists and making lots of noise. At least he was in a room away from other people so he couldn't disturb them. The two police officers were trying to subdue him.

"Actually, I think I will call the warden and have you returned to the prison tonight. Your injuries are not life-threatening and the prison infirmary can handle them." Dr. Mendenhall put another shot into Devin's IV and in moments Devin was subdued. Dr. Mendenhall turned to the officers and told him that he would be back soon. He left, headed to his office and contacted the chief of staff Dr. Parker and filled him in on what Devin said; together they called the warden and asked for Devin to be moved to the prison immediately. The warden said he would send a vehicle. Dr. Mendenhall told him that Devin was currently sedated. He also relayed all the nasty things Devin said. The warden asked if there were police present and Dr. Mendenhall said there were two officers present who took notes on the things Devin said.

By seven in the evening Devin was released from the hospital into the custody of the state, and relocated to the prison infirmary where he was placed in confinement. Devin didn't come out of his sedation until early the next morning. Dr. Mendenhall and Dr. Parker gave their statements to the DA's office, because both them were involved in the care of Devin and Erin, and the police officers added their notes to the DA's file as well indicating that they had already read Devin his rights when he was brought in, before any meds were given, and Devin agreed that he understood the rights.

*****

Erin and her men finished their dinner. Anthony and Erin talked for a bit while Kade and Jake headed back to Kade's to get them something comfortable to sleep in. Jake told Erin he would bring her computer bags up with him when he returned. She told him to leave the camera gear at the house, but she needed her computer and the SD cards, as well as her tablet and notes. She asked him to bring her baggy sweats and oversize t-shirt for when she actually could go home. The goal was also to take Jake's bike back to Kade's so it wouldn't sit in the parking lot all night. The boys were gone a little more than an hour.

In the meantime, a lovely bouquet of pink and white roses came to Erin's room from Kyle and his PR person.   Terry also sent Erin a weeping cherry bonsai tree. She was so excited to have flowers in her room and the bonsai tree was perfect. Dr. Parker checked on her one more time and told her to get some sleep. He told her he would be back in the morning. She thanked him again for taking care of her.

Just before Kade and Jake made it back the rest of the Romano family came into make sure she was ok.

"Erin, my girl." Angelina said and came over for a gentle hug. Anthony moved out of the way.   "How are you doing?"

"Hi mom!" Angelina beamed; she liked being called mom. "I'm doing ok. Mariah helped in surgery, so I was in good hands." Cassi hugged her too. The women stayed and talked with Erin while the men talked across the room.

The three women talked while Roberto, Anthony, Michael and Alex talked over by the sofa. Anthony relayed that Kade, Jake and he were staying here tonight because Devin was also somewhere in the vicinity of Erin's room. After a few minutes the brothers all came back around Erin's bed.

"Alex, Michael, I almost have your video pieces finished. Michael, I talked with Anthony and we decided that in addition to your video piece on your page we would do a dictionary of the types of piercings that you do. It might help to explain the different names so your clients can ask for them by name. Does that sound ok?" He nodded.

"When can we see the finished product Erin?" Alex asked as he put his arm around Cassi.

"Well, when Kade and Jake get back, they are bringing my computer in. So perhaps tomorrow I can show you all the pieces that are finished. Each of the tattoo pieces have a different feel based on your art and your personality. Anthony has already seen his piece, but I want to make sure you are all ok with them." Anthony smiled at her.

"I can't wait." Alex said.

"Erin, how did your shoot go today? What is Kyle like?" Michael asked.

"It was an amazing interview. He's really down to earth. You all would like him and would get along well with him."

"He took Erin out on the ice and showed her how to hold a hockey stick, and hit the puck into the net." Anthony added. Erin blushed a little.

"He even sent flowers! Those roses are from him. He called when he heard about the accident. He said he recognized the car. I had him talk to Anthony because I was still kind of out of things with the meds from the surgery."

"He actually knows the whole story. He was livid with Devin and wanted to do what we've all wanted to do to Devin. He asked if he could send flowers to Erin. I think Erin touched him just like she did all of us!" Anthony supplied. "He seems like a really good guy."

The family didn't stay too long, but promised to come back tomorrow. Alex said that he would try to bring Cassi back with him. Cassi grinned and told them she had things to do with the garden tomorrow and with Mariah. Erin said she hoped to go home on Sunday, but time would tell. After kisses and hugs, the family left and it was once again Anthony and Erin.

"Anthony, my handsome hero, can I ask you a question?" Erin said looking at him with the love in her eyes shining.

"Absolutely sugar." He perched on the edge of her bed and held her right hand.

"I actually finished Michael's piece for the website, but it's missing one picture." He waited. "It's missing the picture of the delicate chain piercing with the rhinestone barbells."

"It would be missing that one honey. Michael hasn't had anyone who he could do that piercing for."

"Not yet. What would you think if I had him do me with that piercing?" He stared wide eyed at her for a moment; she waited for his response. He finally broke into a huge smile. He needed to make sure he heard what she just said. She was thinking about having Michael pierce her nipples. That was awesome.

"Really?" She nodded. "You want Michael to pierce your nipples with the delicate chains and we can use that on the website?"

"Only if you are on board with it my sweet Anthony, and are ok with it. I have been giving a lot of thought to all you have told me – and seeing the art in the piercings that Michael does has made me want to explore it more. You've made me want to do this, and I want to do this for you my handsome hero, my gift to you for loving me, wanting to marry me. The chains and rhinestones are so pretty and I think it would look amazing. Is that ok?" She was blushing.

"Yes my love. I think it's amazing. You are so beautiful and those will just enhance that. Michael will be over-the-moon. You've made me very happy too. I love that you want to do this for me."

"I mean no one who looks at the site will know it's me except you and your family, but I can't do this presentation justice without that one piercing. If you are ok with all of this, Michael can do them both. I just need you to distract me from the procedure and pain." Anthony leaned forward to gently kiss her and hug her to him.

"I am excited Erin. It's going to look so awesome on you and so sexy."

"What's going to look awesome?" Kade asked as he and Jake came back in to the room. Anthony looked at Erin to get permission to answer. She nodded.

"Erin has decided that in order to complete Michael's piercing art piece for the website she's going to have him pierce her nipples with the delicate chains piercing. That's the one piercing that Michael has not been able to do yet."

"Really Erin?" Kade said smiling. "That's awesome." Jake gave her a smile and a thumbs up too. Erin captured her lip into her teeth. She was blushing a lot which just enhanced the bruise on her left side. It made all three men smile. She just asked them not to tell Michael until she had the chance to do it. They agreed. Everyone settled in and soon they were all sleeping peacefully, with Anthony curled around Erin.

Chapter Seven

The brothers all came on Saturday late morning to see Erin. Cassi had things she needed to do with Mariah and her garden so she couldn't join them. Erin had asked permission to connect her computer via Bluetooth to the TV in the room to show the brothers their video pieces for the website. The nurse, Diane, said that would be fine and didn't realize that that was possible.

"Hey Erin, darlin', how are you feeling today?" Alex asked when he came in.

"Better Alex. Thanks. I slept last night in Anthony's arms so that helped." She smiled at him. The all greeted her with hugs. "If you all want to find a seat and watch the TV I will show you your website videos." She invited them all to sit. "I have them all finished, well almost finished. As you watch them, if you have changes you'd like to see, please let me know. I can change pictures around, change the music, whatever you want." She prepared her computer and connected it into the TV. "We'll start with Kade's piece."   She rolled the video and watched all of them and their faces as they watched their pieces play on the TV.

"Erin it's amazing. I love that you picked country music for my piece!" Kade was really excited. She smiled at him. "I don't want to change a thing. That's my work and it's awesome to see it showcased like that! Thank you." He hugged her.

"Cool. I'm so glad you like what I did. Ok. So now let's look at Alex's piece." She rolled Alex's video and again watched them. Alex was enamored with the piece, and he loved that she included her own artwork that he did for her in the piece, and like Kade, loved the music she chose for him and the colorful background. They repeated this process for Anthony's piece too and none of the tattoo artists wanted any changes made.

"Ok Michael, that brings us to your piece. I talked with Anthony and we decided that your page also needed a dictionary of sorts to help explain the different types of piercings." Michael nodded. "Ready?" Again he nodded and she played the piece.

"I love it Erin. But there is one black square. Why?" Michael asked.

"Well, we have one more picture we need to get and put into your piece. It's the piercing with the delicate chains." Erin tried to keep the smile off her face.

"I haven't done that piercing yet. No one has let me do that." Michael looked at his brothers.

"Well bro, you have someone who wants that piercing now." Michael looked shocked. "Erin is wanting you to do those piercings to her."

"Really Erin?" Michael asked, surprised.

"Yes. I asked Anthony for permission last night and I think it would be really pretty, so yes please." Erin smiled at him. Michael rushed over to hug her gently.

"We can do this as soon as you are out of the hospital. That way those piercings will heal as you are healing the rest of your body." He kissed her cheek. "Thanks bro." Michael said to Anthony and hugged him too. "Erin, darlin' do you know when you'll be going home?" Dr. Parker came in as he asked that.

"I'd like to keep Erin here until Monday. That way I can ensure that her leg and arm swelling is down and we can replace the casts." Dr. Parker said.

"Sounds good doc. We'll prepare the house for her to come home." Kade said. "I'm guessing she will be in a wheelchair for a while." Dr. Parker nodded.

"Can I have a moment with Erin guys?" They nodded.

"We'll be in the cafeteria. Erin, honey, just text when we can come back." She nodded and kissed her Anthony.

******

Devin, shackled to a bed in the prison infirmary, was able to meet with his lawyer. Mark came in and they spent some time talking. Devin told him that the police had been to his house and gathered their evidence, and Mark asked what that all entailed. Devin described to him what kinds of things the police would have found. He wrote things down, trying to figure out a defense against all the evidence the police had collected. Mark realized they had an extremely uphill battle. Devin was in so deep and he didn't think they could defend him from all the charges. Devin then asked if it was possible to accuse Erin of assault for the broken bones and the hit to his balls. Mark said she would be served with papers on Monday and have to appear in court on Wednesday. Devin smiled and went back to resting and healing while Mark went to work on how to charge Erin with assault. Mark was debating as to how to go about it, because technically it was self-defense, but perhaps he could use the fact that she was a black belt in judo against her. Mark had already talked with Richard about this charge the last time Devin asked. They didn't know how to pull it off, but she would end up in the courtroom just the same and that might rattle her. Devin was upset that he didn't kill her in the traffic accident he caused. She was still a thorn in his side because she didn't want him the way he wanted her. He couldn't imagine her not wanting to be with him to let him pleasure her and let him take pleasure from her. It was unfathomable to him that she kept telling him no.

*****

Erin and Anthony stayed at the hospital the rest of the weekend and into Monday morning. Now that Devin was in custody and at the prison, Erin was breathing easier so that Jake and Kade could go home. Erin was following doctor's orders and eating her meals, keeping her leg and arm elevated, and resting; Dr. Parker was thrilled with her progress. He had removed the IV early on Saturday morning because she was doing well. She asked if she could get up, but he asked her to stay in bed until Monday. He knew he was asking the impossible because Erin was very active. He brought her some theraband that she could work with it while lying in the bed, and that seemed to appease her. She contented herself with editing on the pieces for Kyle while Anthony watched TV or read his book.   Erin loved having Anthony's arms around her in the nights.

Monday, just before lunch, Kade and Jake came back to take Erin and Anthony home with them. Dr. Parker took Erin to the exam room and changed her casts while the boys headed to the cafeteria to have some lunch.

"Ok, Erin, I'm going to cut off the leg cast first, and then we'll put a new on. Do you still want purple, or do you want a different color?"

"Purple, please." Dr. Parker smiled at her. He got to work and Erin didn't flinch or move. He was able to remove the old cast, check the incision in her ankle and see if it was healing, taking away the bandage but adding more antibiotic ointment, and then he prepared to put on a new cast. First, he checked on her dislocation to see if it was stable. He had her lay back on the table and he moved her leg in various directions to check the hip socket. She could see all the bruising from where the airbags, and her door hit her; she couldn't see the incision because it was on the outside and Dr. Parker didn't turn her leg so she could see it.   After the leg was back and immobilized, he turned to her arm. He took off the old cast, which was just about to slide off on its own, and put a new on. He also checked her shoulder and the range of motion to make sure the dislocation was staying put. Dr. Parker told her he was pleased at her progress. She smiled. She asked if she could work out a little with the right side over the next couple of weeks. Dr. Parker told her yes but to be very careful. He knew the movement would help her heal.

Erin was returned to her room and Dr. Parker told her he would start to work on her discharge paperwork. She thanked him. Erin texted her boys and they headed back to her room. They talked and told Erin that they had made some modifications to the house, but for the most part it was ready for her to come home to. They talked about Alex and Michael's weddings, and Anthony told Erin she had an appointment with Michael tomorrow afternoon which made her smile. As they were talking a knock was heard on her door.

"Come in." Erin said.

"Miss Erin Bradford?" The man at the door asked.

"Yes."

He walked in and handed her an envelope. "Consider yourself served." She took the envelope and he turned and walked out. Erin sat there stunned.

"What does that mean?" Erin asked, when she finally found her voice, as she looked at the envelope.

"He's a process server and he serves papers to people who are being sued, or who have to appear in court for some reason. Erin, let's open the envelope and we'll deal with whatever it is. Breathe honey. Let's not jump to any conclusions until we read the contents. We'll figure this out together." Jake said. The boys all looked at each other wondering what Devin was up to now. They tried to keep their faces passive.

Erin took a deep breath and opened the envelope. She read through the letter and her demeanor changed from happy to angry. "Is he kidding? This is insane!" She looked up at the boys. "Devin is charging me with assault and battery for his broken ribs and broken nose, and the injury to his groin from when he tried to kidnap me! That bastard!" All three men were taken aback at Erin's language, but they didn't blame her. "Sorry for my outburst and my lack of decorum, my bad language. I'm angry. This is never going to end!"

"No worries darlin'. You've just never said those words before. You just caught us off guard. We're rubbing off on you." Kade said, with the hint of a smile and a chuckle. She apologized again to them for her language; she couldn't see past the anger to joke with Kade.

"Erin, may I see your paperwork?" Jake asked. He took it and quickly perused it. "Wow, I agree Devin is a bastard. He's decided that Erin hurt him with the broken ribs and broken nose, and she hurt his groin with her knee, when it was self-defense. There's no mention about it being self-defense, or the reason behind it. So, Erin has to appear in court on Wednesday morning."

"Can I have just two minutes with Devin alone?" Erin asked, her anger clearly still present. "I want to show him what real pain is; he's never going to leave me alone." Kade looked at her stunned. "Sorry Kade, I'm angry with him and this is getting really old. I seem to always have to defend myself around him and that's happening a lot. I just want this nightmare to be over. I want him to listen to me when I tell him no." She was breathing hard and trying to keep herself off the edge of wanting to hit something. This was a nightmare that was never going to end.

"Erin, darlin', we'll get him in court. Get your anger out now and we'll get you an attorney. We'll face this head on. These charges will not hold up because we can show it was self-defense. We can show the judge that there should be no charges against you for assault or battery. We need the footage from your neighbor's phone." Jake said. Erin was simmering under the surface.

"I'll call Uncle Mory." Kade said and stepped to the window to call.

"Anthony, handsome, we need to change my appointment with Michael to Thursday or Friday. I need to make sure I'm ready for Wednesday morning."

"Agreed sugar. I'll call Michael right now." Anthony stepped away and called Michael, explaining what just transpired. They set up for Thursday afternoon instead. Kade got ahold of Uncle Mory and Uncle Mory would come tomorrow with Bill Santo and they would represent Erin. He told Kade that these charges would not stick because they could easily show self-defense. He also asked for the security camera footage from that day. Kade thanked him and hung up. Jake called Dottie and got the footage she took as well.

"I'm sorry for my outburst guys and my unladylike language. This just makes me angry. He can't take no for an answer, and now this. I apologize. This is not how I was raised, but my anger got the best of me today. Please accept my apologies." They assured her all was ok.

Dr. Parker came in to let Erin and her men know she was released to go home. Anthony stayed and helped her get dressed in her baggy sweats and t-shirt while Kade and Jake took her belongings and the flowers to the truck. Dr. Parker sent up a wheelchair and once they were set, they wheeled Erin to the car. All three men told Dr. Parker that they would carry Erin if she needed to go somewhere, so they didn't need a wheelchair. Dr. Parker told them they would want the wheelchair so he was sending one home with them regardless. One of the orderlies brought out a wheelchair that Jake put in the back of the pickup. She sat in the backseat with Anthony and Kade drove them home.

*****

Wednesday morning found them in the court room. Judge Jeremy Jackson was presiding. "Good morning. All rise for the honorable Judge Jackson." The judge seated everyone, looked over his notes and started the proceedings.

"Good morning. Today we are here to determine if enough evidence exists to charge one Ms. Erin Bradford with assault and battery on Mr. Devin Traeger. Mr. Traeger are you present?"

"Yes your honor." Devin said as he stood the best he could in shackles.

"Ms. Bradford are you present?"

"Yes your honor." Erin said from her wheelchair. The judge seemed surprised to see her in a wheelchair. He recovered his demeanor and returned to the folder in front of him.

"Mr. Connor, will you please present your evidence against Ms. Bradford."

For the next thirty minutes Mr. Connor presented the medical reports for Devin's injuries being careful about stating the reasons for his injuries; he also drew attention to her background with her judo training and her black belt. The judge spent a few minutes looking over the materials that Mr. Connor presented him, entered into evidence, and then turned to Erin.

"Ms. Bradford, can you have one of your attorney's bring you forward? I have a few questions." Uncle Mory wheeled Erin so that she was facing the judge. "Ms. Bradford, how tall are you?"

"5'4" your honor."

"How much do you weigh, without the casts?"

"About 110 pounds your honor."

"Ms. Bradford, can I ask what happened to you? Why all the casts and the wheelchair?"

"Your honor, last Friday afternoon Mr. Traeger drove his pickup deliberately into my driver's side door at the intersection of 4th Street and Pier Street."

"I see. Ms. Bradford, did you do these injuries to Mr. Traeger?"

"Yes your honor. In my defense though, those injuries were sustained as a result of self-defense against Mr. Traeger when he tried to kidnap me out of my front yard. I have a restraining order on file against Mr. Traeger which he has disregarded on numerous occasions, and he tried to kidnap me out front of my house that day, so I did everything I could to get out of his grasp, which is when these injuries occurred to him. I have the video footage from my security cameras to show you, as well as footage from my neighbor's phone that she recorded when this happened." Uncle Mory brought the video footage forward along with the restraining order and the court records. These were entered into evidence.

"Thank you Ms. Bradford. You can return to your seat." He then looked up at Devin. "Mr. Traeger can you please come forward?" Devin, with the help of the bailiff, moved to where he was standing before the judge.

"How tall are you Mr. Traeger?"

"6'2" your honor."

"And your weight?"

"240."

"Mr. Traeger, did you try to kidnap Ms. Bradford."

"Yes."

"Did you run your pick-up into her car on Friday afternoon?"

"Yes."

"Why?"

"Because she said no to me; she's repeatedly telling me no. I have been good to her and she keeps turning me down without ever giving me a chance." Erin sat, without breathing, and trying not to show emotion. She was angry and Anthony could see that. Devin sounded like a child who couldn't get his way. Anthony hoped she would keep that to herself and not cause a scene. He wasn't close enough to her to be able to keep her off the edge. He got Jake's attention, and hoped Jake could help.

"Women, including Ms. Bradford, do have the right to say no Mr. Traeger. You claim that Ms. Bradford deliberately hurt you, but what I see in the evidence she provided in her defense is that you provoked her repeatedly and she was only protecting herself."

"She's a black belt in judo, your honor. She shouldn't be able to use that on me." Again Devin was whining and complaining like a child being told no. Erin watched the judge trying to keep the slight smile off his face.

"Mr. Traeger, the evidence I have here in front of me shows that Ms. Bradford has a restraining order to keep you away from her and you have repeatedly ignored the order. You have eight inches in height on her and about 130 pounds, so she did what she needed to do to protect herself. She has a right to defend herself and if that means causing you broken ribs, a broken nose and a knee to your groin, it is not considered assault. It is considered self-preservation. I am appalled at the fact that you deliberately rammed your vehicle into her car. I'm guessing your intent was incapacitate her." He looked up at Devin.

"No your honor, my intent was to kill her. If she won't be with me, let me love her, then she shouldn't be with anyone." Erin's mouth dropped open, she sucked in an audible breath, and she tried to regain her composure. Jake's arm came up and landed on her shoulder, massaging lightly, trying to give her support. She tried to smile at him and Anthony, but they could see the hurt and anger. The judge took an audible breath as well at that remark. He could see Erin's reaction out of the corner of his eye. He needed to stop this hearing now. This was over and he needed to make sure she was safe. He needed to help protect her. The judge made a few more notes in his folder and then looked up and addressed Devin, his attorney and the court at-large. Erin was reeling with the admission that Devin was trying to kill her.

"This court finds the there is no evidence of assault and battery on the part of Ms. Bradford. Mr. Traeger, all that you just admitted to here in my courtroom is public record and will be provided to the DA for your upcoming trial. I am recommending that you be placed into solitary confinement and you will stay there until your trial, which I am also recommending be moved up to start next week, or as soon as the court docket is available. You do not deserve to be free and on the streets. Bailiff, please take Mr. Traeger back to his cell." He turned and addressed Erin. He could see she was still reeling from the words that Devin spoke.

"Ms. Bradford, there is no case against you here. All charges that were presented are dismissed. My apologies from this court for the pain and suffering you have been through at the hands of Mr. Traeger. This system is clearly broken and has failed you tremendously on several occasions. I hope you can heal and get back to normal. We will be working on the case against Mr. Traeger. Court is adjourned." Erin was breathing again, but reeling.   Jake realized that he had more work to do with Erin now that Devin admitted his goal was to kill her. He could see the wheels turning in her mind. He didn't want her to retreat to that dark part of her world again where she paced and let the demons in. Although being in the wheelchair she couldn't pace at all.

Soon they were heading out of the courthouse and driving home. Erin was very quiet, but tense; she was rigid in Anthony's arms. She hadn't said anything since the answers she gave to the judge. She was processing the entire morning and the things she learned in the courtroom. She was trying to wrap her head around the fact that Devin was actually trying to kill her and was outraged that she didn't die in the accident. She always thought she was a good person, but Devin wanted her dead regardless of that fact. That was almost too much to handle. The tension was thick in the cab of the pickup.

"Erin, honey, are you ok?" Anthony finally asked. They couldn't handle the silence anymore. She was projecting her fear and anger throughout the truck. All of them felt it.

"Yeah. I'm just processing the fact that Devin was actually trying to kill me. I can't seem to get my head around that piece of information. I didn't do anything to him except say no which I thought my right. I just need to process hearing him say his intent, putting it into words. Those words are stuck in my mind right now."

"Erin, we're going to talk about all of this when we get back to the house. We need to work through all that you are feeling and thinking. I want to do some more hypnosis with you. We don't want the demons to reappear and drag you under again." Jake said. She nodded her head, but her mind was still reeling and she wasn't focused on what Jake was saying. Jake could see the demons already chasing her; she was pulling away from them, withdrawing. She was devastated with all she just learned and she was trying to make sense of the last couple of hours.

Erin showed all that she was feeling and thinking about on her face; Jake was grateful to be able to see her reactions. He needed that insight to help her. She also built up walls and made them almost impenetrable, so Jake needed to figure out where the weakness in the wall was. She was struggling with the words from Devin's mouth that he was definitely trying to kill her. She heard Devin say that she didn't have a right to tell him no. Devin lived in a fantasy world where he got everything and everyone else got nothing. In Devin's world it was his way or no way. Jake needed her to see that he lived in an alternate reality.

Kade pulled into the driveway and they all piled out of the car. Anthony opted to just carry Erin inside while Jake got the wheelchair out of the back. Erin decided that she wanted to sit outside for a bit and so Jake joined her out under the porch cover. None of them wanted her to be alone with her thoughts. They didn't want her to retreat away from them again. Jake wanted her talk about it all, but Erin was holding back. He suspected that she didn't know how to voice what she was feeling and how to talk about the encounter today. Somehow he needed to reach her and let her know it was better to talk than keep it bottled inside. Jake pulled his chair up close to her and held her right hand in his, stroking it with his thumb. She needed relaxation time. Kade and Anthony pulled out leftovers out of the fridge, and set up lunch while Jake talked with Erin. They had pizza and pasta leftovers. They needed to give Jake a chance with her. Finally, she spoke.

"Jake, I'm just numb right now actually hearing Devin say that he was trying to kill me. I mean I knew all along that was his intent, but when he said the words out loud and with such vehemence, it overwhelmed me and I just need to process it all. Plus hearing him say that I had no right to say no to him just kind of rattled me. I know you want to help but I don't know how to have you help me. I don't know how to let you in my head right now; it's very crowded up there with my thoughts and Devin's voice. I can't fathom the anger that man has against me and how cruel he is. He's sick and he needs so much help. It makes me want to hit something hard to get this anger out of my body, but that won't do anything except hurt my right side, maybe break some additional bones. I'm tense and I'm trying to let things go, but I'm not sure how to do that. I've just endured so much with his mind games already, and his sick, twisted way of doing things, and the pain he's caused me, and I don't know how much more I can take. He's back in my head with his words today and I don't know how to get him out of my head; I don't know how to let you in either."

"I understand that Erin, that's a normal reaction. I understand more than you know honey. He is a very cruel man and the system has failed not only you, to protect you, but its failed Devin as well." Jake watched her for a bit in silence. She hadn't yet made eye contact with him and he needed her to look at him.

"Erin, can you look at me please honey?" She took a shaky breath and finally looked up at Jake. He could see the tears in her eyes. She was trying to be so brave and so together, but inside there was much turmoil. He didn't want her to retreat from him and lock herself into her own world. He held her gaze and used his free hand to hold her chin while his other hand stroked her hand. Touch was important right now. She needed to know they were all there for her.

"Erin, please don't let what he said push you back out on the ledge you were hovering on before. You've known for a while now that Devin is sick and twisted, and what he said today just proves how ill he is. The system not only failed to protect you and Erica, its failed Devin too. He needs a lot of help and he needs an outlet for his clearly mixed up ideas on how to treat women. He needs to talk with a professional. Devin doesn't understand that women are people and not a possession for his enjoyment. You have survived all he did to you over the years and you are stronger for it, and my goal is to keep you here and thriving.   You let me in when Devin was stalking you so please let me in now too. I haven't changed. I'm still Jake, someone who wants to make sure you are ok Erin. You are a survivor. Erica is surviving too with her own support system.   I don't know if there are others, but hopefully with your bravery and testimony we can ensure that Devin can't hurt anyone else ever again. You are a survivor Erin; this is something we already knew, but you need to believe it too honey. I know it's a shock to hear him actually say it out loud, but you are stronger than this. I'm pretty sure you knew what his intent was when he hit you. You told me you saw the anger in his eyes. Remember that if you give into the words he said you let Devin win and the demons will take over, smother you and take you down to the depths with them. Let's not let the words dictate your life honey." She reached over to hug Jake. He wrapped her in his arms. She needed to hold him right now, needed to feel his arms around her, and she held him hard. Tears trickled down her cheeks. He was right, she knew that, but it didn't make it any easier.

"You're right Jake. I know you're right, but that doesn't make it any easier to accept. I think I just needed to process the words and maybe I can work out a little this afternoon to try and relieve the stress of those words. I won't let him win, I won't let the demons back in, that I promise you, and I won't retreat away from you all, but I'm needing to figure out how to deal with what I heard in court this morning, and not let it affect me. It's kind of thrown me off my game again. The words were so clear from his mouth and right now they are lodged in my brain, along with all Devin's anger toward me. I keep asking myself if I did this to Devin and caused him to be this way. I thought I was a good person, but today made me stop and wonder, question all that I am. Did I do this? Did I drive Devin to be this way?" Jake nodded and released her, as she started to pull back, to sit back in her chair. She let the tears trickle down her cheeks and she looked away to the ocean to try and bring herself back to some sort of center. She spent a few minutes deep breathing.

"Erin, this is not your fault, you did not do this; you don't have the much power honey. Please factor that into your thinking. You did not cause Devin to be this way; we don't know what caused Devin to be the way he is. Only Devin and God know the real reason. You are not responsible for his actions. You are only responsible for who you are and what you do, how you react to any situation. Remember the song *'Man in the Mirror?'* You can only change yourself, and you can control your reactions to the words Devin said today in court. This is not on you, and I can see how you think that, but it's not true. Again you don't have that much power darlin'. Please remember that." She nodded but the tears continued to trickle down her cheeks. She just couldn't look at Jake right now; she was embarrassed that she was so weak. She needed time to process and the ocean and beach calmed her considerably. She focused on her breathing.

Anthony and Kade joined them, when Jake motioned to them, and they had some lunch. Erin talked with them and tried to explain what she was feeling. She did eat lunch which was different from last time, but she seemed a million miles away. They knew she was processing the words she heard today. Jake, Kade and Anthony tried to help her sort through everything and she talked herself back into her normal, somewhat. She needed to not worry her guys, so she figured out how to hide the pain and make herself present and somewhat happy. She put a smile on her face and she tried to be present in the moment. She needed to figure this out but she needed to let them know she was ok. Jake told her again that she was not the cause of Devin's illness, but he could see she didn't really believe him. She said she realized that Devin was a monster and she didn't realize just how sick and twisted he was until today. She assured them that she was ok, but perhaps needed a bit of a workout later to try and relieve some of the stress. Jake realized that she said and did all the right things but she really didn't believe it wasn't her fault.

She spent the afternoon talking with Jake under hypnosis and working out in the gym with her boys. She pounded with her good hand on the punching bag, visualizing Devin's face. Jake held the bag so it wouldn't knock her out of her wheelchair. She had to relieve her anger and stress at Devin. While she was pounding the bag with her right hand, she was praying to God for divine intervention; praying for an answer to all of her questions. Jake could see the wheels turning in her head. Finally, after thirty minutes of punching and exerting herself, she broke through her own anger and the tears started to pour down her cheeks. It was like a faucet turning on. Erin stopped punching the bag and Jake watched the rivers of tears pouring down her cheeks. He called for Anthony. Anthony gathered her into his arms, moving her to his lap on the training table, and held her until her tears were done. She clung to him and let the pain wash over her. He rocked her and soothed her. She cried until the tears were spent from her system. She was physically and mentally wrung out.

"Erin, honey, tell us what you're thinking right now." Anthony invited when she quieted down. All three of them were gathered around her. Kade brought her tissues and she tried to pull herself back together.

"Anthony, Jake, Kade, I think I just realized that by holding onto my anger for Devin is only hurting me and making me nuts. I know that's what you were trying to tell me earlier Jake, but I needed to figure it all out for myself. While I was hitting the bag I was asking God for guidance, some divine intervention, maybe answers to all my what if questions. I got my guidance and answers in spades!" She took a deep breath and tried to compose herself. The boys waited patiently.

"I grew up in a world where you learned to turn the other cheek and forgive someone who has wronged you, no matter what they did wrong to you, or how much they hurt you and how many times they continued to hurt you. Sometimes though, that's so much easier said than done." She paused and took another deep breath before she could go on.

"One passage from the Bible kept repeating itself in my head over and over again; that passage said that you have to forgive seventy times seven in any situation. I just realized, after I punched the bag hard enough and long enough, that I need to be the bigger person in this situation and forgive because that's the only way I can move forward." She took a deep shuddering breath. None of them said anything but let her continue when she was ready.

"I think I am finally realizing that Devin is really sick and he needs help in the worst way, but he won't accept help because he doesn't know how to respect people or more specifically, women, he doesn't respect himself either, and he doesn't see the sickness inside himself. He sees women, especially me as a possession to own, something that he can use and abuse for his own pleasure, like he did with Erica. He doesn't think enough of himself either to get help, so he can't see that what he's done is wrong. I can't change him, I can't make him want to get better, I can't help him be a better person, and that's what I was trying to do with the restraining orders, with the times I confronted him, had him arrested. I was naïve enough to think I could change him or convince him to change. But what I realized today is that I can only change myself, I have to be the change agent here for me, and I have to forgive him to move away from this anger and hurt, to let go. Change only comes from the face I see in the mirror every morning; I see that now clearly. I can only change myself. If I can't live with myself, with that face I see in the mirror, then I need to change myself, my thinking, so that I can live with who I am. I'm a good person. I did not do this to Devin. I did hear you Jake." Jake was smiling; Kade and Anthony revealed their surprise.

"Exactly Erin. Devin has no hold over you unless you let him; by you holding onto your anger and hatred toward him, you have given him power over you. I'm so proud of you." Jake said and came over to hug her. "Tears are cleansing aren't they?" He looked at her and held her gaze, held her head between his hands.

"Yep. Thanks Jake, thank you all. I'm sorry for the tears and for making you worry about me yet again. I had to work through all of this for myself. Sometimes I need to wear myself out to see things from a different perspective." She hugged Anthony and tried to let all the stress of the last few months wash over her. "I need to get through Devin's trial, but I can finally see the light in the distance, and this time it's not a train in the tunnel barreling toward me! It feels like the weight I've been carrying on my shoulders just lifted off and I can finally be free. I feel lighter than I have in a long time." She hugged each one of them and they headed to the living room to relax a little. Erin slept through the night with no nightmares and no help from Mariah's magic pills. She was wrapped in the arms of her love. She was healing both physically and mentally.

*****

Thursday afternoon found Anthony, Erin, Jake and Kade at Ink, Inc. Erin was smiling and happier than any of them ever remembered seeing her. She had the weight lifted off her shoulders and she oozed sunshine. Kade was finishing up his client's artwork which was absolutely beautiful, Alex had just finished his last client for the day, and Michael was prepping for Erin. Erin had made lunch of calzones and salad, so they all joined together in the break room to enjoy some food and conversation. Erin realized she had an amazing family and they all loved her. That made her warm and gooey inside, but surprised that she found someone as wonderful as Anthony to love her. She never expected to fall in love, never expected to be happy, but she was out of this world happy!

"Erin, are you ready?" Michael asked, smiling, breaking into her thoughts.

"As ready as I will ever be Michael." She was deep breathing and trying to keep the butterflies at bay.

They ate lunch together and talked about the upcoming weddings. Erin told them her goal was to be up on her feet by the time the two brothers got married. She had a few weeks to do that. Alex told her that even if she was still in a wheelchair it was going to be a great celebration. She asked them about the ceremonies and they told her about what they knew. Cassi wanted to do a lot of the food herself, and Erin told Alex that she would love to help Cassi and him out. Michael said that he and Mariah wanted to do most of their stuff on their own too, so Erin offered her help to them as well. They told her they would pass that along to their ladies. Both weddings were going to be held at their mom and dad's house.

"Erin, darlin', come with me and we'll get set up." Michael took her hand and helped wheel her to his work area. Anthony helped his brothers clean up from lunch and then joined Erin and Michael. "Erin, trust me honey. This is the easy part. You've been through so much pain already honey, this is not going to hurt a bit. I promise." Erin smiled at him; her eyes were sparkling. Michael loved seeing her so happy and her eyes reflected that happiness.

"I'm excited but just a little bit scared Michael. I trust you though."

They spent the next ten minutes deciding on the right chains and the right finials for the barbells. Erin picked the really delicate silver chains and she selected, with Michael's help, the rose shaped rhinestones for the finials on the barbells. The roses had delicate crystals so would match the chains. "Those are going to look amazing Miss Erin." Michael said. "I'm going to take these and put them in alcohol to clean and sanitize them." He got up and put the pieces she chose in an alcohol bath and started to set up his tray. Anthony came in at that moment and walked over to where Erin was sitting.

"Hi beautiful." He leaned in for a kiss.

"Hi handsome. We just picked out the pieces of my piercings." She smiled at him. "Michael is cleaning them now."

"Ok Erin, darlin', we need to get you ready. Shirt off!" He smiled at her.

"Where do I need to be?"

"You can sit in my chair here. Anthony can hold you in his lap. Is that what you want?" She nodded. She reached up and pulled off her t-shirt. She had worn a camisole and no bra under it. Michael loved the shape of her figure; she was so beautiful. Anthony sat in the chair and Michael lifted Erin onto his lap; Anthony helped her get settled in his lap against his chest with her casted leg resting on Anthony's. When Michael was ready, she removed her camisole too.

"Miss Erin, you are so beautiful. This is going to look exquisite." Michael said. She took a deep breath and tried to keep her nerves at bay. She concentrated on Anthony's arm around her and the fact that she was sitting in his lap. She was trying not to hurt him with the cast on her leg, which was resting on Anthony's leg. Her body burned with fire where she connected with Anthony. He had one arm around her waist with his hand resting on her flat belly. "These piercings are going to look amazing on you."

Michael instructed her to relax and breathe normally. He cleaned her nipples and they puckered from the cold and from Michael's perusal. He moved the tray of supplies closer to him and prepared for the first piercing. Erin relaxed her casted arm on the chair's armrest, and grasped Anthony's hand in her right, threading their fingers together. Anthony whispered sweet nothings in her ear and she forced herself to relax while Michael held her breast in his hand and pierced the first nipple. It was a moment of white hot pain and then nothing except cold from the metal. Michael connected the chain and the finials and repeated the process with the second breast. Anthony's grip on her tightened and she tried to keep relaxed. Michael finished the second piercing, cleaned her breasts with alcohol again and put antibiotic ointment on them.

"Wow, you are beautiful Erin. Those chains are sexy as hell. Anthony you're going to love this view." Michael exclaimed. Erin blushed. "Just sit in Anthony's arms for a bit honey. Let your nipples get used to the new hardware." She nodded. "We'll wait a bit, let you acclimate to the piercings, and then I'll get pictures so we can add these to the web site. You did great Erin." Michael kissed her cheek. Erin leaned back and tipped her face to Anthony for a kiss. The cold air was making her shiver just a bit.

"Thanks for holding me my handsome hero. I tried not to move too much and I tried not to hurt you."

"You did great beautiful. I don't think too many people sit that still and let Michael do his work. You did amazing." She smiled at him and kissed him again. She was very aware of his body under hers. His body was responding to her nearness and the fact that she was sitting in his arms shirtless. She missed being in Anthony's arms with being in the hospital and in casts. Anthony was amazed at how comfortable she was in her nakedness in his arms. He was so proud of her. She was definitely his weakness, his addiction.

"Ok Erin. Let's get you set for your picture!" Michael said as he came back in about ten minutes later. "Anthony, Erin, your brothers and Jake want to see how these turned out. Is that ok?" Michael asked them, as he checked his work again.

"Erin, are you ok with Alex, Kade and Jake seeing you and your new hardware?" She nodded and blushed. "I'm here with you. It's just that Michael has not done this type of piercing before, so everyone is curious. You're kind of a novelty right now because you are the first to have this type of piercing." Erin took a deep breath and smiled at Anthony and Michael.

"I'm fine with it. I'm just shy you know, and never thought of myself as anything special, but this is art and I think it needs to be seen. You both make me feel special. As long as you're ok with it my handsome Anthony." She blushed again, he nodded; she sat up straighter in Anthony's arms. Michael smiled and called the three in.

"Nice work bro." Alex said. "Erin, darlin' it looks amazing. Maybe with our website and people seeing how beautiful they look Michael will get more clients to do it." She smiled at him.

"Erin, darlin', thanks for doing this. You look beautiful and those chains are incredibly sexy." Jake said, which cause the blush to deepen on her cheeks.

"Erin, wow!" Kade said. "We didn't hear you scream either! You did great."

"Do you usually hear people scream when Michael pierces them?" She asked shocked. That got a laugh from everyone. Erin had forgotten momentarily she was sitting here amidst five men without her shirt on. She seemed at peace and ok with it; she was really relaxed in Anthony's arms.

"You know Erin, the big football player types usually moan and grumble when Michael pierces them. A lot of them do the nipple piercings with no problems and then come back for the Jacob's ladder piercing. The last one usually gets them and they aren't quiet about it. We didn't hear you at all. We didn't even know Michael had done the piercings." Erin smiled at them.

"Ok I need to get pictures. Usually I have my person standing, but maybe I can do this another way."

"Michael, I can stand on my good leg. You all just need to get me there and once I'm balanced the guys can let go and you can take your pictures." Erin said.

Jake and Kade picked her up out of Anthony's lap so Anthony could get up, Alex moved the wheelchair out of the way, and Anthony moved to where he could hold Erin up in front of Michael's photo board. Erin was very aware of the warm, large hands on her bare skin and she tried to not react. Jake put her gently on her good leg on the floor while Kade balanced her; Anthony held her right hand, wrapped his arm around her waist, and Erin tentatively put her left leg on the floor to balance, and made sure she was standing up straight. Jake held her left arm with the cast up and out of the way; she pulled her shoulders back and lifted her head which raised her chest up and in a good spot for the pictures. Michael moved her to get the best light and prettiest picture, and had the guys step aside, all except Anthony and Jake who were out of range of the camera. He took his pictures and made them look amazing. They moved Erin back to Michael's workspace, Michael checked his work one more time, put more ointment on the piercings, added non-stick bandages with paper tape to hold them in place, and Anthony helped her get dressed. He sat with her while Michael gathered up his tools and then sat down to tell Erin about the piercings.

"Ok Miss Erin, these will take a few weeks to heal completely. You need to use this liquid cleaner every morning and you need to move the bars around too. Roll them and slide them back and forth so that they won't heal into the tissue. Put the ointment on and replace the bandages. No bra for the next two weeks. Ok?" She nodded.

"Erin, honey, I will help you since one of your hands is in a cast." Anthony said. She nodded and smiled at him. All the men in her life were sorry to see her cover up her beautiful body. Alex realized why she wore the loose clothes she did, because of Devin's reaction. Jake realized that Erin drew people to her so it was no wonder why Devin was obsessed with her. She was beautiful and sexy as hell, and she didn't know how beautiful she was, or that she drew people to her. That was the best kind of beautiful in his book. He tried to change his way thinking. He really needed to find a girl of his own. He'd been alone for far too long. Erin and her sunshine just made him ache with want. Kade was thinking the same thing. He needed to get his libido under some sort of control. She was Anthony's fiancée and her close proximity to him was making him nuts. He just reacted to her. It had been much too long since he'd been with a girl too.

Chapter Eight

Erin finished the website for the Ink, Inc. and she finished Kyle's introduction to the city. She spent Friday morning early rendering the pieces and she called Kyle just before lunchtime. He told her he would watch the videos and get back with her before Friday was over! She was so excited. She emailed the pieces to Kyle and turned her attention back to the website. She finished adding all the video components, checked each button that she had created using pictures of the shells and rocks she had collected from Kade's beach, and made sure that all of it worked.

Jake and Kade headed to the impound yard to clean out Erin's car, well what was left of her car, take pictures and prepare for her to go to the DMV. They met the insurance adjuster there to figure out next steps. Jake discovered that the side mirror had come off the car in the impact and they wondered if that was what hit Erin in the head. It had ended up in the backseat, so it was possible based on trajectory and where it landed. He also saw the finial from Devin's truck and wondered if that hit her too. She had two bruises on her face. Her bruises were pretty colorful and evident; still very deep purple so they would take a bit to heal. Uncle Mory helped them to figure out what Erin's next steps were. Once the adjuster was done, Kade talked to the owner of the salvage yard and he wanted to purchase Erin's car. Kade told him they would get back to him soon.

Anthony, Alex and Michael all had appointments at Ink, Inc. on Friday, so Erin was alone in Kade's house. She had figured out how to get from the sofa to her wheelchair, and she used her good foot and arm to get herself around. She was sore in her arm and her leg, and the joints of her hip and shoulder let her know she still needed to let them heal. She wasn't patient, and there were things she couldn't do on her own, but it didn't stop her from trying. Kade and Jake had left her with snacks, water, her diet pepsi and her computer.

After lunch, Erin made her way into the kitchen and started pulling something together for dinner. She hadn't cooked in a week, so it was time to get back to normal. Jake and Kade still hadn't returned from wherever they went, and Anthony wasn't home either. Erin pulled the pork loin out of the freezer, defrosted it some in the microwave while she mixed up a dry rub to put on the pork. She preheated the oven and mixed up her spices, taste testing along the way. She added a bit of brown sugar to make a caramelized crust on the pork too. Once she was satisfied, she pulled the pork loin out of the microwave, scored the top and sides, smeared yellow mustard on it and covered it in the spice rub and brown sugar. She wrapped it in foil, put it in a roasting pan and stuck it in the oven. Next, she washed and prepped her potatoes, which she also put in the oven to bake, and cleaned up the kitchen. Just as she finished prepping dinner her phone rang.

"This is Erin."

"Hi Erin, its Kyle."

"Oh hi Kyle! Did you get the videos?"

"I did Erin. They are fabulous. You really know how to tell a story, my story!"

"Do you want any changes?"

"Nope. It's perfect. I do want you to be at our pre-season game on Friday in two weeks though. I know you're still in casts and a wheelchair from your accident, but perhaps your fiancée Anthony and your protectors can bring you. I'm really hoping you are feeling better!"

"I'd love that Kyle, and I know my Anthony would enjoy it too. I'm healing. I'm not patient and so I push myself to and past my limits, but I'll get there. That's one of my flaws! How do I get tickets?"

"I'll send you tickets. You and your family will be my guests. How many do you need?" They talked for a bit longer, Erin told him she needed eight tickets and Kyle told her he would send tickets over to her. She gave him the address for Kade's house, and she told him she would send the completed pieces to her boss and to the PR folks as soon as they finished their conversation. Kyle asked about Devin and where things stood. She told him about the charges he tried to press against her, the coming trial, and he told her to stay strong. He told her that she was tough and she could handle it!

Kyle was working with his new team not only on his kids' clinics, but also to help advocate for people like Erin and the lack of help restraining orders gave. Erin suggested that the team get in touch with Judge Kafner, telling him that the judge was working to create new legislation. Kyle told her he was proud of her and to keep surviving! Finally, they signed off and Erin sent the video files to Terry. She called him to tell him the first stage of the project was finished. He told her he got the videos and would get them to the PR team. They wanted to launch Kyle's introduction on Monday morning. Terry told her he was sending the second project information for Kyle and the Raptors to her drive. Terry made sure Erin was doing ok and not too much.

Once Erin had completed her work for Terry she returned to the kitchen. She started to pull stuff out of the fridge for a salad, and she grabbed her cookbook to make something for dessert. She made her way to the pantry and discovered she had some cake mixes in there, so instead of making something from scratch she made a chocolate cake. She could just start to smell the pork roast in the oven. The boys would be surprised that she had dinner almost ready. Her phone rang just as she pulled the cake from the oven.

"This is Erin."

"Hi beautiful. You sound busy. What's going on?"

"Hi handsome. I'm making dinner. I just finished my project for Kyle Hunt and that's been emailed to my boss. Kade and Jake are still gone doing whatever they are doing this afternoon and I thought I should make dinner."

"Wow. How are you feeling darlin'?"

"I'm sore handsome. My entire body hurts. It hurts to propel myself in the wheelchair, but it's good for me to move my muscles and keep my strength up. I'm not complaining though. I miss you my Anthony!"

They talked for a bit and Anthony told her he was heading home shortly. She let him know the website was finished and she wanted to show it to him and Kade, and then send it to Alex and Michael for approval. They could launch it as early as Sunday if they were ok with it. They signed off and Anthony told her he was heading out the door to come home. She told him to drive safely.

Erin returned to the kitchen to check on her dinner and to frost her cake. She moved her casted leg off the extension, stood on her good leg, got plates out of the cabinet and then wheeled herself to the table to set it. Just as she finished the setting the table she heard a noise outside in the front yard. It sounded like a vehicle, but not one she was familiar with. She had gotten used to Kade's truck and the motorcycles, but this didn't sound like any of them. It didn't sound like Jake or Kade, or even Anthony. It was a vehicle Erin didn't recognize.   She peered out the window keeping out of site. The person getting out of the vehicle, and walking from the driveway to the door did not look familiar. Quickly she pulled out her phone and called Kade.

"Hey Erin."

"Kade," she whispered. "Someone is coming to the front door and I don't know who it is. Are you and Jake close to home?"

"Erin honey, stay out of sight. I'll answer the ring on my phone and see who it is. Don't panic darlin'." Kade was trying to reassure her and they were trying to get home. "Stay on the phone with me honey." Erin could hear the person coming to the porch. She wasn't breathing and she pressed herself against the wall. He rang the doorbell which rang on Kade's phone. "Hold on honey." He answered the doorbell and the guy said he was looking for Jake. Kade told him that he and Jake weren't home at the moment, but if he could wait about ten minutes they would be back to the house.

The guy said he would wait in his car for them. Kade signed off with the guy at the door and Erin heard his steps retreat. She started to breathe again. She kept thinking to herself wondering if life was ever going to be normal again.

"Erin, darlin', its ok. That guy is one of Jake's SEAL buddies, and Jake's employee. He's here for another job. We're pulling into the driveway right now. Jake will talk with him and I'll use my key and come in. Breathe honey." Erin thanked him and tried to quell her fear.

She headed back to the kitchen to check on dinner but she was on high alert. Her nerves had kicked into overdrive. She knew her fear was irrational because Devin was in prison awaiting trial, but it didn't lessen the impact of someone unknown coming to the door. The pork roast was just about done and the potatoes were fully cooked, so she pulled them out and scooped out the insides to make them into twice baked potatoes. While she was working she heard Kade's key in the lock. It sounded like Anthony was home too. She tried to fight her panic of earlier, but with things still up in the air with Devin it was hard to let down. She kept reminding herself to breathe normally. Everything was good. Just breathe in and out slowly.

"Something smells good in here!" Kade said as he headed into the kitchen. He tried to make sure Erin knew he was headed her way. He knew she was already on the edge of her sanity with everything that happened.

"Just dinner." Came the response from Erin. She was trying to come back to normal and not panicky mode, making her voice conversational and light.

"Wow Erin. We could smell good stuff from the driveway. What's for dinner honey?"

"Seasoned pork roast, twice baked potatoes, salad, and cake for dessert."

"You even set the table." Anthony exclaimed. "I'm not going to ask how you got the dishes down from the cabinet." He walked over and leaned down for a kiss. She smiled and bit her bottom lip. Erin wrapped her good arm around him and pulled him closer. He could feel her nerves, her trembling. "Thanks sugar." She smiled at him.

"I need to check on dinner and get the roast out of the oven." She let go of Anthony and tried to move to the oven. Kade intercepted her and took the hot pads from her lap.

"I've got this Erin. You've done a lot today. Let me help you honey." She smiled up at him and backed her wheelchair up. Anthony headed to put his stuff away and wash his hands. Erin loved that all of the brothers knew how to cook.

"Kade, does Jake's guest want to join us for dinner? I made more than enough."
Erin asked. "Sorry I panicked earlier." She smiled at him.

"I'll go ask him once I get all this out of the oven. Are you sure Erin?" She
nodded and headed to the cabinet to get another plate down. Kade headed to intercept
Jake and Ryan. Anthony watched in fascination as Erin positioned her wheelchair,
locked the wheels, moved her casted leg and stood up on her good leg. She took down
another plate, and a glass. She sat it on the counter while she rearranged herself back in
her wheelchair. She then grabbed the plate, silverware and glass off the counter,
putting it in her lap, and headed to the dining room. Anthony just shook his head. She
was so independent and it was amazing to watch her. She took such good care of him
and his brothers. It was slow going because she didn't have both hands to use for the
wheelchair, but she was creative. Anthony had to give her that much.

Kade knocked on the cottage door and Jake welcomed him inside. Kade invited
Ryan to join them for dinner. Jake had briefed Ryan on Erin's situation. Ryan was here
for another case that just wrapped up and was reporting to Jake, but also wanted to
help if possible on this one. Jake and Ryan accompanied Kade to the main house. Jake
introduced Ryan to Erin and they all sat down to enjoy the dinner that Erin prepared.
Kade watched Erin. She was more settled with everything since her tearful breakdown
the other evening. She conversed easily with everyone and she made Ryan feel at
home. Once dinner was done Anthony helped her clear the table and do the dishes.
Jake and Ryan headed back to the cottage and Kade headed to his office to work on
some paperwork. Anthony then helped her with laundry, sheets this time.

*****

"Kade," Erin said as she knocked tentatively on the office door an hour after
dinner. "Are you busy?"

"Just doing some much needed paperwork. What's up Erin?"

"Well, if you and Anthony have a few minutes, I finished the website for Ink, Inc.
and I'd like for you both to walk through it and see if it works. It doesn't have to be
now if you need to finish your paperwork, but when you have time. I don't want to
interrupt you; you look very busy." She felt really bad that she interrupted him.

"You finished it?" She nodded as he looked up at her, and smiled at the awe in
his voice. She could see the surprise in his features too.

"I have it set up in the living room. Perhaps when you finish your paperwork
later, or need a break, you and Anthony can go through it and then I can send the mock
up to Alex and Michael. Once you all have approved it we can launch it." She started
to back up out of his office to give him space. She was trying to get the wheelchair

maneuvered so she could leave him to do his work, but she wasn't being successful in getting herself out of his office. She was exhausted and sore. She really wanted him to have whatever time he needed.

"Wow." He finished two pieces of paper on his desk, filed them and stood up. "Lead the way Miss Erin." She smiled at him and turned her chair around slowly, Kade reached out to help, and they headed to the living room. Anthony had not yet told Erin that the four brothers owned their own winery too, so that was the paperwork Kade was finishing up. They just did the inking and piercing as a hobby, but it was a profitable hobby. Their wines were served all over the world and in high demand from some of the world's best restaurants and bars. Erin had never asked why the KAMA Mission Mountain wines were the only wines in the wine fridge. Kade knew Erin was perceptive and it wouldn't take her long to figure it out. He hoped Anthony would tell her before it became something between them.

She brought up the splash page on the TV and handed the mouse to Anthony. Kade and Anthony clicked on all the links and looked over every piece of the website including the final video for Michael's piercings. Erin had taken the pictures of the shells she collected and made them into the buttons for each artists' page. She used the rocks for the guest book, the rate card, and the appointment schedule, and she use sand as the background. They were impressed that she "cut out" the pictures of the shells and made them step off the page with shading. They almost looked 3-D. Kade clicked on the guest book link and was surprised to find seven comments already on the site.

"Erin, honey, how did we get these?"

"I asked Michael if any letters or cards had come in to the shop for you all and your work. He gave me these seven which were recently received and I thought it would be good to pepper the site with comments already added from satisfied customers." She smiled at her two boys.

"That's good thinking. I like this." Kade and Anthony read through them. "I wonder why Michael never told us we had these letters from customers."

"Maybe he was saving them for me to use on the website?!" Erin added. "I mean I asked Michael if any comments or letters had come in. I told him I would like to start the guest book with some comments."

Kade and Anthony told her they really liked what she did and asked what the next step was. Erin told them she needed to send the website to Alex and Michael, and then they all needed to decide what they wanted their internet address, their domain name to be. Neither of them understood, and Erin could see the confusion, so Erin took her mouse and keyboard and searched for domain names based on their shop's name.

She showed them what was available and let them know that once they chose a name she would purchase the domain name for five years, with renewals, and could upload the site and launch it. That would be the address they put on their business cards. She told both of them they also needed to determine if they wanted email addresses associated with the site. She explained that she had connections with a hosting location and would add their website to the space where her own current website was located. Her contract allowed her three websites on the server and she only had one currently. Kade didn't understand a word she said, but nodded at her. Erin could see the confusion and tried not to smile. Both Kade and Anthony needed to just trust Erin with the work. They had no idea what any of what she just said meant.

"Erin, let me call Alex and Michael and see if they can either come over tonight or talk with us all on the phone. We can settle this tonight and maybe launch the site tomorrow. Not sure how to do that, but I'm sure you can help us with that too." Erin smiled at him. Anthony called his brothers and they were out and about. They told Anthony they would be there in thirty minutes.   All the brothers approved the site, selected the domain name they wanted, and were giddy when Erin told them she would make it live tomorrow morning. She did her magic, while they were watching, to purchase the domain name and prepared to FTP the pages so it would be there and ready. It would be live in the morning. Erin told them she would make sure the site popped up as people searched local businesses too. All the brothers were impressed that she could actually do that.

******

The DA had contacted Kade on Friday afternoon to let him know the trial would begin on Tuesday morning and he needed all of them present in the courtroom. Kade told his family and asked Michael to not schedule Kade or Anthony until they knew exactly how long they would be out. Kade and Jake told Erin and all three of them worked to keep Erin sane. They couldn't take a motorcycle ride this time, but Erin suggested that they go over and pack up some of her personal belongings at the house. Erin worked to launch the Ink, Inc. website early Saturday morning and then texted all the brothers to let them know it was live! She also told Michael he would need to check the email daily because people could now request an appointment there! She told him if he needed her help she would set it up on his computer in the office.

Saturday afternoon Erin's phone rang and it was Drake. They were at her house packing up some of her belongings. He really wanted to see her house. She asked if he was free, and he said he was heading their way now. Erin let her boys know that Drake was coming to see the house. Jake, Ryan and Kade worked to pack up Erin's electronics that she had disconnected for them, while she sorted through her files and packed up her kitchen with Anthony's help. Drake arrived and Anthony and Kade walked him through the house and the yard. He asked lots of questions that Anthony was able to answer from living in the house with Erin. Drake told him how much he loved the yard and the location. Drake said the house was perfect.

"Erin, this is an amazing house. I love it." Drake exclaimed.

"I'm glad you like it. Is it what you are looking for?"

"I think it is, it's so homey. I have a wonderful lady in my life, and we need a place to call home. We really need to get settled. My lady has been through a lot of late." She told him that she could relate.

They talked a bit more and Drake asked if she was taking the furniture or leaving it. She asked if he wanted it, and so he wandered through the rooms to determine what he wanted of her furniture. Drake told her that he didn't have much yet, and if she was willing, he would take all the furniture she was willing to leave with the house. They decided that they could do this sale with Uncle Mory's help, avoiding a realtor's fees. That made both Erin and Drake happy. Erin told him the inside and outside was recently repainted and the inspection of the house earlier in the year showed no damage, so it was in really good shape.

Erin asked about his girlfriend and if she might want to see the house before he decided. Drake told her that Erica was dealing with some heavy duty stuff right now and with the trial looming, he didn't want to burden her with any more decisions. In the course of their conversation Erin realized that Erica was Drake's girlfriend; Erin asked if she was ok. Erin told Drake that the person that hit her on Friday was the person who abused Erica. Drake was shocked and angry. Erin and Drake talked at length about what she and Erica were going through and she let Drake know she was here if Erica needed to talk as well. Erin told him that Erica and she were going to make sure Devin paid for the crimes. They shared a lot and Drake told Erin he was trying to help Erica heal. She thanked him for that.

They decided that they would work on the house sale after the trial, since all of them needed to be in court on Tuesday. Erin told Drake that her goal was to take clippings of all her roses and start them for her new life with Anthony. Drake told her that was cool with him. They would see what all Drake wanted her to leave in the house, and would make decisions on everything after the trial was settled. He told her he would be in court when Erica testified and wished her the best. Drake left and her guys put boxes into Kade's truck.

"Erin, honey, you said you wanted to take starts of your roses. How do we do that?" Kade asked.

"Kade, I need to figure out where I can plant them once they root. They will root fast and I don't want be without a place to plant."

"You can plant them around my house, your house for now! I haven't done a lot with landscaping and I would love to have your beautiful roses all around my house." He smiled at her.

"I would love that. I have been kind of designing your gardens. Sorry Kade. It's what I do. I see a blank canvas and I have to fill it!" She blushed and pulled out a piece of paper from her pocket and showed Kade what she wanted to do in his yard. He looked over her drawing and smiled.

"You can fill my yard with flowers Miss Erin, anytime. I would love that." He hugged her. "So, how do we do this?" Anthony, Jake and Ryan gathered around too.

She explained that she needed twenty potatoes, a plastic tub that was rectangular and deep, kind of like a dish pan, and water. Kade, Anthony, Jake and Ryan looked at her puzzled. She went on to tell them that she would take a nice size cutting from each of her roses and stick them into each potato on one end that she cut off. She would mark on the potato which rose it was. She would cut off the other end and stand all the potatoes up in the bucket and add water. The roses would use the potato as soil to root and grow, and the potatoes would absorb the water. Once they had roots she could plant them in the gardens at Kade's house. The potato would eventually disintegrate leaving the roses to bloom and grow. All of them were very impressed with what she described.

"Erin, we'll pick up potatoes on our way home and tomorrow we can come back and do all the cuttings. Does that work?" She nodded and smiled at them.

They finished packing up Erin's personal stuff, taking the pictures off the walls, and loaded all of that into Kade's pickup. They swung through a drive-through on the way home and had dinner together. Kade made room in the back empty bedroom to store her boxes. He also told her she could move her kitchen stuff into his kitchen. She was almost free of the house that held so many bad, as well as good, memories. They could all see the relief in her shoulders as the weight was leaving her. Erin was settled with her decision to sell her home and move her good memories to Kade's house.

Sunday afternoon the boys arranged to have Cassi and Mariah come over and spend a couple hours with Erin. They talked about the trial, and how Erin was feeling, and then Erin changed the conversation to the upcoming weddings. Cassi said that her baker had pulled out from doing their cake, so Erin offered to make her cake. Erin pulled out pictures of the two wedding cakes she had already made and Cassi was thrilled. Cassi chose the champagne-orange cake flavor, and after the trial they would go to the party store and pick out the decorations. Erin asked about the groom's cake, and Cassi asked if that was a thing! Finally they agreed that Erin would make that cake too in Alex's favorite flavor, Red Velvet.

Erin asked Mariah if she wanted Erin to make her cake too. Mariah jumped at the chance to have Erin make both cakes for her wedding. Mariah decided on champagne-orange with French vanilla alternating layers, and Dutch chocolate for the groom's cake. She asked them to think about the decorations for both cakes, and if they wanted round layers, square layers or octagonal layers. They told her they would have the pictures of the cakes they wanted after the trial was over. Erin was pretty excited. She loved to bake and she loved to create with frosting, fondant, modeling chocolate and more. She loved to help her girls.

*****

Tuesday morning found the group heading to the courthouse. Anthony helped Erin dress in a t-shirt dress because none of her pants would fit over the cast, but she opted for a pair of running shorts underneath to make her feel a little more secure in the wheelchair with her leg up. She was healing well from her piercings and today she was able to put her corset on under the dress. Anthony was helping her every day to move and clean the piercings, and she told him they didn't hurt at all. Anthony took a bed pillow from her boxes in the storage room and put that into the wheelchair with her for her arm. She was trying to stay calm and centered and she made herself smile, breathe and relax.

"Ready to go?" Jake asked. They piled into the pickup and headed to the courthouse.

*****

"All rise. The honorable Judge Kafner presiding." Everyone around her stood and she prayed for a good outcome, and everyone to stay safe. She found herself praying for Devin too; she wanted him to get help when this ordeal was all over.

For the rest of the morning the judge and the attorneys seated a jury made up of mostly women. After lunch Mr. Donaldson presented the opening remarks for the prosecution that outlined all the charges against Devin and that the evidence would show beyond a shadow of a doubt, the guilt of the defendant, followed by the opening remarks of the defense. Richard and Mark were both present to help Devin; Richard received a waiver from the Ethics Committee to handle this trial for his client. Devin again pleaded not guilty, but the list of charges had grown with the vehicle accident. Erin was prepared for Devin to be in the courtroom and she did her best to stay centered on Anthony and her team. Devin looked terrible; Erin could see that when she risked a glance his way. Jake told her that Devin had been in solitary confinement since the last hearing and the car accident. The judge told the two sides that she wanted the prosecution to present their case and be wrapped up by Wednesday of next week, and then the defense had their time to present. Both sides agreed.

During the next three days Erin and her protectors were called upon in the presentation of the evidence against Devin. The defense lawyers grilled Erin on all facets of the charges and asked multiple questions about the evidence presented in the cross-examination. She never wavered from her story with all the questions they asked her, no matter how they were worded. She spent a lot of time on the witness stand for both sides. The defense was trying to trap her with their questions. She told the truth and listened intently to what they were actually asking. She didn't offer any more and didn't get upset at all. They asked her about how she protected herself and her crew, and the defense tried to make a case out of that, but the judge overruled them stating that Erin was not the one on trial here. She answered each question posed to her and she didn't lose her cool, or react other than to provide the answers. Jake was so proud of her for her professionalism.   She handled everything well.

Each night Erin was exhausted from the questioning and sitting in the wheelchair. Her team worked out with her and helped her to relieve the tension in her body. Jake did therapeutic massage, so once she was done punching the bag, they laid her on the training table and Jake rubbed her arms, shoulders, and legs, and then worked on her shoulders, hips, and range of motion. He used theraband to put pressure on her left hip and leg, and her left arm. At least they had the game on Friday night to look forward to which helped Erin get through all the days. Jake knew that the work he did with her would help her to heal faster and maybe get out of the casts sooner. Tickets for the hockey game had arrived on Thursday by courier which gave them all something fun to round out a very stressful week. Anthony invited Alex and Michael to join them. Erin invited Ryan.

Friday morning Erica was called to the stand to testify about Devin and Drake was in the courtroom to support her. Erin tried to give her support too; she squeezed Erica's hand as she went by her. Devin had two outbursts while she was testifying and the judge admonished him. The second time it happened Judge Kafner told him that the next time he would be removed from the courtroom. Richard and Mark were doing their best to keep Devin contained, but everyone could see how badly Devin needed help. Someone needed to get to the bottom of why Devin was the way he was. Something must have happened in his past to make him react this way, treat women this way. It didn't appear that Devin had much of a support system; no family was there for him. He seemed to be self-sufficient and had the money to live on and buy a house without working too much.   Yet no one in the course of the questioning ever asked the question of why Devin was the way he was, or the why behind what he did.

Friday afternoon found Erin back on the stand to answer more questions for the defense. Devin had one last outburst, demanding that Erin tell him why she kept telling him no. His lawyers could not still him at all. Devin's eyes were glassed over and he demanded an answer from Erin. Erin didn't respond, didn't react beyond a quick shocked look, waiting for the judge. She did her best to recover her professional face. Jake and Anthony watched her carefully. The judge had had enough and she asked for Devin to be removed from the courtroom. The bailiff and his assistant did that and the trial continued. Around 4 pm Judge Kafner called for a recess for the weekend. She instructed the defense to talk with their client. Court would resume at 9 am on Monday. Erin was escorted out of the witness box and she and her boys headed home. It had been a very long week.

They had dinner and changed into comfortable, warm clothes. Erin changed into sweats and a long-sleeve shirt with the Raptors jersey over the top. Anthony helped her get dressed and she rewarded him with a kiss. He helped to put one of her footies on her toes to keep them warm while they were sitting close to the ice tonight. He worked to tuck it into her cast so it would stay. Alex and Michael arrived, and soon they were ready and they piled into Kade's truck. He drove them to the stadium. Kyle had given them a parking pass too so that it would be easier to get Erin and her wheelchair into the arena.

There were people waiting to assist Kade, Jake, Ryan, Alex, Michael and Anthony with Erin. Anthony told them he would carry Erin down to the box if they could bring her wheelchair, so one of the stadium people grabbed the wheelchair while another led the way to the seats. Soon they were seated and their seats were next to the ice! In the box were stadium hotdogs in a warmer, chips and drinks for everyone. They were being treated like royalty. It was amazing.

"It's time for Raptors Hockey!" The crowd that was seated was up on their feet shouting and clapping. Erin looked around from her wheelchair and was totally amazed at the crowd. The seating in the venue was really raked so those near the top had just as good a view as she did from the ice. She wondered if they had vertigo up that high. She had her camera and took video of the arena, focusing on every angle of the venue.

"I'd like to direct your attention to center ice. This year the Raptors have a new center forward – please meet and welcome Kyle Hunt." Kyle skated to center ice and the crowd went absolutely nuts. "Some of you have seen the PR on Kyle from our website. Kyle was able to meet with a television producer from TK Productions to tell his story. Kyle, do want to say a few words?" The spotlights found Kyle from two directions and the house lights were turned off. Erin watched him standing at the center of the rink and was just amazed at how poised he was. Nothing seemed to rattle him. He was just like when she interviewed him to introduce him for the PR firm that hired TK Productions. It was amazing to watch.

"Thank you all. I'm Kyle and I'm so excited to be here with the Raptors team. As you all know every year we focus on one or two things to help with and put our team behind, in and around our community. This year we have two projects on our radar. The first is an outreach with clinics for our community youth to teach them to play hockey, how to be part of a team, and get them moving away from video games and computers, getting some exercise and fresh air." Applause from the crowd, and shouts of excitement. Kyle waited for it to settle down so he could continue.

"The second project is near and dear to my heart because it affects someone I know personally in this audience tonight; it might affect more that I am not aware of." He took a moment and waited for that to sink in. The stadium got very quiet.

"Our special guest this evening has been dealing with a situation where she had a restraining order that should have been designed to protect her, but it didn't. So, the Raptors are working with Judge Kafner, Mory Romano, the state bar association, and our legislators to design 'Erin's Law' to help protect people from those who want to hurt them. My special guest tonight is Miss Erin Bradford, the face of this legislation. She brought this to our community's attention by surviving repeated attempts by the one person who has hurt her over and over. You may have seen this in the papers and on the evening news. She's involved in the court case right now so we can't talk too much about it, but Miss Erin is the television producer who helped to introduce me to this community. As our special guest tonight she will be riding the Zamboni between periods so she can meet you all and wave to the crowd, and if I can talk her into it, she will come out on the ice with me and take a couple of laps. She's in casts on both her arm and leg from a recent car accident, but hopefully she'll allow me to bring out on the ice and introduce her to you." The crowd was cheering as Kyle left center ice and skated toward the home team's box seats. The spotlights followed him. Erin was staring at Kyle, her eyes wide and in shock, and she wasn't breathing normally. Her family was all smiles. Her hand gripped Anthony's harder. She didn't expect this at all. Her eyes never left Kyle's.

Kyle skated to a stop in front of Erin and her entourage. His microphone was still on. "Miss Erin, will you accompany me onto the ice for a couple of laps?" He held his hand out to her and the crowd chanted "Erin! Erin!" She swallowed hard and put her good hand in his. Anthony picked her up out of her chair and handed her to Kyle, telling him to take good care of her. She wrapped her non-casted arm around his shoulders so she could wave to the crowd, and prayed that Kyle wouldn't drop her.

"Ready?" Kyle smiled at her. She nodded and held on. Kyle held her like she weighed nothing and skated around the entire rink three times ending up at center ice, spraying up ice crystals when he stopped, where they were surrounded by the entire team. Their competitors, the Kings, also came out onto the ice and rallied around them. Erin stayed with Kyle through the introductions; he stood her on her good leg in front of him and she leaned on him for support. Her family smiled – Erin was so small compared to all the players. Kyle's left arm was around her waist holding her up. She high fived all the players on the team. The Kings' captain told them all, using Kyle's mic, that his team wanted to get involved too because too many women they knew had been hurt by the restraining order process. It was something every community dealt with and it needed to come to the public's attention. Every team member on both teams gave Erin a high-five and thanked her for her bravery. Erin was a little shocked, but warmed by the care and concern of all these players.

Kyle skated back to the box and handed Erin back to Anthony. She was overwhelmed but she had a blast. While she was skating with Kyle one of the stadium officials came to let Anthony, Kade, and the others know that they would come back to get her just before the end of each period and take her to the Zamboni. The official told them she would be seat belted in, could sit or stand, and would be safe. Kade relayed that to Erin when she was back with them. Finally, the game was underway. Erin had her camera and took lots of video and some stills. She had a great view of the ice and the action. The Raptors won 3 to 1. It was a hard fought victory, but the team played very well.

During one of her stints on the Zamboni a couple of ladies and their protectors came to talk to Erin's family. They told them that they too had been hurt because of the restraining orders not protecting them and wondered how they could help with making restraining orders stronger. Jake asked them to come forward to Judge Kafner after Erin's trial was over, because the legislation needed to have faces that represented it. They both agreed. Jake and Kade asked them questions to determine how vulnerable they were, and if they were safe in their life now. Both of them had their situations resolved because the men that were trying to hurt them were arrested and imprisoned on other charges. It was amazing to see the support when a team like the Raptors put their energy behind it and pushed it into the spotlight.

*****

The trial went through Thursday of the following week. All the evidence was presented and all the witnesses had been heard from, and the defense presented their information as to why Devin wasn't guilty of the charges. Again Erin wondered why Devin never took the stand in his own defense and no one asked the why behind his actions, but she had no control over that. Closing statements were made by both sides and the Judge instructed the jury for their deliberations. Court was recessed and the judge asked all parties to stay at the courthouse until 4 pm. Deliberations continued into Friday and at 3 pm Friday afternoon the jury sent a note to the judge that they had reached a unanimous decision in the case. The judge gathered everyone back to the courtroom and at 3:30 the jury foreperson read the jury's findings.

"In the matter of the state vs. Devin Traeger, this jury finds that Mr. Traeger is guilty of all nine counts charged against him."

"Thank you jury members for your work here in this case, we will decide on the sentencing next week, thank you for your service to the state. Mr. Traeger, please stand." Judge Kafner waited while Devin got to his feet. "This court, a jury of your peers, has found you guilty of all charges.   You are hereby remanded back into custody and your sentencing hearing will be held on Monday next week. Court is adjourned for the weekend."

Erin was clearly breathing again and she and her boys headed home. Her injuries were healing but she still had the bruising on her face; she was getting around much easier with the wheelchair, and she was maintaining her muscles by working out with the boys each night. Jake wondered again if the side mirror was the cause of her bruised cheek and the finial from Devin's truck the one on her forehead. It kind of had that shape to the bruise and he suspected it was a very deep bruise. Erin wanted to find time to just be with Anthony.   They hadn't had any downtime or time to be alone together. She wanted to make tonight special for him. She had been doing research because of her inexperience, and she wanted to make him feel loved and wanted.

They arrived back at the house and Erin got to work on dinner. She took the leftover pork, cut it up, added onions, celery, bean sprouts and eggs and made egg foo young with steamed rice. She even whipped up a sauce to put over it with soy sauce, orange juice, and hoisin sauce. Everyone seemed to enjoy it. After dinner Kade, Jake and Ryan headed to their favorite country bar to dance, shoot pool, relax and have guy time. That gave Anthony and Erin time to themselves.

"Anthony, my sexy handsome fiancé, do you have time to sit and talk for a bit?"

"I do sugar. What's on your mind?" He picked her up out of the wheelchair and sat with her on his lap on the couch.

"First I want to say thank you for all you have done for me and for always being there for me, your support. You are amazing and I love you so much." She leaned in and kissed him.

"Sugar, there is nowhere else I'd rather be. I love you too honey and just want to keep you safe, love you, and hold you." She kissed him again.

"My sweet, sexy, handsome Anthony," she started and he watched the blush creep into her cheeks. "I don't know how to accomplish this exactly, but I want to pleasure you tonight, make you feel good, maybe help you relax some, relieve the tension. We haven't had a lot of us time with the trial and my healing. I know I can't make love to you with these casts on, but I have researched how I can make you feel good, if you'll let me and maybe teach me what you like, we could have a wonderful night together." She was really red by the time she finished saying that. Anthony smiled.

"You've been doing research, like on the internet?" He asked, with humor and laughter in his voice.

"Yes. Don't laugh at me Anthony. I'm new at this! I needed help to figure out how to do this, how to make you feel good, what was right. I needed to know how to please you with these dreaded casts on my leg and arm." She continued to blush, but she didn't break eye contact with him.

"You are so cute honey. Yes, we can enjoy each other tonight. I would love that. I've missed you so much and I didn't want to hurt you with all the injuries. It was hard to keep my hands off your beautiful body. Plus you needed to heal from your piercings." He hugged her and pulled her closer to him. She reveled in the feel of his body under her hands. He picked her up and carried her upstairs after making sure the doors were locked. He wanted nothing more than to feel her body lying alongside his. He was trying to picture in his mind what kind of research she had done, but he'd try very hard not to embarrass her further and let things play out. He would let her lead and then he would help as needed. She was getting braver and more settled with their relationship. He knew she was inexperienced, but she was responsive, a quick learner, and game for just about anything. She was planting feather-light kisses along his jaw and down his neck to his shoulders. Her non-casted hand was rubbing his shoulders, threading through his hair, as he carried her. Anthony was trying to restrain himself. She made him want in the worst, but best way possible, and his body was definitely responding to her ministrations.

Anthony helped her get settled in bed, removing both of their clothing, and then he stretched out beside her. He marveled at how beautiful she was. He let her take the lead to show him her research, which was amazing. She found unique ways to pleasure him and she enjoyed letting her hands roam over his body. He helped when she couldn't move very well with the casts, but she had a unique way of pleasuring him. She had learned well through her research. She massaged his shoulders, and the rest of his body, her hands roaming over all of him, then concentrated on making him feel good with her one good hand and her mouth. She struggled a bit with the casts on her left limbs, but she found a way to maneuver and made Anthony writhe with pleasure. Her research had paid off. Anthony had never experienced love like this. Erin was incredible and she wanted him to feel good and loved, tension free. She was amazing. She definitely knew how to relieve the stress. He had release and was so totally relaxed after all she did for him.

They spent the night in each other's arms with Anthony teaching Erin more ways to pleasure him, and him finding ways to pleasure her too without the casts getting in the way. He watched her face in the throes of passion, and loved the feel of the piercings on her nipples. She was so responsive and she found amazing ways to make him feel good. They drifted off to sleep in each other's arms, totally sated and so much in love with one another. Anthony was so glad she was his. The tension was definitely lifting. They both slept well.

Chapter Nine

Saturday morning Erin woke early and realized she was lying the arms of her handsome, sexy Anthony. She was warm and sated, completely relaxed. She tried not to wake him, but he had been watching her for a bit. He loved the feel of her in his arms; they were skin-to-skin and totally relaxed. She risked a glance up to his face.

"Good morning sugar." He whispered, smiling at her.

"Morning handsome. Did you sleep well?" She smiled up at him. She realized her casted leg was laying on his leg and she didn't want to hurt him, so she stayed still.

"I slept amazingly well. You did your research well!" She blushed which made him smile even more. "Did you sleep?"

"I did. You know how to make me forget everything. Last night in your arms was incredible! I'm glad you enjoyed it too." She was still blushing and trying to figure out how to move her leg without hurting him. She lifted it slightly and tried to move it over, but the cast got caught in the covers and she couldn't use her left arm. "Sorry handsome, I'm trying not to hurt you, but I think I'm stuck."

"Let me help Erin. Hang on." He reached under the covers and helped to untangle her leg from the sheet. Together they managed to move her leg off his, and he helped her straighten up in his arms.

"Did I hurt you?" She asked, very concerned and very aware that she was not wearing any clothes. The bed sheet slipped down below her breasts and her blush increased. Anthony was just enjoying the view. The piercings were definitely sexy on his Erin. Michael was right, he did enjoy the view of her in the piercings with the delicate chains.

"You didn't hurt me beautiful." Anthony reached and brought her closer to him kissing her senseless. She ended up laying on his chest, kissing him passionately. Her hands roamed over his body and it was another hour before they were ready to get up and get dressed. She relished the time she spent with her Anthony, in his arms and skin-to-skin. She was so in love with him and she was so glad he was in her life. He was so patient with her and helped her learn about lovemaking, how to please him. He even let her try out her research on him and he encouraged her to explore. She was over-the-moon happy with Anthony and couldn't wait to marry him, start a family with him. Anthony helped her in the bathroom later, they showered together, and got dressed; he carried her downstairs. The house was quiet; Kade had gotten in late and was still not up. Anthony put her in the wheelchair and she headed to the kitchen to get the coffee on and start breakfast. Anthony headed to the office.

Erin checked her messages and she had one from her good friend Laurel. She was really excited to hear from her. Laurel had been out of town for quite a while. While her casserole was baking she called to see if Laurel was up. They talked about life in general and Laurel told Erin she had just moved back to town. She had a new job, which she described in detail, and she wanted to know how things were. Erin filled her in on the goings on with Devin and the fact that she was engaged to the most handsome man on the face of the planet. Laurel was really concerned about the situation with Devin and glad that things were resolving. She also asked Erin if she could help her find a guy of her own. She wanted someone who enjoyed the things she enjoyed. Erin told she might know one that could be her match. After a few more minutes they signed off and Erin promised to keep in touch. Laurel told her that Kiera was looking too and maybe Erin could set them both up! That got Erin to thinking about Jake and Kade. She'd have to work on a plan.

While she was musing about the girls and Jake and Kade, she headed to the cabinet to get dishes down to set the table. Jake came in the back door as she was trying to get herself up and out of her chair by moving her leg off the extender. Her arms were sore and she realized she had overdone things again. All her extra-curricular activities from last night had depleted her. Her energy was just not there! She was struggling a bit to stand up on her good leg. This was not good at all. She tried four or five times to hoist herself up, but she wasn't able to do it.

"Whoa there Miss Erin. Let me help you please!" Jake rushed over and put a hand on her shoulder gently guiding her back to the wheelchair, and put her casted leg back onto the extender. "I'll set the table. You don't have to do it all by yourself darlin'." She smiled up at him and Jake's body reacted to her. He really needed to find a girl of his own. He tried to stop his reaction to her nearness and concentrate instead on something more like helping to set the table for breakfast.

"Thanks Jake. Did you, Ryan and Kade have a good night last night?"

"We did. We spent some time shooting pool and having a couple of beers. It was nice to spend time with Ryan. Ryan took off this morning early to head home to his wife and kids." Erin seemed surprised.

"I'm glad I got to meet him." She moved back to let Jake have space in the kitchen. "Jake, when we get done with breakfast can I talk with you about what happens on Monday when Devin is sentenced?" He nodded. He watched her a moment; she was chewing on something in her mind.

"I can see you have something on your mind Miss Erin." He grabbed the plates and coffee cups, setting the counter for them. He then went back to the silverware drawer and the napkins. She nodded and headed to the refrigerator to get a canister of biscuits out. She grabbed a cookie sheet, peeled the label off the can gingerly holding the can as far away as she could, and Jake watched her with fascination, as she closed her eyes, crinkled her face up, as she made the biscuit can pop. "Does that pop bother you darlin'?" Jake had a smile on his face. He just had to know.

"Yeah. It's like popping a balloon. It sets me on edge. It also sends shivers down my spine. I don't like it!" She smiled up at him visibly shivering. She put the biscuits on the cookie sheet with parchment paper and slipped them into the oven.   "I haven't seen Kade yet, but breakfast will be ready in about twenty minutes."

"Coffee?" Jake asked. She nodded. "Did you and Anthony have a good night last night?" He turned to see her blushing several shades of red. He wondered momentarily what that was about, but then it hit him what he asked her. She was mortified and didn't know how to answer. He forgot how inexperienced she was and he just embarrassed her. They left them alone last night so it must have been a good night. He tried to hide the smile on his face; she was so cute. Quickly he turned back to his coffee cup.

"We did." She managed to squeak out. She tried to turn away, but Jake knew something was up. He didn't want to embarrass her further, so he stirred his coffee intently, keeping his eyes averted from her. He busied himself getting her a cup of coffee and adding creamer. She was taking numerous deep breaths and thought she needed to explain the blush. "Sorry Jake, it's just that I'm really inexperienced with relationships, being with a man is new to me, and talking about last night makes me blush. Just know we had a great night." That made Jake chuckle, the laughter bubbled up and he just couldn't keep it inside. He kept his eyes locked on his coffee to give her time to pull herself back together. She was really trying to control the blush, but nothing was making it disappear. She was completely mortified.

"I'm glad you had a good night darlin'. You needed release." He winked at her as he handed her a cup of coffee. He just couldn't help himself. She was so funny and definitely out of her element talking with him about what happened last night. She was taking in lots of breaths of air, and the blush kept deepening on her cheeks, down her throat too. She needed to change the subject.

"So Jake, do you have a girl?" She was slowly coming back to her normal.

"No. I'm ready though to find that one special person, though. These last few weeks being with you, Anthony, and Kade have made me decide it was time to settle down. I found some land close to Kade's place that I purchased a few weeks ago, just to the east of here, and am ready to put down some roots. I'm moving my security business here and perhaps we can talk about a website for me too! I want to build a house like Kade's." She nodded and then Erin smiled like she had a secret.

"Ok Erin, spill it. What's in your head honey?" Jake smiled back. He leaned against the counter and waited. She looked like a kid that just got caught with their hand in the cookie jar! Jake just sipped his coffee.

Erin sucked in a deep breath. It was time to tell him. "I have a girlfriend that just moved back to town, she's here to stay now, and she's one of my oldest and closest friends. She's a lot like you Jake, shares the same interests, and I think you two would get along great. Excuse my language for a moment, but she's a badass and she is also in security. She's a bit tougher than I am. She rides a motorcycle and is covered in tattoos. She might be your match!" Jake laughed out loud at that and almost spit out his coffee. Erin watched him, fascinated, as he tried to compose himself. He glanced again at Erin and she was really serious.

"I think I'd like to meet this girl. What's her name?" After he had pulled himself back together and swallowed his coffee.

"Laurel. She left town about a year ago chasing a job. It didn't pan out for her so she's back and she's ready to settle down too. I'd like to introduce you to her. She's experienced with relationships, more than I am. My girls are all more experienced than I am. I also have another friend Kiera for Kade." She threw that last part in as she turned away.

"Do we call you Matchmaker Erin now?" Jake laughed at her.

"I just want everyone to be happy and settled Jake. You're like a brother to me Jake and so I want you to be happy too. I'm also really glad you're staying here! I like you a lot." She smiled her sweetest smile at Jake and fluttered her lashes at him. That just made Jake laugh even deeper. He walked over to her chair and gave her a hug.

Together they finished prepping breakfast and put everything on the counter. Jake called to both Kade and Anthony. It turned out they were in the office working on some paperwork. Anthony had designed the house for him and Erin, and they were working with an architect to get it drawn up. Kade cautioned Anthony to make sure that Erin liked the rooms and the placement, especially the kitchen. Erin still did not know about the vineyard and winery. Anthony needed to tell her soon. It had come up at family dinners and Kade saw Erin's puzzled looks, but Erin was too nice to ask about it. Anthony agreed. He told Kade he would talk to her after the hearing on Monday.

After breakfast Jake, Erin and the two brothers headed to the back porch to talk about Monday. Once they were sitting down and sipping their coffee, Jake mentioned that Erin had questions.

"Go ahead Erin, what's on your mind?" Kade invited.

"Well, I'm thinking about Monday's hearing and since Devin's been found guilty I'm guessing this thing on Monday is for him to know how long he will be in prison. Is that right?"

"Yes, sort of." Jake said. She looked up at him. "It's a hearing of sorts where the prosecution, in this case the DA, will present information on why the state feels Devin should get a specific amount of years for the crimes – these years that he has to serve for each count he was convicted on. Then, the defense will present why Devin should do less time and their justification as to why that is. The jury and the judge will listen to everything and then render a decision including rehabilitation and restitution."

"Are there any witnesses?"

"Sometimes." She looked questioningly at Kade for that remark. "Erin, sometimes the victims in the case, like you and Erica, can make a statement on behalf of the state to tell the court why Devin should be locked away. It makes for a stronger argument for the jury and the judge if the victims are able to speak to the hurt, the fear and more that was caused during the time Devin did what he did." All three of them watched Erin for a bit wondering how she would respond to that. She sat and thought about Kade's statement.

"Wow. I don't know if I'm prepared to speak on Monday, but some thoughts regarding Devin have been going through my head that I need to share with you all. I think after my breakthrough, maybe more accurately my breakdown, about Devin the other night, I have all these jumbled thoughts in my head. I'm probably not going to express this right or so you can understand what I'm thinking, so please bear with me, but here goes." She took a breath, looked down in her lap, and then made eye contact with them, and started. "I am wondering if the prosecution can ask that Devin get mental health help while he's serving his time. It's the judge, along with the jury that makes the determination as to Devin's future, right?" Jake nodded. "He really needs to talk about all of this with a professional and he needs to not just be locked away, forgotten about. There has to be a reason why Devin is the way he is. I heard Jake say a couple of times, through the haze of my anger and confusion that the system not only failed to protect Erica and me, maybe others too, but it also failed Devin, failed to get him help. So I was curious."

"Erin, do you want to speak at the sentencing?" Jake asked.

"I don't know how to answer that Jake. I wouldn't know what to say or how to say it if I did speak. I just wanted to know if part of his sentence should be or could be to get him psychiatric help. I know he won't seek if for himself, so perhaps if it was ordered as part of his sentence." She paused and took a breath. They let her gather her thoughts and tried hard not to derail her.

"I think way deep down Devin is a good person who just got off the track somewhere, derailed maybe through circumstances or through something that happened in his life, in his past, and he needs help in the worst way to get his life back in the right lane. I realized in court that there was no one there to support him, no family, and that made me wonder. He started snowballing out of control, gaining traction into his slide out of reality, and he needs help to stop the slide. I have forgiven him for what he's done to me, because I can't move forward without letting my anger go. If I hold onto that anger, then I am letting Devin still control me; I did hear you Jake, but somewhere the system didn't see who Devin was becoming, or simply turned a blind eye to who he was becoming, and no one reached out to try and help him get him help, not even his lawyers. His lawyers didn't ask why Devin did what he did repeatedly, they just found a way to get him off the charges and out of jail. That says something to me. It says his law team was just there to take the money and not really help Devin, which speaks of unethical behavior on their part. Does this make any sense or have I gone off the deep end again?"

"It makes perfect sense Erin. I'm just amazed by you. You were hurt repeatedly by this guy and instead of wishing that he would just be locked up, put away, and the key thrown away, you are advocating for him to get medical help. That's awesome." Jake said.

"Someone needs to advocate for him, it doesn't seem like he has any support system or family in place. I know a bit about being an advocate because I did that with my mom. I don't know if Devin has family or a support system or not, and no one was there for him throughout the trial, but part of this is that I feel a bit responsible for where's he at now."

"You are not responsible for his behavior Erin!" Anthony said shocked, his anger barely concealed below the surface. Erin laid her hand on his arm and looked at him with the love in her heart for him. She didn't react and didn't snap back at Anthony. She just tried to explain what she said.

"I know that, handsome. I think perhaps I used the wrong word or in the wrong context. Let me see if I can explain what I meant." Anthony nodded at her. She took a deep breath and kept her hand on Anthony's to reassure him and maybe calm him down some. "Someone has to speak up and ask the hard questions about Devin's slide to the dark side. I learned all about advocating for someone when my mom was sick, but that's getting us off track. During the trial all that got presented through the evidence and the entire string of events were the things that Devin did wrong and no one ever asked why he acted that way? He never took the stand to answer to any of the charges or why he did what he did, but he had outbursts during the trial, including demanding an answer as to why I told him no so many times. He is clearly needing help and that to me was his way of asking for help, but it wasn't addressed, except for the judge to remove him from the court room." She took a breath and her guys watched her, waiting.

"Let's look at Quatro, I think that's his name, because he's a good example of what I'm trying to say." Jake nodded to her. She took a deep breath, gathered her thoughts and then proceeded. "He was trying to save his sister from pain, trauma, and injury, and the guy harassing her ended up killing her because the restraining order failed to protect her, so Quatro killed him and ended up in prison. That speaks to me of a very broken system. Quatro could have easily given up on life while serving time for what he did, but he took responsibility for his actions and here he is helping from the inside, trying to help fix the system that didn't take care of his sister and that put him in prison. He helped me in a roundabout way by questioning and befriending Devin. I don't condone what Quatro did, please understand that; violence is not the way to solve a problem, even though I wanted to hit Devin too and make him hurt because I was frustrated and angry, but I'm guessing Quatro couldn't get help through the legal channels; he couldn't get protection for his sister or protect her himself, and I'm guessing he didn't have the support system I have in all of you. That speaks volumes to me of an intensely broken system. How can it be fixed, changed? That's kind of what I'm getting at. It's like when I told you during my tearful breakdown if Devin were punished earlier and sooner because of what he did, he would be able to change and see where he went wrong before it got so far out of hand. No one looked at the why behind what Devin did, or asked him why he did it, and nothing changed his behavior. His lawyers just placated him and helped him do the things he did, while working to get him off of the penalties, basically giving him free rein to continue to hurt people. You said it yourself Kade, Devin had a rap sheet a mile long, but nothing ever stuck. I truly believe that someone has to advocate for Devin and get to the real reason he is acting the way he is. Is it drugs? Did something happen with his family? Was he raised to abuse women? What happened in his past to make him the way he is?"

"I'm so proud of you Erin." Kade said. "You are speaking to things that have been on-going for quite some time and I agree with you. The system is very broken because it let Devin continually break free and hurt you, hurt Erica, and maybe other young women. While you aren't responsible for Devin's actions or who he became, I see what you are saying. You feel that the restraining order, and the times it was enacted, were more of a catalyst for Devin to further slide into the dark side." Erin nodded at him. "I don't know how to fix it or if it's possible to fix, but perhaps we need to talk with Uncle Mory who can talk with the DA. If you were to speak on Monday Erin, it might have a huge effect to get the ball rolling and change the system. At least it would bring it into the light and make it known, make it public record; it might also get help for Devin and get to the bottom of why he turned out the way he did. Just know the system is very broken, flawed, all around the world and you can't fix everything, but you may be able to change things here in our little corner of this very big world!" Erin nodded, but the wheels were still turning in her mind about how to fix the situation. It was part of Erin's nature to fix things.

"Erin, honey, Judge Kafner talked to me last week when we were on break in the court case, on recess, and she asked me if you would help to be a face for the legislation." Anthony started. "I think with your passion about the advocacy for mental health help for people like Devin, you would be a good spokesperson. You have the Raptors and Kings behind you too. You have an uncanny knack of drawing people to you, so you would be a great spokesperson. People tend to listen to you when you speak. Erin you would be the public face, be able to tell your story, and maybe make a difference. Maybe you can make people hear you and really understand what happened and how it needs to be changed and repaired. You've lived it."

"As long as I have all of you by my side I can do that!" She smiled at all of them and took Anthony's hand in hers, raising it to her lips to kiss his knuckles. They sat sipping coffee in companionable silence for a bit.

"Ok, I'm changing subjects now." Erin said. All three of them looked up at her and smiled. "Kade, can I plant the roses today? They are blooming in the potatoes and water and I think I need to get them into the ground. I think I even saw some buds on them."

"Absolutely. What do you need to do that?"

"I need first to go get my drawing and show you what I've worked on for your gardens. You saw my initial design but I've refined it and expanded it." Erin said. "I want to spread the roses out around the house on three sides, and add in some calla lilies, tiger lilies and carnations. I've already called the nursery and they've put things aside for me. Maybe even some flowering bushes."

"Where is it honey?" Anthony asked. "I'll go get it and then we'll find you some gardening gloves and tools."

"It's in my computer bag, in the front pocket. There is a file folder called Kade's house." Kade smiled at her.

"You're going to fix up my yard aren't you Miss Erin." Kade said smiling broadly.

"That's my plan. You know, you might meet that special someone soon and decide it's time to settle down and start a family. This way your yard is ready to go!" She smiled at him, her eyes twinkling with unsaid words. Kade just shook his head.

"Kade, Erin and I talked this morning while making breakfast and she has two girlfriends she wants to introduce us to."

"Uh oh. Are you matchmaking Miss Erin?" She smiled sweetly at Kade and once again fluttered her eyelashes with a look that said 'who me?'

"She told me the girl she picked out for me is in security and is a real badass! Her words! She drives a motorcycle and is covered in tattoos. I don't know much about the girl she picked for you. We didn't get that far in our conversation, but she's getting to know us too well if she's picking out girls for us." Jake smiled at her.

"What's all this? My Erin is matchmaking for you two?" Anthony said as he came and sat back down. Erin just smiled up at him. Anthony leaned in for a kiss. He handed her the folder and she showed Kade, Jake and Anthony what she was thinking. Erin had drawn Kade's house and added in all the gardens showing what each plant was. Kade was very impressed. She drew the house in three dimensions and it looked like an architect had drawn it, it wasn't just a floor plan, it was like one was standing at the far corner of the property and seeing the house in real life and in full color; an elevation drawing. They talked through the three sides of his house and where she planned to put each of the different colored roses, as well as the calla lilies and tiger lilies. She told him her plan was to put carnations around the area where they were sitting now, maybe adding in spring flower bulbs and some flowering bushes for greenery, and asked if all of that was ok with him. She watched Kade looking over her drawings. He was smiling and really pleased with what he saw.

"I love this design. It's so colorful. You are so creative Erin and you put my favorite rose color by the back door! How can we help?" Kade asked. She told them she would need garden tools, gloves, and the roses, and then they would need to go to the nursery and get the lilies and carnations next weekend. She told them she had already called the nursery and had the plants set aside for them. She would call them back and finalize the order. Jake and Anthony headed to the shed to the get the tools and Kade moved Erin to the first location. He went to get the roses. Anthony picked Erin up out of her chair and set her in the grass near the garden bed. He handed her the tools and her gloves while Kade brought the roses container. Anthony stayed with Erin while Kade and Jake headed inside to call Uncle Mory about Monday's hearing.

Erin spent the next two hours in dirt therapy planting all the roses exactly where she wanted them to give the most color and the prettiest garden possible. Anthony helped her and together they made Kade's yard come to life. She was sore when they finished. Next weekend they would go to the nursery and get the remaining plants so she could put them in the ground too. Erin had already done her research and had the nursery put away the plants and bushes she wanted. Anthony loved how the roses just brightened up Kade's yard. He couldn't wait to see what she did with their yard! Of course, he still needed to tell her and show her what he had planned for their house.

*****

Kade and Jake talked with Uncle Mory and Mory thought it would be good to have Erin speak on Monday. Jake cautioned that they would need to convince her, but her apprehension came because she didn't know what to say or how to say it. Uncle Mory said he would take all the info that Kade and Jake gave him and write up a statement for Erin. He would call the DA and share the information with him and then perhaps later today or tomorrow they could come by and they could convince Erin to speak in court. Kade and Jake signed off with Uncle Mory and debated on how to bring all this up with Erin. They had planned for Mariah and Cassi to come by later this afternoon to spend a couple hours with Erin, but Cassi and Mariah had other things going and asked for that to be next weekend instead. Jake reminded Kade that they also needed to talk about the car and the salvage yard, and Erin had an appointment with Dr. Parker on Wednesday this week. It was shaping up to be another busy week. Both of them headed back to the yard. They just wanted to be there for her through all of this.

*****

Saturday afternoon, after lunch, the four of them sat back outside admiring the roses and the start to Kade's landscaping adventure. Erin had made cookies and ice tea. Jake and Kade told her that Mariah and Cassi weren't coming today. Erin just smiled at her men. Everyone had things to do and she didn't want to disrupt their lives.

"So guys, it's been four weeks since my accident and I think I need to do something with the insurance and my totaled car, but not sure what the next steps are. Can any of you help me with what I need to do?" Erin asked.

"Erin, do you remember the day Ryan showed up and Jake and I were gone for a bit?" She nodded. "Well, we met the insurance adjuster at the salvage yard and on Monday afternoon, after the sentencing, we need to take you to the DMV and you can sign off on the title and sell your car. The salvage yard wants to buy your vehicle."

"Why would the salvage yard want to buy my totaled car?" Erin was shocked.

"They will use it for parts Erin. There are lots of people who come to salvage yards looking for parts to repair cars; you still have viable parts in the car, and the salvage yard wants to purchase what's left of your car so that they can sell off the parts."

"Wow. Ok. Will the insurance company then just cancel my policy on that car? Not sure how to do all this. Sorry for all the questions." Erin was trying to process everything. She wanted to take care of things but had no idea how to go about it and how to ask the right questions.

"The insurance company is working with Devin's insurance company to get you a settlement because the accident, for lack of a better word, was Devin's fault and we can put that money toward a new car when you are ready." Jake said. "Devin will more than likely be paying restitution for all the harm he caused both you and Erica which will include your car, the hospital bills and the medical costs. I'm guessing that the state will sell his house and use that as part of the settlement."

"Honey, when we get everything resolved and you get back on your feet, we'll look into another vehicle for you. In the meantime, can we talk through the schedule for this week? I think we need to plan how to accomplish everything." Anthony asked. She told him it would be their vehicle and so they could find something together.

They spent the next hour going over the schedule. They had court on Monday morning, the DMV in the afternoon, and all three of her guys would be with her. Tuesday Erin had a shoot at the ice hockey arena for the Raptors' practice and a couple of interviews with players and coaches. Wednesday she had her follow-up appointment with Dr. Parker in the morning and then practice again in the afternoon with interviews, and the same for Thursday afternoon. She would be editing in the mornings on Tuesday and Thursday. Friday night they had another game she needed to video at. Erin said her hope was to be out of the casts on Wednesday, and into splints so she could move a bit easier, and not be so reliant on the boys. She apologized for taking up all their time to help her with her work. She was also prepared for Dr. Parker to set up PT appointments. She knew her ankle would take a while to move again. Jake would accompany her to all the practices and all of them would be there for the game. Jake would also take her to see Dr. Parker. Kade and Anthony needed to do work at the shop.

"Erin, honey, can you tell us a little bit about your life before Devin, maybe about your mom and growing up?" Anthony asked, once they ironed out the calendars for the week.

For the next hour Erin relayed to all of them that it was just her and her mom growing up, and her mom worked very hard to make ends meet, sometimes two and three jobs. Erin told them that starting at age 12 she got really good at making cakes and desserts and she started her own baking business, helping her neighbors plan parties and such. She baked for them and she was good at it. All the money she was able to bring in helped to keep them in their apartment and pay the bills so her mom didn't have to work so hard. She even managed to put some money away for college, investing it so it would grow. When she was 16 she went to work for a party planning business and put more money away for college, as well as helping with all the bills since her mom had gotten sick. Her mom didn't have a college degree, so she worked a lot of jobs that only paid minimum wages, and no health benefits, but her mom worked very hard to put food on the table and a roof over their heads. Erin tried to help as much as she could when she was old enough.   All three asked her questions and Erin answered them easily. She clearly loved her mom very much and worked hard to make sure her mom was comfortable and take care of.

Erin went on to tell them that she managed to get scholarships for college which enabled her to work and take care of her mom, pay for their apartment. By Erin's junior year in college her mom had taken a turn for the worse in her health condition and could no longer work, so Erin took on more jobs to pay the bills and help her mom with the care she needed. She told them she pretty much worked around the clock and slept very little, to make sure she and her mom could stay in the small apartment they had, and she could complete her school work. Anthony and Kade felt really bad for all that Erin had been through. Jake was pretty impressed with all that Erin had been through; she worked hard and didn't shy away from anything. That was impressive. Jake realized that Erin was independent because she had to be and she didn't know how to accept help because she didn't complain or stop working, she didn't know any other way. She was constantly moving, which explained the pacing.

She told them that she started her own production business her senior year and used all that money to pay off the medical bills while working on a payment plan for the rest of the bills, for the oncologist, the cancer treatments, medications, and the doctors. She brought in a home-health nurse and found ways to pay for that too, to help her mom while she was in class or doing her jobs. By the time she graduated she had lined up the job at TK Productions and was negotiating a job with the TV stations. She found her house, had good enough credit rating to get a loan and then worked her butt off to pay off the house, her mom's final expenses, the car loan and the rest of the medical bills. The house was a fixer upper, so she learned about repairs, interior decorating and worked to make the house very livable for her and her mom.   It took her four years of scrimping and saving but she managed to get everything paid off and started to put money away for the future.

"Erin, wow I am so amazed by you. You took what you had and made it work to help your mom and to help yourself. I am so proud of you." Kade said.

"Kade, Anthony, Jake, I did what I had to do to survive. My mom provided for me as best she could while I was growing up and I needed to be there for her no matter what. She needed me to step up because it was just us, and I wanted her to be comfortable as her condition deteriorated. The house was our dream and I was glad I could manage to get us a house before she died. We struggled and there were many days when all I ate was top ramen and peanut butter so I could keep her strength up with healthy foods and her meds, but I survived and I could make my mom comfortable through her illness. My goal was to make sure she didn't have to worry when I was old enough to help out. We made it and we were happy."

"Erin, what about your father?" Jake asked.

"I don't know who my father is. My mom told me that he left when he found she was pregnant. That's a blank on my birth certificate. So it's been mom and I against the world for all my life. You all would have loved her. She was an amazing woman, so caring and giving. She made me who I am." Erin drifted off and a peaceful look came over her face, but it was mixed with sadness too. Tears were balanced on her lashes but she didn't let them fall. She was taking deep breaths of air to try and quell the want to cry. All of them realized that Erin worked so hard that she didn't really have time to grieve her mom's loss, and Devin stalking her on top of all that made it hard for Erin to let down. Erin was amazing, but everything that happened made her keep a lot of it bottled up and sometimes it just spilled over into her breakdowns. She had no one over the years to share this with and so she tried to keep it all to herself. Jake understood even more why it was so hard for her to share with him, open up to him.

"I wish I could have met her." Anthony said as he wrapped his arm around her shoulders.

*****

Sunday late morning Uncle Mory and the DA Mr. Donaldson showed up at the house. Jake and the brothers had prepared Erin that they were coming. She had baked a coffee cake and made sure the coffee pot was on and ready. She had Anthony help her dress in yoga pants and a big t-shirt. The guys realized that Erin was the most settled they had seen her. She seemed to be comfortable with everything and her own body. They attributed that to giving her an outlet to talk about her past and her family, and being able to unload some of her burden.

"Hi Miss Erin." Uncle Mory greeted her with a hug.

"Hi Uncle Mory." She tried to be bright and happy, no stress.

"Miss Bradford," Mr. Donaldson started, getting right to the point, "we wanted to talk to you about tomorrow and perhaps having you make a statement at the sentencing. Your men here told us about your passion with Devin needing mental health help and you being his advocate." Mr. Donaldson was a formidable man. He didn't mince words and was very forthright.

"Mr. Donaldson, I don't know what to say or how to say it." Erin was panicking.

"Miss Bradford, no reason to panic. We took the information that Mr. Kasper and Mr. Romano gave us and we've crafted a statement for you." He handed her a piece of paper. "We'd like you to read this over and if you want to change any wording we can explore that, but this is what we'd like you to say tomorrow." He just laid all that out there and she swallowed hard as she accepted the piece of paper.

Erin looked at the paper and in stunned silence read through the words. Jake and Kade told them, in great detail, what Erin had said about the system being broken and that it had failed not only her and Erica, but it had failed Devin too. Kade served everyone coffee and cake, and the men talked while Erin read the words. Erin was impressed with all the words she read. Kade and Jake had really listened to her. Anthony sat with his arm around her letting her know he was there for her. She read the words three times at least making sure she truly understood exactly what she would be saying. There were a few words that didn't sound like her, and one place she wanted to rearrange the words in the sentence because it didn't work, but the for the most part they captured what she had talked with Jake, Kade and Anthony about. She grabbed her pen and circled what she wanted changed. She waited for a lull in the conversation before she spoke.

"Thank you for putting this together. There are a few words that I don't think are me and how I talk, and one sentence that I'd like to rearrange to make it more speak-able, but overall it is what I told my wonderful guys here about my experiences with Devin and the system." She took a very deep breath and tried to bring herself back to her center. "If we can change the words I've circled to something different and rewrite this one sentence that I've noted, I think I can get through this tomorrow." She handed the paper to Mr. Donaldson.

"Miss Bradford, what words would you prefer to use?" The DA asked her. She pointed out words that would feel more comfortable for her and after a bit the DA agreed, made the changes and told her he would print out a new copy for her in larger print for tomorrow. Mr. Donaldson made Erin work hard for the changes she wanted, but she stood her ground and pushed. Erin didn't think Mr. Donaldson was used to being told someone wanted to change what he had written. He also told her he would arrange for a podium that might fit the wheelchair better when she spoke.

"If it's possible Mr. Donaldson, I'd like to stand on my good leg and have some support from one of my guys here. I think I would feel more comfortable if I could stand up at the podium and it might make for a stronger statement from me."

All of them agreed and they would allow one of her men to be with her. All three of her guys talked and decided that Jake should be the one bringing her forward and getting her standing, staying with her. She was thinking about small victories. Mr. Donaldson was a force to be reckoned with, he didn't mince words, and she wasn't comfortable with him. He also seemed like he didn't like to be questioned about his words or his way of doing things. She was happy that she could stand up tomorrow and do her statement. It was a small victory, but a victory nonetheless.

After a bit more conversation, Uncle Mory and the DA left them and Erin was breathing again. She kept her mantra to herself that she could do this. She stretched and tried to keep the smile on her face for her boys. She didn't want to worry them.

They spent the rest of Sunday curled up on the couches watching movies. Erin needed some downtime and she needed to prepare for tomorrow. Kade suggested they order pizza for dinner; that decision met with rave reviews from everyone. Once dinner was done they once again spent the evening watching more movies. She let the boys pick the type of movie and she lost herself in the time with her new family. She was thinking of her mom and hoped that her mom was happy with all the things that Erin had done. Erin sat with Anthony's arm around her, her head on his shoulder, after dinner, and she promptly fell asleep. Kade and Jake were talking about the movie they were watching and Jake mentioned that Erin was asleep.

"She's so relaxed in my arms." Anthony said in whispered tones. "I think we'll just stay like this for a bit and then I'll carry her upstairs. She wore herself out with the work on the gardens and trying to be independent." That made Kade smile. They enjoyed the movie and finally a little after nine Anthony carried her upstairs to bed. All of them slept well and prepared for another long week.

*****

Monday morning found the four of them heading once again to the courthouse. Erin was deep breathing and preparing to speak at this hearing. The guys in her life were trying to keep her calm. She had made them breakfast sandwiches with the leftover biscuits, bacon and eggs. Jake was amazed at her creativity in the kitchen. He hoped he could make it work here and be near to this woman who had changed his life in so many good ways. He had to admit that he was also looking forward to meeting Laurel, the girl Erin had picked out as his match. He was intrigued.

"Good morning. All rise for the honorable Judge Kafner." Everyone stood, except Erin.

"Be seated. Mr. Donaldson are you ready to present your arguments?" He nodded.

Mr. Donaldson gave information from the prosecution side as to why Devin deserved the maximum sentence for each count he was convicted on. Then the judge called on the defense lawyers to present why Devin should receive minimums in this case. This was about an hour in the courtroom.

"Mr. Donaldson, is there anyone who wants to speak on behalf of the state in this case?" Judge Kafner asked.

"Yes your honor. I'd like to bring Miss Erin Bradford to the podium to speak." She nodded. Erin could feel Devin's gaze boring into her as she was brought forward. Jake got up and pushed Erin to the podium, then he helped her to stand on her good leg at the podium. Jake stood right behind her and she leaned against him for support. She took a deep breath and Jake's hands tightened at her waist giving her as much confidence as he could without saying anything. She pulled out her piece of paper, and slowly read her statement telling the court that the system had failed her and Erica, and it failed Devin too, she was asking the court to consider mental health help to get to the root of what was causing Devin to act the way he was acting. She made eye contact with the judge, with Devin's defense, briefly connecting with Devin, and with Mr. Donaldson. Devin was very subdued this morning, but as she spoke on his behalf, he seemed surprised. She asked the judge to make sure that Devin had help and was not just locked away or forgotten about; she requested that they get to the why of what he did. When she finished she thanked them all and Jake helped her back to her wheelchair. They returned to their seats. The judge asked if anyone else needed or wanted to make a statement. Judge Kafner paused and no one else moved to the podium.

"This court will be in recess while the jury members and I confer. Please stay in your seats. I'll be back to render our decision shortly."

"All rise." The judge left the bench and everyone stayed put.   Devin looked over at Erin, but she didn't glance his way. She could see him out of the corner of her eye, but she kept her focus on her men. His life was about to change with the jury's decision. Erin was engaging in conversation with her team trying to ignore Devin's glare. He looked at her with questions unanswered in his features. He seemed surprised that she advocated for him and he wondered why she did it. She wasn't sure what else he was thinking or where all of this would go, but her hope and her prayers were that Devin would get the help he needed.

Devin sat with his defense team, but he wondered why Erin wanted him to get help. He didn't believe he had anything to gain now that he was convicted of all these crimes; it was her fault he was here. He was trying to figure out her angle. She had nothing to gain from him getting help. Was there another angle to this? Devin couldn't imagine that she had any feelings for him at all, except feelings of hatred. Her statement didn't indicate that though. Her statement made him feel like he might still be worth something, that his life still had meaning. Devin's mind was churning with possibilities of what Erin was up to. This couldn't be simply out of the goodness of her heart. No one functioned like that. There must be some ulterior motive.

*****

After thirty minutes of everyone sitting in the courtroom, the bailiff had everyone stand again. Judge Kafner entered, along with the jury members, and seated all. Erin realized there were news stations there waiting for the verdict too. By tonight everything that happened would be all over the news.

"Mr. Traeger, will you please stand?" Devin and his defense team stood and waited for the worst. Devin stared straight ahead.

"Mr. Traeger, you were found guilty by this jury of your peers in this trial of nine counts ranging from statutory rape to attempted vehicular manslaughter. All of these counts come with sentences that encompass many years in prison. I have heard from both sides in this case and from Ms. Bradford and her request that the court consider the cause behind all of this behavior. The jury and I are inclined to agree with Ms. Bradford, and so the jury and I are recommending you serve a total of 65 years in the federal prison. You will have mental health sessions daily with a prison psychiatrist to help with discovering the why behind all of this behavior, and perhaps helping you to see why all of this behavior was wrong. You will also be required to pay restitution to both Ms. Bradford and Ms. Stanton; that figure will be determined at a later date. You will be required to serve at least 30 years before you will be eligible for parole. Do you understand the scope of this sentence?" She waited for an acknowledgement from Devin.

"Yes your honor." Devin said. He was much more in control and much more calm than during the trial. Devin was wondering if he might actually have a chance at a real life after prison. Erin was advocating for him and so he needed to make an effort. Maybe this was his wake up call.

"Mr. Traeger, you are hereby remanded back into custody. You will be moved to the Federal Penitentiary this afternoon. Thank you jury for your work on this case. This court is adjourned." The bailiff had everyone rise and Devin was taken away by the bailiff and the court officers. Erin sat for a moment and tried to absorb everything that just happened. The court listened to her and actually took her seriously. That was pretty cool. She may have made a difference in this instance. Kade, Jake and Anthony watched her for a moment.

"Is this the end?" Erin asked as she looked up at them.

"It is for today Erin." Jake said. She looked at him questioningly. "If, and that's a big if, Devin's team decides to appeal this decision, there could be more hearings."

"So even with this part today, it's never going to end." Erin just shook her head, and looked into her lap. Life was not easy. Jake could see her devastation.

"Erin, look at me." Jake said as he knelt down beside her. "There is every possibility that Devin and his team will choose not to pursue an appeal. The judge gave him a very lenient sentence for the pain and suffering he caused. Each of the counts for rape and vehicular manslaughter alone come with life sentences. He got off fairly easily and I know that both of Devin's lawyers are tied up with the State Bar Ethics Committee to explain their actions over the course of their careers." She tried to smile at him, but she was clearly torn that this wasn't the end. "We are all here for you and will always be here for you darlin'. Let's not worry about tomorrow and what that could bring, let's focus on today and the good things that happened here. This was a victory for you and for Erica, for anyone with a restraining order. You made a difference by speaking up, and now maybe Devin will get the help he so desperately needs."

"Ok." She smiled at Jake, hugged him and then hugged Kade and Anthony.

The bailiff came back in and let them all know the reporters were downstairs and they wanted to talk to Erin. Erin took a deep breath. She knew this was coming, so she put a smile on her face. She was the face of this so she needed to be professional and try to answer questions.

"Ok – let's get this over with and then we can go do our other stuff for today." Anthony was so proud of her. They pushed her wheelchair to the door and headed to the elevators. Erin was preparing to answer the reporters' questions. She asked her men to make sure they didn't stay too long. They agreed. She answered questions from the reporters and lots of photographers were capturing pictures of her and her protectors. Erin didn't waiver; she answered questions like a pro.

*****

The four of them headed to the DMV after lunch. Anthony told her how proud he was of her for the statement today and how she handled the reporters. She was feeling a bit better and they headed inside to get the paperwork resolved. Jake grabbed the file folder that held all Erin's documents and they cleared security, then headed to the right office. Kade had called the salvage yard owner and he met them at the DMV.

"Erin, this paperwork is to sell your car, I guess what's left of it from the accident, to the Bern's Salvage Yard for parts. Is this what you intend to do?"

"Yes ma'am." Erin answered.

"Very well. Let's sign off on the paperwork and the title and we'll remove the registration for this vehicle from your record. Because you had just recently paid the registration on the license plates you will receive a refund in six to eight weeks. Is this the right address?"

"No ma'am. I have a different address right now, temporarily. Can I change it or give you a new address?"

Kade went on to explain about the trial and the need to move Erin to a new, secure location. The clerk at the DMV said she had heard about the trial, followed most of it and wanted to know what happened at the sentencing. Kade and Jake told her about Erin's statement, bragged on her a bit, and how the case ended up. After a few more questions and answers, the clerk was able to change to a different mailing address for Erin. After another fifteen minutes they had signed the title and registration to the Salvage Yard owner and he handed a check to Kade for Erin's car. Finally, this day was wrapping up and they could go home and relax. Erin was tying up the loose ends of her life. Again, she sent up thanks to God for his help in her life and she prayed that her mom was happy with how she was living her life.

Chapter Ten

On Wednesday Jake took Erin to see Dr. Parker. Dr. Parker was very pleased at her progress and after the x-rays determined that she could move to a splint for the arm and then to crutches and a walking boot for her ankle. The femur was healed and looked to be in good shape. Jake told him about their workouts and that he used theraband with her on the shoulder and hip. Dr. Parker was impressed and decided that Jake could be her PT person. Dr. Parker showed him a few more exercises, and asked Erin if she was ok with that. She told him that was great. Jake practiced with Dr. Parker on Erin for the next forty minutes. Dr. Parker and Jake helped her get up on the crutches and they worked with her to get her used to walking again. Jake realized he needed to work on strength for her left arm, but she was doing pretty well for the first time up on crutches. Dr. Parker gave him a belt to hold Erin up as she walked with the crutches to ensure that she didn't face plant and do more damage. They practiced in the exam room for a bit.

They headed to Ink, Inc. after the time with Dr. Parker, bringing lunch with them, and had lunch with Kade, Michael and Anthony, then Jake took her to her shoot at the ice hockey rink. She had more footage of the practice to get this week and she would set up for additional interviews through the next several days. Jake carried all the gear and helped Erin set up her shots; Jake helping as much as possible, and as much as Erin would let him. Erin realized that he was a great production assistant and so she let him do more of the work as the week progressed. She interviewed more players, took footage of the practices and then came up with a brilliant idea for the open to the pieces. Kyle came over to talk with them and was pleased Erin was now out of the casts and up on crutches. He handed her an envelope with tickets for all the boys and her for the next three home games. Erin was thrilled.

"Kyle, I have a thought for the opening of the pieces that we are doing and I need your help to make it reality." Erin said. Jake was listening intently too.

"What are you thinking Miss Erin?" Kyle asked with a smile on his face.

"I have a very small camera called a lipstick camera and I'd like to attach it to a puck, and have you hit it into the net. Not hard enough to dislodge the camera, but to give the impression of the puck sliding on the ice from the puck's point of view, and going into the net and then do it again from the view of the stick coming into contact with the puck."

"Okay, that sounds intriguing. I don't know if I understand where this is going, but I can certainly do that."

"I would take that footage and then create a graphic that would start with the puck moving from the stick hitting it to sliding along the ice, and dissolve to an animated puck moving on the ice that I would create later. It would slide across the screen, move in curlicues and wrap around the screen as we introduce each starter, by the movement, or each new segment. The puck and its movement would create the tie between all of the segments. From there I would dissolve back to the puck entering the net and using pucks to spell the word RAPTORS, one letter at a time. I would use fast-paced, driving music to pull it all together and cut the images to the beat of the music."

"I can picture that now that you have described it. I like it! What a great way to tie the pieces and segments together. We can do that here or we can do that at my ice rink at my house. Your choice. Once we see it in reality we might be able to use that as our open for the live games too, to tie in and make the segments and live games mesh." Erin smiled at him.

"I don't have the camera with me today and I need to experiment with a puck and connecting my camera to it, making it stay, but perhaps we could do that on the weekend. Early Saturday morning. It wouldn't take too long." Erin was hopeful.

"We can do that. Can you be at my place at 8 and we can set up and do the shoot?"

"I can do that. I do need to take a puck with me so that I can attach my camera to it." Kyle smiled at her and skated away across the rink. He came back with three different pucks for her to experiment with. "Thanks Kyle. We'll see you Saturday morning."

*****

Saturday morning Jake and Erin headed to Kyle's house. Jake was impressed with Kyle's set up. He led them to the ice rink and gave Erin time to set up her gear. Her tablet was connected via Bluetooth to the camera on the puck and so she could start the video from off the rink. She had Jake turn the puck with the camera facing the hockey stick and asked Kyle to skate up to it and then hit the puck. They did that three times before Erin was satisfied. Then, they turned the puck around and she had Kyle hit the puck towards the net, it skated along the ice and finally ended up in the net. They did that two or three times too. She was happy with the shots so Jake carried her out to the net on the ice, helped her get to her knees in front of the net and she set up the pucks to spell out Raptors. Once she was set with that, she had Jake shoot stills and video after she set the camera where she wanted it. She wanted to have the last puck slide into place for the top of the S. Kyle helped her and they managed to get it videotaped with the puck sliding into the right location. She then had Jake take stills as she removed one letter at a time. Jake and Kyle were impressed with her creativity.

They finished the shoot in just under an hour, and Erin put the pucks back into the boxes that Kyle had for her. She just stayed on the ice on her knees for the duration, but Jake could see she was shivering. Forty minutes of ice and cold would do that. The cold was seeping into her joints, she was very stiff. She was trying to hide that, but Jake knew. She was going to hurt to walk when they got her up. She would be stiff from the cold and quite possibly her knees wouldn't straighten out. He wrapped up her gear for her, putting things away. Erin handed the boxes back to Kyle, removed her small camera from the puck and handed that back to him as well.

"Erin, that's yours!" Kyle said crouching down beside her. "You keep it for inspiration and maybe something you might need as you create your graphics. And, when you have it all done can I see it?" He was smiling at her.

"I will share it with you when I finish it!" She smiled at him. "Thanks Kyle for all your help this morning. We'll get out of your hair now so you can have the rest of your day. Thank you." On impulse she reached over and hugged him.

"Miss Erin, can I help you up off the ice?" Kyle asked. He put the boxes of pucks on the net.

"That would be great. Otherwise I'm crawling to the edge from here!" She smiled at him.

"We don't want you doing that!" He stood, still on skates, reached down and scooped her into his arms and skated to the edge where Jake was waiting. Kyle could feel her shivering but he didn't say anything. She was so tiny that the change in temperature affected her and caused her to shiver. He hoped he could give her some warmth as they headed to the side. She curled into his arms absorbing his warmth. They thanked him again, gathered everything and headed home. Jake watched Erin as she used the crutches to get around. She had no range of motion in her leg and she was unstable. She was also very stiff from the cold of the ice. They needed to work on that tonight.

Cassi and Mariah came to Kade's house at 10, picked Erin up, and the three of them headed to the party store. Cassi and Mariah both picked out the decorations for the grooms' cakes and they selected the colors too so Erin knew what color to put on the cakes. Erin found the pans she wanted to use for their wedding cakes based on their drawings, and she purchased the cardboard pieces to put the cakes on, parchment paper, and the columns and plastic holders that would separate the layers. The ladies were pleased with how Erin was going to decorate the cakes and they made sure they gave her all the details they wanted. Both girls picked out their cake toppers. Finally they had everything they needed and the girls took Erin back to Kade's. Erin was getting very excited. She just needed to ask Kade for pink champagne.

Saturday afternoon Erin was making the groom's cake for Alex. Anthony was still at Ink, Inc. She had the big cake, a full sheet cake, in the oven. She had finished a smaller version for dessert after dinner, and she was mixing up her frosting and her glaze. Kade came out of his office and wandered into the kitchen and found Erin perusing closely the bottle of wine from last night's dinner. She looked like she was trying to solve a puzzle.

"Hey Erin. Something smells good!" She looked up and smiled at him.

"I am making Alex's groom's cake. It's in the oven now. Oh, Kade, I wanted you to know that I rearranged your freezers in the garage. I took stuff out of the upright freezer so that I had the shelves for the cakes. I hope that's ok."

"That's great Erin. This is your home too!" Erin shifted her gaze back to the wine bottle. "What are you thinking about honey?"

"Can I ask you a question?" He nodded. "I have been looking at this bottle and its label for weeks now. This is probably going to sound insane, because it sounds crazy in my own mind. The mountain drawing looks like Anthony's artwork, his style, the lettering with the colors looks like your style of artwork, the design of the overall label looks like Alex's artwork and the wine charms look a lot like Michael's piercings. I also have been thinking about the KAMA and to me that stands for Kade, Anthony, Michael, Alex. Is that crazy? Have I lost it again?" She looked back up at Kade.

"No honey it's not crazy. We four brothers own a vineyard and winery. That is our wine." He watched her face as she put things together. Kade could see realization hitting her.

"So when your dad asked about it at the dinners/gatherings, I wasn't imagining that you four own this winery." He nodded. "I think that's so cool. Do you make champagne too?" He nodded again. "I need pink champagne for the wedding cakes."

"I know. I have four bottles in the wine cellar put away for you to bake the cakes with." She smiled at him. "Honey, I told Anthony he needed to tell you about this, but he wanted to wait until the trial was over and things were more settled. He didn't want to add any additional pressure to you. Our business, Ink Inc., here is more of a hobby than a need to do."

"I understand Kade. He really didn't even need to tell me. But I had to ask. Is your vineyard and winery here in the states? I'm just inquisitive, and sometimes nosy, and I've been staring at this label for so many weeks now. You do make good wine! Thanks for letting me know and answering my questions. At least I know I'm not crazy!" She looked like she wanted to say more so Kade stayed still a moment. "Wait you have a wine cellar?" Kade nodded. "Can I see it sometime?" Again Kade nodded. He knew by the look on her face that she wasn't finished. So he waited a beat. Since she didn't offer anything else at the moment, he answered her first questions.

"Our vineyard and winery is located in Italy, just outside of Rome. We go there at least twice a year to check in and we keep in close contact with our vintner and growers. We also have a vineyard here in the states to put different grapes in our wines, as well as fruits, and we ship our wines all over the world. Do you have a favorite kind of wine Erin?"

"I love a good buttery Chardonnay, but would love to see one that has peaches and vanilla as added flavors, or with a Rosé that contains cherry and vanilla." Kade watched her for a moment. His mind was whirling with possibilities of those two wines to add to their collection. She knew how to pair flavors and that was amazing to Kade.

"That sounds amazing. I need to work with our vintner and see what we can do. We can do a special blend for you! Those flavors sound really great and could make a new set of wines that could be heavily requested too." Kade paused and watched Erin's face. "Erin, honey, is there something else on your mind?"

"Yeah. I haven't talked to Anthony yet, but would you be ok with us getting married on the beach south of your house? And use your backyard too?"

"I would love that. Is that what you want?" She nodded.

"What I really want is to have the groomsmen in khakis with Hawaiian shirts, bridesmaids in sundresses with Hawaiian lotus flowers on them, and everyone being comfortable in either flip flops or bare foot. I would wear a wedding dress, because I think the white dress thing would be cool and because my mom never got to do the white dress thing, but I'd love to be barefoot in the sand and have my groom in khakis and a matching shirt like the groomsmen. I just needed a beach to make it all happen." Kade smiled at her.

"I love that idea. That sounds amazing. I can picture it now. Yes you can use the beach. You know, Anthony owns the land next door and so we will all share that beach!" She smiled at Kade. Just as they finished talking the timer on her oven beeped. "Oh, my cake is done!" She turned and Kade was worried about her, so he quickly came around the counter to help get the cake out. He waited while she checked the center with her toothpick, and once she was satisfied he nudged her out of the way to get the cake out of the oven. Erin ran her butter knife around the edges, put the cake board on top with parchment paper and asked Kade to help her turn it over.

"That smells divine!" Kade exclaimed.

"Thanks Kade. I made a smaller version for dessert tonight, just to make sure I have the recipe right. Let's move the pan off the cake and then I can glaze the cake while it's warm." He helped her remove the pan once the cake was centered on the board, and they let it cool a bit. She gave him a taste of the icing that was in the mixer bowl. Kade was impressed with Erin. She had these little tasting spoons that were disposable so it helped as she baked and cooked. She would always know if she had enough flavoring or needed some additional ingredient.

"Wow, this is really good!" Kade said excitedly.

"What's good?" Jake and Anthony said as they came in. "Whoa, something smells really good too."

"Erin just made the groom's cake for Alex. We just took it out of the oven." All three of them watched as she glazed the warm cake and frosted the one she made for dessert for tonight. It was fun to watch her. She gave them all a taste of the frosting she was using. She left the cake on the counter to cool. She told them she would cover it later and then they could put it in the freezer. Jake really needed to start on her PT so it was now or never!

"Miss Erin, do you have time to work on your PT with me?" Jake asked. Apprehensively Erin nodded. Jake smiled. "I am not planning to torture you Erin. We do need to get your ankle moving though. We also need to work on your muscles and strength. Ok?" She nodded again and grabbed her crutches to follow Jake to the workout room.

Erin knew this was coming so she had on shorts and tank top under her sweats and t-shirt. Once she was in the workout room she took off her t-shirt and sweats and waited for Jake. Jake seated her on the training table and removed the arm splint. His goal was to start with the least amount of pain and get her moving.

For the next hour Jake worked on her arm, checking range of motion and then adding a little weight to help her rebuild her muscles. He had her lift the weights in three different ways to try and strengthen her forearm and upper arm. He corrected her form and helped her to move in the right way. He massaged her shoulder, adding in warming oil, and then using the theraband to help with resistance. She was moving pretty well, but her muscles were still lacking on the left side. Jake would help her get that back. They just needed time, and Jake had a plan to add more weight each week to help her get that strength back, and they would build that up slowly. They needed to work on her PT daily. She would do well if they could do the therapy sessions at least once a day, but maybe she would let him do twice a day.

"Ok, Erin, let's move to your ankle." She tensed up. "Honey, it will be ok. I know it's still sore, but I will work to massage it and warm it up and we'll start slowly. I'd like to help rub the bruising out of it. Ok?" He helped her get in position on the training table and he removed the walking boot, sitting on the stool near her foot. He turned her ankle and smoothed his thumb over the incision and Erin sucked in a deep breath seeing the red scar line. Jake did his best to reassure her that it was healing fine. She was still pretty bruised too, but she tried to breathe and let Jake work. She tried to pull herself into her zen place so that she wouldn't tense up as he worked. He laid a towel over his leg and put her heel on his knee.

He poured some warming oil in his hand and then started a deep tissue massage on her ankle. She was sucking in air and trying not to pull away. Jake knew it was tender, but he needed to massage it and try to help it heal. The massaging would help the bruising go away, but he knew she was hurting. As he massaged, he moved the foot down and up slightly, watching Erin's face. She had no side-to-side movement on the ankle, but that would come in time. Having her ankle completely rebuilt made it so it was very stiff. She tried really hard to not tense up and let Jake work. He finished his massage on her ankle. She didn't flinch and she didn't tense up but he could see the pain written on her face, and her eyes were swimming with tears. She was trying to be so strong and brave.

"Ok Erin, I'm going to slide you back onto the table and have you lay down. I want to work on your hip and massage your entire leg. You're doing great honey. I know it hurts like hell. You are so brave." She nodded, not trusting herself to speak, and started to slide herself back so she could lay down. One or two tears slid down her cheeks as she scooted back. Jake brushed them off her cheeks and told her again she was doing great. He helped her and laid her on the table, making sure she was comfortable. She did her deep breathing while Jake worked her hip and flexed her knee, massaged her leg over the bruises. Finally, after another twenty minutes Jake finished up. In the kitchen, meanwhile, Kade wrapped up the cake because it was cool and he didn't want it to dry out. He would ask Erin how she wanted it wrapped before sliding it into the freezer. He also wrapped the one she made for dessert.

"Erin, I have pain meds for you. You need to keep the inflammation down now that we've worked it, so we'll head back to the living room, and I want your foot up with ice for the next thirty minutes at least." She nodded. A few more tears escaped her eyes. She was trying to keep the pain tolerable with the breathing and focusing. She didn't have any energy left in her body to move. She was trying to sit up. She really didn't want to ask for help either. Jake waited, he knew she was debating how to move to the living room; he cleaned his hands and the equipment. He watched her and was ready to help. He knew she wanted to do this on her own, but her body was not yet ready for that. He knew he had worn her out.

"Jake," Erin started, finally. He looked up at her as he was putting tools away. "I don't have the energy to get to the living room. I barely made it to sit up on the table. I'm really sorry, but I have nothing left. Everything hurts." Tears were still sliding down her cheeks. He perched on the training table next to her and wrapped his arm around her.

"Thanks for telling me Erin and sort of asking for help." She smiled at him. He knew she was independent and stubborn. "I know you want to do all this on your own Erin, but it's really ok to ask for help and I would be glad to help you. This is going to be slow going and will take a lot of your energy. All you have to do is ask me. It's not a weakness to ask for help." She took a deep breath. Jake waited. She was trying hard to clear the tears and process everything. He kept her wrapped in his arms.

"Jake, can you please help me get back to the living room? My arms and my legs feel like jelly and I can't do this on my own." She looked up at him with liquid eyes.

"Absolutely Miss Erin." Jake smiled at her. He handed her the pain meds and a bottle of water. She swallowed the pills and waited for Jake. "Was that so hard honey – to ask me for help?"

"Yes." He smiled at her. She giggled. "Thanks Jake for putting up with me. I'm not trying to be a pain or a thorn in your side. I really do need you and you take such good care of me. I can't do this without you. It's just hard to ask for help. I've been independent for so long. It's hard to be reliant on everyone." She hugged him and he brushed more tears off her cheeks. He picked her up and her head dropped to his shoulder. She was completely spent; the pain had overtaken her small body. He carried her to the living room and put her in the recliner. Anthony heard them coming and brought out the ice pack and Kade gathered some pillows; together they took the boot off, elevated her leg on the pillows and added the ice pack to it. She laid her head back and in no time was sound asleep. Jake knew it was exhaustion as well as a defensive mechanism to deal with the pain. Anthony covered her with a blanket so she wouldn't get cold. She was still just in her shorts and tank top, and it was cool in the room. Jake just smiled at her and shook his head. She was something else. She needed rest though in order to heal.

*****

Kade, Anthony and Jake sat on the back porch relaxing with ice tea and cookies. They left the door open, with the screen shut, so they could hear Erin if she needed something. Kade asked how the first round of PT went. Jake told them that he had lots of work to do on the ankle, but her arm and shoulder were doing very well. He told them she had a few tears too because of the pain, but they would get there. Anthony said that her incision area looked a little angry. Jake told him they needed to leave the boot off it and allow air to circulate around it to heal better. Jake also suggested that she sleep without the brace so that it would heal. It was all going to take time. They just needed to work every day and try to help her get her range of motion back. They talked about Alex and Cassi's wedding, and Jake said that Erin was concerned about standing up for Cassi with the bruises and the splints.

"Anthony, I wanted to let you know that Erin figured out about the winery on her own." Kade said and Anthony was surprised. "She was looking really intently at the label this afternoon when I came into the kitchen; she asked me if she was crazy to think that the mountain graphic looked like your artwork, and the overall design looked like Alex, the wine charms for Michael and the lettering like mine."

"She's really observant. I should have told her sooner."

"Actually, she said that you really didn't need to tell her at all. She was curious though and wanted to know if she was crazy thinking the KAMA stood for the four of us. She also gave me a couple of good ideas for new wines – a buttery Chardonnay with peaches and vanilla, and a Rosé with cherry and vanilla." Kade smiled at Anthony. "She also asked me, and she hasn't talked to you yet Anthony, if you guys could get married on the beach that our properties share."

"She wants a beach wedding?!" Anthony asked smiling.

"She said her perfect wedding would be to have the groom and groomsmen in khakis with Hawaiian shirts and her bridesmaids in Hawaiian print sundresses, and everyone either barefoot or in flip flops."

"She's a woman after my own heart."

"That's why you two are a match. She said that she wanted to be in a white wedding dress, but barefoot in the sand." Anthony was smiling. This was his Erin. She was so amazing. Anthony was so in love with his Erin. He wanted to do all he could to help her through the PT and the pain. He knew this was going to be a long road for her and would take all her energy. She wanted to do so much to help everyone in the family and her poor body needed rest and help.

Their conversation moved into Jake's life and they talked about his business and about him moving here, buying land and preparing to build a house. Both Jake and Kade were excited to meet the girls Erin had picked out for them. Jake told them he had asked Erin to help him create a website for his business too. They all smiled at that. Erin was so good for them. They thought that perhaps they could do dinner out with the girls on Sunday. They'd have to talk to Erin about that. Jake and Kade wanted to meet Laurel and Kiera.

*****

Two hours later Erin woke and the boys heard her groan. Anthony was the first one in the house. She was struggling to move and not having any luck. She was so tiny in the large recliner and she couldn't set the recliner back up. She was really struggling.

"Hey sugar." Anthony said as he got to her side. He reached to brush her hair back from her face. He was also trying to calm her down and let her know he was there for her.

"Anthony, handsome, I hurt everywhere. I can't move. I feel like I got run over by a truck." She groaned again.

"It's ok honey. Let us help you. But, you kinda did get run over by a truck." Kade took the ice pack off her leg, chuckling at Anthony's remark. It was no longer cold so he took it to the freezer. Because of the haze of pain she couldn't see the humor in Anthony's statement. Her brow was furrowed with pain.

"Sorry guys, but I have to go to the ladies' room. And I can't move at all. It all hurts, and I have no energy. I've lost all my independence." Jake helped to set the recliner up and he put her walking boot back on. Jake knew that was the crux of what was eating at Erin, her lost independence. It wasn't lost at all, just on hold for a bit.

"I've got you sugar. I'll take you upstairs and help you. It's ok." She tried to smile at Anthony, but she was in lots of pain. She was trying to be brave but she was hurting. Jake helped Anthony get her in his arms and he took her upstairs. She groaned with all the movement.

"Kade, do we still have those muscle relaxants from Mariah for Erin?" Jake asked as he headed into the kitchen.

"Yeah. They are right here Jake." Kade handed him the bottle he took out of the small cupboard. "Is this because of the PT you did earlier?" He nodded.

"When we finished she finally asked for help. She told me her arms and legs felt like jelly and she had no energy. I gave her ibuprofen to help with that, but I'm guessing with all she's been doing, productions and making cakes, and all the stress, we need to help her recharge her batteries tonight." Kade agreed. "She wants to do everything on her own and her poor body can't always keep up. She's also bemoaning the fact that she is reliant on all of us."

"Perhaps I should pull something together for dinner. She isn't going to be able to do that." Kade started looking through the refrigerator. "It looks like Erin took out steaks to put on the grill. She always pre-plans for us. Let's do that and we can do a salad to go with it. Sound good?"

"Yeah it sounds great. I'll go set up the grill and get it heating." Jake went out the back door to get the grill ready. Anthony came back downstairs with Erin in his arms. He kissed her and whispered to her. She was trying to smile at him. He sat her at the kitchen counter. She had a little more color and looked like she was feeling a bit better. Anthony arranged her leg on the stool next to her.

"Kade, did you cover the cake for me?" She asked surprised. He nodded. "Thank you! We need to put a big plastic garbage back over it and seal it, then it needs to go to the freezer." Anthony got a garbage bag out and Kade helped him get the cake into the bag. They sealed it after getting the air out of it and Anthony took it to the garage. She cautioned him to hold it under the middle so the cake wouldn't crack.

"I pulled out steaks for dinner tonight Kade. I thought we'd have the rice pilaf – those boxes on the counter by the toaster. And I thought I could make a salad." Kade smiled at her.

"Jake is starting the grill. What do you need for the rice?"

She told him and he got everything out for her. She prepared the butter and rice and had Kade put it in the microwave for the right amount of time. Soon it was ready for the water and the seasoning packets. Anthony helped Kade and they got the casserole dish into the microwave to cook. Anthony had put Erin's leg up on the stool next to her with a soft pillow, and she was adjusting, trying to get comfortable. Erin cautioned them that they needed hot pads to hold the glass dish because it would be very hot. Anthony got out the salad fixings and he helped Erin get the salad made.

"Erin, could we do dinner out tomorrow night with your two girlfriends, Laurel and Kiera?" Kade asked.

"I'll call them after dinner and find out. Where do you want to have dinner at?"

They decided on Mama Luisa's Italian Eatery. Erin just smiled. This was going to be a great evening. It gave her something to focus on rather than the pain from the PT. Kade took the steaks out and worked with Jake to get them cooked. Anthony set the table and Erin texted Laurel and Kiera. She got an immediate response from both of them that they could make it. She told them to meet at Mama Luisa's at 6 and it was going to be casual, get to know you kind of thing. Laurel told her she was super excited to meet Jake.

The four of them had dinner and Jake made sure Erin took one of Mariah's magic pills. Soon Erin was relaxed and sound asleep. Anthony took her upstairs and put her to bed, taking her brace off. She needed her rest. Erin was pushing so hard to be on her feet for her girls. Alex and Cassi's wedding was coming up on the weekend. Erin really wanted to be more independent. She grew frustrated when it seemed like nothing was progressing. Jake kept trying to reassure her and he told her that she was making progress, but he could see her doubt! She didn't want to be patient, but she pushed herself to do the PT and the exercises.

*****

Dinner was a success! Laurel and Jake seemed to be getting along very well, as were Kiera and Kade. They were deeply involved in conversation and animated as they got to know one another. They had a lot in common and so could find things to talk about. Anthony and Erin watched both couples and Anthony realized Erin picked out amazing matches for both of them.

"Erin, honey, you did great picking out girls for my two brothers here." He smiled at her.

"I just wanted everyone to be as happy as we are handsome." She smiled at him and leaned in for a kiss. "Anthony, I'd like to talk about our wedding. I know you've been busy at work, probably because of the website, and worrying about me, and I've been busy too keeping up with all my work, but I can't wait to marry you my sweet hero." He smiled at her.

"Can we do that later tonight? Kade already told me about your beach idea. I love that idea!" She was giddy at that comment; she leaned into kiss him. They returned to the conversation at the table and just enjoyed a nice night out. It was nice not to have to cook or worry about Devin.

*****

The week flew by. Kade, Anthony and Jake watched in wonder as Erin finished the groom's cake and the wedding cakes. She had each cake all separate on their dividers for the layers, and she used her turntable to decorate. Kade watched as she frosted each layer with the final coat, smoothed it out with a bench scraper, and created roses out of the icing; she made rose buds for the edges and full roses for the layers. She placed the plate on the top of the bottom layer and decorated around it, and did the same with the next two layers. These plates had places for the columns to connect to when she put the cake together.   Kade asked her about the space between layers and Erin told him that Cassi wanted a small bouquets of silk flowers in her wedding colors. She showed him what she had created for that space. Kade was impressed.

The cake was going to be amazing when it was all done and set up. She let all the roses dry in the delicate pink color that Cassi had requested. While all the decorations were drying, she turned her attention to the groom's cake. Using the pictures of Alex's motorcycle, she used edible food paint and colored the white modeling chocolate motorcycle decoration to look just like Alex's. She sat at the counter and painstakingly painted the motorcycle with a teeny tiny brush.

The boys watched in wonder as the motorcycle took shape and Anthony was really surprised at how much is resembled Alex's bike. Erin could take a picture and replicate it in candy. It was amazing. She then created his workspace from Ink, Inc., and put the tools of his trade on the work areas she built out of modeling chocolate, and painted them. The boys were awestruck at her work and level of detail. Cassi also wanted the words *always and forever* written on the cake. The colors were light green and light pink. Erin asked Kade to do the lettering on the cake; she showed him how to operate the decorating tip and he practiced on wax paper. Kade did a phenomenal job on the lettering. He had a steady hand and such a fluid motion that the lettering looked absolutely awesome.

"Erin, honey, how do we transport this cake?" Anthony asked. He was concerned about the layers and how it would work.

"Well handsome, we'll wrap each layer separately after they dry, put them in these boxes, and I'll take all the parts with me, as well as touch up frosting if I need it and my tools. We'll set the cake up completely with the bride and groom on the top, the bridesmaids and groomsmen in the center, as well as the filigree bridges at your mom and dad's. I have all the decorations for the wedding cake, so we should be good." She looked up him.

"It's going to look amazing Erin." Jake said. She smiled and captured her bottom lip in her teeth. These three men loved to watch her work. She was so precise and so creative. She told them she wanted pictures to add to her portfolio of cakes when it was completely set up. Jake told her he would help her take pictures. She smiled at him and thanked him.

Throughout the week she worked twice a day with Jake on her PT. She was getting stronger and her ankle was starting to loosen up. Jake made sure that each night she took one of Mariah's magic pills to help with relaxation and recharging of her batteries. Erin didn't have nearly the tears as the first day, and her bruises were starting to fade as Jake massaged the area and he could put a bit more pressure on her bruises. He could, however, feel all the screws and pins, which worried him some, and he could see the scar starting to recede in its redness too, so they were making progress. The screws and pins were pushing against her skin. She had really tiny ankles, but the screws and pins were making themselves known. She flinched though, every time he hit the spaces with the screws and pins. He needed to watch that part on her ankle. It was almost as if the screws were pushing their way out of the ankle bones. They may need to go back and see Dr. Parker. He massaged steering clear of those spaces and trying to reassure Erin even though he wasn't convinced it was ok.

Saturday morning Erin was up early. She made breakfast and gathered all her tools. She didn't want to wake Anthony, he was sleeping so peacefully, so she figured out how to get down the stairs all by herself. She put the coffee on and she opened up the curtains. She and Jake made an agreement that he could torture her after the wedding, when they got home later tonight. She had already gathered her dress and what she needed to be Cassi's maid of honor. The three girls had decided early on that Erin would serve as Cassi's maid of honor, Cassi would be Mariah's and Mariah would be Erin's. Now, she just needed to make sure she had all her decorating tools, the items to finish the cakes, all the decorations, and extra frosting. She had purchased cake boxes which would make the transport easier. She started moving cakes to the boxes from the refrigerator.

Erin bustled around the kitchen without her crutches as she worked to put each cake layer in the appropriate box. She couldn't think about the pain in her ankle. She labeled each of the boxes and placed the wrapped cake in it. She set each cake box on the table as she finished and crossed stuff off her list. Jake came in the back door watching Erin in her zone. He was pleased to see that she was walking pretty well without the crutches. She didn't see Jake because she was wrapped up in her country music and her cakes. He loved watching her and listening to her sing to herself. He just stood there, fascinated. Anthony made his way down the stairs and stood next to Jake. Both of them were smiling. Kade joined them.

"Good morning gentlemen." Erin said when she noticed all three looking at her. "Breakfast is just about ready and the cakes are all ready to go."

"How long have you been up and why didn't you wake me for help sugar?" Anthony said as he came to her and wrapped her in his arms.

"You needed your sleep handsome. I'm getting stronger thanks to Jake's torture, I mean PT, and I needed to do this. You all have taken such good care of me, but you also need your rest." She kissed Anthony and smiled at all of them. "We have two very busy weeks starting today. I have more cakes to make after this wedding is over!" She smiled again at her men. They were so good to her and put up with all her hair-brained ideas. She didn't know how she deserved them all, but she was deliriously happy with her life and her family.

They all ate breakfast and then Anthony helped Erin to shower and get ready for the day. By ten they had loaded the pickup with the cakes, their garment bags with their clothes, and themselves. They arrived at mom and dad's house and the boys carried all the boxes inside. Erin bustled around and carefully unwrapped each cake, setting it up in the right order. She had Kade help Jake unbox the groom's cake because it was a full-sheet and she didn't think she could manage it by herself. The two were far steadier than she was.

By 11:30 Erin had both cakes up and completely decorated. Jake was taking pictures of her setting up the cakes, and he took more pictures of all the cakes once it was completely set up. She stood back after she placed the bride and groom atop the cake, and made sure everything was perfect. She grabbed her camera from Jake, snapped several more photos, getting close-ups of the details, and then moved to the groom's cake to take pictures of it. She had to go get dressed soon because the photographer would be here to take pictures.

"Erin, dear, the cakes are beautiful, works of art!" Angelina exclaimed and came over to wrap Erin in a hug. "You do beautiful work." Erin smiled at her.

"Thanks mom! I have to go get dressed now. Can I put my camera bag somewhere safe?"

"I'll put it in the spare bedroom where my boys are getting dressed." Angelina took the camera bag and Erin made her way to girls' dressing room. Mariah and Kiera helped her get dressed. She had to wear her boot, but a heel on the other foot. She told Cassi that she didn't want to ruin her photos with the bruises and her splints, but Cassi assured her that the pictures would be beautiful. They had already told the photographer and he would position Erin so that they had really pretty pictures. She was determined to have Erin be a part of them. Mariah made sure Erin was stable on her feet. It was an amazing wedding! Cassi and Alex looked so happy and Cassi was thrilled when she saw the wedding cake. Alex was overwhelmed seeing the groom's cake and all the details. There were lots of murmurs about who made the cake and Angelina bragged on Erin. Alex and Cassi were flying to Italy for their honeymoon in the morning. It was Alex's turn to visit the winery so they would spend their time exploring Italy.

*****

They arrived home and Erin changed into her shorts and tank top. She headed to the gym and waited for Jake to join her.

"Jake, before you get started," Erin said. Jake came over to listen to her. "I don't know what is going on with my ankle, but something was rubbing and really hurting at the wedding; and it feels wet now. I just wanted you to know before you get started."

"Ok Erin. Let me get all my stuff set up and then I'll take a look at your ankle." She adjusted herself on the training table and worked to sit where her leg was dangling over the end near where Jake would be working on her. "Was your ankle hurting throughout the whole day?"

"No. It was ok as I made it through the service, but then at the reception, when Anthony and I danced the last time, I could feel something pulling and almost like a tearing sensation." Jake was worried. Those screws may have created a problem.

Jake removed the splint and saw the torn skin on her ankle. Erin looked down and sucked in air. "OMG!"

"Ok honey. We talked about the screws and the pins. I told you I could feel them all." She nodded, clearly in shock at what she was seeing on her ankle bone. He cleaned off her ankle and both of them could see the heads of the screws and the pins sticking out. "I need to call Dr. Parker. We need to get this taken care of tonight honey. The screws not only tore through your skin but they did a number on the inside of the boot." He stood and moved her back on the table so her leg was extended on the table and not hanging down. He tried to reassure her with a hug. "Please sit here honey. I am going to take a picture and send that to Dr. Parker. We'll see what he wants to do." Erin was a little bit panicky at seeing hardware sticking out of her ankle. Anthony came in to see how things were going.

"Anthony, I'm calling Dr. Parker right now. The screws and pins he used on Erin's ankle have punched back out through her skin." Anthony came over and wrapped his arm around Erin sitting behind her on the table. Jake stepped to the side to call Dr. Parker.

"Hey honey. I'm so sorry. Is this what you said you were feeling earlier?" She nodded, but her eyes were still glued on her ankle. Jake came back over.

"Ok Erin. Dr. Parker wants to see you now. He thinks he may need to take you back to surgery and remove all the hardware." Jake said.

"More surgery?" She was devastated.

"Erin, we need to get your ankle repaired. So yes. Anthony, can you carry her and I'll bring her boot. We need to keep the boot off her ankle. Let me wrap it with a bandage before we go." Jake sat down on his stool and Anthony helped Erin slide down so Jake could bandage her ankle. Anthony told Kade what was happening as they headed out the door with Kade's truck.

*****

Dr. Parker was waiting when they arrived. Anthony carried her inside and Jake followed with her boot. Dr. Parker led them to a cubicle and once Erin was comfortable on the gurney he removed the bandage. It took him a bit to get the bandage off her ankle with all the pieces sticking out.

"Wow. Ok this is something I don't think I've ever seen. It appears that your ankle is rejecting the screws and the pins Miss Erin." Dr. Parker was examining the ankle and feeling all around the broken skin area. Erin was sucking in air to keep the pain at bay and Anthony was holding her hand. "We need to head to the OR. I need to remove the screws and pins and then I'll repair the skin. It will look as good as new. Don't worry Erin."

"Doc, how long will she be in the hospital?" Anthony asked.

"I think we can just keep her here overnight tonight and she can head back home tomorrow. Is that ok Miss Erin?"

"Yeah I guess."

"Ok Erin. We need to get you prepped for surgery. I'll send a nurse in to help you change into a hospital gown." He turned to Anthony and Jake. "You two can come with me and I'll take you to the surgical waiting room."

"Anthony, here's my ring so I don't lose it, and my phone. I'll see you after." Anthony leaned in and kissed her. "Jake, thank you for taking such good care of me." Jake hugged her. Both of her men told her they would see her after. Erin tried to be brave and smiled at them. They left and followed Dr. Parker and soon a nurse appeared. Anthony called Kade to let him know what was happening.

"Well, Miss Erin, I didn't expect to see you again so soon." Henry said as he came in.

"Hi Henry. Yeah I guess I didn't get enough of this place the last time I was here." She smiled at him.

"More surgery?" He asked.

"Yes. The screws in my ankle decided they didn't want to be there anymore." Henry looked at her ankle.

"Wow! I guess not. Ok, so let's get you changed and I'll put your clothes in a bag." Henry helped her change from her street clothes which was pretty easy since she was in shorts and tank top, into the hospital gown. "Miss Erin, you have new accessories since we last met." Erin blushed.

"Oh! Yeah, my soon to be brother-in-law did that for me. It was a gift for my Anthony."

"Very nice. It looks beautiful on you." Henry smiled at her and she blushed even more. "I need to let Dr. Parker know. I'll put tape over them for surgery. Ok?" She nodded.

"Henry, can you make sure that Dr. Parker does some sort of magic so I won't want to throw up again after surgery?"

"I will indeed. Let me note that in the chart and then I'll put you on the telemetry for your vitals." He asked her for her name and date of birth then proceeded to connect her to the pulse ox, blood pressure and heart monitors. He added tape across her piercings and then headed out to find Dr. Parker. Erin sank back into the bed and let the day wash over her. It was so weird about the screws in her ankle. She must just be weird. Dr. Parker said he'd never seen that before.

Erin breezed through surgery and ended up in the corner room on the fifteenth floor again. She did better with the nausea cocktail added to her IV. Anthony and Jake stayed in the waiting room until Henry directed them upstairs. Jake headed back home and Anthony stayed the night. Jake said he would be back in the morning to help them get home. Erin once again asked him to bring sweats and a baggy t-shirt. She hugged him and thanked him for taking care of her.

*****

Sunday morning the sun was streaming in the windows of Erin's room. Dr. Parker made sure she had the same room as before and Anthony stayed with her. Erin awoke and stretched, realizing she was in the arms of her handsome Anthony.

"Morning handsome." She leaned in to kiss him. She was laying on her right side with her left leg up on pillows. Anthony had his arm around her waist and she was using his shoulder for a pillow.

"Morning sugar. Did you sleep?" She nodded.

"Did you get some sleep my sweet hero?" He nodded and kissed her again.

Dr. Parker came in followed by dining services with their breakfast trays. He examined Erin's ankle, changed out the bandage and told her he was working on her discharge paperwork. He also told her he was changing her splint to something different and if she used the crutches for a couple of days she should be up and around for the wedding on the weekend. They ate breakfast and Anthony helped Erin shower and get dressed. Jake arrived and before eleven they were heading home.

Erin checked her phone and email when she got home and returned several messages. She was propped up in the recliner with her leg up and ice on it. She called Kyle back and they talked at length about the open she had created. He told her how impressed he was with her skills. He also told her that the live game crew wanted to use her open and give her credit for it. She told him that was great! She filled him in on her latest escapade with the surgery and the screws, and he told her that the Raptors wanted her to speak to *Erin's Law* after the game on Friday. She made notes in her calendar and let the boys know.

Sunday afternoon Anthony moved Erin outside to soak up some sun on the beach. He set her in a lounge chair and the boys doted on her. She had her laptop and her phone, and she had all the diet pepsi she could drink! They took such good care of her. While Erin was soaking in the sun she made her lists for Mariah's wedding and noted when she needed to make the cakes. They had until the following Saturday. Cassi and Alex would be back from their honeymoon on Wednesday before the wedding.

Anthony came and sat with her for a bit and she talked with him.

"Anthony, when I get better will you do an ink for me?" Anthony smiled at her.

"I'd love to Erin. What are you thinking about?"

"I'd really like to have your family dragon crest with your name on it as my ink."

They talked for a bit and Anthony wanted to know if she wanted it on her shoulder, her hip or her side. Erin chose her right hip, well upper thigh on the outside. Anthony was thrilled and told her they could do that before the wedding!

Chapter Eleven

Erin finished the cakes for Mariah's wedding. Michael did MMA style fighting so the groom's cake had his piercing station, piercing pieces like barbells, jewels and chains, and his fight ring. Erin had pictures to go by but Kade was a really big help in figuring out the angles to make the mesh for the ring. She tempered chocolate and piped the parts of the ring around a glass covered with parchment paper to make it round. She made two halves and then joined them with more melting chocolate. It took a lot of work, but once it dried and was painted, it looked amazing. Mariah also wanted a medical exam room set-up too. She met Michael while fixing his broken ribs, and fractured wrist, after one of his many fights, so Erin used modeling chocolate to create all the pieces. The word *"speechless"* was requested by the couple to be written on the cake. Erin once again had Kade do the lettering in light blue frosting.

Jake and Erin worked on PT through the week. They worked in the morning on weights and theraband, and in the evenings on the punching bag and more resistance training. Jake put her through the paces but it paid off. She was walking almost normally and would be able to be in two shoes this weekend at the wedding. Jake practiced with her and helped her gain her steadiness because it wasn't just shoes but stiletto heels. She would just need to watch the dancing and the uneven ground. Jake worked on weights and allowed Erin to use the punching bag with both hands this time. She was getting her strength back on the left side and she was light on her feet. He was very pleased with her progress. She spent part of her time sparring with Jake and Kade in the ring. Erin was coming back to being herself completely.

*****

The wedding was beautiful and Mariah looked so happy; she was glowing! She loved the cakes that Erin had created for their ceremony. Jake took the pictures for Erin of the cakes. She was very pleased with her work. Erin actually had requests from several people in attendance for cakes for special occasions. Mariah had also asked Erin if it was possible to videotape the ceremony. Erin set up two cameras and gave the remotes to start them to Jake. He proved to be a great help with the cameras and the technology. She was thrilled that he had some production knowledge to help out. He took great pictures too to add to Erin's cake collection. Mariah made sure that the guys could walk the bridesmaids down the aisle. Anthony walked Erin down and held her steady across the grass in the backyard. When they danced, later at the reception, Anthony held her in his arms and her feet didn't touch the floor. She made the same deal with Jake that he could do the PT after the ceremony. Mariah and Michael were heading to Hawaii for their honeymoon. They were catching the red eye flight and would be in Hawaii for breakfast! It was exciting.

Meanwhile, Erin and Anthony were planning their wedding. They had worked through most of the details already. The colors would be light purple, light teal and silver. Anthony was totally on board with the beach wedding. Erin had let her bridesmaids know that they would be in sundresses with lotus flowers in bright colors of purple and magenta. Anthony wanted the teal color, so the matron of honor Mariah and the best man, Kade, would be in purple, with the rest of the bridal party in magenta. The men would be in Hawaiian shirts in magenta and purple colors. Erin found the perfect wedding dress that accentuated her figure and showed off her ink too! It was strapless and looked amazing on her. She also opted for a ring of white baby roses with pearls for her hair with a veil down the back only. Erin told Anthony that she'd like to have Jake give her away, so the two of them asked him together.

"Jake, do you have a few minutes to talk with us?" Anthony asked. He nodded and they headed outside to talk around the table with Kade. They had a conversation about the weather and about the flowers in Kade's yard. Jake asked if Erin would consider helping him when he got his house built with the landscaping. She agreed. He told her he would have the plans back from the architect next week and then they could talk about that. She asked him what kind of flowers he liked and he told her wanted roses for sure and whatever else she might suggest. They would go take a look at his land and that would help Erin decide for his gardens. Erin then asked if she could change the subject. All of them agreed.

"Jake, will you give me away at our wedding?" Erin asked.

"Really?! You want me to give you away?" She nodded and smiled at him. "I would be honored to give you away Erin." She stood and hugged him. She whispered her thanks to him.

"Speaking of architectural plans, Erin, honey, can you sit with me and let's look over the plans for our house?"

"Our house?" She climbed into Anthony's lap. Jake and Kade moved their chairs around so they were all on the same side of the table.

"Yes! I own the land next door to Kade's, and I've been working on plans for a house for us. I want to make sure that you like it and we can break ground." He pulled out the plans and unrolled them. "It will be a two story house with bedrooms upstairs, a gym, kitchen, living room, laundry room downstairs. We even have a space for a wine cellar like Kade's. I was trying to put together all the things I thought you and I would need, and we can change them as you see fit." She watched as he revealed the plans.

"This is amazing!" She looked over both levels and for the next hour they talked through the plans. Erin asked for a couple of changes to the kitchen and the master bedroom, but most of the changes were minor. Kade and Anthony helped with what she was trying to do, but her biggest change came when they added in an island in the kitchen. She wanted a large space with counter space to cook, bake and more. They decided on a four bedroom house with three bathrooms. Erin also said that since her house was sold she was prepared to invest in their new house.

"Honey, we're going to put that money into an investment for our future." Anthony said. "I've been living with my mom and dad until I moved in with you. I've put away my shares of the winery over the years to build a permanent house and have more than enough for the house. We'll put the sale of your house into a retirement portfolio." She smiled at him. She leaned over and hugged him to her.

"Also, Erin, you got a certified letter this morning. I'm guessing it's a settlement for your car, medical bills, etc." Kade handed her the envelope. She took it hesitantly from Kade, stared at it, but made no move to open it.

"Erin, darlin' what's wrong?" Kade asked.

"Not sure I want to open this. It's been so nice not to have to think about Devin and all the past stuff, and I know you think this is a settlement, but what if it isn't?" Erin looked up at them. They could all see the fear in her eyes.

"Erin, we're all here with you. We'll deal with whatever is in the envelope together ok? We're all in this together. You have all of us to watch over and protect you." She tried to erase the fear off her face, but she was very guarded. She sat looking at the envelope for a bit, but finally took a deep breath and slid her finger under the flap to open it. She pulled out the paperwork and started to read it. They watched her as her eyes revealed her shock at what she was seeing. Her free hand came up over her mouth trying to cover the surprise in her face.

"Honey, what is it?" Anthony asked, very concerned. She didn't have the words so she passed the paper over to Anthony to read.

"Wow. It says here that in the settlement, Devin paid for the totaled car, a settlement of $45,000. He also paid all the medical bills directly to the hospital and doctor, including the most recent surgery. His settlement also includes $100K for pain and suffering." Kade and Jake were nodding in agreement. Jake looked back at Erin.

"Erin, honey, is there something else with the settlement in the envelope?" She nodded. She pulled up another envelope. "What is it Erin?"

"According to this second letter that I haven't handed to Anthony yet, there is a note of apology from Devin in this envelope. He was required to write this to me as part of his psychiatric treatment." She held the envelope like it might explode. Her eyes were huge. "I can't open this you guys. There's no telling what is in here."

Kade reached over and took the envelope from her. "Erin, let's put this away for now. Are there any instructions? Do you have to respond to the note from Devin?" She shook her head.

"I don't think so. Here's the other letter." She handed that to Kade. He quickly scanned it.

"It says here that Devin was required to write this letter to you to apologize for what he did. It further states that no one vetted it; the judge did not see it before it was sent." He kept reading. "It also invites Erin to respond to the letter once she has read it." He paused. "I'm inclined to agree with Erin. I don't know what is in here and I don't know that we want to dredge anything up from the past."

"Erin," Jake said and waited for her to look at him. "Can I open the letter and read it on your behalf? If it's bad I won't share it with you. I think we need to know what has happened with Devin over the last eight weeks. I can work with Mory and write a response if required. But this way, it's just me seeing the words." Erin looked at Jake with fear etched on her face and took a deep breath.

"Ok. I don't want to put you through that though. There's no telling what Devin said in this letter." She took another deep breath as she was processing. "You have my permission to open and read it. If it's not good please don't make me read it." She was pleading with him. "I'm happy and I'm settled. I don't want to relive all of that. I don't have the energy to relive all of that pain." Jake agreed and took the envelope. Erin got up and went to start on dinner. She needed to keep herself busy so she didn't go back to the dark place.

"Jake, eight weeks is not enough time for him to be rehabilitated. I think it's odd they would send that letter without someone vetting it. Maybe we need to contact Drake in case Erica got a letter too." Kade said. They all agreed with that.

Erin peeked back out the door. "Hey guys," they all turned and looked her direction. "I don't know if Erica got a letter too, but I'm guessing she shouldn't read the one from Devin. She doesn't need any more pain either. She's trying to heal and get past all of this too."

"We were just talking about that Erin. I'm calling Drake now." Kade said. He pulled out his phone and stepped away, wandering down to the beach. Erin turned and headed back inside. Her phone rang and it was Kyle. She took a really deep breath and tried to center herself.

"Hi Kyle." Erin said, trying to keep herself smiling and happy.

"Erin, hi. I'm calling because the team and our PR folks are thrilled with the open you created for the website segments and the production team that does our live games, well they want to use it for the opens to the games, as you already know. You will receive credit for creating it every time it plays. Can you be at our game on Friday night and talk with the production crew?"

"That would be awesome. Yes!"

"Good. I'll send the tickets. Erin, we also want to do a follow-up on *'Erin's Law'* and do a segment with the production crew and you about these last several months. Will you agree to an interview? We want to keep this in the spotlight, keep it in front of the public, and need you to make that possible."

"I'm happy to do that. I don't want anyone else to go through this ever. Just tell me what time to be there and I'll be dressed for an interview. Will this be part of the pre-show for the game?"

"Thanks Erin. Yes, and it will be done on the ice so those in the stadium will also hear the interview too. I'll send tickets to you and your men. I will also have our producer send you a list of questions so that you can be better prepared. You will come out onto the ice with me to start the game. We'll talk about where things are at center ice. Can you skate? Are the casts off?"

"Yes! That's awesome. I may need a hand to hold because I'm still getting my steadiness back and I don't want to fall down in front of everyone, but I can skate. That will be amazing." They talked for a bit longer and signed off. While she was on the phone she had a couple of text messages. She read them and smiled. Laurel and Kiera were enjoying getting to know Jake and Kade. Laurel told her that Jake was the man of her dreams and she was falling in love with him. Erin was thrilled that things seemed to be working out. Now, more than ever, they needed to move out and give Kade back his space. It was hard to have them living underfoot and being in the way. She put her phone away and got her rolls going. She wanted stuff on hand for breakfast. Her mind was going a mile a minute and trying to figure out how to give Kade his life back and his house. She no longer had her house, it was Drake's now. But maybe they could find an apartment. Kade came in the backdoor. He could see that she was deep in thought.

"Hey Erin. What're you making?" She looked up and smiled.

"I'm making some cinnamon rolls for tomorrow morning. I thought I might make orange rolls too. Does that sound good?"

"It sounds amazing. You are such a great baker! Thank you for all of this." He hugged her. He could see she was thinking about something so he decided to ask. "Honey, is there something on your mind? Are you worried about something?"

"Yeah." She took a deep breath. Kade held onto her shoulders and she finally looked up at him. "Kiera said things were going well with you two." Kade nodded. "I was thinking that Anthony and I need to get out of your way so you can actually think about a life with Kiera if that's what you want. We're sort of in your way living here and being underfoot."

"I'm not in any hurry and neither is she. She understands everything that is happening with you and Anthony and my having you both here. This is not something to worry about Erin. I love having you both here; you can cook and you are so creative with my gardens; you are so much fun to have around, I love sparring with you when we work out. You aren't cramping my style darlin'. Everything is good. Ok?" He held her shoulders so she would continue to look at him. She nodded and smiled at him. She hugged him again.

"I just felt bad that we are still here and I didn't want to keep you from exploring things with Kiera, having time to yourself without us underfoot. You've been so good to us, me in particular, and I love that we have a great place to live, but I also want you to have your life to live on your own terms." She smiled at him and went back to work. "Kade, when my ankle is healed enough with the scar will you do an ink for me over that area?"

"I would love that Erin. Do you have a design in mind?"

"No. This is your choice. We both like country music, the beach and flowers. I'll trust you to come up with something and then maybe it will hide the scar!" He smiled at her and watched her work.

They talked while Erin worked on the rolls. He watched her efficiently roll out the dough, add the butter and cinnamon mixture, and roll them up. She cut them and put them in pans, then put them into the warm oven to rise. She cleaned up the cinnamon parts and then rolled out the orange rolls. Kade just watched in wonder as she made four dozen rolls for them to have for breakfasts or whenever they needed a snack. It was a good thing they all liked to work out!

*****

Over dinner Erin filled them in on Friday and the game. She told them that Kyle and the team wanted to splash the *'Erin's Law'* thing to keep it in the public's mind, that she would be skating with him prior to the start of the game and that she needed to do an interview with production team at center ice during the pre-game. She also told them about the team wanting her open that she created to use as the open for the games. Jake and Kade asked if they could see how she created it. After dinner she pulled up her computer and showed all three of them the video with the driving music. Erin played it for them a couple of times. All of them were impressed with her talents.

Jake left the trio shortly after dinner and headed to his cottage. He had a phone meeting with Uncle Mory to discuss the letter that Devin had sent to Erin.   The letter basically accused Erin of making him get psychiatric help and that he wasn't crazy. Drake said that Erica received a letter too and he took it. Jake asked if he could come and get it and then provide an answer for both of them. Drake agreed. Jake headed there and came back to deal with the response.   Devin basically said that Erin was the cause of all his problems and the fact that he was in prison; she was the reason behind everything that happened. Jake needed to have Mory respond without Erin getting dragged back into the demons.   He knew this was too soon to see anything other than accusations toward Erin. Mory would be able to formulate a response and make sure that future letters were vetted. Maybe Devin needed a different psychiatrist.

*****

Friday night Erin and her entourage headed to the ice hockey venue. Erin had her skates in hand and Jake had taped her ankle to give it some stability. She had prepared the best she could for the interview using the questions the production team sent. Jake, Anthony and Kade helped her with answers and what sounded the best. Once they were seated in the box she put her skates on and prepared to be called out onto the ice. Anthony, Kade and Jake were reassuring her that the interview would go well. She smiled at them and tried to just be present in the moment. Cassi and Alex joined them tonight. Cassi had never seen a hockey game so was looking all around. Once again the team provided them with stadium dogs, drinks, chips and cookies! Erin watched as the crew set up at center ice. She wasn't sure how to navigate the carpet.

"Hey guys, what do I do with the rug that's out there?" Erin asked.

"Erin, darlin', once you get to the edge of the carpet, stop skating using your toe pick, then step up on the carpet and walk to the seat they have for you. Ok?" Jake said. "You can do this honey."

"Thanks Jake. I don't want to look like a klutz out there."

"You'll be fine sugar." Anthony said.

"Good evening ladies and gentlemen. Welcome to Raptors Hockey!" The crowd was cheering and on their feet. "Tonight, as we prepare for the start of the game, we want to talk with Erin and share some details with you on our progress for 'Erin's Law'. Kyle, can you bring Erin to center ice?" Erin watched as Kyle skated toward the box. Erin stood and Anthony helped her by lifting her over the box onto the ice. Kyle took her hand, put his arm around her waist and together they skated to center ice. The crowd was still cheering and chanting Erin's name. It was a heady feeling. Kyle helped her negotiate the rug and seated her on the stool near the interviewer; Kyle sat in the other empty stool. The Raptors skated out and stood behind her.

Erin and Kyle talked with the producer about the trial, and advocating for change with the restraining orders. She invited those who had been affected by restraining orders to come forward to Judge Kafner, and she shared her story openly and honestly. The questions revolved around how she protected herself and her support system. She told them she was afraid to tell people in the beginning, but once she had help it became easier; she relayed that before Anthony and her guys she really didn't have a support system. She also shared that she didn't want to put anyone else in danger so she tried to keep things to herself which was the wrong approach. Erin encouraged anyone who was in a similar situation to trust their support system and share the details because help was needed to stay safe. She could see Jake nodding in agreement. The teams both came out for introductions and to thank Erin for her bravery. Kyle skated her back to the box and the game commenced. During one of the intermissions the production director came and told Erin they would re-run the interview from the beginning after the game. They also wanted to do more productions with Erin to keep the focus in front of the community and the legislature. Erin agreed.

*****

Life got back to normal for all of them and Erin was back to work at TK Productions, Terry telling her that in a month she would be full-time with benefits there, and stringing for the news stations on the weekends when she wanted to. She had become a news story too with all the work she did in her spare time for the legislation. Drake and Erica got settled at Erin's house and got married; Erin and Anthony continued to live at Kade's. They broke ground on their house and Jake broke ground on his. Erin took both sets of plans and developed a landscape plan that included roses in all the yards, lilies of many varieties, hostas in Jake's yard, flowering shrubs and green bushes in both yards, and carnations in theirs. Jake was pleased with the effect the plants would have on his yard. She also designed grape vines in both of their yards and an arbor to handle the vines. Erin also developed plans for weeping cherry trees and more palm trees in both yards.

They continued to work out every day and Erin was back to 100 percent. "Erin," Jake said when he came into the house. "I am planning a small celebration for Laurel's birthday on Sunday evening. Can you make me a cake?"

"I'd love to make you a cake Jake. What kind of cake do you want?"

"She loves something called rainbow chip. Can you do that?" Erin smiled.

"Yes Jake. I can do that easily and I'd be happy to do it for you! What kind of decorations do you want on it? I mean besides 'Happy Birthday Laurel."

"Can you make it look her tattoo, the maze looking one?" Erin nodded.

"Can you get me a picture of it?" Jake told her he had one and would email it to her. Erin found her recipe for the cake and got the layers made so she could decorate them when they were frozen. Jake watched her, impressed at how fast she was at getting the cakes made and glazed. By dinnertime she had the cakes glazed, cooled, wrapped and ready for the freezer. He helped her get them into the freezer and she returned to her editing project.

Saturday afternoon Erin took the cake layers out of the freezer and added the final layer of frosting, and a raspberry filling, and put the cake together using plastic dowels so it wouldn't slide. She used a saw tooth tool and created ridges in the side of the cake's frosting to give it some depth and dimension. Because she had all her boxes of cake tools, she had everything she needed to make sure that Jake would have an amazing cake. She filled those ridges in with thin lines of rainbow colors to enhance the rainbow chip effect. Then, she spent a couple of hours creating the tattoo on the top of the cake. Jake and Kade watched her work for bit then headed to watch the game in the living room. Anthony was at Ink, Inc. working on a client. By three in the afternoon Erin had the cake almost fully decorated. She asked Kade if he could print the words Happy Birthday Laurel on the cake board around the base. He created the effect she wanted with his steady hand and his artistic flair. Jake was sitting on the back porch while they finished up the cake.

"Jake," Erin called. "Can you come in here for a minute?" Jake got up and headed inside. "What do you think?" She turned the cake toward him.

"Wow. That's amazing Miss Erin. It looks just like her tattoo. You are an artist darlin'." Jake was still staring at the cake. "She's going to love it." He looked up finally and saw both Kade and Erin staring at him.

"Jake, can I ask you a question?" Erin said. He nodded. "Are you and Laurel in love with one another?" Jake sort of blushed.

"Yeah Erin. I want to ask her to marry me." He finally confessed. Erin was over-the-moon happy.

"I'm so happy for you Jake. That's awesome." She ran around the counter and hugged him. He held her to him and looked at Kade. He smiled at her. Kade told him he was happy for him too. The three of them talked for a bit and Jake shared that he was thrilled to have Laurel in his life. His house was getting finished and soon Erin could work on the landscaping, and then he could look at getting married if Laurel said yes!

****

Mory took the response from Jake to the court. Jake had the two letters Devin had written; he formulated a response on behalf of Erin and Erica. The judge was furious that the letters left the prison without being vetted. She contacted the warden and told him that she wanted a different psychiatrist on Devin's case, one that wouldn't succumb to Devin's charms, and she wanted all future letters to be sent to her first to be vetted. The warden asked about the letters. Judge Kafner told him that letters had been sent that Devin wrote to both Erin and Erica and accused Erin of creating the reasons behind why he was in prison. The warden was also outraged. He told Judge Kafner that Devin's eight weeks was in no way long enough to be rehabilitated to the point of writing a letter. The judge agreed. Together they found a new, more attuned psychiatrist and the warden said he would change the meetings so that Dr. Morton would be able to work effectively with Devin. The judge cautioned that a guard needed to be present in case Devin tried to hurt Dr. Morton, as she was female and Devin seemed to have problems with women. The warden agreed.

****

Erin made a dinner for Jake to take with him and the cake to Laurel's house. He wanted to make it a very special evening, so Erin created a pasta dish for Jake. He asked her for the fettucini Alfredo and the parmesan crusted chicken. She made him more than enough for two. She added red peppers, onions and artichokes too. They had the cake for dessert and she made him a loaf of fresh French bread. She packed everything up, so it would stay hot as he traveled, and Kade helped him load the items into Kade's truck. Erin sent up prayers that this dinner would go well. She made dinner for Anthony and herself.

Kade had a date with Kiera. They were headed to Mama Luisa's and then to dancing afterward. Erin and Anthony had the night to themselves. It was going to be a night to finish the plans on their wedding, and to spend some quality time with each other. They had exactly two weeks. Erin was getting more and more excited. She thought they had just about everything planned out. Erin had their cakes in the freezer.

They decided to do the champagne-orange cake too. Anthony's favorite flavor was buttercream yellow. So Erin created that as his groom's cake. It had a beach theme with shells, rocks, and starfish on one corner, his inking station on the other corner and the words *'you had me from hello'* and *'hero'* across the bottom. Erin made sand from buttery crushed graham crackers, and created water with a teal-colored glaze. The cake was amazing.

On Saturday Erin accompanied Anthony to Ink, Inc., and after he finished his buddy's ink, he started to work on Erin's dragon with Anthony's name. She didn't move much as he worked on her upper right thigh. Anthony did the outline first then filled the dragon in with teal, purple, and yellow colors. He used red to put his name into the design. It took the better part of the afternoon to do the ink. He wasn't finished, but he didn't think Erin could take much more. A couple of times he saw her wince, but she didn't move and she didn't complain. Anthony decided he could finish the ink on Monday after giving her a bit to recover from what he had already done. She was wearing her bikini bottoms so he had ample space to work. It looked amazing already. He rubbed the salve into it and covered it with a clear protector.

"Ok Erin, honey, we'll finish this on Monday. Your leg needs a break and I'm guessing you need one too!" She nodded and leaned over and kissed him.

"Anthony, my sweet hero," Erin started. Anthony stopped working and looked at her. "I just wanted you to know that I asked Kade to do an ink for me around my scar on my ankle. This way, I have part of all four of you with me always."

"That's awesome honey. Is it healed enough for that?"

"You know, I think it might be, but I want to finish this ink with you and then give it a bit to heal. Maybe next weekend I can have Kade to my ankle so it's ready for our wedding." She smiled at him.

Anthony finished her design on Monday and it looked amazing. Erin was thrilled with the design. They put the last touches on their decorating around Kade's yard and with Kade and Jake's help built the arbor where they would do their vows. That arbor would go into their yard to hold the grapevines. Erin had ordered a second arbor for Jake's yard for the same purpose. Both Jake's and their houses were almost complete. The construction crew had finished the outside, and cleaned up so that it would look nice for the wedding. Kade, Jake, and Anthony set up chairs on the beach, and Erin finished up the cakes and all the food in the house. They decided to small sandwiches, canapés, mints and nuts, as well as the cakes. Champagne was courtesy of KAMA vineyards.

*****

Kade and Erin headed to Ink, Inc. and Kade created a beautiful tattoo for Erin around and through her scar. For their shared love of country music, the beach and roses, Kade designed a beach sunset with cowboy boots featuring a rose design. It was amazing and Kade's use of color, and design made her ankle look incredible. Erin was so thrilled. All of her ink was done and mostly healed before the wedding.

*****

Erin and Anthony's wedding was amazing and so much fun. Jake gave her away and the entire starting line-up for the Raptors was on hand to celebrate their wedding. Erin danced with everyone, but saved several special dances for her new husband. She danced the father/daughter dance with Jake, and she danced with Anthony's father too.   Anthony planned a Caribbean vacation for them for their honeymoon. They were leaving the next morning, and Erin couldn't wait. Everyone enjoyed the beach with bare feet or flip flops. It was a perfect wedding, with the ocean and waves gently lapping at the shore. Kade's backyard, and their own backyard, was set up for the reception. Everyone had a grand time.

Towards the end of the reception, just before Anthony and Erin headed away from the house, they got everyone's attention to say thank you. Erin was pretty sure that Kade and Jake both needed to say something, so she started out the speaking, and they thanked their guests for coming. She alluded to love and the magic of the night. Kade asked if he could speak next and Erin yielded the floor to him. Kade proposed to Kiera and Jake proposed to Laurel. Both ladies said yes and Erin hugged them all. It was an amazing celebration of love.

Epilogue

Kade and Jake each had their weddings on the beach as well. Erin made their cakes and helped her girls with their planning. She was working full-time at TK Productions, stringing for the news stations when she could, and she built a website for Jake's business. Erin enjoyed her honeymoon and almost two months to the day they were married Erin discovered she was pregnant!

"Anthony, do you have a minute?" Erin started. They were settled into their house and everything was moved in.

"Yes sugar. Is everything ok?" She smiled at him.

"It is. I just have something for you." He came over to where she was sitting. Once he was sitting down she handed him a small package.

"What's this sugar?"

"Just open in handsome." She was smiling and incredibly happy. Anthony opened the package and stared at the contents. "You're going to be a dad!"

"Really?!" He looked again and then grabbed her in a huge hug. "This is amazing. We're going to be a family! Mom and Dad are going to be over-the-moon happy."

"Should we tell everyone tonight?" Anthony agreed. He hugged her again to him. "Are you happy my handsome hero?"

"I am so happy honey. This is amazing!"

Later at dinner, once everyone was eating, Anthony asked if he could say something. Everyone stopped eating and looked at Anthony. Erin was pretty sure that Mariah knew because of the smile on her face, but she didn't say anything.

"Mom, Dad, family, Erin and I have, well will have a new addition to our family in a little over seven months! We're pregnant!" Erin couldn't keep the smile off her face.

"Congratulations!" Mariah and Cassi squealed. All of them hugged Erin and Anthony. Angeline wanted to know if they knew what they were having.

"I think it's too early to know that, but I don't know." Erin said.

"Erin, Anthony, if you want to know the sex of the baby you can do that the next time you go in for your appointment. I'm guessing in another month you'll have an ultrasound, so they can tell from that." Mariah said.

Dinner resumed and everyone chattered about the news and all the weddings. Jake and Laurel were so in love as were Kade and Kiera. Erin asked Jake how the gardens were doing and he showed her some pictures. It was a fabulous night. While the ladies were doing dishes, Erin took Mariah aside to talk with her.

"Mariah, since I don't know what to expect or what I'm doing, is there any way you could be my doctor?" Erin asked.

"Erin, I would love to do that. I have privileges at the hospital, so if you want me to be your physician, we can do that. Have you seen anyone yet?"

"No. I went to the women's health care center just to make sure that my home test was accurate, but I wasn't ready to schedule an appointment with them. I trust you and you've taken such good care of me. Is that ok?"

"I would love that Erin. Yes I can and will be your doctor. We'll need to set up monthly appointments for you and if you want I can help you find out the sex of the baby. Are you leaning one way or the other?"

"I would really like a little boy, but a little girl would be awesome too. I'm just excited to be a mom!" She hugged Mariah.

"This little one is going to be spoiled! It's so amazing. You and Anthony will be great parents."

*****

May of the next year Erin gave birth to twin boys! Anthony was the proud daddy and the family rallied around to help. Mariah and Cassi were both expecting too, so soon the Romano clan would be growing again. Erin continued to work productions, but her hours were reduced for a time. Antonio and Giovanni were thriving and being loved by their grandparents, aunts and uncles. Erin and Anthony worked out a schedule where Erin could be home while Anthony was working at the tattoo shop and Anthony would be home with the boys while Erin was on video shoots.

The state legislature passed 'Erin's Law' and strengthened the restraining order process. More than twenty-five ladies had come forward with stories and that spurred Erin into creating a website to provide resources, and a social media presence to help others who were fighting for their own lives with stalkers or others who wanted to do them harm. Having the Raptors and Kings behind them helped to bring the legislation to the national level and Erin became a spokesperson for that as well.

*****

In December, more than year after Devin was incarcerated, he completed two stages of psychiatric help. At the end of that second stage he was once again ordered to write an apology to Erin and Erica.   He had given the female psychiatrist a hard time in the beginning, accusing her of being out to get him, but over the months he grew in his awareness and was able to figure out what caused him to slip into the pattern of continually hurting women. The letters were first vetted by the psychiatrist, then sent to the warden and finally to Judge Kafner. Judge Kafner saw that Devin was finally getting to the root of his actions and this letter actually was an apology, rather than being accusatory. Judge Kafner called Mory, who brought Jake with him to her office.

"Mory, Jake, here are the two letters, written by Devin and vetted by three of us, that are actually apologies to both Erin and Erica. Once you both have read them and agree that they can be given to the ladies, we will proceed."

Jake and Mory read the words that Devin had written. Devin explained to both of them that he learned the behaviors from his father and he was genuinely sorry about his actions and the fear he caused them both. He explained the why behind his actions and what he has learned about himself, and he further explained that he was doing his best to be rehabilitated, and perhaps one day he could be a positive influence on society. He told them he was sorry for all the hurt and pain he caused them too. He hoped that in time they could forgive him. In Erin's letter Devin apologized for slamming into her car with his pickup and he apologized for scaring her, attempting to hurt her production crews and for all the times he sent her graphic emails, texts and packages. He told her he now realized that he was just like his father and he was doing his best to get well and become the man he should have been from the beginning. He told her agreed with her when she told him no and that he had no right to expect forgiveness, but he thanked her for making sure he could get help with his problems. Jake was pleased with what he read, as was Mory.

"Judge Kafner, I think Devin's had a real breakthrough here." Jake said.

"I agree Jake. Do you think this letter will be received well by Erin? I know she's happy now and married with twins. Will this letter upset her?"

"You know, Erin was the one who advocated for Devin. I think she will be ok when she reads this letter. I'll be there with her and so will Anthony. Judge, do you want a response from the ladies after they have had time to digest this?"

"I guess I would say if that is something they want to do, then yes, but it's not necessary. We don't need to dredge up something or push a relationship that doesn't need to be there."

"Agreed Judge Kafner. You picked a good psychiatrist for Devin. Thanks Judge. Will Devin continue to be in therapy?" The judge nodded, confirming that Devin would still have weekly sessions and continue to move forward. Jake was glad about that.

Jake took both letters from the Judge and headed home. He called Drake on his way to let him know he had a letter for Erin and this one was a true apology. Drake told him to bring it by, or he would come get it. Jake made a turn and headed to Erin's old house to drop off the letter. Jake advised Drake to be there for Erica, but this letter was good and a true apology and it did not require a response. Drake thanked him and Jake asked how Erica was doing. Drake told him they were getting married and he asked Jake to give Erin a hug and a congratulations on her twins. Jake headed to Kade's. The group was having dinner together and perhaps he could sit with Erin while she read the letter.

*****

Dinner was a happy and joyous occasion. Erin was busy with the twins who were now seven months old and crawling, but had lots of help from both Kiera and Laurel. She made homemade pizzas and salad, and everyone seemed to be having a good time. For dessert she served an assortment of cookies and bars and after dinner the group sat outside enjoying the beautiful night. Erin put the twins down to sleep after their baths, and came back with the monitor. She loved her life. Everything was amazing and she had an amazing man who loved her and the boys.

"Erin," Jake started as he came over to where she stood. "Can you sit with me for a bit?" She nodded and handed Anthony the baby monitor.

"What's up Jake?" They had moved to the smaller table and were away from everyone else. She suspected this had something to do with Devin, but she needed to let Jake tell her. She was settled and happy and determined not to let things bother her.

"Erin, honey, earlier today I met with Judge Kafner and Uncle Mory." Jake watched her. Erin was so settled that she didn't react except to wait for him to finish his thoughts. She had a smile on her face and she was very much in a good place. "I have a letter here; I've already read it, as has Uncle Mory, and it's a true apology, to you from Devin. He's turned a corner in his life and I think you should read this. Just know that I am here for you, and we can talk about it after, but it is something you need to read."

"Ok." She said that simply still smiling. "Thanks for reading it first." She held out her hand and Jake put the letter there. She took a deep breath. Life had sure changed and Erin was doing really well; she didn't overreact before she knew what it was about, and she tried to take things one step at a time. She opened the letter and read the words printed there. She didn't think that Devin would ever change, but she realized that her advocating for him had made a difference.

"Jake," she said and looked up at him. "We did it! We made a difference and Devin seems to be getting help to get his life back on track. It looks like he has finally examined what made him do the things he did and he is taking responsibility for his actions." She smiled at him.

"Not we, Erin." Devin said. "You, honey, you made the difference. You advocated for him and you put yourself out there in the public eye. This state has a new law regarding restraining orders, the national level is working the laws too, Devin is getting help to get back on track, and he realizes what he did wrong; he is working to fix that and get his life back on track, and you are thriving. I am so proud of you."

"Jake, I couldn't have done it without you. Please know that. You helped me more than you will ever know. This family accepted me and made me feel wanted and loved, you helped me to see that it was ok to ask for help and to lean on people, that I didn't have to do it all by myself." She gestured to everyone gathered at the big table. "I am so lucky. Everything worked out and we are a force to be reckoned with. But, I could not have survived all of this without you; truly you are my hero just like my Anthony. Thank you." She reached over and hugged him. "Do I need to respond to this letter?"

"Only if you want to." Jake hugged her again and they sat for a bit. Erin was settled, she was happy and she was going to be ok. Life was good. She had an amazing husband, two wonderful little boys, a family and soon another child!

The End.

www.ingramcontent.com/pod-product-compliance
Lightning Source LLC
Chambersburg PA
CBHW071246150726
48001CB00018B/203